FORSAKEN Dreams

ESCAPE TO PARADISE
BOOK 1

MARYLU TYNDALL

BARBOUR
PUBLISHING

Cover design: Faceout Studio, www.faceoutstudio.com
Cover Model Photographer: Tyler Gould

Published by Barbour Publishing, Inc., P.O. Box 719, Uhrichsville, Ohio 44683,
www.barbourbooks.com

*Our mission is to publish and distribute inspirational products offering exceptional
value and biblical encouragement to the masses.*

 Member of the
Evangelical Christian
Publishers Association

Printed in the United States of America.

To obey is better than sacrifice.
1 Samuel 15:22

Dedicated to every Jonah running from God.

Cast of Characters

Colonel Blake Wallace—leader and organizer of the expedition to Brazil and a decorated war hero wanted for war crimes by the Union. He suffers from post-traumatic stress disorder.

Eliza Crawford—widow and Confederate army nurse who signed on to nurse the colonists, married to a Yankee general, and disowned by her Southern, politician father.

James Callaway—Confederate army surgeon turned Baptist preacher who signed on as the colony's only doctor but who suffers from an extreme fear of blood.

Hayden Gale—con man who has been searching for his father to execute revenge for the death of his mother. Believing the man is heading toward Brazil, Hayden stows away on board the *New Hope*.

Angeline Moore—signed on as the colony's seamstress, Angeline is a broken woman who wants more than anything to put her past behind her. Unfortunately, there are a few passengers on board whom she recognizes from her prior life.

Magnolia Scott—Georgia plantation owner's pampered daughter who doesn't want to go to Brazil and will do anything to turn the ship around. Constantly belittled by her father, she is obsessed with her appearance.

Mr. and Mrs. Scott—once wealthy plantation owners who claim to have lost everything in the war, yet they still retain their haughty, patrician attitude toward others. They hope to regain their position and wealth in Brazil.

Sarah Jorden—seven months pregnant and a war widow, she signed on to teach the colony's children.

Wiley Dodd—ex-lawman from Richmond who is fond of the ladies and in possession of a treasure map that points to Brazil as the location of a vast amount of gold.

Harman Graves—senator's son and ex-politician from Maryland whose hopes to someday run for president were crushed when the South seceded from the Union.

Captain Barclay—old sea dog who was a blockade runner in the war and who captains and owns the ship *New Hope*.

Parson Bailey—signed on as the colony's pastor and spiritual guide.

Emory Lewis—the colony's carpenter who took to drink after losing his wife and child in the war.

Moses and Delia—a freed slave and his sister who, along with her two children, want to start over in a new land away from the memory of slavery.

Jesse and Rosa Jenkins—simple farmers who, with their young daughter, Henrietta, hope to have a chance at a good life away from the ravages of war.

Mable—slave to the Scotts.

CHAPTER 1

May 29, 1866
Somewhere in the Caribbean

We shall all be in heaven or hell by night's end!" Parson Bailey shouted above the din of the storm. "God save us. God save us." His pudgy face swelled with each fateful phrase, while his eyes as wide as beacons, skittered around the tiny storeroom with each pound of wave and wind.

Eliza Crawford extracted herself from her friends huddling in the corner and made her way to the parson, intending to beg his silence. It did no good for him to say such things. Why, a parson of all people should comfort others, not increase their fears.

Thunder shook the ship. The deck canted, and instead of reaching Parson Bailey, Eliza tumbled into the arms of the very man she'd been trying to avoid since she boarded the *New Hope* almost three weeks ago— Wiley Dodd. Though of obvious means, evident in the fine broadcloth coat he wore and the gold watch he so often flaunted, something in his eyes, the way he looked at the women, made her stomach sour.

"In need of male comfort, Mrs. Crawford?" he asked. That sourness now turned to nausea as his arms encircled her. Not that she needed much assistance in the squeamish department. Her stomach had been convulsing since the storm began a few hours ago. But the perfumed Macassar oil Mr. Dodd slicked through his hair threatened to destroy all her efforts to keep her lunch from reappearing over his posh attire.

"We are done for. Done for, I say." The parson continued his rambling as he clung to the mast pole.

"I beg your pardon, Mr. Dodd." Pushing against his chest, Eliza snapped from his clawing grip.

The lizard-like smile on his lips belied their dire situation. "You're welcome to stay with me if you are frightened, my dear."

"Yesterday you called me a Yankee whore, sir!"

His smile remained though he gave a little shrug. "Desperate times and all that, you know."

Lightning flashed through the porthole, masking his face in a deathly gray.

"Why are you not frightened?" she asked him.

"Naught but a summer squall," he shouted over the ensuing roar of thunder. "I have experienced many such storms."

Eliza wondered how often a sheriff would have been to sea. Even so, he'd still chosen to remain below instead of help above with the other men. The ship careened upward as if it were but a toy in a child's hands. Eliza stumbled again and struck the bulkhead. A wall of water slammed against the porthole, creating a perverted dance of seething foam that lasted far longer than it should.

Was the ship sinking? Her lungs seized at the thought.

"The end is near. Near, I tell you!" the parson ranted.

The wave retreated. Leaden sky took its place, and Eliza scrambled on hands and knees back to her position beside a massive crate strapped to the bulkhead. Back to her only friends on this ill-fated ship. Mrs. Sarah Jorden and Miss Angeline Moore received her with open arms, neither one sobbing as one would expect of genteel ladies in such harrowing circumstances. Besides, there was sobbing enough coming from the other side of the room, where the wealthy plantation owners, Mr. and Mrs. Scott, and their pampered daughter, Magnolia, clung to each other in a desperate barbarism contrary to their elevated station. In fact, Mr. Scott had not opened his eyes in hours. Perhaps he attempted to drown out his wife's incessant howling, which elevated to a piercing level after each of the parson's decrees of doom. Tears streamed down Magnolia's fair cheeks, pricking Eliza's heart.

She should be angry at the young lady for exposing Eliza's ruse. But all she felt was pity.

Sitting beside the wealthy planters, Magnolia's personal slave hunched with folded hands and moving lips as if she were praying. Eliza hoped so. They needed all the prayers they could get. She had already lifted her petitions to the Almighty. Still, she whispered one more appeal, just in case, as she scanned the rest of the passengers crowded in the tiny storeroom—sent below by the captain when the seas had grown rough.

Farmers, merchants, lawyers, people of all classes and wealth. Jessie and Rosa Jenkins and their young daughter, Henrietta, had not uttered a peep since they'd tied themselves to a large table anchored to the deck. Mr. Harman Graves, a politician from Maryland, sat with his back against the bulkhead and a pleased look on his angular face, as if he knew something they did not. He rubbed an amulet between thumb and forefinger, lips moving as if in prayer, though Eliza doubted it was directed at God.

Next to him, Mr. Emory Lewis, a carpenter, if Eliza remembered correctly, kept plucking a flask from his pocket, taking a sip, and putting it back, only to repeat the ritual over again.

The eerie whistle of wind through rigging tore at Eliza's remaining courage. She shivered, and Sarah squeezed her arm, whispering something in her ear that was lost in the boom of another wave pounding the hull.

A child's whimper brought her gaze to her left, where Delia, a freed Negress, hugged her two young children close. A flash of lightning accentuated the fear tightening the woman's coffee-colored face. The fear of death—a fear they all felt at the moment. A fear that was no respecter of class or race. A fear that broke through all social barriers. For yesterday, the Scotts, as well as some of the others present, would not have agreed to be in the same room with a freed slave.

Or even with Eliza.

Thunder bellowed, barely audible above the explosion of wind and wave. How did this tiny brig withstand such a beating? Surely the timbers would burst any moment, splintering and filling the room with the mad gush of the sea. Locking her arms with the ladies on either side, she closed her eyes as the galloping ship tossed them like rag dolls over the hard deck.

"And the sea gave up the dead which were in it; and death and hell delivered up the dead which were in them: and they were judged every man according to their works." Parson Bailey had taken to quoting scripture, which only caused Mrs. Scott to howl even louder.

Eliza's thoughts shifted to Blake and the other men struggling to save the ship up on deck. Well, mainly to Blake, if she were honest. Which was something she hadn't been of late. But that was another matter altogether. *Oh fiddle, Colonel Blake Wallace,* she reproved herself. She shouldn't be calling him by his Christian name. Though the last nineteen days she'd spent in his company seemed a lifetime, in truth she hardly knew the man.

Then why, in her darkest hour as she faced a suffocating death in the middle of the Caribbean, was it Colonel Wallace who drew her thoughts? Not just her thoughts, but her concern—fear for his safety. Fear that she wouldn't have a chance to explain why she had lied, wouldn't have a chance to win back the affection that had so recently blossomed in both their hearts. She rubbed her tired eyes.

But what did it matter now? He hated her for who she was. No, for whom she had married. In fact, as she glanced over the terrified faces in the room, only loathing shot back at her. To them she was the enemy. An enemy they were risking their lives to escape. And now they were all going to die. Together in the middle of the sea. With no one to mourn them. No one who would know their fate. Not even Eliza's father or Uncle James and Aunt Sophia or little Alfred, Rachel, or Henry. Not that they would care. To them, she was already dead.

Disowned. Disinherited. Forsaken.

The brig twisted and spun around as if caught in a whirlpool. Angeline's trembling body crashed into Eliza on one side while Sarah's smashed into her from the other, making Eliza feel like a garment run through a clothespress. An explosion of thunder cracked the sky wide open, followed by an eerie silence, as if all of nature had been stunned by the angry shout of God. Or maybe they were all dead. But then the wind outside the hull and the whimpers of fear within resumed. Angeline pressed Stowy, her cat, tightly against her chest while Sarah's free hand clutched her belly swollen with child. Seven months along. How worried she must be for her wee one!

"Repent, for the end is at hand!" Parson Bailey's flashing eyes speared Eliza with a look of hatred. She knew what he was thinking. What they all were thinking.

That she was the reason for the storm.

Another thunderous blast and Eliza squeezed her eyes shut again, wishing—praying—this was only a bad dream. How did she get herself into this mess? Why, oh why, did she ever think she could start afresh in Brazil?

She opened her eyes and stared at the oscillating shadows: light and dark drifting over the bulkhead, crates, boxes, and tables. And over the hopeless faces. A torn piece of rope tumbled back and forth across the deck. Parson Bailey still glared at her. Something maniacal glinted in his eyes as he shared a glance with Mr. Dodd and Mr. Graves.

"It's you!" he raged, glancing over the others. "God told me this Yankee is the cause of the storm!"

Though all eyes shot toward the parson, no one said a word. Hopefully they were too busy holding on and too frightened for their lives to do anything about it. Mr. Graves, however, staggered to his feet, slipped the amulet into his pocket, and glanced at Eliza like a cougar eyeing a rabbit.

She tried to swallow, but her throat felt like sand.

Mr. Dodd grinned. "I say we toss her over!"

"Aye, she's our Jonah!" Mr. Graves added.

"Precisely." Parson Bailey nodded.

Though the freed Negress's eyes widened even farther, only the farmers, Mr. and Mrs. Jenkins, offered any protests. Protests that were lost in the thunderous boom of the storm.

"Don't be absurd, Parson!" Sarah added from beside Eliza. "God cares not a whit whether Eliza is a Yankee or a Rebel!" Yet, no sooner had the words fled her mouth than thunder exploded so loud it seemed God disagreed with the young teacher's pronouncement.

Eliza frowned. For goodness' sake, whose side was God on, anyway?

The ship bucked, and Eliza's bottom lifted from the deck then slammed back again. A rope snapped, and a crate slid across the room. Mr. Dodd halted it with his boot then glanced at Mr. Graves while jerking his head toward Eliza.

"Jonah must go overboard for the seas to calm!" The parson howled above the storm, though he seemed unwilling to let go of the mast pole to carry out his depraved decree.

Angeline squeezed Eliza's arm. "I won't let them take you!"

As much as she appreciated her friend's courageous stance, Eliza knew what she must do. She must leave, get out of this room, out from under these incriminating eyes, before these men dragged her above and did just what they threatened.

Terror stole the breath from her lungs, but she tugged from her friends' arms nonetheless and lunged for the door. She was prepared for the angry slurs behind her when she opened it. She wasn't prepared for the blast of wind and slap of seawater that shoved her flat onto her derriere and sent her crinolette flailing about her face. Pain shot up her spine. Humiliation at her exposed petticoat and stockings reddened her face. But when she glanced around, everyone's eyes were closed against the wind and spray bursting into the room. Shaking the stinging water from her eyes, Eliza rose, braced against the torrent, gripped the handle with both hands, and heaved the door shut behind her. Then leaning her head into the wind, she forged down the narrow hall. She had no idea what she intended to do. Toss herself into the sea? She shivered at the thought. Yet if that was God's will, if He wanted her to throw herself into the raging waters, then so be it!

But then again, when had she ever obeyed God?

The burning prick of conscience was instantly doused by a cascade of seawater crashing down the companionway ladder. The mad surge grabbed her feet and swept them from beneath her. Gripping the railing, she hung on for dear life as she floated off the deck. Seawater filled her mouth. Thoughts of her imminent demise filled her mind. But then her body dropped to the sodden wood. Eliza gasped and spit the salty taste from her mouth.

Thunder roared, shaking the railing beneath her hand. The brig jerked and flung her against the ladder. Struggling to her feet, she dragged her dripping gown up the steps, unprepared for the sight that met her eyes.

Waves of towering heights surrounded the ship, their foamy tips scattering like spears in the wind. Rain fell in thick panels, making it nearly impossible to see anything except blurry, distorted shapes that surely must be the crew hard at work. Wind crashed into Eliza, stealing her breath and howling in her ears. Rain pelted her like hail. The ship pitched over a swell. Eliza toppled to the deck then rolled as if she weighed no more than a feather. She bumped into a small boat and gripped the slippery moorings anchoring it to the deck.

Salt! Salt everywhere. It filled her mouth. It filled her nose. It stung her eyes. It was all she could smell. And taste. That and fear. Not just her own. Fear saturated the air like the rain and waves. It boomed in the muffled shouts ricocheting across the ship. Buzzed in the electric charge of lightning. Clinging to the moorings, her gown flapping like a torn sail, she squinted and searched for the captain, hoping his calm expression would soothe her fears. Yet from his rigid stance on the quarterdeck and his viselike grip on the wheel, Eliza's hopes were swept away with the wind.

Which did nothing to ease her terror. A terror that numbed her heart as she accepted her fate. A wall of water slammed into her. She closed her eyes and hung on as the ship angled to port. Why did she always make bad decisions? Why did she never listen to her conscience? Stubborn, rebellious girl! If she hadn't married Stanton, if she had listened to her father and her uncle, she would be home now with a loving family. She wouldn't have been forced to become a nurse in the war, forced to witness things no lady should witness. Forced to take care of herself in a man's world.

Sailors, ropes tied about their waists, crisscrossed the deck in a tangled fury. By the foredeck, Hayden, their stowaway, his long dark hair thrashing around his face, held fast to a line that led up to the yards. In the distance, Eliza made out James Callaway clinging to the ratlines as he slowly made his way up to the tops. How could anyone hold on in this wind? Especially James, who was a doctor, not a sailor.

But where was Blake. . .Colonel Wallace? Fighting against the assault of seawater in her eyes, she scanned the deck, the tops. *Dear God, please. Please let him be all right.*

She must find him. Or discover his fate. She must talk to the captain. If they were going to sink, she'd rather know than cling to false hope. Bracing against the wind and rain, she rose to her knees, struggling against her multiple petticoats and crinolette. Inconvenient contraptions! If she stayed low, she may be able to crawl to the quarterdeck ladder and make her way up to the captain.

The ship rolled then plunged into a trough. The timbers creaked and groaned under the strain. Rain stabbed her back. Wind shrieked through the rigging like a death dirge. A massive wave rose before the ship. The bow leaped into it. Eliza dropped to the deck and dug her nails into the wood. *Oh God. No!* The ship lurched to near vertical. Lightning etched a jagged bolt across Eliza's eyelids.

She lost her grip. Tumbling, tumbling, like a weed driven before the wind. She threw her hands out, searching for something to grab onto. Anything. But the glassy wood slipped from her fingers, leaving splinters in her palms.

And terror in her heart.

Her body slammed into the railing. The ship canted. She rolled over the bulwarks, flung her hand out in one last effort to save herself. Her fingers met wood. She latched on. The salivating sea reached up to grab her legs, tugging her down.

Her fingers slipped. Pain radiated into her palms, her wrists. The brig heaved and canted again like a bucking horse.

God, is this how I am to die? Perhaps it was. She'd run from God long enough.

Rain slapped her face, filled her nose. She couldn't breathe. Her fingers slipped again. She couldn't hold on much longer.

A strong hand grabbed her wrist. A face appeared over the railing. "Hang on! I've got you."

CHAPTER 2

May 10, 1866
Nineteen days earlier
Charleston, South Carolina

*T*he hand that gripped Eliza's was strong, firm, rough like a warrior's, yet gentle. He lifted her gloved fingers to his lips and kissed them while eyes as gray and tumultuous as a storm assessed her. "Welcome aboard, Mrs. Crawford." The voice equaled the strength that exuded from the man. No, not any man. A colonel, she had heard, a graduate of West Point. Though he was not broadcasting that fact to the Union authorities scouring Charleston.

"I'm"—he coughed into his hand—"Mr. Roberts, the overseer of this expedition. You are a nurse, if memory serves?" He assisted her from the plank onto the deck of the brig, where the scent of perspiration, tar, and aged wood swirled about her.

Mr. Roberts, indeed. She knew his true identity to be that of Colonel Blake Wallace, a decorated hero of the war, but his secret was safe with her. She smiled. "You are correct, sir." Thankful for his firm grip, Eliza steadied herself against the motion of the ship. Her heart needed steadying as well, as the colonel continued to gaze at her as if she'd sprouted angel wings. A flood of heat rose up her neck, and she tugged from his grip.

"Forgive me, Mrs. Crawford." He shook his head as if in a daze and turned to welcome another passenger on board, giving Eliza a chance to study the man who'd organized this daring adventure. In the early morning sunlight, his hair glistened in waves of onyx down to his stiff collar where the strands curled slightly. Drawn along the lines of a soldier, his body displayed a strength only hinted at by the pull of his white shirt and black waistcoat across broad shoulders. Matching trousers stretched over firm thighs before disappearing inside tall leather boots. He turned and caught her staring at him. And then smiled—a glorious smile that was part rogue and part saint, if there was such a thing. Either way, it did terrible, marvelous things to her stomach. Or was that the rock of the ship?

Oh fiddle! He was heading her way. With a limp, she noticed. A slight limp that tugged at her heart.

"Do you have luggage, Mrs. Crawford?" Dark eyebrows rose over those stormy eyes, and Eliza thought it best not to stare at the man any longer. She was a widow, after all. A single woman. And she wouldn't want anyone getting the wrong impression of her character. "Over there." She pointed her gloved finger to a large trunk perched on the edge of the dock.

"Very well." Turning, he shouted to a man standing by the railing. "Mr. Mitchel. Would you bring that trunk to the master's cabin?"

"Aye, aye." The man darted across the plank.

The colonel nodded toward her and seemed about to say something when a burly man with a tablet stole his attention with a question.

Another man sped past Eliza, bumping into her and begging her pardon. Clutching her pocketbook, she stepped closer to the capstan, out of the way of sailors who scrambled across the deck of the two-masted brig, preparing the ship to sail and helping passengers and their luggage on board. The squawk of seagulls along with the thud of bare feet over the wooden planks accompanied the shouts of dockworkers and crewmen. Beyond the wharf, a group of citizens huddled on shore watching the goings-on from Bay Street.

Furniture, sewing machines, and a plethora of farming implements, along with trunks, lockers, and crates were soon hauled aboard. A pulley system, erected over the yards above, lowered a squealing pig through a hatch into the hold below.

Adjusting her bonnet to shade her eyes from the rising sun while fanning herself against the rising heat, Eliza studied the oncoming passengers. An elderly couple, dressed far too elegantly for sailing, boarded with a lady about Eliza's age whom she assumed to be their daughter. Wearing a pink taffeta gown with a low neckline trimmed in Chantilly lace, the young woman drew the attention of nearly every man on board, including several sailors who stopped to gape at her. Eliza couldn't blame them. With hair that rivaled the luster of ivory and skin as creamy as milk, she was the epitome of a Southern belle. Only her red-rimmed eyes marred an otherwise perfect face. That and her frown. She seemed oddly familiar to Eliza, as if they'd met before. Behind them, a young Negress, bent beneath the burden of a large valise, dragged a portmanteau as she struggled to keep up.

A tall man with light, wavy hair and wearing a gray three-piece suit, round-brimmed hat, and a pleasant smile on his face leaped from the walkway onto the deck and glanced over the ship, followed by a young couple with a small child, a foppish man all dressed in black with dark sideburns and a goatee, and finally a pregnant woman. Alone, with no husband at her side.

All strangers, yet soon they would become her bunkmates, her neighbors, her companions—perhaps even her friends.

That was, if she could keep her past a secret.

The colonel turned her way again, snapping his fingers at another man crossing the deck. "Forgive me, Mrs. Crawford. Max will see you to your cabin, where"—he scanned the deck—"I believe Mr. Mitchel has already taken your trunk. I trust we shall have a chance to become better acquainted after we set sail?"

She wanted to say she would enjoy that, but that would be too forward. Instead, she merely smiled and thanked him as the man led the way below deck. Standing at the companionway ladder, Eliza cast one last glance over her shoulder and found the colonel's eyes still on her. Ah, so he had taken note of her. As if reading her thoughts, he chuckled, coughed into his hand, and limped away.

Eliza had never been on a ship before. Born and raised in Marietta, Georgia, she had no reason to take to the sea. As a war nurse, she'd traveled on a train or a coach. Now as she descended below deck and the sunlight abandoned her and the halls squeezed her from both sides, her nerves spun into knots. And they weren't even out at sea yet! Her skirts swished against the sides of the narrow corridor, and she pressed them down, lest she snag the fabric on the rough wood. They passed another hatchway leading below, and the scent of something altogether unpleasant filled her nose. Thankful that the man didn't take her in that direction, Eliza followed him to an open door.

"Here ye go, miss. Used t' be the master's cabin, but the cap'n reserved it for the single ladies on board." Max pressed down springs of unruly red hair that circled an equally red face while he allowed liberties with his gaze on Eliza. She took a step back, unsure if it was safe to enter the room with this man in tow. His body odor alone threatened to stir her breakfast into disorder.

"That's very kind of him. Thank you, sir." She hoped her curt tone would drive him away. It did. But not before he winked above a grin that revealed a jagged row of gray teeth.

Sunlight filtered in from a small porthole, casting oscillating shafts of light over the cabin as small as a wardrobe. A woman, sitting on the only chair, looked up as Eliza stepped inside.

"Hello, I'm Angeline Moore."

"Eliza Crawford." Untying the ribbons beneath her chin, she eased off her bonnet. "Pleased to meet you. I suppose we shall be bunkmates?"

"Yes, and one other lady, I believe." Angeline stood. Copper curls quivered about her neck. Her smile was pleasant, her cheeks rosy, and her violet eyes alluring. And what Eliza wouldn't give for such feminine curves as hers. Or would she? Despite her dalliance with the colonel above, she had no interest in attracting men. She'd already tried her hand at marriage, and that had ended miserably.

"One more lady. . .in here?" Eliza glanced at her trunk, which took up nearly half the room. "With your luggage and the other lady's, we will be packed in here like apples in a crate." Her stomach tightened at the thought.

"I don't have a trunk. Everything I own is right in here." Angeline pointed to a small, embroidered valise on the table beside her.

Eliza thought it strange to have so little, but she didn't want to pry. Setting down her pocketbook, she planted her hands at her waist. "But where are the beds?"

Angeline pointed to three pairs of hooks on the deck head. "Hammocks, I believe." Her lips slanted.

"Oh my."

"We are better off than most." A voice coming from the hallway preceded a brown-haired woman with a belly ripe with child. A ray of sunlight speared the porthole and struck the gold cross hanging around her neck, causing Eliza to blink.

"Aside from those who can afford it, most passengers sleep together in the hold," the woman continued as she set down her case, pressed a hand on her back, and gave both of them a wide grin. "Good thing we are all single women. I'm Sarah Jorden."

Pleasantries were exchanged between the ladies whom Eliza hoped would soon become good friends.

"I am a nurse," Eliza offered, sitting down on her trunk. "And you, Mrs. Jorden? What brings you on this adventure?" She patted the spot beside her.

"Please call me Sarah. And I am the teacher." She smiled, sliding onto the seat. Brown hair drawn back in a bun circled an oval face with plain but pleasant features.

"Are there children coming aboard?" Angeline asked.

"I believe so. Several, in fact," Sarah said.

Angeline returned to her seat and began fingering the embroidery on her valise. "A teacher and a nurse." She sighed. "I fear I bring no such useful skills to our adventure. I am only a seamstress and not a very good one at that. In fact, it is unclear why I was even accepted for the journey."

"Oh rubbish, dear." Sarah tugged off her gloves. "We shall simply have to discover what talents God has given you."

A wave of red washed over Angeline's face. Odd. Perhaps she was just nervous about the journey—the unknown, the new beginning in a strange land. Certainly, being a single woman all alone made it all the more frightening. Or it should. Yet Eliza felt more excitement than fear. The sparkle in Sarah's eyes indicated she felt the same.

Reaching over, Eliza pulled the pamphlet out from her valise. The pamphlet she'd read so many times during the past two weeks, she knew it by heart. The pamphlet she had prayed over, thought about, agonized over.

Brazil! Brazil! Land of dreams. Land of hope. Land of beginnings! Fertile land available at only 22 cents an acre. Farmers, bring your tools; bring your implements, household items, and furniture; bring as many varieties of seeds as you can. People of every age and skill needed to recreate the Southern utopia stolen from us by the North. Become wealthy in a land of plenty, which Providence has blessed more than any land I have seen. Brazil welcomes you with open arms, a land of mild temperatures, rich soil, and perfect freedom. A land where dreams come true.

From the first time Eliza had read the pamphlet handed to her by a man on the street, three words continued to leap out at her, sealing her decision. *Dreams.* She'd had so many of those as a child. None of which had come true. *Hope.* Something she had lost during the past five years. *Beginnings.* A place she could go where people didn't know who she was—didn't know what she had done. A place where she wasn't shunned, hated, insulted, and rejected. Where she could start fresh with new people. A new society. A Southern utopia.

Was there such a thing outside of heaven?

Blake Wallace squeezed his eyes shut, not only to block out the sight of the port authority officer but to give himself a moment to think. He wanted another five hundred dollars?

That was nearly half of his remaining savings. He couldn't very well ask his passengers to pay more than the forty-two dollars he'd already charged them for the trip. Most of them were as poor or poorer than he was. In fact, many of the wealthiest families in the South had been stripped of their money, their belongings, even their property. Their homes had been ransacked and burned, their servants and slaves scattered, their dignity stolen. His jaw bunched at the memory of his own white-columned, two-story family home in Atlanta burned to nothing but ash and debris. And then two months ago, the land purchased by Yankees for pennies.

His family dead.

Most people had nowhere to live and little food to eat. They sought refuge under trees or in borrowed tents. Railroads were torn up, schools closed, banks insolvent, towns and cities reduced to rubble, and jobs nonexistent.

Now as he stood before this Yankee port authority officer in his fancy brass-buttoned jacket, it took all of Blake's strength, all his will, not to strangle him on the spot.

"There is the alternative. . . ." The man's voice was as slimy as his character.

Blake opened his eyes. A drop of tobacco perched in the corner of the man's mouth.

"And that is?"

"I could inform the new lieutenant colonel in town that you are a Rebel officer."

Though his stomach churned, Blake allowed no reaction to reach his stoic expression. Was it that obvious?

"Yeah, I can tell." The man spit a wad of tobacco to the side. "I can spot you Reb soldiers a mile away, and you officers give off a certain stink." He scrunched his nose for effect.

Blake narrowed his eyes, flexing his fingers at his sides to keep them from fisting the buffoon. A drop of sweat trickled down his back.

The port officer shrugged. "Have it your way. The new colonel in charge of Charleston won't rest till he ferrets out all you Rebs and either imprisons you or, better yet, hangs you."

Blake resisted the impulse to rub his throat. He didn't relish dangling at the end of a rope or rotting in a Union prison. And he knew if he stayed, that would be his fate. He'd been too visible in the war, had inflicted too much damage on the enemy. So it had been no surprise that a month ago, his name had appeared on the Union's most-wanted list for war crimes.

Which was why he changed his name, moved to Charleston, and decided to leave the States. Organizing and leading an expedition to Brazil, where he hoped to start and head a new colony, seemed the opportunity of a lifetime. And his last chance at a new life. At a good life. If such a thing even existed anymore.

Blake counted out the gold coins into the man's hand, clamping his jaw tight against a volcano of exploding anger.

"Where do you think you're going anyway, you and your pack of mindless Rebs? 'Specially in that old ship?" The port master jerked his head toward the brig. "You ain't even got steam power."

"Brazil," Blake said absently as he watched a dark-haired man hobble over the railing of the *New Hope* and drop below. Probably one of the passengers. Regardless of its age, the ship was a beauty. Fine-lined and sturdy, a square-sailed, two-masted brig of 213 tons, refitted with extra cabins for passengers, and owned and sailed by a seasoned mariner, Captain Barclay, an old sea dog to whom Blake had taken an immediate liking.

As he scanned the deck, Blake caught a flicker of brown hair the color of maple syrup. Mrs. Eliza Crawford stood against the larboard railing, the wind fluttering the ribbons of her bonnet.

"Brazil! I hear there's nothin' there but mosquitoes and malaria." The port officer's caustic voice drew Blake's gaze once again. "Not to mention everyone knows Brazilians are crossbred with Negroes!" He shook his head and chuckled. "Poisonous insects, scorching heat, too much rain, diseases like leprosy and elephantiasis—no wonder we won the war. You Rebs are dumber than a sack of horse manure."

Ignoring him, Blake finished counting the coins. "This is robbery, and you know it."

"You're the ones that robbed our country of her young men. Seems fittin' justice."

Sunlight glinted off something in the distance, temporarily blinding Blake. Two Yankee soldiers strolled down Bay Street, their dark blue uniforms crisp and tight, their brass buttons and buckles shining, and their service swords winking at Blake in the bright light. His heart lurched.

A nervous buzz skittered up his back. "Are we settled?"

"Yes, sail away, dear Rebel, sail away!" the man began to sing, but Blake didn't stay to hear the next chorus, though it haunted him down the wharf.

"Good riddance to ye, ye Rebel, sail away!"

Halfway to the ship, Blake sneaked a glance over his shoulder.

The soldiers had stopped to speak to the port authority officer. Would he turn Blake in? Of course he would. And keep the reward money as well as Blake's extortion fee.

Blake rubbed his neck again at the thought of his impending fate. He tried to swallow, but it felt like the rope had already tightened around his throat. Even so, hanging would be a kind sentence. The Union had done far worse to some of his fellow officers. Which was only one more reason for Blake to leave his Southern homeland.

That and the fact that everyone he knew and loved was dead.

The memory stabbed a part of his mind awake—the part he preferred to keep asleep. The part that, like an angry bear, tried to rip the flesh from his bones when disturbed. This bear, however, seemed more interested in tearing Blake's soul from his body as clips of deathly scenes flashed across his mind. Cannons thundered in his head, reverberating down his back. Men's tortured screams. Blood and fire everywhere.

24

No, not now! He gripped his throat, restricting his breath. He must jar himself out of the graveyard of memories. *Think. Think!* He had to think. He had to focus!

But his mind was awhirl with flashes of musket fire, mutilated body parts, the vacant look in a dead man's eyes. He stumbled. Shook his head. Not now. He could not pass out now. His passengers needed him. They'd put their trust in him to lead them to the promised land. Besides, he wasn't ready to die.

Blake thought about praying, but he'd given that up long ago. The day he'd received word that his baby brother had been killed at the Battle of Antietam. His only brother. The pride and joy of the entire family. He was only seventeen.

Blake drew in a deep breath and continued onward. The visions faded and his mind cleared. Perhaps God was looking out for him after all. He marched—limped—forward as nonchalantly as he could, trying to signal Captain Barclay on the quarterdeck to begin hoisting sail. But the old sea dog must've already assessed the situation, as sailors leaped to the tops to unfurl canvas. The plank had been removed, and men lined the railing, their stances and faces tight, their eyes suddenly widening at something behind Blake.

Only then did he hear the thumping of boots and feel the dock tremble beneath him.

A hand clutched Blake's arm and spun him around. Two Union solders stared him down. "And where do you think you're going, Johnny Reb?"

CHAPTER 3

Grant was sure the beat of his heart was visible through his chest. Yet with the control and experience gained from years in command, he faced his enemies with a look of authoritative aplomb. One, a mere sergeant, by the stripes on his coat, was busy gazing at a group of young ladies standing by the millinery shop across Bay Street. The other, a lieutenant, shifty-eyed, thickset, with a mustache that dripped down both sides of his mouth, stared at Blake as if he were a toad.

"Where are your papers, sir?" He jerked a thumb toward the *New Hope*. "You can't leave port without proper papers."

Blake's stomach churned as he reached into his waistcoat and handed them to the man. "Everything is in order. Surely the port master informed you."

"Port masters take bribes, Mr."—he examined the papers—"Roberts." He squinted as he glanced over the document. His friend finally lost interest in the ladies and faced Blake as well.

"Where are you heading?"

"As you can plainly see, Lieutenant, Brazil."

The sergeant chuckled. "I've seen the signs posted around town. You're starting a new colony, ain't ya?" He pointed a finger at Blake, nearly poking him in the chest. "'A Southern utopia,' the pamphlet said." He exchanged a look of disgust with his partner and continued laughing. "But what else should we expect from Rebs? Always running away like cowards."

Blake ground his fists together behind his back. Out of the corner of his eye, he saw the crew of the *New Hope* loose the lines that tied the ship to the wharf. Thankfully, the soldiers hadn't noticed. Blake's stomach tightened. Captain Barclay would leave without him. He'd instructed him to do just that should Blake be arrested. But he was so close. Just ten more yards and he'd be on board.

Just ten yards between him and freedom.

A dark cloud swallowed up the sun. A portend of bad things to come? Shifting weight off his bad led, Blake scratched his neck, feeling the cinch of the noose already. A breeze coming off the bay brought the scent of rain and freedom, but it did nothing to cool the sheen of sweat covering his neck and arms.

The lieutenant slid fingers down his long mustache and thrust the papers back at Blake. "Prepare your ship to be searched, Mr. Roberts."

Blake's chest tightened. "For what purpose?"

"Slaves, Rebel soldiers, valuables that belong to the Union." He thrust his face into Blake's, dousing him with the smell of alcohol. "I'm sure we'll find plenty of contraband to confiscate." He faced his friend. "Go assemble a band of men. Tell them to arm themselves. We wouldn't want our Rebel friends to forget themselves, would we?"

"I assure you, Lieutenant, we aren't carrying anything illegal."

"Then you have nothing to fear." His gaze pierced Blake before he turned toward the sergeant ambling down the wharf. "Bart!" The man didn't turn. The lieutenant marched after him. "Sergeant Bart!" he yelled, finally getting his attention. "Bring me the list of war criminals again." He jerked a thumb toward Blake. "This one seems familiar. . . ."

But Blake didn't stay to hear the rest. The *New Hope* drifted from the quay, and the crew beckoned him on with anxious gestures, their faces pinched. He didn't have time to check how wide the expanse of sea had become between dock and hull. He didn't want to know. It mattered not anyway. He had no other choice.

Ignoring the pain shooting up his right leg, he bolted down the remainder of the dock and leaped into the air. His feet spiraled over murky water. His arms flailed through emptiness, scrambling to reach the rope the crew dangled down the side of the brig.

Curses and shots fired behind him. A bullet whizzed past his ear. The rope loomed in his vision as if it were at the end of a long tunnel. Larger and larger it grew. And yet farther and farther away it seemed. His lifeline. One scraggly rope that would either save him or hang him. The crew shouted encouragements, but their voices seemed muffled and distant. So did the pistol shots and the voice of the lieutenant damning him to hell from the wharf.

Pop! Pop! Pop! More shots exploded around him.

Tiny holes appeared in the hull of the ship, shattering the wood into chips. The brig drifted farther away. Blake's feet touched water. It was all over. He wasn't going to make it. Then his hand felt rough hemp. He closed his fingers. His shoulder snapped hard. His arm ached. He slammed into the hull with a jarring thud. Swinging his other arm up, he clutched the rope.

A shot zipped past his head. Its eerie whine catapulted him into action. He yanked his feet from the water and began to climb up the oaken hull. Someone pulled the rope from above.

A storm of boots thundered over the wharf, releasing a hail of bullets. A woman screamed. The wind snapped in the sails, and the water began a soft purl against the hull as the brig pulled out of port.

Almost there. Almost there. Blake released the rope and grabbed onto the bulwarks. Hands hauled him on board just as the soldiers on the dock unleashed hell.

Eliza backed away from the group of sailors as they dragged Colonel Wallace over the railing and onto the deck. She had not gone below as ordered. Not when a man's life was at stake. Not when their entire journey was at stake. She knew trouble was afoot when those soldiers had stopped the colonel. Nothing good ever came of a chat with Union officers. Certainly not in the past year since the war had ended. They were out for blood. Pure and simple. They wanted nothing but to punish the South for her sins. And as self-appointed judge and jury, they wielded the whip of revenge with the utmost cruelty.

Remorse and sorrow flooded her at the thought that she had once associated herself with the North. Quite intimately associated.

The colonel landed with a thump on the deck as a torrent of shots peppered the sky and the ship, and seemed to rain down on them from everywhere.

"In the name of the Army of the United States and by command of Lieutenant Colonel Milton Banks, I order you to stop and drop your anchor at once!"

Eliza glanced at the dock. At least twenty Union soldiers stood in line, some firing pistols and rifles at the *New Hope*, others furiously reloading their weapons.

So stunned by the sight, she could only stand and watch as sailors ducked and slumped to the deck all around her. Strong arms grabbed her shoulders and pulled her down just as a bullet struck the mast behind her. The acrid smell of gunpowder bit her nose. Still, the firestorm continued. But it was Colonel Wallace's body atop hers that caused her to tremble. Not any fear of death.

"Stay low, Mrs. Crawford." His hot breath wafted over her cheek as he cocooned her with his body—his muscles hard and hot from exertion.

Eliza couldn't breathe. Her skin buzzed. He smelled of man and sweat. Oh how she'd forgotten what it felt like to be held by a man. The shame of it! She must stop this at once. Here she was in the middle of a battle, her very life on the line, and all she could think of was how wonderful it felt to be in the colonel's arms. Sails flapped and thundered above her until, suddenly, they bloated with wind. The ship jerked, and the rush of water grew louder. Shots popped and cracked in the air, but they no longer struck the ship.

Colonel Wallace gazed down at her for a moment, uncertainty in his gray eyes, and something else. . . . He jumped off her as if she had a disease. A breeze swept his body heat away, leaving a chill behind. And the all-too-familiar feeling of being alone in the world.

He offered her his hand and helped her to her feet. "Forgive me, Mrs. Crawford."

But before she could thank him, he turned and hobbled to the railing where sailors lined up to watch the Union soldiers shake their fists in the air and growl at them from the quay. With a sweep of his hand, he gave a mock bow. "It's been a pleasure, gentlemen!" he yelled, eliciting chuckles from the crew.

Eliza could only stare at him like a silly schoolgirl. Such courage, this man. The way he had jumped across the wide gulf without hesitation beneath a barrage of bullets. Then the gallant way he protected her with his own body. Dare she admit that her skin still tingled from the encounter? And now, his lively sarcasm toward his enemy made her smile.

"Back to your stations!" Captain Barclay shouted from the quarterdeck. "We've still got to get past Fort Sumter and Fort Moultrie."

The sailors scattered like rats before light, some leaping into shrouds, others handling lines on deck.

"Praise God! Praise God!" A tall, gangly man with tiny eyes and thick sideburns emerged from the crowd, Bible clutched to his chest. "He has saved us!" He slapped Colonel Wallace on the back. "Excellent jump, my dear man. Excellent jump!"

Other passengers popped up from below to congratulate the colonel. He received all their accolades with a wave of his hand as if embarrassed at the attention. But there was one man not rejoicing. One man, dressed all in black, who leaned against the starboard railing, eyeing the proceedings as a scientist would a specimen beneath a microscope. His angular face nearly matched the odd-shaped stone he rubbed between two fingers. When his dark eyes latched on hers, he snorted and ambled away.

Eliza rubbed her arms against a sudden chill. Or maybe it was just the hearty breeze that now blew across the deck, filling sails and fluttering the hem of her gown. Making her way to the railing, she spotted the soldiers slogging down the wharf in defeat, far out of range now as the ship picked up speed. A kaleidoscope of tall ships anchored at wharfs and quays passed before her eyes. Warehouses and taverns cluttered the docks. Mills and shops stretched into Charleston, where citizens began to emerge from their homes. A loud horn startled her, drawing her gaze to the other side of the brig, where a steamship made its way into port, white smoke pouring from its stack. If only they had steam power, they'd make it to Brazil much quicker. The sooner the better, to her way of thinking.

She glanced back toward Charleston. A string of quaint homes stretched across East Bay Street, reminding Eliza of her family home in Marietta, a faint memory these past years.

Colonel Wallace slipped beside her, following her gaze to the city. Her heart skipped a beat as the wind showered her with his scent. "Take a good look, Mrs. Crawford. We shall not see Charleston in a long while, if ever again."

"Does it sadden you, Colonel?" She gave him a sly grin.

He blinked and raised his brows. "You know who I am?"

"I know *of* you, sir."

"No wonder those soldiers suspected me." He chuckled, his eyes sparkling. "It would appear my charade fooled no one."

"It is hard to hide the look of a warrior."

"Hmm. I wasn't aware there *was* a look."

Eliza dragged her eyes away from him to view Shutes' Folly Island off their port side.

Blake swung about, placing his elbows on the railing. The breeze toyed with the black hair at his collar. "Ah, Castle Pinckney." He pointed to a small masonry fortification on the island. "We used it as a prisoner-of-war camp during the war."

Eliza studied the crumbling structure and thought of all the Confederate soldiers still being held in prisons in the North. An ache weighed on her heart. Enough was enough. Why couldn't the Union forgive and forget? Build instead of destroy? What good would it do this great nation to foster even more hatred and bitterness? She sighed, squinting against the sun. Yet prejudices ran deep, fueled by the agony of loss. She, of all people, knew that firsthand. It would be years, maybe even decades, before the wounds of this horrid war healed. Which was why she must leave her beloved country, her beloved South forever. She swung back around as they passed the South Battery at the tip of Charleston. Charred, cold cannons lined the park like sleeping soldiers. Dormant until the next war woke them into action.

Colonel Wallace gripped the railing, lost in his own thoughts. Finally, he said, "No, I am not sad to leave what has become of the South. It will never be what it once was. The North has seen to that." Spite bit his tone, but he wiped it away with a smile. "And you, Mrs. Crawford? Are you sad to say good-bye to your homeland?"

"I have not belonged here for quite some time, Colonel." She cast a glance toward Fort Sumter up ahead, a sudden nervousness rising. "They won't fire upon us, will they?"

Following her gaze, he shook his head, but not before she saw a flicker of trepidation cross his eyes. "We are no longer at war. And, to them, the *New Hope* is but another merchant ship leaving Charleston. The soldiers would have no way to get word to them in time, for I see no telegraph wires connecting the mainland." He hesitated a moment, as if hoping to gain reassurance from his own words. Finally, he breathed a sigh then leaned one arm on the railing and assessed her with an intensity that caused a flush to rise up her neck. "You did not go below with the other women during the shooting."

"I don't fare well in cramped spaces."

His laughter bubbled over her, pulling a grin to her lips. "Then I fear you have chosen a rather uncomfortable voyage, Mrs. Crawford. There is no place on a brig that is not cramped."

"Except on deck," she said.

"Indeed. Then I shall be privileged to see you often."

She lowered her gaze.

"Forgive my boldness." His tone was contrite.

"No Colonel. It's simply been awhile since I've received a compliment."

Her comment brought a perplexed look to his face, but he smiled nonetheless. "Still, it was a rather brave thing to do. Staying above amidst the shooting."

Eliza gazed over the white-capped wavelets in the bay. The wind picked up, stirring the loose strands of her hair about her neck until they tickled her skin. She pressed a hand over them, suddenly embarrassed that she'd never been able to put up her own hair properly without a maid. "I must thank you for saving my life, Colonel. I'm not quite sure why I didn't duck like everyone else."

"Shock does odd things to people." He rubbed his jaw as sullenness overcame him. "I've seen that firsthand."

"I imagine you have, Colonel." Eliza had witnessed that as well. The shock of men who woke to amputated limbs and disfigured bodies. The shock of watching their friends and companions die beside them.

His gray eyes turned inquisitive and sad. "You no doubt endured much"—he seemed to be searching for a word—"unpleasantness, being a nurse on the battlefield."

"More than I cared to." More than she would ever forget. The ship bucked, and she grabbed the railing for support.

"You have my sincere admiration, madam, for volunteering for such gruesome service. Many of my own men would have died if not for the hard work and care of our nurses."

"It was the least I could do." The very least after what she'd done.

"And signing up to be part of a new colony in Brazil. A widow? I do believe your courage and tenacity surpasses many of the soldiers under my command."

"I fear I've always been too adventurous for my own good." Eliza laughed even while her heart swelled at the colonel's praise. Especially coming from a man like him. She'd done her research on him before joining his expedition. Hailing from a prominent family in Atlanta, he was a West Point graduate who rose to the rank of colonel within only a year after his first commission. Being a nurse, she'd had many contacts among soldiers, many of whom had served under the colonel. All had the same story. His men adored him and happily risked their lives for him, and all who knew him spoke of his honor and integrity.

"Still, Colonel. You flatter me too much. It is I who should sing your praises for the sacrifices you made on the battlefield."

He glanced across the deck, his lips tight. "We have all sacrificed."

His humility only added to her regard.

He faced her. "You sacrificed your husband to this horrid war."

Eliza nodded and shifted her gaze to the bay, suddenly feeling like she had no right even to speak to such a man.

"Forgive me. I'm far too blunt at times."

Eliza could now add kindness to his list of exemplary qualities.

"But let's talk of more pleasant things." He studied her. The tone and expression on his face made her wonder if he, too, felt the overwhelming attraction between them. Another flush heated her neck. Oh fiddle! She was behaving like an innocent girl, not a widow who knew the intimacies of marriage. But then again, men had not paid her much notice in the past three years when she'd been covered in blood and filth on the battlefield.

"What do you hope for in Brazil, if I may ask, Mrs. Crawford?"

"A new start, like most of us, I imagine. But most of all peace. I long for peace, and a place to nurse cuts and colds not amputations and bullet wounds."

He nodded his understanding.

"And you, Colonel? Aside from desiring any place where you aren't hunted by authorities, that is."

"You said it all so succinctly in that one word. *Peace*." He gazed across the bay, such pain burning in his eyes, it nearly brought tears to her own. Pain and something else. A hint of hope, a longing. He faced her, snapping out of his daze. "Yes, peace. And to start a colony. Be there at the beginning of a new city, a new community, just like our forefathers. Very exciting!"

"And I have no doubt you'll find yourself as equal to the leadership of a colony as you were to the leadership of a regiment."

He looked down as if embarrassed by her compliment. How unusual and yet utterly charming for a man who was used to being in command.

"Now it is I who am flattered, madam. However, I'm quite pleased to have such an advocate on board."

"Then you can count on me, Colonel." Eliza smiled as they stared into each other's eyes a bit too long for being so newly introduced. Yet she couldn't seem to pull herself away.

Until thankfully, the snap of a sail broke the trance. With topsails spread to the rising wind, the *New Hope* approached the neck of the bay. Silence permeated every plank and timber as all gazes bounced between Fort Sumter on their right and Fort Moultrie on their left. Colonel Wallace stiffened. He slipped even closer to Eliza, as if he could actually protect her from a cannon blast. An endearing sentiment that brought a smile to her lips.

Though the American stars and stripes waved proudly above the fort, most of the buildings were nothing but crumbling ruins. Hammer and chisel echoed over the waters as soldiers worked to repair the once magnificent fort. Some of them stopped to gaze at the passing ship. One man even raised his hat to wave at them. Captain Barclay and a few sailors waved back, chuckling. As they sailed past, the remaining intact cannons merely winked at them in the sunlight.

Colonel Wallace released a breath. Captain Barclay ordered more sails raised, and within minutes, the unfurled canvas caught the wind in a jaunty snap, and the *New Hope* burst onto the open sea, free at last.

Other passengers emerged from below, among them the finely attired older couple Eliza had seen come aboard earlier.

"Mr. and Mrs. Scott," the colonel said in a low voice, following the direction of her gaze. "Wealthy plantation owners from Roswell, Georgia. Their daughter, Magnolia, must still be below. And behind them, there"— he pointed to a man in a striped shirt and suspenders. His rosy round face reminded Eliza of an aged apple. "Mr. Lewis, our carpenter."

The poor man's hands shook as he clasped them together and made his way to the foredeck. "He seems a bit unnerved," Eliza said.

"We are all unnerved, Mrs. Crawford. It is not easy leaving everything we know."

A gasp sounded from the Scotts' direction, and Eliza glanced to see Mrs. Scott, hand over her mouth, pointing across the deck at a Negro man and a woman with two small children.

"Ah yes." The colonel frowned. "The only freed Negroes coming on the journey. Moses; his sister, Delia; and her children, Joseph and Mariah."

Though many freed slaves had been wandering the streets since Eliza had come to Charleston, she'd never actually spoken to one. Her parents had kept a few house slaves in their home in Marietta, but Eliza had no idea whether freed slaves would be relieved, fearful, angry, or even hostile toward whites. Yet the kind look on Moses' face did much to ease her apprehension.

"And there is the doctor."

Eliza snapped her attention to a tall, brawny man with light brown hair and a scar angling down the side of his mouth. "Doctor?" She felt immediate relief that she wasn't the only medical person on board.

The colonel shifted his weight. "James Callaway. Well, at least he used to be a doctor in the war. He says he hasn't tended patients since. Became a preacher after that."

Eliza was about to comment on how odd a transition that must have been when a woman's scream blared from below.

All eyes shot toward the companionway hatch. Excusing himself, the colonel headed toward the sound when another scream pierced the air. Eliza followed him, fearing that her new roommates were somehow in trouble. Before they even reached the companionway, a man emerged. The wind caught his dark hair and blew it around him as he stumbled above, clutching his side. The plantation owner's daughter, Miss Magnolia, popped up behind him, her face awash with rage and fear. "He attacked me! That man attacked me in my cabin!" She dashed to her mother, who gathered her up in her arms and tried to console her daughter amid her hysterical sobs.

But the man didn't look as though he could attack anyone. Hand pressed to his side, he dropped to his knees before tumbling backward to the deck. Only then did Eliza see blood oozing in between his fingers.

She knelt beside him and studied the wound. "This man's been shot!"

CHAPTER 4

The night before

Hayden Gale sauntered into McCrady's Tavern, squinting as his eyes adjusted to the dim lighting. He scanned the mob of merchants, fishermen, gamblers, and ne'er-do-wells who frequented his favorite Charleston haunt, searching for the man he was to meet. Mr. Wilbur Ladson, Hayden's latest mark. Worth more than four thousand dollars a year and owner of more than five hundred acres of farmland in Ohio. The wealthy landowner had come to Charleston on a business deal, or so Hayden had heard. But Hayden's business with him had nothing to do with a deal and more to do with a sham—a sham that would make Hayden rich. Which was why he'd purposely made Mr. Ladson's acquaintance and, in the process, found him to be a man of oversized paunch and undersized intelligence. Add to that his excessive greed, and he was the perfect target. A target who would provide Hayden with both the means and the freedom to focus on a far more important goal.

Spotting the ill-bred, fatwit in the corner, Hayden headed his way, spiraling through tables laden with flickering lanterns, cards, and foamy mugs of beer, while waving off greetings tossed his way. It was good to be back in Charleston, the town of his birth, despite the memories that lurked in every corner, tugging at what was left of his heart. The heart he'd left behind when his mother had died and those same memories had banished him from town. But he was back now on a tip, a very reliable tip, that his father, Patrick Gale, had returned.

Hayden swept a gaze over the bawdy mob, looking for that face that was forever planted in his mind from a tintype of his mother's. He'd been searching for his father for fifteen years, and he wouldn't give up until he found him—and planted him six feet under for what he'd done. Even if it took the rest of his life. He scanned the faces one more time. His father wasn't here.

Just as well. Hayden had business to attend to. Besides, it was only a matter of time before he found the man. He'd nearly caught him in Galveston—had been in the same room with him, but the charlatan had slipped away. It was as if the man knew Hayden was looking for him. Which was impossible. Zooks, he probably didn't even remember he *had* a son.

Hayden stopped before Mr. Ladson, who was devouring a plate of shrimp and grits, grease sliding down his chin. A skinny man with spectacles perched atop a pointy nose sat beside him, sipping a drink. Odors of lard, alcohol, and tallow blended unpleasantness in Hayden's nose.

"Ah, Mr. Jones. Please join us." Mr. Ladson gestured toward a chair. "I'll order you a plate. Charleston excels herself in grits and seafood."

"No thank you." Hayden slipped comfortably into the phony name he'd given Mr. Ladson, as easily as he slipped onto the seat and gestured for the barmaid to bring him some port.

The three men drifted into conversation about the weather, the high price of goods in the South now that the war was over, the ease with which one could purchase Rebel land, all topics that conversely bored or angered Hayden. Though he'd spent some time during the past few years in the North, he was Southern bred through and through and hated what the "Reconstruction" was doing to his home. Reconstruction, indeed. More like destruction.

Mr. Ladson finished his feast, wiped his mouth with his napkin, and sat back in his chair. Someone began playing a piano on the other side of the room.

"We should get down to business, Mr. Jones." The skinny man, whom Hayden now remembered was Mr. Ladson's accountant, slid his spectacles up his nose. "Mr. Ladson and I have another business dealing later tonight."

"Another venture, sir?" Hayden smiled at Ladson. "It would seem your visit to Charleston has been quite lucrative."

"Indeed, Mr. Jones. First your deal involving a hundred acres of cultivated farmland and then another deal with Mr. Haley involving a grand investment in a railroad. The South is indeed prime for the picking!"

Hayden ignored the man's ravenous glee. In fact, he ignored everything else but the name Haley—a name that sent his stomach into his throat. "Mr. Martin Haley?"

"The same. Do you know him?"

Hayden painted a nonchalant mask on his face to disguise the hatred roiling within, something he had grown quite adept at doing over the years. *Haley.* One of his father's aliases. "I've made his acquaintance." He tapped his fingers over the rough wood.

The skinny man's eyes lit up. "Do you vouch for his integrity, Mr. Jones?"

Hayden could barely restrain his laughter. As it was, he coughed into his hand to hide any telltale expression sneaking onto his face. "Of course. He's a fair man. In fact, I have some business with him myself."

The men exchanged a glance before Mr. Ladson said. "Well, you best hurry. I believe Mr. Haley said he was leaving town tomorrow."

"Leaving?" Hayden kept his tone nonchalant.

"Yes, headed for Brazil on some wild scheme to buy up land so the South can rise again"—he lifted his mug of ale in mock salute—"or some such nonsense."

Hayden sifted this new information through his mind, pondering the implications. It sounded just like his father to run off to Brazil on some harebrained enterprise. The barmaid returned with his port. After flipping her a coin and sending her a wink that made her giggle, he downed the drink in a single gulp.

The skinny man pulled out a leather satchel that Hayden hoped was full of money, while Hayden withdrew the writ of sale from his coat pocket along with a pen and ink and laid them on the table. Cultivated farmland, indeed. The property Mr. Ladson had toured was such, but the land he was purchasing was nothing but a swamp.

The accountant grabbed the document and scanned it in the lantern light, his beady eyes shifting back and forth. A drop of sweat slid from his slicked-back hair onto his forehead.

"I assure you everything is in order," Hayden said. Mr. Ladson picked up the pen, dipped it in ink, and anxiously awaited his friend's approval.

Just sign the paper and give me the money. Hayden hid his urgency behind a placid smile. Once this deal was completed, he would leave a far richer man than when he'd arrived. And just in the nick of time. He was down to his last twenty dollars. And the crème de la crème of this fortuitous night would be that afterward he would follow these slatterns to their meeting with his father. Finally, he would have his revenge.

He shoved down a pinch of regret over swindling Mr. Ladson. The man was a Northerner who hated the South. He certainly deserved far worse. Besides, he had plenty of money. Yet even those excuses did not stop the accusations that constantly rang in Hayden's ears day and night, the words that stabbed his conscience and haunted his dreams.

You're just like your father.

A shadow drifted over the table, causing the lantern flame to sputter and cower. Mr. Ladson hesitated, pen poised over the document that would free Hayden to pursue his father without any encumbrances.

A voice accompanied the shadow. "Hayden Gale?"

Hayden gazed up into a pair of seething eyes set deep in a pudgy face. Hair bristled on the back of his neck. "I'm afraid you are mistaken, sir. There is no one here by that name. Now if you don't mind." He batted him away. "We have personal business to discuss."

Gruff hands grabbed Hayden by the coat and hauled him from the chair, slamming him against the tavern wall. Dust showered him from above. Spitting it away, Hayden held up arms of surrender. "My name is Elias Jones, sir. You have the wrong man." He tried to make out the man's features in the shadows, but he couldn't recollect him from the many men he had swindled over the past years. How was Hayden supposed to remember each one?

"Do I now?" The man gritted his teeth and hissed like an angry cat. "You're the one, all right. You defiled my wife and swindled my family out of our last two hundred dollars. No, no, I'd know you anywhere." Releasing Hayden, he slugged him across the jaw.

Hayden's head whipped around. His cheek stung. Ah yes, now he remembered the man. Rubbing his face, he glanced over at Mr. Ladson, who had put down the pen and was frowning at Hayden. *Blast it all!* Hayden released a foul curse. "I have no idea what you are referring to, sir." Drawing back, Hayden slammed his fist into the man's rather large belly. "But I will not stand by while you attack me and my character without cause." He shook his aching hand, but the man barely toppled over before he righted himself.

The music stopped, and a crowd formed around the altercation. Hayden wiped blood from his lip. He supposed he deserved the man's rage and worse for what he had done, but why did he have to find Hayden now when he was on the cusp of a huge deal?

Fist raised, the man charged Hayden again. This time Hayden blocked his blow with one hand while shoving the other across the man's jaw. Cheers erupted from the mob as more of the besotted gathered around to be entertained. But Hayden had no desire to provide said entertainment. He had no beef with this man, and he certainly didn't relish dying on the sticky floor of this hole-in-the-wall. Hayden's strike barely caused the burly man's head to swivel.

Shaking out the pain in his hand once again, Hayden backed away, studying the room for the best escape route. The man pulled out a pistol. Hayden barely heard the hammer snap into place over the raucous cheers, but the sound of it spelled certain doom.

"I'll kill you for what you've done, ye thievin' carp."

Hayden had no doubt he would do just that. "Now, calm yourself, sir. If you kill me, you'll go to jail, hang for murder. Then what would become of your lovely wife?"

The man seemed to be pondering that very thing as the shouts of the throng grew in intensity. *This can't be the end.* Hayden could not die for one night with a lady he barely remembered and a measly two hundred dollars. It just didn't seem fair. He'd done far worse than that in recent years. Several of those incidents now passed through his mind like a badly acted play—a play that would no doubt be performed before God on judgment day. Shame burned within him.

The ogre smacked his lips together. "Naw, killin' you will be worth it." He fired his pistol. Searing pain struck Hayden's side. Gunpowder stung his nose. The mob went wild, some rushing toward Hayden, others toward the man, while some broke into fistfights among themselves.

Gripping his side, Hayden ducked and wove a trail through the frenzied mob, finally blasting through the front door into the cool night air. He stumbled down the street, wincing at the pain and ignoring the horrified looks of passing citizens. He couldn't risk someone helping him. They would ask too many questions. Besides, his ruse was blown.

He must leave town as soon as possible. The pain of losing the fortune hurt nearly as much as his bullet wound. Nearly.

He slipped into a dark alleyway and slid to the ground by a rotting barrel. A rat sped across a shaft of moonlight. Hayden removed his hand. Blood poured from the wound. He peered into the shadows and grabbed a paper lying nearby. He intended to press it over his wound when a word at the top caught his eye. Brazil. He read further. A ship called the *New Hope* was leaving tomorrow at sunrise for Brazil to start a new Southern colony. Despite his pain, Hayden smiled. There could only be one ship leaving Charleston for Brazil tomorrow.

Perhaps fortune shone on Hayden after all.

Back to the present

Eliza glanced over the crowd of sailors and passengers closing around the wounded man. "Doctor, please help!" She addressed the man whom the colonel said was a physician, but he stood gaping at the patient as if he'd never seen blood before.

The colonel gripped the doctor's arm, drawing his gaze.

"That man assaulted me!" Magnolia Scott whined from across the deck.

"So you shot him?" the colonel barked.

"Of course not!" She huffed. "He was like that when he came in my cabin."

The crowd grew silent, their gazes shifting from Magnolia to the wounded man as if trying to imagine how he could have pulled off such a feat.

"I doubt he could assault anyone, Miss Scott." Eliza put voice to their thoughts as the captain barged through the mob and began spouting orders for the sailors to take the wounded man below.

"Do you have a sick bay, Captain?" Eliza stood.

"Aye, miss. But it's small and has few medicines. My man, Wilkes, will take you down."

"I'll show her," the colonel spoke up, dragging the doctor behind him.

Sinking down into the bowels of the ship once again, Eliza felt as though she were being smothered alive. At least the cabin in which the sailors put the wounded man was a bit larger than her own shared quarters, though not by much. They laid him in the center of the room on a wooden table that took up nearly the entire space, save for a cot, a work shelf, and a glass-enclosed cabinet sparsely stocked with bottles and vials. He groaned. Fear skittered across his green eyes. The doctor and the colonel entered behind her.

"I need a bowl of freshwater and some clean cloths," the doctor said to the sailors as they were leaving. "Remove his shirt, if you please, Miss, Miss. . ."

"Mrs. Crawford," the colonel interjected. "She's the nurse I told you about." He lit a lantern and hung it on a hook on the deckhead.

Eliza began unbuttoning the man's shirt. "Only a volunteer nurse. No formal training." The metallic odor of blood filled the air.

"The war?" the doctor asked.

She nodded, removing the soaked cloth.

"Then that's all the training you need."

"I did not. . .assault. . . ." The wounded man spoke, his voice strained and weak.

"Don't worry about that now." Eliza brushed strands of dark hair from his face. "We're going to remove the bullet and dress your wound."

"How did you get shot?" the colonel asked.

Oddly, the doctor remained at a distance. "And by whom?" he added.

The man had no answer.

"It didn't happen on board." Eliza examined the bloody opening. "Looks to be a day old at least."

The deck canted, and she gripped the table as the lantern sent waves of light over the patient. She didn't envy the doctor. It would not be easy to operate under these conditions. She faced him, awaiting his next command. He ran a hand through his brown hair streaked in gold and shifted his broad shoulders beneath a cutaway coat. The masculine lines of his chin quivered, stretching the scar angling down the right side of his mouth. But it was his eyes that drew her. The color of bronze. They would be striking except for the terror flashing across them at the moment.

"We must remove the bullet," the doctor said numbly as the sailors returned with the basin of water and cloths.

Eliza knew that much. Grabbing one of the cloths, she pressed it against the oozing gash. The man groaned, the sound joining the creak of timbers as the ship plowed through the sea.

The doctor gestured toward the wound, his eyes on the bulkhead. "You've dealt with these before, Mrs. Crawford, have you not?"

"I've assisted, but I've never extracted a bullet myself." It was then that she noticed his hands shaking. Which caused her pulse to rise.

"Then I will supervise," he said.

Colonel Wallace glared at him. "I agreed to your passage because you were a doctor, James."

"And I did not lie to you. I am a doctor. I simply haven't"—he halted and ground his teeth together—"I don't perform surgery anymore. Not since I left the battlefield. I told you I'm a preacher now. Been preaching the Word of God for the past two years."

"So, *Preacher*"—the colonel's tone was biting, his eyes raging— "you're telling me we have no doctor. No one to fix the broken bones and heal the diseases that will be inevitable in the jungles of Brazil?"

James took a deep breath in an effort to compose himself then flattened his lips. "I did not mean to mislead you, Colonel. I can instruct Mrs. Crawford. She can be my hands. But that is all I can offer you besides counsel in spiritual matters."

"What the dickens—I already have a parson aboard!" The colonel took up a pace while a look of contrition folded onto the doctor's face.

Eliza swallowed as the realization set in. She glanced at her patient. His fate rested in her hands and her hands alone.

CHAPTER 5

$\mathcal{B}$lake ran a comb through his hair and studied his reflection in the cracked mirror hanging on the bulkhead of his cabin. A fleeting question regarding his sudden interest in appearances taunted his mind, but he already knew the answer. It was the lovely Mrs. Crawford and his expectation of seeing her within moments in the captain's cabin. It was why he had washed the grime from his face and donned a clean shirt and waistcoat. He only wished he had more fashionable attire and perhaps some of that bergamot or cedar cologne women seemed to love. But he had no such thing—he was a simple man with simple tastes.

Except, he realized with surprise, when it came to Mrs. Crawford.

There was nothing simple about her. After the good doctor had declared his inability to operate, she had gone to work, steady-handed and determined, moving like a fine-tuned instrument beneath the doctor's instructions. Only her trembling voice gave away her fear. Still, she had continued until the bullet was removed, the wound stitched, and the patient resting.

Where other women would have swooned at the horrors of digging through human flesh, she performed her duty with courage, a courage Blake had not often seen, even on the battlefield. That any woman could endure the nightmare she no doubt suffered as a war nurse only made him respect Mrs. Crawford all the more. That any woman who'd lost her husband, who was alone in the world, would venture to an unknown land to start a new life only increased that rising respect.

And did he mention she was also beautiful? Not in a Magnolia Scott stunning sort of way, but in the kind of beauty found in a field of flowers: delicate yet strong. Fresh, uncontainable, and wild.

His cabinmate, the good doctor—or should he say preacher—entered,

44

hat in hand and hair tossed about his face, severing Blake's musings. James heaved a sigh. "I can't imagine what you must think of me, Blake." He tossed his hat onto the table. "I did not mean to deceive you. I knew you already had a parson and wouldn't sign another. So, once I discovered a nurse had joined the venture, I knew she could be my hands."

Blake stared at him through the mirror before turning around. The ship rolled over a wave, and he leveled himself against the shifting deck. "And what if there had been no nurse on board?"

"I wouldn't have signed up." James shrugged. "I would have sought another ship. One that needed a pastor." He dropped into a chair and leaned forward, elbows on his knees. "In truth, I didn't want to wait for the next ship. I wanted. . .no, *needed*, to leave everything behind."

A sentiment Blake could well understand. "Regardless"—he huffed—"you've left these colonists in a rather precarious situation."

"I still have the knowledge up here." James poked his head and gave a sheepish grin. "It's the hands that don't work anymore."

Blake rubbed his eyes and sighed, listening to the rush of seawater against the hull. It did much to soothe his nerves. "Well, I'm thankful Eliza could handle things." He studied his new friend for a moment, noting the way he clasped his hands together before him and stared at them as if they were foreign objects. "What's wrong with them?"

"I can't seem to stop them from shaking. Been like that since I left the assault on Petersburg in '84."

"Petersburg? I was there. Got a bullet in my leg to prove it."

James snorted. "Odd that it might have been me who tended your leg, but I don't remember."

"But you said you left?"

James nodded, his gaze still lowered.

"We won that battle," Blake said.

A moment passed in silence. "Still we lost nearly three thousand men that day." The trembling in James's hands increased. He clamped them together. "I couldn't stand it another minute. The blood, the agony, the mutilation of so many young men. Boys, really. I had to get away. So I ran away. Threw myself back into God's arms, into the preaching my father planned for me to do all along." He finally glanced up, a haunted look in his eyes, and rubbed the scar on his cheek. "But even that didn't help. Brazil is my last hope."

Emotion burned in Blake's throat. How many times had he felt like running away from the war, the stress and horror of battle after battle? But he was a colonel. His regiment depended on him. He had to do his duty. As a civilian doctor, James's situation was different. He'd dealt with amputated limbs and disgorged bowels and anguish and death all day and night with nothing but conscience to keep him at task. How could Blake blame him for leaving when he doubted conscience and duty would have been enough to keep him in such a hell?

He liked James. Straightforward, honest, humble. Blake had commanded enough men to recognize strength and goodness in a man's eyes. Besides, he could hardly fault James for trembling hands when Blake had his own visions and blackouts. "Brazil is the last hope for many of us," he finally said, his tone softening. Smiling, he gripped James's shoulder then grabbed his coat from a hook on the wall. "Come along, the captain will be waiting on us. I, for one, am looking forward to our first meal on board the ship."

James rose, straightened his string tie in the cracked mirror, and followed Blake down a long corridor and up a hatch where they emerged onto the main deck to a blast of wind and a magnificent starlit sky. Both stole Blake's breath away. Catching his balance on the rolling deck, he halted and gazed up at the million glittering diamonds spread across a black velvet curtain.

"Incredible, isn't it?" James said.

"Indeed."

All seemed quiet on deck. Most of the sails had been lowered and furled for the night, keeping only topsails faced to the wind. The first mate stood at the helm. Other passengers mulled about, but it was Mr. Graves, the ex-politician, who drew Blake's attention. He leaned over the starboard railing, cigar in hand, babbling something at the sea. Blake hoped the man wasn't mad. He had chosen him for his knowledge of government, which they would desperately need as their colony grew into a city. But it wouldn't do to have a lunatic organizing things.

It also wouldn't do to be pursued by a Union ship. The dark horizon offered Blake no glimpse of what dangers lurked beyond even as the smell of gunpowder still haunted his nose from his close encounter leaving Charleston. Still, the Union had better things to do than chase down one war criminal. And if Blake's memory served, there were no navy ships anchored in Charleston ready to depart at a moment's notice. The war was over, after all.

Shrugging off his worries, Blake hurried up the quarterdeck and down the companionway to the captain's cabin, where he was greeted by the fragrant scents of mutton stew, cheese, and buttered rice. His stomach growled. Far too loudly, for everyone in the room swept their gazes his way.

But it was only one gaze he was interested in. And her golden eyes sparkled when they met his.

Eliza hoped the captain had invited Colonel Wallace to dinner. She so wanted a chance to get to know him better. Now as he stood in the doorway, looking quite dashing in his suit of brown broadcloth, she could hardly take her eyes off him. He limped into the room with more authority than most did without disabilities to impede them. She lowered her gaze, hoping he hadn't noticed her staring at him, hoping he didn't find her too bold, and wondering if she hadn't lost her mind. After Stanton, Eliza wanted nothing more to do with marriage. She found the institution confining, restricting, and far too empty of the promises of love and romance she'd read about in Jane Austen novels. She had also found that she wasn't good at it. To even think of entertaining attentions from a man could only lead to disaster and heartache for them both. No, all she wanted was to escape her past and start over in a community in which she could use her nursing skills to help others. Then why, oh why, did Colonel Wallace affect her so? He was a Rebel officer! Of all the men on the ship, he was the one man she should avoid at all costs.

Introductions and greetings abounded between those in attendance: Mr. and Mrs. Scott, the wealthy plantation owners, and their daughter, Magnolia; Eliza's cabin mate Angeline Moore, whom she'd had to all but drag out of the cabin to attend; a man Eliza hadn't met, Mr. Dodd who was a sheriff from Richmond with an apparent problem keeping his eyes off the ladies. Then there was James Callaway, the doctor, of course, and Parson Bailey, who seemed too tiny a man to evoke fear of damnation from the pulpit.

A slave girl stood against the bulkhead behind the Scotts. Across from her, squeezed between a large chest and enclosed bookshelves stood two sailors awaiting commands.

Everyone took a seat around the table laden with bowls of stew, various cheeses, rice, and platters of biscuits and greens. Much to her delight, Colonel Wallace pulled a chair out for her right beside his own. The doctor, or should she say preacher, held out a chair for Angeline, placing her beside Eliza while he took the seat on her other side. Angeline thanked him and slid onto her chair, but her tone was strangled and her normally rosy cheeks had gone stark white as her gaze flitted between the doctor and Mr. Dodd.

Eliza laid a hand on her arm and gave her a concerned look, but the girl waved her off with an attempted smile.

The parson said grace in a rather loud and oversanctimonious tone that grated over Eliza, though she quickly reproved herself. She shouldn't think poorly of a man of God. Yet before he'd even intoned his lengthy "Aaaaaaamen," the captain had already scooped a healthy portion of rice onto his plate.

"We won't be dinin' so well for the remainder of the trip, I'm afraid." Captain Barclay glanced across the table. Though his voice was as rough as rope and his face wore the age of the sea, his demeanor was pleasant and his eyes kind. "But I thought for our first night, it would do well to enjoy a hearty meal with some of my guests."

The ones paying for a cabin, from the looks of things. All except Sarah, who had begged off with an excuse of an unsettled stomach.

"How fares this stowaway of ours?" the captain asked.

"His name is Hayden Gale, Captain," Eliza offered, grabbing a biscuit from a passing platter. "At least that's the name he gave me in his delirium."

Through the stern windows behind the captain, moonlight cast sparkling pearls over the ocean, swinging in and out of Eliza's vision with the rock of the ship. How the plates and bowls managed to stay on the table was beyond her, but aside from a little shift here and there, they were as sturdy as sailors under heavy seas. Candles showered the linen tablecloth, pewter plates, mugs, and silverware with flickering light, creating a rather elegant dining table for being out to sea.

"And he isn't on the passenger list, Colonel?" the captain asked.

"No sir." The colonel took the plate of biscuits from Eliza. Their fingers touched, and a spark jolted up her arm. His eyes shot to hers, playful and inviting. She looked away. *Oh fiddle! He knows how he affects me!*

"Of course the miscreant isn't on the manifest!" Magnolia scowled and turned down a bowl of corn her mother passed. "I told you he attacked me in my cabin. He's nothing but a lecherous swine!" She sniffed, and Eliza got the sense the girl's histrionics were purely for show. Her mother threw an arm around her and drew her close. "There, there, now."

Mr. Dodd looked as though he wanted to hug the girl himself, though not for the same reasons, Eliza was sure.

"Well, we can't be turnin' the ship around now." The captain chomped on a biscuit, crumbs scattering across his full gray beard. "If he has money, he can pay. If not, he can work."

Eliza helped herself to some greens and handed the dish to Angeline, who passed it on, staring numbly at her plate as if in a trance.

"You can't seriously allow him to join us. He could be a criminal!" Magnolia twirled a lock of hair dangling at her neck, candlelight firing in her sapphire-blue eyes.

The brig canted, sending a brass candelabrum and several plates sliding over the white tablecloth. The creak and groan of wood seemed the only answer to the young lady's outburst.

Until the colonel spoke up. "Never fear, Miss Magnolia. I'll have a chat with him when he recovers. We will get to the bottom of this. I won't allow any harm to come to you"—he glanced at Eliza—"or anyone aboard this ship."

Eliza tore her gaze from his as the warmth of being cared for flooded her—a feeling she hadn't felt in years.

"Magnolia!" Mr. Scott all but shouted, startling Eliza. "Quit fiddling with your hair. It's a disgrace as it is." He glanced back at the slave girl as if Magnolia's coiffure were her fault, failing to notice that his daughter melted into her chair at his admonishment. Facing forward again, he adjusted the jeweled pin on his lapel as a scowl deepened the lines curving his mouth. "And speaking of harm, I had no idea I would be traveling with freed Negroes." His gaze shot to the captain. "I simply must protest."

The stew soured in Eliza's stomach. "They are freedmen now, Mr. Scott." She abhorred slavery, always had. Though her father had treated their slaves with kindness, her aunt and uncle, who had taken over the hotel after her father's law practice became successful, had not. Now that the war was over and the Negroes were free, she wondered if they were any better off, for she'd heard that nothing but lynch mobs and starvation awaited them.

"It is the law now." The captain shoved a spoonful of rice into his mouth, but Eliza got the impression his sentiments lay more with Mr. Scott's.

"They have a right to start over just as we do," Eliza added.

The colonel turned to her, but she couldn't tell if the expression on his face was shock or admiration.

Mr. Scott gave an incredulous snort. "Start over! What nonsense. Start over from what? For what purpose?"

"I couldn't agree more, sir." Mr. Dodd took a mouthful of stew then dabbed a napkin over his lips. Tall, well-dressed, with blond hair, a lopsided, pointy nose, and deep blue eyes, one could almost consider the sheriff handsome. Even his manners and speech indicated good breeding. But something about the man gave Eliza the quivers. And not in a good way.

Mr. Scott nodded his approval toward Dodd.

The colonel cleared his throat. "As much as it may unsettle some of us, Mrs. Crawford is right. They are free as we are and must be treated with respect."

"Respect? They were not created for respect." Mr. Scott's fork clinked a bit too loudly on his plate. "I say we drop them off at the nearest island."

His wife's gaze remained lowered, though a whimper escaped her lips. A breeze squeezed beneath the door, sputtering the candles and playing a symphony of lights and darks across the deckhead.

The colonel set down his glass. "We will do no such thing, Mr. Scott. And that is the end of it." His commanding tone brooked no argument, and Eliza could see why men obeyed him. Even Mr. Scott seemed momentarily speechless, though she was sure the pleasant reprieve wouldn't last.

Captain Barclay took a swig of wine, wiped his mouth with the tablecloth, and leaned back in his chair. "As much as I don't approve of freeing the beasts, it is the way of things now. They are hardworking and will no doubt be an asset to your colony."

Mr. Scott huffed his displeasure. Magnolia frowned and picked at her food.

Eliza wondered how the Scotts' servant felt about the conversation, but when she glanced her way, her face was as bland as the stew they were eating. Did she know she could be free? Why hadn't she left the Scotts? Eliza had heard that several slave owners had threatened to hunt down and kill any slaves who ran away. She hoped that wasn't the case with this sweet girl, who looked to be no more than fifteen.

Angeline pushed food around her plate, oddly keeping her face turned from James, who sat beside her. Finally, she joined the conversation. "And what is your opinion, Parson Bailey? Does God have something to say about slavery?"

The parson's scrawny shoulders rose. He set down his fork and took a drink, drawing out the moment. With a receding hairline, thick muttonchops, and tiny close-set eyes, he looked more like a mongoose than a man. A chuckle bubbled in Eliza's throat at the comparison, and she hid her smile behind a napkin.

"The Bible says much about slavery, Miss Angeline. Slavery was well accepted in biblical times, even encouraged."

James plopped a chunk of cheese into his mouth. "I beg to differ with you, Parson. Accepted, yes. Part of the culture of the day, indeed. But hardly encouraged. Not by God nor by Jesus. In fact"—he shot a glance over the table—"in the Jewish tradition, if a man was a slave to another, he was freed every forty-nine years during Jubilee."

The parson's face twisted in a knot. "And who are you, sir, to dare interpret scripture?"

"He is a preacher like yourself." The colonel smiled.

"Indeed." He turned condescending eyes on James. "From what church?"

"My father pastored the Second Baptist Church in Knoxville, Tennessee. I took over the parish when I"—he coughed—"returned from the war."

"Humph." The parson wiggled his nose as if some unpleasant smell had invaded it. "Baptists, of course."

James was about to respond when Mr. Dodd leaned forward and addressed Angeline. "I know you from somewhere, Miss Moore."

Angeline choked on the first bite of food she had taken. She coughed into her napkin, not facing the man. "Mine is a common face, sir."

"I would hardly agree with that!" James said so emphatically a few of the men chuckled. A blush rose up his neck, and Eliza smiled.

Angeline was indeed a beauty. With hair the color of copper and violet eyes framed in thick lashes, she rivaled Magnolia in comely appearance. Yet unlike Magnolia, Angeline had a sweet demeanor about her and something else, a strength hidden by weakness.

Yet now, the poor girl seemed to be having trouble breathing. Eliza pressed a hand on her back.

"No, no, no." Mr. Dodd nodded, still studying her. "I'm sure we have met. It will come to me in time."

Angeline swallowed her meat and drew a deep shuddering breath as Eliza's gaze swept to Magnolia. She felt the same way about the Southern belle—as if she'd seen her before. But where?

"I don't see why we have to go to silly old Brazil anyway," Magnolia said, drawing her lips in a pout. "The South will eventually rise again, and all my friends are still in Roswell." Her eyes moistened as she glanced over the dinner guests, searching for an ally.

A growl emanated from Mr. Scott's direction.

Mrs. Scott bit her lip and laid a hand on her daughter's. "Now, dear, you know your father spoke to you about this."

"Brazil is the new Eden!" Mr. Dodd exclaimed. "A paradise waiting to be harvested." He leaned forward, a sly look in his eyes. "With plenty of gold, I hear."

"Gold, humph." James smirked, causing Dodd to go on rather forcefully. "Pirate gold, my good doctor, pirate gold. You'll see."

"Gold or not," the colonel interjected, "it is a land of freedom and new opportunities, and Lord knows, after what we have all endured, we need both."

"Here, here!" Captain Barclay slouched back in his chair and sipped his wine, assessing his guests. His gaze landed on Angeline who was still toying with her food. "Where are you from, Miss Moore?"

"Norfolk, Captain. My father was the owner of several shipyards there."

"Norfolk?" Mr. Dodd exclaimed. "Then that's where I've seen you. I was born in that fair city."

At his statement, some of the tightness seemed to leave Angeline's body.

"But you said *was*, Miss Moore," the captain pressed.

"Yes. He's deceased." She paused to collect herself.

The table grew silent for a moment. Not even the clink of a fork or the slosh of drink. Nothing but the rustle of the sea against the hull and the gentle creak of wood.

Eliza laid a hand on Angeline's arm. "I'm sorry for your loss." She wanted to ask her if his death was due to the war but thought it best not to dig any deeper into the lady's sorrow, especially in front of the others.

"The dear man is in heaven now." Parson Bailey offered the expected platitude.

The colonel finished his last bite of stew and set down his spoon. "I'm sure there is not a person at this table who has not lost someone close to them in this horrendous war."

Nods of affirmation and vacant eyes attested to the truth of his statement. All except Dodd, who cleared his throat and poured himself another glass of Madeira.

"Ah, Mr. Dodd," Captain Barclay said, "perhaps you knew Miss Moore's father?"

"No, I do not seem to recall a shipwright named Moore. However, I left town when I was but eighteen to pursue my profession."

"Which was?" Mrs. Scott asked.

"I was a sheriff in Richmond for several years." His shoulders rose.

Angeline broke into a fit of coughing. Her face turned red, and Eliza grabbed her arm and patted her back. "Hurry, something to drink," she said.

The carafe of wine was passed, and Eliza poured some into her friend's glass and held it to her lips. "Here, take a sip."

Magnolia licked her own lips and grabbed the carafe, filling her cup.

"What are you doing?" Mr. Scott snatched the glass from his daughter's hand. "Ladies do not drink. It is most unbecoming. And, for God's sake, sit up straight."

The poor girl straightened her spine immediately, placed both hands in her lap, and stared straight ahead as if she were a soldier.

Their eyes met, and Eliza saw an emptiness in them before they flashed in recognition. So the young woman remembered Eliza as well. A lump formed in her throat, and she prayed silently that her association with Magnolia had only been in passing. Otherwise, if the lady knew who Eliza had married, this trip would be over before it started.

At least for Eliza.

CHAPTER 6

*E*liza was beyond exhausted. Many of the passengers had become seasick as the ship moved farther out to sea, and she'd done nothing but run back and forth from passenger to passenger, trying to ease their discomfort. Which of course she couldn't really do. Thank God she had not succumbed to the debilitating condition herself. Although being forced to traverse the cramped bowels of the ship like a gopher caused her stomach to clamp so tight, it forbade all passage of food anyway. It grew even worse when she had to visit the hold where most of the passengers were berthed. And where most of those who were still ill groaned and moaned and gripped their stomachs in agony. All she had on hand to help relieve their symptoms were mint tea and words of comfort. But that seemed trite in light of what they suffered.

Now, as she made her way to the captain's cabin to witness the stowaway's interrogation by the captain and Colonel Wallace, despite her exhaustion, despite her hunger, her heart fluttered in her chest. Rebellious traitorous heart! Of course she'd seen the colonel on deck during these past three days, busy helping the captain, but they'd not had an opportunity to speak. Which was for the best, of course. Yet something about him tugged on her, drawing her thoughts and heart like the needle of a compass to true north. And as with a compass, there seemed to be naught she could do to change its direction.

Maybe it was the sorrow that seemed to hover about him like thick, dark clouds gorged with rain. She'd seen many men afflicted in the same way during her years as a nurse. She'd also seen some of them find relief by simply sharing their horrors, their heartache and pain, with someone who cared. Perhaps she could be that someone for the colonel. Strictly as a friend, of course.

Pressing down her blue tarlatan skirts, she squeezed through the corridor, thankful recent fashions had flattened the wide crinolette and moved it around back, or she might get stuck like a fat mouse in a maze in these narrow hallways. After knocking and hearing a call to enter, she opened the door and slipped inside the captain's cabin. Her patient, the stowaway Hayden Gale, sat in a chair, looking none the worse for the pistol shot in his side. His long hair, the color of dark coffee, hung just below his collar, and though he pressed a hand over his wound, color had returned to his cheeks. Not an ounce of fear crossed his green eyes as he stared straight ahead at the captain.

To his left stood Colonel Wallace, arms crossed over his chest. His black string tie hung limp over his white shirt as if he'd done battle with it and lost. James was behind him, while two of the captain's officers guarded either side of the desk. Magnolia and her mother sat in the far corner, and Parson Bailey leaned against the bookshelves, nose in the air. Absent their coats—no doubt due to the rising heat—the bands tied around the men's arms appeared stark against their white shirts. Black bands that had become such a familiar, yet depressing, sight throughout the South this past year. Bands of mourning that represented a loved one lost in the war. Every man in the room had at least one, save Hayden. The colonel sported five as far as Eliza could tell. *Five.* Her heart went cold at the sight.

"Ah, there you are, Mrs. Crawford," the captain said, shifting her attention his way. "We thought you should be here since Hayden is your patient."

The colonel approached and gestured toward an empty chair by the Scotts, giving her a smile that sent her heart spinning again and making her wonder what he had looked like in his uniform. Quite handsome, she imagined.

"Now, Hayden, how did you come to be on my ship?" Captain Barclay leaned back in his chair, moving a pocket watch in between his fingers with astounding ease. Behind him, glittering shafts of morning sun bounced over the desk and the bulkheads, and over the stowaway, who snapped his hair from his face and huffed his displeasure at the question.

"As I told you, it was purely by accident. I got shot, became delirious, and wandered on board unwittingly."

"Crawled all the way up a swaying plank and onto a ship, did you?" James snorted. "You must have been quite out of your head!"

"I was, sir." Hayden gave the doctor a sardonic look then cocked his head in scrutiny. Seconds ticked by as the two men stared at each other, and Eliza began to wonder if perhaps they had met before. Although James seemed more annoyed than pleased. Then for no apparent reason, Hayden gave a hearty laugh and faced forward. "Yes *Doctor*. Quite delirious. And feverish, in fact."

Eliza didn't recall noting any fever, but she kept that to herself.

Magnolia stood and pointed a trembling finger his way. "I assure you, his assault on me was no accident!"

Hayden's interested gaze took her in. "Princess, though your beauty may warrant such an action from a desperate man, I, myself, have never had to beg, force, or steal affections from any woman."

A grin lifted the corner of Hayden's lips as he continued to gaze at Magnolia. Eliza agreed. He was far too charming to have to beg for feminine attention. Not only was the man appealing to look at but he had a dark, mysterious quality about him that, coupled with a roguish charm, made him quite alluring. Magnolia, apparently, was not of the same opinion, for the Southern belle stomped her tasseled boot on the deck, her eyes seething. "You have your proof! He is a beast!"

Mrs. Scott drew her daughter into an embrace. "Captain, you must do something to ensure my daughter's safety." The deck tilted, sending the ladies back down to their seats and the gentlemen bracing their boots.

Parson Bailey gave Hayden a look of pity. "God can forgive any sin, son. You have only to ask."

The colonel took a step toward Hayden. "What were you doing in Miss Scott's cabin, sir?"

"I was searching for something with which to bandage my wound. What else would I be doing?" Hayden stretched his broad shoulders beneath what had once been a fine, silk-lined, wool coat but was now torn and marred with blood.

"Mrs. Crawford and I can vouch for his condition, Captain," James offered, rubbing his chin. "He'd lost a significant amount of blood and could hardly stand."

"That doesn't mean he didn't have vile intentions." Mr. Scott's jowls quivered with his pronouncement.

"The heart is inherently evil," Parson Bailey added. A sail thundered overhead.

Hayden rolled his eyes. His jaw hardened beneath a sprinkling of dark stubble. "I did not mean to frighten the lady."

"Very well." Captain Barclay scratched his scraggly beard. "But there is the matter of why you were shot, sir."

Hayden hesitated, staring at the canvas rug beneath his boots. "Tavern brawl."

Magnolia huffed. "Mercy me. Does that not attest to his character?"

He gave her a sideways glance, a hint of a grin toying with his lips.

"That doesn't answer the question." The colonel's commanding tone had returned.

"A misunderstanding."

James rubbed the scar on his cheek. "Then why didn't you seek medical aid?"

"Like I told you, I was delirious. I don't even remember coming on board."

"Very well." Captain Barclay stood, opened and shut his pocket watch, then placed it on his desk. "There's naught to be done about it now. I'm afraid you're stuck with us, Hayden, all the way to Brazil. As soon as I drop off these fine people, I'll take you back to Charleston if that is your desire."

Hayden shifted in his seat and glanced over those present, his eyes softening for the first time since Eliza had entered. "I wouldn't mind trying my luck out in Brazil, seeing what she has to offer."

"She has nothing for you, I'm afraid." The colonel's gray eyes hardened around the edges. "You have not paid for your voyage, nor have you passed the criteria for joining our new society."

Hayden chuckled then clutched his side with a wince. "Zooks, what criteria? I'm strong and capable. You'd be fortunate to have me." The ship suddenly bucked over a wave, causing those standing to stumble. The parson struck the bulkhead with a thud.

"Not if you're a thief or murderer." Mr. Scott stiffened his jaw.

"Or a ravager of women," Magnolia spat.

Hayden snorted. "So what's it to be? Clapped in irons and locked below for the entire voyage?"

"That's for the captain to decide." The colonel deferred to Captain Barclay with a gesture.

The old sea dog circled his desk, stuffing his watch into a pocket. "When you've recovered from your wound, you may prove your strength and capability by joining my crew. That way you can at least pay for your passage."

Hayden flinched. "I know nothing about sailing."

"You'll learn quickly." The captain winked at his two officers, one of whom chuckled.

"I suppose I have no choice." Flattening his lips, he released a sigh. "Though, the work is beneath me." He tugged at his cravat, the lace of which was not only out of style but stained.

"And just what is your normal enterprise, Mr. Hayden?" Eliza spoke up, though she had yet to make up her mind about the man.

Eyes the color of jade assessed her. "Investments, Mrs. Crawford. I deal in land and commodities, foreign and domestic."

Something in the quirk of his lips and flash of his eyes made her wonder if he was being forthcoming.

Colonel Wallace shifted his boots over the deck and glared at the man. "If you so much as look at a lady for more than two seconds, or if I find anything missing on this voyage, I won't hesitate to feed you to the sharks."

Instead of cowering beneath the colonel's authority, Hayden gazed up at him, a playful sparkle in his eyes. "Such drastic measures, Colonel. Won't I even get a trial?"

"God sees all things done in the darkness," Parson Bailey interjected.

"I'm the law here," the colonel replied.

Hayden sat back in his chair with a huff. "You won't have any trouble from me."

This seemed to satisfy all present, except the Scotts, who approached the captain's desk spewing further complaints. The captain dismissed them with a wave and a hearty declaration that all would be well, sending them leaving in a stew of huffs and "I nevers." Just as quickly, he released Eliza, the parson, and Hayden with the excuse that he needed to discuss business with James and the colonel. The latter glanced forlornly at her as she left the cabin, his eyes full of promise. Was he as disappointed as she was at not having a chance to speak to each other? Or perhaps God was protecting her from her own foolish heart—a heart that had led her astray once before.

Just as Eliza was leaving, a sailor brushed past her and barreled into the cabin. "Captain, the compass is crushed. Broken clean through."

Her ears burning from the resultant curses behind her, Eliza headed toward the galley for some tea, wondering who would destroy a compass and why.

With a hot cup in hand, she finally entered her cabin to the moans and groans of Sarah, swinging in her hammock. The poor dear had also succumbed to the cruel whip of mal de mer, and Eliza hated that she couldn't do more to ease her suffering. Halting beside the pregnant woman, she wiped sweaty strands of hair from a face as white as the foamy wake off the stern. The foul stench of sickness emanated from the chamber pot on the table.

Slipping an arm behind Sarah's back, Eliza helped the woman sit, bunching pillows behind her and lifting the cup of mint tea to her lips. Her gaze wandered past the sunlight winking off Sarah's gold cross down to her distended belly, so round and firm with child, and a sad thought jarred Eliza. She would probably never have children.

When she'd first married Brigadier General Stanton Watts, she'd hoped to have a houseful. She could still see him standing at the altar the day of their wedding in his crisp blue uniform with sparkling brass buttons and the single gold star adorning his shoulder board, denoting his elevated rank. So handsome! At that moment, she'd believed she was the luckiest girl alive. That was until news of war interrupted their honeymoon.

After depositing her at his family home in Harrisburg, Pennsylvania, he'd thundered away on his horse to meet with a Union war council. During the next year, she'd only seen him twice when he'd made brief visits to their home and even briefer visits to their bed. Then he was gone forever, leaving her a widow at only nineteen.

She doubted she'd ever marry again.

Sarah sipped her tea, the sweet mint fragrance rising to sweep away Eliza's foul memories.

"Oh my, your face looks a fright!" Sarah breathed out between gulps. "The way you are staring at my stomach as if the child will burst through at any moment. I assure you"—she ran a hand over the bulge—"she isn't ready yet."

"Forgive me." Embarrassed, Eliza snapped from her daze and withdrew the cup. "It's just that I have always wanted children." She blinked. "Wait. You said, 'she.' How do you know?"

"I just know." Sarah caressed her belly with fingers born to love a child.

Eliza set down the cup. "Well, you needn't worry. I've delivered wee ones before. And the doctor is more than experienced, I should imagine."

Yet it was another voice that answered. "Yes indeed. James does seem more than competent." Angeline burst through the door, her face aglow with sun and wind, and her voice cheery.

When both ladies gaped at her, she lowered her lashes. "I meant to say, he seems highly intelligent. And kind." She brushed a curl from her forehead and frowned, her mood shifting as rapidly as the rays of sunlight through the porthole. "Which surprises me, actually."

Eliza and Sarah's stares turned into smiles, causing Angeline to continue babbling. "He makes a better doctor than a preacher, I think."

"How would you know such a thing? Are you acquainted with the man?" Eliza asked.

Angeline's eyes widened, and she let out a little laugh. "Of course not. No. I've never. . .no, no. Of course not."

Eliza helped Sarah lie back down, perplexed at Angeline's sudden nervousness.

Which abandoned the lady when she heard Sarah groan. Dashing to the hammock, Angeline squeezed her hand. "I'm so sorry you are sick. You must be miserable."

As though on cue, the deck seesawed, sending the hammock swinging and both Eliza and Angeline stumbling. Sarah threw a hand to her mouth, her face blanching, and Eliza quickly grabbed the chamber pot, but the woman waved it away.

Though Eliza had never been seasick, she knew from her experience these past three days how debilitating it must be. Men, far stronger than Sarah, had been reduced to whimpering sacks below decks, while she, on the other hand, put them all to shame with her kind smile and noncomplaining attitude. Even now she squeezed Angeline's hand and said, "Don't concern yourself with me. I'll be well soon enough."

Releasing Sarah's hand, Angeline stepped toward the porthole, where sunlight dusted her hair in waves of fiery copper.

Eliza was reminded of James's interest in the girl. Fiddle, if Eliza couldn't get married, she could certainly aid in finding agreeable matches for her friends. "Doctor or preacher, I do believe James has taken notice of you."

"Me?" Angeline gave a nervous chuckle. "No." She sank into a chair, her shoulders lowering. "He is simply kind to everyone."

Eliza raised a brow. She'd seen the way the doctor looked at Angeline at dinner and then several times on deck. "We shall see. And you"—she dabbed a moist cloth on Sarah's head—"I don't want you fretting over your upcoming delivery."

The woman gave a weak smile. "I'm not worried. God is with me, Eliza. He has never let me down."

Eliza nodded. God had been faithful to her as well, though she had not always been faithful to Him. Still, she wondered how this woman could say such a thing when she was about to bring a child into the world with no husband to care for them.

Sarah's gaze traveled between Eliza and Angeline. "Since I'm sure you are both wondering, my husband, Franklin, fought with the Sixth Georgia Volunteer Infantry." She paused and ran a hand over her extended belly, sorrow clouding her features. "After the war ended, he came home a different man. Wounded more on the inside than on the outside."

Eliza swallowed down a burst of angst at what the woman would say next. She reached for her hand.

"He hung himself in our barn just last Christmas."

Angeline gasped.

Moisture flooded Eliza's eyes.

Yet Sarah's expression was full of peace. "Don't look so sad. He's doing far better than we are now. I miss him, but I'll see him again."

Angeline's brows scrunched. "How can you know for sure?" When both Eliza and Sarah once again stared at her, she bit her lip. "Please forgive me, Sarah. I'm sure your husband is in heaven. It's just that. . .that"—she gazed out the porthole—"I fear my faith has slipped away over the years."

"We shall have to rectify that, shan't we, Eliza?" Sarah said.

Ignoring the woman's declaration, Angeline jumped to her feet. "Oh sweet saints, I almost forgot. Mr. Scott is reading portions of *Hunting a Home in Brazil* on deck. The air is clear and fresh, and it may do Sarah well to go above."

When they all agreed, Eliza and Angeline assisted Sarah out of the hammock, into a simple gown, and up the companionway ladder. A group of passengers huddled around Mr. Scott, who sat atop a barrel, reading from an open book. The constant bucking of the deck tried to disband the mob, but they clung as steadfastly to each other as they did to every word the old plantation owner uttered. Words that, through the sieve of wind, wave, and the thunder of sail, reached Eliza as naught but garbled grunts. The deck rose then dropped, nearly toppling the ladies and sending salty mist over their faces. Shaking it away, Eliza finally managed to settle Sarah against the railing closer to Mr. Scott, where they all could hear him better.

Wind gusted over them, sneaking beneath their skirts and puffing out the fabric until they appeared like three lacy bells dancing on the deck. In fact, as Eliza took in the scene, all the women's skirts were similarly bloated. Restraining a chuckle at the sight, she held her hat down and endeavored to hear Mr. Scott when she spotted the colonel on the quarterdeck beside Captain Barclay. He stood, hands clasped behind his back, with as much authority as if he were captain of the ship. His gaze shifted to her, and she thought she saw a smile touch his lips before the captain leaned to say something to him. No doubt the compass had either been repaired or replaced, for neither the captain nor the sailors seemed alarmed.

James, the good doctor, stood across the deck talking with a sailor, but his eyes had already found Angeline. Beside him, Mr. Graves, his ebony hair tossed in the wind, leaned against the starboard rail, puffing on a cigar and assessing the crew and passengers with the disinterested attachment of one watching a play.

"Have you been to Brazil?" one of the passengers asked Mr. Scott, drawing Eliza's gaze away from the distressing man.

"No, I haven't had the pleasure. But it says right here that Brazil is a Garden of Eden. A paradise of temperate weather, abundant fruit, and rich soil."

One of the women clapped her hands in delight.

"And the land's only twenty-two cents an acre!" another man shouted.

"An' there ain't no Yankees!" a man beside him said, eliciting a round of applause.

"Yes." Mr. Scott closed his book. "Rivers as wide as cities and filled with all manner of fish, and flowers as big as my hand that smell sweeter than a Georgia peach."

"May God bless our journey and our new colony." Parson Bailey, ever-present Bible clutched to his chest, gazed up at heaven as if the Almighty would shower him with good fortune at that very moment. Instead, the deck tilted and he staggered.

"And we can have slaves if we want," a man shouted, causing a few uncomfortable glances to find Moses and his sister standing up on the foredeck. Up until that point, the black man's face had been beaming at the descriptions of Brazil, but now he merely stared at the crowd without expression. Eliza found his courage admirable for a man who only a year ago would have been whipped for looking a white man in the eyes. Delia, his sister, however, lowered her gaze and gathered her children into her skirts.

"But you will *not* enslave Mr. Moses and his sister." Colonel Wallace's thunderous voice blared with authority as he leaped down the quarterdeck ladder and approached the group. Even with his limp, his gait reminded Eliza of the prowl of a lion. Mr. Scott scowled and dabbed a handkerchief over his brow.

"He has been freed and will remain free," the colonel added, fists on his waist. "However, I'm told you will be able to purchase slaves once we are on Brazilian soil if you have the intent and the coin. They allow no importation of slaves."

"What about Mr. Scott?" The blacksmith jerked a thumb toward the elderly plantation owner. "He has that slave girl with him."

Mr. Scott stuck out his chin. "She is my daughter's lady-in-waiting. Nothing more."

Eliza wondered if that was true. She'd not seen the girl do anything but shadow the spoiled woman since she'd come aboard.

One of the farmers removed his hat and dabbed the sweat on his brow. "What happens when we arrive, Colonel? How do we know where to buy land?"

The deck jerked to larboard, and Colonel Wallace shifted his weight from his bad leg. "We will sail into Rio de Janeiro, where we will meet with Brazilian authorities, perhaps even the emperor himself."

Gasps and glances sped through the crowd.

"I'm told," he continued, "they will assist us with scouts and interpreters to help us choose the best land."

"Oh, it all sounds so marvelous," Rosa Jenkins, one of the farmers' wives, exclaimed as she hugged her young daughter.

Dodd slunk through the crowd and stopped before the colonel. "I hear tell there's a hidden lake of gold guarded by monster crocodiles." His eyes flashed with excitement as he glanced over the mob. Some stared at him as if he'd lost his mind. Others ignored him, while interest lingered in a few gazes. In fact, more than one sailor stopped what he was doing and inched closer.

"Did you say a lake of gold?" a woman exclaimed.

"Just a myth, Mr. Dodd." James joined the group. "An old tale meant to fool the greedy."

Dodd looked him over with a sneer and patted his pocket. "Maybe the lake is a myth, but I have a map." His brows arched. "An old pirate map that describes the location of buried treasure."

The colonel chuckled. "If there were any treasure, I'm sure it's long gone by now, Mr. Dodd. Pirates don't tend to leave their gold for long."

"If they all got killed off, they do." Wind blew Dodd's blond hair into a frenzy and doused Eliza with the scent of his Macassar cologne. "Besides, I got this map from an old sailor who frequented pirate haunts in the Caribbean. Paid good money for it."

"I hope not too much." James chuckled, and several colonists joined him.

"Is that why you signed on with the colony?" The colonel's tone grew strained. "And here I brought you along for your experience as a sheriff."

"I'll be your law when the occasion calls for it." Dodd opened his pocket watch and gazed at the time as if he had an appointment. "But that won't stop me from looking for gold."

The colonel shook his head and snorted before returning to his post. Yet several passengers crowded around Dodd, wanting to know more about this mysterious treasure. Others continued prodding Mr. Scott for more information about Brazil, prompting from him further descriptions of exotic fruits, wild chickens that all but leaped into pots of boiling water, forests filled with mahogany and cherry, plenty of wild game for the taking, and sap as sweet as honey. But Eliza grew bored at the fanciful talk. For that was all it was. There was no paradise this side of heaven. No utopia. She'd forsaken whimsical dreams when her family disowned her and left her to rot on the street. When she'd been forced to witness horrors no woman should see. Brazil was a new start for her. A place where people didn't know who she was. Nothing more. She raised her face to the sun, feeling its warm fingers caress her skin. A breeze tugged strands of hair from her chignon, but she didn't care. Though her father had forbidden her to wear it down, saying, "Only women of questionable morals wear their hair loose," Eliza had tossed aside her pins at every opportunity. Here in the relentless wind, she had the perfect excuse. She smiled as her curls tickled her neck and tumbled down her back. Free.

She was free at last.

No more loathing glances from the citizens of Marietta, no more being banned from shops, hotels, eating houses, and even from church. No more falling asleep hungry in tavern rooms not fit for pigs, selling her nursing skills for pennies to desperate souls who tolerated her presence. It had not mattered where she went or how far she ran, or even that she had changed her name, it seemed everyone knew the famous solicitor Seth Randal's traitorous daughter.

She drew in a deep breath of the briny air and smiled. The rush of water against the hull combined with the snap of sail and creak of timber into a soothing symphony that swept over Eliza, loosening her tight nerves. The ship lunged and sprayed her with salty mist.

Closing her eyes, she waited for the sun and wind to dry the moisture away when a voice crashed down on her from above. "A sail! A sail!"

"Where stands she?" Captain Barclay shouted as Eliza glanced across the horizon.

"Two points off our larboard stern, Captain!"

Spinning to face the back of the ship, Eliza spotted half-moons of snowy canvas floating over the azure sea about a mile astern.

Clutching her skirts, she crossed the deck to where the colonel stood, spyglass to his eye. "Who are they?"

"Unclear." He continued to study them. "I can't spot their flag."

Eliza's throat went dry. "You don't suppose the Union sent a ship after us."

He lowered the scope and gave her a reassuring smile. "They wouldn't waste their time. I'm the only contraband on board this brig."

Though the colonel's voice was strong and confident, his gray eyes held a hint of alarm. The wind flung Eliza's hair into her face. She swatted it away and glanced once again at the ship.

"Most likely a merchantman or a fishing vessel," he continued. "Nothing to trouble yourself over. See, even Captain Barclay isn't concerned." He pointed to the quarterdeck where the captain calmly studied the ship, his first mate by his side.

Eliza nodded, tension fleeing her as she drew a deep breath. However, that tension returned when off the bow of the ship, a wall of fog ascended from the sea, blocking their path.

Graves, the brooding ex-politician, caught the direction of her gaze and smiled at her from his spot by the foremast. But she hadn't time to wonder at the reason. Instead, she alerted the colonel, who upon seeing the fog, called to the captain. The sailors had been so intent on determining the origin of the other ship, they hadn't noticed the coming haze.

"Odd," the colonel said, shaking his head. "I've never seen a fog so thick when the sun shines."

"It seemed to come out of nowhere." Eliza gripped the railing.

"Still, it's just fog. If anything, it will keep us well hidden." Yet his tone seemed hollow and distant—unsure. She followed his gaze to the captain, who unleashed a string of orders for the crew to shorten sail. When she faced the colonel again, he assessed her with eyes as stormy and gray as the incoming fog. "But I perceive you are not a woman easily frightened. Neither plucking a bullet from a man's flesh nor traveling all alone to a new land seems to trouble you."

Warmed by his compliment, Eliza noted that James was assisting Angeline and Sarah below, out of the chilled mist. "I have never been accused of being timid, Colonel."

He shoved the telescope into this belt and leaned back on the railing, arms across his chest. His charcoal-colored hair danced over his collar in the wind. "War has a way of stealing one's innocence. As well as strengthening their character. However, in your case, this pluck of yours seems more something you were born with than something acquired."

She slipped a bit closer, allowing his large body to block the wind. Something about the man made her feel safe—a masculine assurance, confidence, and protectiveness that dripped from every pore and hovered in the air around him. And she hadn't felt safe in quite some time. Besides, she could stare into those piercing, gray eyes for hours—the ones that now looked at her with adoration. Adoration she didn't deserve. "I fear you may be right, Colonel. Though my fortitude has caused me much trouble through the years."

A mischievous twinkle crossed his eyes. "I should like to hear of your daunting adventures, someday, Mrs. Crawford."

Did any man have a deeper, more symphonic voice? It resonated through her in low, soothing tones that melted all her defenses. She backed away and lowered her gaze. "I would never want to disparage your good opinion of me, sir."

He took her hand in his. "You never could."

She tugged it away. What was she doing? She'd never been the flirtatious type. Perhaps three days of navigating wobbling decks and cleaning up vomit had warped her good senses. Senses that told her there could never be anything between a Southern colonel and a Yankee by marriage. Unless. . .after hearing her story, after hearing her reasons, perhaps there was a chance he would understand, a chance he could see beyond her past.

Another chill struck Eliza, and she hugged herself as the ship thrust into the fog bank. Gray roiling mist enveloped them, condensing in drops on the woodwork and lines.

"Stand by to take in royals and flying jib!" Captain Barclay's orders ricocheted over the deck. "And light the lanterns fore and aft!"

Colonel Wallace gripped the railing and gazed at the gray curtain. "Odd. Very odd."

Most of the passengers scrambled below out of the cold as deathly silence devoured the ship. Even the creak of wood and purl of water against the hull sounded hollow and distant. Above them, the tips of masts disappeared as they poked through the head of the vaporous beast.

Sailors stood on deck, wide-eyed. Some climbed aloft to adjust sails. Moses, Delia, and her two children hunkered together beneath the foredeck. Eliza couldn't blame them for not wanting to join the others below, considering their attitude toward the former slaves. Turning, she clutched the railing. Droplets bit her hands and spread a chill up her arms as white foam licked the hull beneath her.

Motion drew her gaze to Mr. Graves, who was still leaning against the foremast, one boot crossed over the other as if he hadn't a care in the world. A satisfied smirk sat upon his lips before he began to whistle. The eerie tune snaked over the deck, sending the hair on Eliza's neck bristling even as the mist thickened, obscuring him from her view.

Heavy moisture coated her lungs, making it hard to breathe. She felt the colonel stiffen beside her as his intent gaze took in the fog on both sides of the ship. He cocked his ear and closed his eyes as if listening for something. The lines on his forehead deepened.

Something was wrong. Eliza knew it. One glance at the colonel told her that whatever it was, he sensed it too.

He took her hand. "You should get below, Mrs. Crawford." His tone brooked no defiance. With a nod, she turned to leave when jets of yellow and red flashed in the distance.

"A shot! All hands down!"

CHAPTER 7

*O*nce again Eliza felt the colonel's firm body against hers. This time, instead of landing on top of her, he'd forced her to the deck and pressed her head against his chest while he hovered over her like a human shield. Cocooned within a barrier of warm muscles, all she could hear was the *thump thump thump* of his heart.

Or was that the crew diving to the deck?

An ominous splash quivered the air around her. Curses flew. A blade of sunlight cut through the fog, piercing the wooden planks to Eliza's right. Pressing a hand on her shoulder—no doubt to prevent her from standing—the colonel rose and glanced over the ship. She felt the loss of his body heat immediately. Along with his masculine scent—both replaced by a chilled wind that smelled of fear and cigar smoke.

"Stay down," he ordered before marching to the quarterdeck, parting a fog that was already scattering beneath the sun's rays. Eliza peeked at Captain Barclay, his face a mass of angst as he raised the telescope to his eye.

"Lay aloft and loose fore topsails!" The captain's shout broke the eerie silence, startling Eliza. Immediately, sailors jumped up and dashed in all directions. Their bare feet thrummed over the wooden planks, sounding far too much like war drums on the battlefield.

"Man the weather halyards and topsail sheets!" Captain Barclay's booming tirade of orders continued. "Helm-a-starboard! Steady now!"

Rising to her feet, Eliza peered behind them, squinting as sunlight shoved away the mist. Off their larboard quarter, the ship they'd seen earlier burst out of the fog, foam flinging from her bow and the American flag flapping at her foremast.

She was heading straight for them.

"Bloody Yanks!" One sailor shouted as he passed Eliza and leaped into the ratlines.

The deck buzzed with sailors dashing here and there, clambering aloft or grabbing lines. Hayden, their resident stowaway, emerged from below, followed by James and a few other male passengers.

"Do you have shot for your guns, Captain?" The colonel's face had tightened like a drum, his eyes focused.

"Aye." The gruff seaman pointed forward where some men were removing canvas from two small guns on either side of the foredeck. "I only have these four-pounder swivels, as you can see." His hardened gaze swept to the oncoming ship. "We are a civilian ship, not a privateer. Those white-livered curs!" He slammed his fist on the quarter rail and barreled down the ladder.

Pressing his wounded side, Hayden led a group of men to the captain. "What can I do?"

In the mayhem, Eliza seemed to have been forgotten. She faced the oncoming ship as it rose and plunged through the sea, its ivory sails gorged with wind. Not a speck of fog remained anywhere. Instead, golden streams of sunlight poured upon the *New Hope* as if highlighting their position for all to see. For the Union ship to see. What did they want? More importantly *who* did they want? Fear curdled in her belly at the thought they were after the colonel.

Perspiration slid down Eliza's back. The ship pitched over a wave, and her feet skipped across the deck. Above her, sails caught the wind in a boom nearly as loud as a cannon. She'd heard more than her share of the monstrous beasts on the battlefield and seen the devastation they could wreak, but she had never been in the middle of a battle. Especially at sea.

The brig swung to port. Her timbers creaked and groaned as the ship tacked away from their enemy. The railing leaped toward the sky. Eliza clutched it lest she tumble across the deck. Her mouth went dry. *Why didn't the blasted Union leave them alone?* Hadn't they done enough damage?

The ship righted again. Wind whipped strands of Eliza's hair into her face. She brushed them aside just in time to see a yellow flame jet from the Union ship.

"Hands down!" the captain yelled, but Eliza had already anticipated the command and lowered herself to the deck planks. The smell of dank wood and tar filled her nose. A heavy body pressed against her back, barricading her from danger. The colonel again. She knew his scent, the feel of his steely muscles.

The snap and crack of wood split the air. Curses ricocheted over the brig. Captain Barclay loosed another string of orders, something about tacks and sheets and the helm. But Eliza was more concerned that someone may have been injured. Thankfully, she heard no screams.

"Go below, Mrs. Crawford." Colonel Wallace's breath wafted on her cheek before he jumped to his feet and assisted her up. Gone was the warmth in his gaze. Instead, steel coated his eyes, his mannerisms, even his voice. He'd slipped into command, ready for battle, as easily as one slipped on a coat.

"Can you manage a ship's gun, Colonel?" the captain asked, stealing the colonel's gaze from Eliza.

"I can."

"Then take command of one of them. My boys are bringing up shot, gunpowder, and a fire wick."

The colonel nodded, gestured with his head for Eliza to go below, and leaped up the foredeck ladder.

"I can handle a cannon as well." Hayden jerked hair from his face.

"And I can handle a pistol or sword." James joined him, standing before the captain.

"And us too!" several of the male passengers shouted.

Captain Barclay nodded in approval. "Very well, arm yourselves, men. I hope"—he stared at the Union ship—"we'll not be gettin' close enough to use them."

Sails thundered. The deck rose as the ship thrust boldly into the next roller, sending white spray aft. It swirled around Eliza's ankle boots before escaping through scuppers, joining a sea that roared against the hull as if it too had joined the fierce call to battle.

Clinging to the railing, Eliza faced the enemy ship. Closer now. She could make out the naval officers manning the gun at the bow.

"Get below, Mrs. Crawford!" Captain Barclay's voice startled her, and she swung around, nearly bumping into the beefy man. He sent her a warning glance before he charged across the deck, blaring orders as he went.

Eliza knew she should go below. But she had never been very good at obeying authority. Besides, she'd rather be blown to bits on deck than die below cramped in the rank belly of the ship. Or worse, sink to the bottom of the sea with no way to escape.

Balancing herself on the heaving deck, she headed toward the companionway but slunk into the shadows beneath the quarterdeck instead. From there she had a good view of the front portion of the ship. The colonel included. With his shoulders stretched taut, his body stiff, and his face like flint, he commanded the men working on the cannon with authority, assurance, and determination. Wind flapped his shirt as he unbuttoned his cuffs and rolled up his sleeves, ready to do his duty. Here was a man accustomed to getting dirty in the trenches right beside his men. A rarity among other colonels Eliza had met.

Movement caught her eye, and she spotted Graves slinking around the foremast. Why hadn't he gone below with the other passengers? Or better yet, if he was going to stay on deck, why wasn't he helping, arming himself? Instead, he leaned against the mast and began to whistle as if he were taking a Sunday stroll.

"Fire as you bear, Colonel!" The captain bellowed, pacing across the oscillating deck, his hands clamped behind his great coat. How he maintained his balance was beyond Eliza. Sails roared as they sought the shifting wind then snapped their jaws upon finding it. The brig jerked and listed sideways. Foamy seawater clawed at her larboard bulwarks. Yet still the Union ship gained.

Eliza drew a shaky breath and clung to the wood of the quarterdeck. If they couldn't outsail the frigate, what was to become of them? Would they be sunk to the depths, or would the Union navy escort them back home? Where Eliza would face a lifetime of scorn and hatred. And what would become of Colonel Wallace? Surely his fate would be worse than hers. Even as he filled her thoughts, his voice drifted her way.

"Fire into her quarters. On the uprise, men!" he shouted. Raising spyglass to his eye, he studied the enemy. "Steady now. Steady." He lowered the scope. "Fire!"

One sailor tapped a wick to the gun's touchhole, and Eliza covered her ears. *Boom!* The deck quivered beneath her feet. Smoke swept over her. Coughing, she batted it away. "Oh Lord, please save us," she muttered, only now remembering to pray. Fiddle! Why did she always wait until things were beyond hopeless?

Blake peered through the gray smoke as the all-too-familiar blast of gunpowder assailed him. He squeezed his eyes shut against the sting as memories crept out from hiding. *No, not now!* He must maintain control. Shoving them back, he gazed toward the enemy as the *New Hope*'s shot plopped impotently into the sea just yards from the frigate's hull. Too short. But in line for a good hit. Blake frowned. He was an expert at cannons. But on solid land not on a heaving ship. How did the navy do it? Still, luck had smiled upon him, for his timing of the rise and fall of wave had not been too far off.

"Good shot, Colonel." One of the sailors turned, his face lined with soot.

"Not good enough. Reload!" Not that they had much chance against a U.S. frigate armed with what appeared to be Dahlgren guns and 32-pounder Parrott rifles. Besides speed, of course. Being smaller, the *New Hope* should be able to outrun a frigate. Blake shifted his gaze to the captain and his first mate leaning over a flapping chart held down by pistols. It would seem from the captain's expression, he was of the same mind.

"Max, Simmons," Captain Barclay shouted at two passing sailors. "Have you seen my sextant, protractor, and Gunter's scale?"

The men shrugged. "Last I saw, they was in your cabin."

"They aren't there." Captain Barclay scratched his beard, frowning. "Get below and search for them at once!" The two men dropped through a hatch while the captain returned to his chart.

The navigation instruments were missing? Along with the damage to the compass? Blake's gaze darted to the frigate as a cold fist slammed into his gut. The Union must suspect war criminals were on board. Otherwise, what reason would they have for so intent a pursuit? And if they caught and boarded them, they'd no doubt discover Blake's identity and haul him back to Charleston to be hanged. He'd never go to Brazil. Never have a chance to escape the memories of war. Never pursue the rising interest he had in Eliza.

Wind tore at his collar, tossing his necktie over his shoulder. The brig slid into a trough, and Blake braced his boots on the deck. He glanced back at the captain.

Orders, Captain! What are your orders? Urgency spun his heart into a knot. Oh how he longed to take command! But he knew nothing of sea battles. And he began to wonder whether Captain Barclay did either. Though the man appeared calm, he seemed trundled in uncertainty as his gaze sped from the charts to the Union frigate and then behind him to some distant spot on the horizon. Regardless, he must make a decision. And fast! On land, Blake would already be spouting orders. But he knew no such order to give here. Except to go faster!

The ship bounced, and he caught his balance. The sailors fumbled with powder bag and priming rod as they reloaded the gun. Amateurs. The men in his regiment would have had it loaded already.

Blake glanced over his shoulder where Hayden stood at the ready in command of the other swivel gun. They exchanged a nod. The stowaway's confident demeanor and his readiness to not only jump into the fray but take the lead elevated Blake's opinion of him. Clearly he'd served in the military. And then there was James, the doctor-preacher, standing before a group of brave passengers and sailors all armed with musket, swords, and pistols. Even Moses, the freed slave, stood among the pack, receiving no complaint from the others at his presence. Blake didn't have time to be amazed as a thunderous blast shook the sky. He ducked. The air sizzled. The shot zipped by his ear. Wood snapped. Splinters flew from the damaged foremast.

More explosions sounded. Distant and muted. Coming from everywhere, yet only coming from within him. Squeezing his eyes shut, he pressed his hands over his ears. *No!* Wails of agony pierced his skull. Flashes of light and dark traversed his eyelids, luring him into a nightmarish stupor. But he couldn't let them. Grinding his fists to his thighs, he punched to his feet, forced his eyes open, and inhaled a burst of salty spray. The cool seawater slapped him back to the present— slapped his gaze to the hole the last shot had torn in the foremast.

Too close. Far too close. Anger rippled up Blake's spine. He wiped the sweat from his face, leaving soot on his shirt. He would not allow one Yankee to set foot on board this ship! Not only for his sake but for the colony. The Yanks would steal all their goods, take him and probably others prisoner. And God knew what they'd do to the women. No, not on his watch.

"Loaded and ready, sir," one of the sailors said.

Blake swung about. The Union frigate dipped and bowed over the churning waves as if nodding its glee over an impending victory. Closer and closer she came. If only she'd present more than her narrow bow, Blake may be able to fire a shot that would do some damage.

Captain Barclay had abandoned his charts and marched across the deck, gazing aloft at the sails. A volley of orders spewed from his mouth. Sailors scampered above, and soon the *New Hope* veered to larboard, sending a curtain of spray into the air. Blake stumbled across the deck to the captain. "What is the plan?" he shouted over the roar of the sea just as a hail of grapeshot peppered the deck, punching holes in the sails above.

The men ducked. All except the captain. Instead, he frowned at his damaged sails then lowered his gaze to Blake. "The plan, Colonel?" He snorted. "Why, to tuck our scraggly tails and run!" His grin revealed a single missing tooth Blake had not noticed before. Yet at his lighthearted tone, armed sailors and passengers turned to listen. Hayden joined them from the foredeck.

Captain Barclay scanned the anxious faces. "We are faster than a frigate. If we fill all our sails, we can outrun them."

"But to where? They'll follow." Hayden cast a harried glance at the frigate as if he, too, had something to fear from the Union.

The captain's eyes flashed. "We are near the Bahamas, Mr. Hayden. There are hundreds of shoals off the windward islands. I expect our friends won't be followin' us, or they'll risk bein' grounded." He winked.

James quirked a brow. "How can you be sure?"

"Because I was a blockade runner in the war. Why, once I slipped through a fleet of Union war ships surroundin' New Orleans. Slunk right past them as if we were a ghost ship. By the time they saw us, we were too close to the shoals for them to follow. Never fear, gentlemen."

"But your instruments," Blake shouted into the wind. "Are we heading in the right direction?" He searched the captain's dark eyes for any hint of uncertainty but found only confidence.

"Never fear, Colonel. I know these seas like a pirate knows his booty." And without further ado, Captain Barclay turned away and cupped his mouth. "Sharpshooters to the tops. If they get any closer, fire at will!" He stormed toward the quarterdeck, muttering, "Those bedeviled muckrakers!"

James slung his musket over his shoulder and started for the ratlines when Blake clutched his arm. "But your hands."

"Only when I see blood." Grinning, he grabbed the rope and swung himself up. "I spent my childhood hunting. I'm actually a crack shot. Never miss," he yelled as he continued climbing above.

Several orange flashes drew Blake's gaze to the enemy frigate. Blood drained from his face. They had fired a broadside. *Boom! Boom! Boom! Boom!* He dove to the deck, hands over his head. Not that it would do any good. In battle, getting hit or not hit was a matter of chance. He'd seen men get their heads blown off on either side of him while he suffered not a scratch. After that, Blake had decided that either God did not exist or He simply didn't care about the affairs of men.

The crunch and snap of wood and chink of iron rang across the ship like death knells. Yet no screams sounded.

Blake would never forget the screams.

"Those blaggards!" The captain spat before marching across the deck to inspect the damage. A portion of the fore rigging hung in a tangle of slashed rope, and part of the gunwale was shattered. But the ship still sped onward. Jumping to his feet, Blake leaned over the railing where a smoking hole rent the hull.

"Above the waterline." The captain slapped his hands together. "Steady now, men. We'll be at the shoals soon! Martin, trim sails to the wind!"

Blake gazed at the oncoming frigate, angry foam exploding at her bow. Men lined her decks, hovering around cannons. Their captain stood on the foredeck, pompous arms crossed over his brass-buttoned blue coat. Blake could make out the gold band on the captain's hat, feel his determination span the sea to swallow up Blake's hope. He gazed at the sun now dropping in the western sky. He hoped the captain was right, for another expertly aimed shot might fell one of their masts.

And then all would be lost.

Shaking his head, Blake returned to man the swivel. The next few hours sped by in a chaotic jumble of cannon shots, shouts, maneuvering, veering, sails thundering, sea roaring, and muskets peppering until the muscles in Blake's legs felt like pudding and his heart sank like iron. The ache in his left leg joined the ever-present one in his right, which now felt like someone held a branding iron to it. At least he'd not had any episodes to add to the mayhem. Perhaps, as he had hoped, the more distance he put between him and the war, the more his memories would fade.

But what did it matter? The frigate was nearly upon them, and the islands were nowhere in sight. Captain Barclay's assured tone had faded to one of gloom as he paced the deck, uttering curse after curse. Even the most hardened sailors' faces paled in horror.

Clouds lined the horizon like gray-uniformed soldiers, fringed in red and gold by the setting sun. The frigate swept alongside the *New Hope*, not thirty yards away, giving the signal for them to put the helm down and heave to. Dark smoking muzzles of a dozen guns gaped at Blake from their main deck.

"Reload!" Blake urged his crew to hurry while they had a clear shot. He could not give up now! Not when his life was at stake. But Captain Barclay's loud "Belay all firing!" rang from the quarterdeck, freezing the sailors in place.

Wiping the sweat from his eyes, Blake stared at the captain, seeing on his face what he'd already heard in his voice. They were defeated. He swept his gaze to the Union frigate where one of the officers stood staunchly on the quarterdeck, a speaking cone raised to his mouth.

"Rebel ship, surrender or die!"

CHAPTER 8

$\mathcal{B}$lake spun on his heels, his face hot and pinched. A flash of blue caught his eye, and he glanced to see Eliza standing against the quarterdeck. How long had she been there? Fear overtook his anger. Even now Union sailors were preparing to board and search the ship. Blake's fate was set in stone. Eliza's was not. Nor were the passengers'. Their future depended on the kindness and mercy of the Union captain. Something Blake hadn't much faith in at the moment.

Still, though his journey had come to an end, there might be a chance for the rest of the colonists. The thought of them thriving in freedom in Brazil would bring him a modicum of comfort when the rope cinched around his neck.

Terror clawed up his throat at the thought. He coughed and drew a deep breath. He must focus. He must do all he could to ensure the future success of the colony.

While the captain issued orders for the white flag to be raised and all sails to be lowered, Blake blasted out his own orders. "Parson Bailey." He approached the preacher, who had crept above when the firing ceased. The poor man stood against the main mast, face stricken and Bible clutched to his chest.

Blake wondered if he could trust anyone who had such tiny, shifting eyes. But the man was a preacher, after all. Reaching into his pocket, he handed the parson a key and leaned to whisper in his ear, "Go to my trunk. Find the four large leather pouches. We need to hide them." For within them lay the future of the colony—every cent and dollar each passenger had paid, along with Blake's own dwindling fortune.

Blake would gather the money himself, but the Yankees would be here any minute, and he could not ensure the safety of both money and passengers—the single ladies being his top priority at the moment. He'd seen firsthand the abuse they endured beneath the hands of angry Union soldiers.

Parson Bailey took the key in his trembling hand. Sweat dotted his forehead. "What do they contain?"

"The wealth of our colony. Our very future."

"Where should I hide them?" he asked, avoiding Blake's gaze.

Good question. Blake scanned the deck and hailed Captain Barclay, who immediately approached and stopped before them. Once Blake posed the question, the captain's understanding gaze shifted from the key in the parson's hand back to Blake. "I have a secret compartment in my cabin." He glanced at the frigate, where the sailors were lowering a boat. "Quickly, I'll show you, Parson."

The two men slipped down the companionway, giving Blake a chance to speak to Eliza. She stared at the frigate off their port side, the heaving of her chest the only indication of her fear.

Frowning, he approached her. "I told you to go below."

"Would it have made a difference?" Her voice was strong, controlled, as if being attacked by a Union frigate was an everyday occurrence.

Blake shook his head. What he wouldn't give to have more time with this astounding woman. He raised his hand, wanting to touch her, to remember the feel of her skin, but hesitated at the impropriety. When her eyes gave him no resistance, he gave in and caressed her jaw with his thumb. So soft. He would remember it forever.

She closed her eyes. Thick lashes fanned over her cheeks like silken threads floating on cream. "They'll take you back to hang, won't they?" she said on a sigh.

"Yes."

She sucked in a breath and gazed up at him, alarm tightening her features.

He wanted to tell her how astonishing she was. He wanted to tell her he'd never forget her, but Angeline dashed up to them in a flurry of gingham and angst. "What is happening?" Her voice emerged in a high-pitched squeak.

Easing an arm around her new friend, Eliza drew Angeline close. "It will be fine."

She exchanged a glance with Blake, prompting him to add, "Nothing to worry about. It will be over soon enough, and we shall be on our way."

However, their assurances seemed of no avail as the poor lady suddenly took to trembling. "But they fired upon us. Do you suppose they're after someone in particular?"

Yes, me. Blake offered a feeble smile. "Perhaps. Yet I'm sure you are safe in that regard, miss."

Still, the lady's face showed no relief. Even Eliza's whispers of comfort bore no effect on the poor woman as her fearful gaze locked on the frigate. Her behavior mimicked the terror raging through Blake's own gut—as if she, too, feared being arrested.

That same terror now threatened to blast away his resolve to remain in control—to ensure the safety of the colonists before he was hauled away in irons. His vision clouded. Flames shot toward him from all directions. He clenched his fists and shook them away. Across the deck, he spotted Hayden and called him over.

As the stowaway approached, his green eyes widened at the sight of Angeline then squinted in confusion. Soot blotched his skin in grays and blacks from his face down his neck and arms.

"Hayden," Blake said, drawing the man's gaze from the woman. "Find Sarah, the woman with child, and stay with her. If you are asked, you are her husband."

Hayden nodded, swung a musket over his shoulder, and after one last glance at Angeline, headed below.

"James!" Blake swung in the direction he'd last seen the doctor and nearly bumped into the man. James's bronze eyes burned with anxiety amid a face flushed and streaked. "Can you look after Miss Angeline? It would be best if she were married, if you get my meaning." Blake raised a brow.

Angeline turned her face from the doctor as if embarrassed. "No, that's quite all right. There's no need for that."

James nodded his understanding. "I'll take care of her." He took a spot beside her and extended his elbow. "Stay close to me, miss. There's nothing to worry about."

The lady uttered a trembling sigh but finally looped her arm through his.

Blake faced Eliza. "I'll be happy to step in as your husband if you have no objection."

He thought he saw a hint of a smile lift her lips before she nodded shyly. The entire scene would have been delightful if his head weren't thrumming like a drum.

And he weren't about to be captured and hanged.

The captain returned from below and nodded toward Blake before he faced the frigate and scowled. "In all my years as a blockade runner, I ne'er was caught. Until now, after the war is over. Blast them Yanks!"

Across the agitated sea, two jolly boats filled with Union sailors headed their way. The crew of the *New Hope* lined the deck, awaiting their guests, rifles and pistols in hand.

"I'm not letting those Yanks take us back!" one sailor shouted.

"We have no choice." Captain Barclay marched forward, hands on his waist. "Lower your weapons at once!"

A shot fired above them. All eyes snapped to the tops where a lone gunman straddled a yard, musket in hand.

"Stand down, Gibbs!" Captain Barclay bellowed, his alarmed gaze shifting to the frigate. "D'you want to get us all killed?"

The man swung through the shrouds and slid down the backstay to the deck with a thud. "Sorry, Cap'n. Was an accident."

But the men in the jolly boats had already stopped rowing, their muskets at the ready. Aboard the frigate, sailors loaded one of the Parrott rifles lining the deck.

Blake's world exploded. The sound of the sea and wind and shouts of men all faded into the background, replaced by the roar of explosions and the *pop pop pop* of hundreds of muskets. A scream curdled in his ears. Was someone hurt? He crouched, holding his head against the blaring noise. *Boom! Boom! Boom! Boom!* Cannon blast after cannon blast rocked the dirt beneath him. The crack of pistol and musket rained down on him. Why wouldn't they stop? He dared a glance over the deck, and instead of wooden planks and hatch combings and masts, a field of tall grass spread in every direction. Mist hovered over it like a death shroud. Lifeless bodies in twisted formations littered the mud. Something warm and wet dripped from Blake's fingers. He looked down. Blood pooled in his palms.

Somewhere in the distance a female voice called his name. That was the last thing he remembered.

The warning shot flew over their bow and plunged into the sea on the other side of the ship. Its deafening roar still vibrated in Eliza's ears when she noticed the colonel had collapsed to the deck, his hands over his ears. Kneeling beside him, she laid a hand on his back. He jolted and shouted, "No! Jeremy!" Sailors and passengers crowded around, confusion and fear mottling their faces. Beyond them, the captain shouted toward the frigate, attempting to persuade them that all was well.

The colonel moaned. His eyelids twitched, and his jaw was clenched so tight, Eliza feared it would burst.

James, the doctor, felt the colonel's face with the back of his hand.

"What's wrong with him?" One of the sailors who'd manned the gun with the colonel leaned forward, hands on his knees.

Captain Barclay shoved the crowd aside. "Clear away! Assume your positions! We are to have visitors soon." He spotted the colonel and halted. "What's the meaning of this? Odd's fish, is he shot?"

"No Captain." Eliza exchanged a glance with the doctor. She had a good idea what was happening to the colonel, and from the look in James's eyes, he agreed with her assessment.

"Jeremy! Jeremy!" the colonel shouted, planting his forehead on the deck.

"Let's get him below." The doctor rose and pointed to a few sailors, who grabbed the colonel by his feet and shoulders and carefully lowered him down the hatchway ladder.

No sooner had Eliza followed them into the sick bay than she heard the grinding thump of boats slamming against the hull, and soon after, the pounding of boots on the deck above.

"Take care of him, Mrs. Crawford." James gave her an unsettled look. "I must look after Angeline."

"Please do take care of her," Eliza said. "She seems quite out of sorts."

Nodding, he took off, leaving Eliza alone with a delirious man and her own nerves strangling her senses. Lowering herself into the chair beside the colonel, she took his hand in hers. "Oh God in heaven, please save us. Please don't allow the Yankees to do us harm or steal from us.

Enough of this war." She swatted a tear from her cheek and straightened her shoulders. "Enough!"

Leading an unusually calm Sarah up from below decks, Hayden ushered her to the starboard railing where the Yankee captain had ordered the passengers to line up for inspection. He'd found her in her cabin, kneeling awkwardly—due to her condition—before a chair, hands folded on the wooden seat. Though an admirable attempt to be sure, her appeal to God most likely vanished in the air above her, for Hayden believed the Almighty had wiped His hands of His creation long ago.

With a smile, the lady had taken his hand, expressing gratitude for his chivalry, and followed him above. Now she stood beside him, examining the proceedings with no trace of fear on her face.

"Never fear, God is with us," she whispered.

Hayden repressed a snort and scanned the pompous bluecoats strutting across the deck while their captain questioned Captain Barclay. Thank goodness he recognized none of them. It would not do well to cross paths with any navy officers he'd dealt with in his past. Nor would it do to cross paths with any civilians he'd done so-called *business* with either. But of course, what would they be doing on a navy frigate? He faced Sarah. "I am not afraid, madam. What astounds me is that you seem not to be as well."

"As I said, God is with us." She pressed a hand over her rounded belly. Plain brown hair held back in a bun framed an equally plain face. Yet her eyes, the color of the sea, exuded a serenity and kindness that made her almost attractive. For a woman bulging with child, that was. A bit too prissy for him, however, with her high-necked gown and continual chatter of God.

The doctor slid beside them, arm in arm with Miss Angeline, a woman whose comely face and copper curls were not easily forgotten. Even if the last time Hayden had seen them was on a WANTED poster in a police station in Virginia. Which would explain why her hands were now shaking and her breath came hard and fast. Whatever she'd done, it was none of Hayden's business. Besides, he'd probably done far worse. Still, he should inform her she had nothing to fear from the navy, but there was no reason to destroy her ruse. Along with his.

Just when these people were beginning to accept him.

Unfortunately, none of them was his father. Hayden had spent the last three days inspecting every inch of the brig, searching each passenger's face for the one that matched the tintype he'd carried in his pocket for fifteen years. He doubted Mr. Ladson had lied to him about his father heading to Brazil. The man's limited intellect and shoddy foresight forbade him the ability to swindle someone like Hayden. Besides, he had no reason to do so. Which meant Hayden's father either was taking a later ship or had changed his mind. Either way, Hayden was on the voyage for the long haul. Once at Rio de Janeiro, he would inquire with the authorities and discover if his father had already arrived. If not, Hayden would give him a month to show his face before he set sail for home.

His gaze shifted to the Scotts, who were hovering around their pretentious sprite, Magnolia. He'd never seen such silken, ivory curls. She was a stunner, he'd give her that. Until she opened her mouth.

The brig lopped over a wave as Union officers gathered weapons from grumbling sailors and began loading them into their boats.

"Wait. We will need those in Brazil." James stepped from the line, drawing attention his way.

A lieutenant approached, measuring him with disdain. "And you are?"

"James Callaway." He moved in front of Angeline as if he could hide such beauty from the man. The officer peered around the doctor, assessing the lady with hungry eyes. Clasping her hands together, she lowered her gaze.

"Did you serve in the Rebel army, sir?" The lieutenant addressed James, who was squinting at the sun's reflection off the two gold leaves and silver anchor on the officer's blue cap.

"I'm a preacher."

Hayden coughed, hiding a rising snicker. *Preacher, indeed.* Yes, he'd heard James preach before. And witnessed his hypocrisy shortly afterward—a hypocrisy that put the final straw in the haystack of Hayden's unbelief and set it ablaze. The good news was the man didn't seem to recognize Hayden from the one time he'd slipped into the back of his church on that cold night in January.

"Ah, two preachers on board." The lieutenant's gaze swerved in Parson Bailey's direction, but the man was hidden behind a group of farmers. "You Rebels are certainly religious sorts, but then you'll need the extra prayers of repentance, I expect."

Blood surged to Hayden's fists. And from the look on his face, the doctor's as well.

"Well, *Preacher.*" The officer poked James in the chest. "I have found that weapons in the hands of Rebels are a danger to all that is good and free. Ergo, we will confiscate yours." He gave a caustic grin and spun on his heels.

"Then how will we hunt and defend ourselves?" Hayden knew he should keep his mouth shut, but his anger overcame his good judgment.

Halting, the man cast Hayden an impudent glance over his shoulder. "I don't have a care, sir. You should have thought of that before you tore our country apart." He continued onward.

"And you should—"

Sarah clutched Hayden's arm and drew him back. But thankfully the flap of loose sails above had drowned out his foolish outburst. The last thing he needed was to get into an altercation with a Union lieutenant.

Thunder grumbled in the distance where dark clouds amassed on the horizon. Captain Barclay handed the Yankee captain some papers. He leafed through them with a scowl as the *New Hope*'s sailors stood in haphazard rows on the main deck, some shifting their feet, some clenching and unclenching their hands as if anxious for a fight. Hayden would love nothing more than to get in a scrap with these feather-brained braggarts and put them in their place, but at the moment they held the advantage. And besides, there were innocent civilians to protect, farmers and teachers and blacksmiths—people far more innocent than he.

Most of whom now huddled on the foredeck, some shivering in fear, others staring straight ahead. Ever the politician, Mr. Graves leaned against the railing, a placid look on his face. Something about that man ate at Hayden's insides. Beside him, Mr. Lewis, the carpenter, sneaked swigs from a flask within his coat, reminding Hayden he could use a drink about now as well.

Two Union sailors hauled Moses, his sister, and the Scotts' slave before the frigate captain, who looked them up and down with so much disgust, Hayden wondered if the man realized he had fought a war to set them free. After ensuring they had, indeed, been released from their chains—a lie the Scotts' slave pronounced after repeated glares from her owner—the captain waved them off.

"Mr. Vane, Mr. Harkins," he barked at two sailors nearby. "Take a crew below and search every nook and cranny of this old bucket. I want everyone brought above. Even the rats. Do you hear me?"

"Aye, aye, Captain." Both men saluted and got to task.

"And Mr. Staves," the captain addressed the lieutenant who had recently spoken with James, "take ten men to the hold and haul up anything of value."

James leaned toward Hayden. "They are looking for someone in particular—a Rebel officer, no doubt."

"Where is the colonel?"

"In the sick bay with Eliza."

Hayden turned to Sarah. "If you're of a mind to pray, madam, now would be a good time."

Chapter 9

*E*very shuffle of boots, every shout, every pitch and inflection of a Northern accent, sent Eliza's heart into her throat as she paced the sick bay's narrow deck. She could hear the Yankee sailors searching the hold, the cabins. She could hear them rummaging in every corner and closet, and by the sound of their moans and grunts, hauling things above. She gazed at the colonel, envious of his unconscious bliss.

He'd been all but blissful up on deck when he'd crouched, hands to his ears, against phantom missiles, screaming the name Jeremy over and over.

She knew exactly what was happening to him. She'd seen it in military hospitals more times than she could count. Men reliving the horrors of war, reliving moments on the battlefield with such clarity it seemed they were still in the midst of the fighting. Hallucinations of brutality, death, terror. Usually the symptoms faded with time, but more often than not, these men ended up in asylums.

Tears pooled in her eyes at the thought of that happening to Colonel Wallace. She'd watched him through the entire chase—hadn't been able to keep her eyes off him. She'd met many officers in her years as a nurse, married one in fact. They were not all created equal. Stripes and pins and ribbons did not a warrior make. The true mettle of a soldier was measured on the battlefield. Eliza had seen officers knowingly send their men to their deaths while saving themselves. She'd seen others who froze and cowered when facing the full arsenal of an enemy advance. Even worse, there were those who gloated over heroic deeds not their own but performed by men of lower rank.

But not Colonel Wallace.

Though certainly unfamiliar with sea battles, he had taken immediate command of the gun crew, issuing orders as if they were second nature, staring down the enemy and facing death side by side with his men. No hesitation. No fear. Even when the frigate fired round after round at them, his concern had been for his men.

Now, lying on the cot, his nankeen trousers stretched tight over muscular thighs that still twitched from battle, his hair dark against the cream-colored pillow, his open shirt revealing a dusting of black hair, Eliza felt a stirring within her she'd never felt before. Not even with Stanton. She looked away. She shouldn't be staring at him while he slept.

Voices drilled down the halls. She could hear Captain Barclay bantering with the Union captain. She hoped Angeline and Sarah were safe. Water slapped against the hull, grating Eliza's nerves and making her stomach feel as though she'd swallowed a brick. Sinking into a chair, she gripped her belly and willed the terror to subside.

The colonel stirred, and she glanced his way.

She'd done all she could. The blotches on his cheeks and neck looked so real, she shivered in remembrance of the disease. And the moisture she'd dabbed on his skin did, indeed, appear like sweat from a fever. If only one didn't look too close. Which was what she was counting on. Close up, anyone could tell the marks were nothing but a paste of powder and a few drops of iodine. She sighed. Hopefully, Blake would remain unconscious and not disturb them. *Oh Lord, let him remain unconscious.* She wrung her hands together. The thud of boots approached, and she grabbed a cloth.

The door swung open, and two men entered. One a lieutenant and the other an unrated seaman.

"Well, look what we have here."

Settling her nerves, Eliza slowly rose and stared at the tall, lanky officer. "What can I do for you, Lieutenant?"

He laughed, took a step inside, and planted his hands at his waist. "In case you aren't aware, miss, your ship has been captured and boarded by the U.S.S. *Perilous.*"

Perilous, indeed. Eliza raised her chin. "In case you aren't aware, Lieutenant, we are no longer at war."

"In case you aren't aware, miss, we are searching for war criminals trying to escape their due justice."

"In case—" Eliza snapped her mouth shut. This was ridiculous. "As you can see, Lieutenant. There are no war criminals in here."

The man took another step inside, his lackey nipping at his heels. "Sir," the lieutenant shouted in the colonel's direction. "You are to go above at once!"

"Any fool can see this man is ill." Eliza huffed.

"Rather bold tongue for a defeated enemy, miss." His sordid gaze raked her. "However, ill or not, he must go above. Along with you." Snapping his fingers, he gestured toward the door.

"Very well." Eliza raised a brow and stepped aside, hoping they didn't notice her trembling legs. "If you want to be exposed to the pox, be my guest. Pick him up and take him above." She tossed the rag into a basin of water. "No doubt you've already been exposed just by coming aboard."

The lieutenant halted.

"Oh?" Eliza went on. "Captain Barclay didn't warn you?" She gave a sweet smile and clicked her tongue. "How uncivilized of him."

The man's mouth hung open, and he quickly drew a hand to his nose. The other sailor retreated toward the door, his face chalky white.

"Who is he?" The officer took a step back.

"Henry Crawford, a farmer from Savannah. I'm his wife, Eliza."

"A farmer? Did he serve in the military?" The ship rocked, and he pressed a hand to the bulkhead.

"No."

"Would youu swear to that?"

"I believe, sir"—Eliza raised her voice to cover the quaver in her voice—"I would know whether my own husband had been home the past four years."

His horrified gaze bounced between her and the colonel. "Very well," he coughed into his hand and glanced behind him, no doubt looking for the other sailor, but the man had already disappeared into the hallway. Rushing out the door, the officer slammed it behind him.

Boot steps faded down the hall. Eliza's breath fled her lungs as she slumped into the chair, willing her heart to return to a normal beat.

"Well done, Mrs. Crawford."

Eliza jumped at the sound of the colonel's voice. She threw a hand to her chest as his eyes popped open and a smile curved his lips.

"You were awake?"

"Not the whole time." His glance took in the room. Then swinging his feet over the cot, he sat and rubbed his face. "But long enough to know I should remain unconscious. What is this?" He stared at the paste on his fingers then swiped his cheek, depositing more of it on his hand.

"It's smallpox, and you should have left it in place should they return."

But they weren't returning. Even now, Eliza could hear the jolly boats hammering the hull as they grew heavy with goods and men. The colonel's gaze drifted above. "Very clever, Mrs. Crawford." He assessed her, admiration pouring from his eyes. "I imagine your ruse is the reason for their sudden departure."

But Eliza no longer cared. Nothing mattered but the way he was looking at her. And the way it caused a pleasurable eddy to swirl in her stomach. Retrieving the cloth from the basin, she turned her back to him as she wrung it out then handed it to him. "It was a simple trick."

"But not one that most would have considered." He wiped his hands and face. "I've never seen a lady so brave."

Eliza's insides buzzed at the compliment. "I am not easily intimidated."

He flashed a grin. "Indeed."

"I fear it has oft gotten me into trouble in the past."

"But this time your bravado saved me from certain hanging." He released a breath and ran a hand through his hair. Lantern light swayed back and forth over him as if it were dancing to the creak and groan of the ship. He stared at the rag in his hands. "Because I collapsed like a weakling."

Anguish lined his face, coupled with a flush of embarrassment.

"Not a weakling, Colonel. A witness of horrors unimaginable." Paste smeared his left cheek where he'd missed a spot. Giving in to an urge, Eliza took the cloth and knelt before him. Their eyes met, just inches apart. She could smell his scent, strong and musky, could feel his breath on her cheek. A storm brewed in those gray eyes, so vibrant, so intense, it seemed she could dive in and swirl among the tempest. If only she could. She would do everything in her power to calm the storm within him.

"I am familiar with your symptoms, Colonel." She wiped his cheek.

He merely stared at her in wonder as if she had descended from heaven.

"Many soldiers suffer as you do," she continued. "There," she added, "no more pox." She rose, but his frown had returned.

"I am not *many soldiers*." He pushed to his feet, avoiding her gaze. "Sounds like the Yanks have left. I should go above to see if I can help."

Eliza didn't want him to leave.

He found his coat hanging on a hook and grabbed it as shame weighed heavy in the air between them. His shame. Unnecessary shame.

"You really ought to sit and have some tea before you leave."

He glanced at her then—an apologetic glance. "You are a kind woman, Mrs. Crawford." Then weaving around the operating table, he headed for the door.

"Who is Jeremy?"

He froze. The deck tilted. Eliza grabbed the table for balance.

"Where did you hear that name?"

Eliza nearly cried at the sorrow in his voice, the anger. "You spoke it in your delirium."

He turned. His Adam's apple slid down his neck as he studied her, assessing her—assessing her worthiness, perhaps. "My brother," he finally said.

"I'm sorry."

Tossing his coat on the table, he said, "Perhaps I will have that tea, after all, Mrs. Crawford."

❧

Her smile swept the gloom from the cabin. Her understanding touched a place deep in his heart he thought long since extinct. She brushed past him to retrieve the pot of tea, making apologies for her wide skirts and saying something about how ships were not made for women's fashions. It brought a much-needed chuckle to his lips and stole away a smidgeon of the embarrassment from his episode. Episode. For he knew not what else to call them. They'd started after the Battle of the Wilderness in '64 and had only gotten worse when the war ended. He hated that Mrs. Crawford had witnessed his weakness, hated that anyone had. He was the leader of this expedition and must be in control at all times. But, heaven help him, he could use a friend on board. And Mrs. Crawford filled a void he'd long since assumed was dead and buried.

She handed him a cup and squeezed past him to take her seat in the chair once again, apologizing for the cold, stale tea. But Blake could not care less. Heat trailed his skin where their arms had touched ever so briefly. He was starting to enjoy the ship's tight quarters.

He leaned back against the wooden slab that served as an operating table. His leg ached, and he rubbed the familiar pain.

"I can have a look at your leg, Colonel."

He sipped his tea, examining her. "It's nothing. Old bullet wound."

"But it pains you." Eyes as golden and glistening as topaz showered him with concern.

"Now and then." Blake reached for his coat on the table, plucked out the belt plate he'd been carrying around for four years, and handed it to her.

She examined it. "A military belt buckle. Georgia, if I'm not mistaken." She flipped it over, no doubt noting the initials *JSW* etched in the metal.

"Jeremy Steven Wallace."

She swallowed and cupped it in her hands as if it were precious. "What happened?"

He shrugged, fighting back the pain, not wanting it to show. "The same thing that happened to thousands of other young men—he died in battle."

She said nothing, only gazed at him with as much pain in her eyes as he felt in his gut.

"He was only seventeen." He set his cup down on the table with a *clank*, feeling the familiar anger scorching his belly. "Wounded at Antietam, then finished off by a Union officer while he lay on the field. Or so I heard."

Her eyes glassed with tears, causing his own to rise. Standing, he turned away and crossed his arms over his chest, seeking anger instead of sorrow. Anger was much easier.

"And the rest of your family?" she asked.

He clenched his jaw. "Died in our home in Atlanta when Sherman burned it to the ground. My sisters were only five and twelve." He stared at the shadows of light and dark oscillating over the divots marring the deck. He heard her stand, heard the swish of her skirts, felt her touch on his arm where all that remained of his family were five black bands.

She leaned her head on his back as if she were trying to absorb his pain. The gesture eroded the fortress around his heart. He wanted to embrace her, run his fingers through her hair, cry until the pain ceased, but instead he stepped away. "I'm sorry," he said. "I shouldn't have burdened you with my sad tale."

"It helps to talk about it."

"Not for me." His temple throbbed. "The Yankees took everything: my family, my home, my leg. And as you saw earlier, my sanity." He gripped the edge of the table until his fingers hurt. "I hate them. Loathe them, in fact. All Union officers and their families should be hanged. No, worse. Quartered and then hanged. And anyone who had anything to do with them."

✸

Eliza shrank back. The hatred spewing from Blake's mouth filled the room, sending its venom into every crack and crevice. She'd seen plenty of anger during the war, and plenty more hatred over the past years, but she'd never seen such malevolent contempt. The man's eye even began to twitch. She wanted to tell him that forgiveness was the only way to peace. But that hadn't worked with her own family, why would it work with this raging beast before her? For that was what he'd transformed into. A beast with the gleam of murder in his eye.

But then he drew a breath, lowered his shoulders, pried his fingers from the table, and the old colonel was back. "Forgive me, Mrs. Crawford, I've distressed you."

"I don't distress any easier than I frighten, Colonel." She offered him a smile.

One which he returned. "But I've gone on and on about myself. I know you lost a husband in the war, probably other family members as well. I've met very few who haven't."

Eliza clasped her hands before her. "No, my family still lives. My father and an uncle and aunt. My father is Se—" She slammed her mouth shut, shocked that she'd almost given his name. A name any military officer who had dealt with President Davis would know. A name that had been tainted by his traitorous daughter. "A. . .good man. He and my aunt and uncle"—she babbled on in order to cover her stutter—"own a grand hotel in Marietta." Fiddle! She was giving him too much information.

93

"Hmm. I hear the town was occupied in '64." Lines deepened on his forehead. "Lots of destruction."

Eliza had heard as much as well. And although she'd not been allowed home, she had prayed for her family daily. "We suffered through it." She looked away.

"And your mother?"

"Died when I was twelve." That much was true. The words still stung as if it happened yesterday. She pressed a finger on the locket hidden beneath her bodice and tugged on the chain to pull it out. "My mother," she said, opening it to reveal the portrait and the lock of hair that were all she had left of the woman who had meant the world to her.

Leaning forward until she felt his body heat, Blake studied the picture. "She's beautiful." His eyes shifted to the lock of hair attached to the inside of the lid. "And your hair is the same color."

Eliza swept back a tear. "Thank you. My father gave the locket to me on my sixteenth birthday." She snapped it shut and allowed it to dangle down the front of her gown. "I haven't taken it off since." Her life had changed drastically the day her mother died. "After Mother's passing, Father became quite obsessed with my safety. Barely let me out of his sight." Smothered her was more like it.

"Odd that he allowed you to run off to the front lines as a nurse."

Eliza realized her mistake too late as skepticism flickered across his face. "I fear when I get something in my mind, it is hard to stop me." She gave a nervous giggle. Oh how she hated bending the truth to this man.

He smiled. His gray eyes studied hers. The air between them heated, and Eliza swallowed at his intense perusal. He was so close, she could smell him, hear his breath, see the pulse throbbing in his taut neck. "And your husband. May I ask what happened to him?"

"Killed in action." She wouldn't tell him for which side. Could never tell him. The past few days, she'd harbored a small hope that perhaps he wouldn't fault her for her marriage, that perhaps they had a chance at building on what was obviously a strong mutual attraction and admiration, but after hearing his rage at Yankees and everyone associated with them, that hope was crushed. She pressed down the folds of her skirt and took a step back, if only to break the spell he cast on her. Regardless of the way this man made her feel, regardless of her admiration for him, there could never be anything between them. Ever.

She would be his friend. Help him with his condition if he allowed her. That was it.

Blake took her hand in his. His warm strength folded around her fingers, and she hadn't the will to pull away. "I'm sure he was a hero. What is his name?"

CHAPTER 10

*E*liza bit her lip, trying to think of a name, any name but the one the colonel asked of her. But in her fear, her mind became a vacant hole with only one name filling it: Brigadier General Stanton Watts, commander of the 106th Harrisburg brigade—Union army. So loud did it ring in her thoughts, she feared it would slip past her lips and her guise would crumble, leaving her an enemy to all on board the ship.

But God took pity on her yet again in the form of a knock on the door and the cheery face of James, who eyed their locked hands with upraised brows and a slight smile. "Ah, you're on your feet, Colonel. The captain wishes to speak to you. If you're up to it."

The colonel released her hands, cleared his throat, and took a step back. "The frigate?"

"Gone. Along with half of our weapons, a good portion of our rice and fresh produce, and all of our pigs."

"The passengers and crew?" The colonel grabbed his coat.

"All present and accounted for. Thank God." The doctor scratched his chin. "However did you elude them? They seemed quite intent on finding any Rebel officers on board."

The colonel and Eliza shared a glance and a smile that caused a tingle all the way down to her toes. "It would seem I had a guardian angel," he said, his eyes remaining on hers as if held there by some invisible force. Finally, he cleared his throat, thanked her for the tea, and sped out the door. Without his masculine presence, the cabin grew large and cold. And it felt less safe somehow.

Picking up his cup, she ran her fingers over the brim where his lips had been, remembering his pain, the agony in his voice when he spoke of his family. All of them gone. *Lord, why? How could You allow so much suffering?* It was too much to bear. Too much for one man. No wonder he hated the Yankees. And anyone associated with them. Which meant her, of course. No, even if her past was never revealed, it would be unjust, even cruel to befriend him, let alone consider anything beyond friendship. She must put the colonel out of her thoughts.

Setting the cup on the tray, she began to tidy up the cabin when a knock on the open door turned her around to see Magnolia, an anxious look on her face.

"Magnolia. You startled me. Are you ill?" Eliza started toward her, only then noticing that the young woman's hands trembled.

Pressing down her skirts, Magnolia floated into the cabin, her sapphire-blue eyes skittering over the sideboard containing medicines and surgical implements. "It's my nerves, Eliza," she said in that accentuated Southern drawl that was as sweet as warm molasses. "I cannot seem to relax."

"Understandable." Eliza studied the young woman as she squeezed her own skirts through the narrow space between table and bulkhead. "It was a most harrowing day. I trust you've not been in a battle at sea before."

This drew a smile from Magnolia as she shook her head, sending flaxen curls bouncing over her neck. "I was wondering if you had something to soothe my nerves." Her gaze sped to the medical cabinet once again before her face crumpled. "I simply cannot tolerate another moment on this ship."

"You don't have seasickness, do you?" Eliza took her hand in hers.

"No." She tugged from Eliza's grasp and plopped down in the chair. Then dropping her face into her hands, she began to sob.

Eliza knelt before her. "Oh dear, there's no need to cry. Everything will be all right. The Union ship is gone, and we are on our way to our new home." Evidenced by the flap of sails above and the increasing purl of the sea against the hull.

"It's not that." Magnolia raised her gaze to Eliza, tears spilling down her cheeks. "I want to go home!" Her pout turned into a scowl as a streak of defiance scored her eyes. "I'm engaged to marry Samuel Wimberly." She swiped the remaining moisture from her face and raised her chin. "He's a prominent lawyer from Atlanta. Why, he was even an adviser to President Jefferson Davis."

Eliza flinched. No doubt he knew her father, then, both being solicitors and both working with the president. But she could never mention the connection. "I'm sure he's a wonderful man." Eliza handed her a handkerchief.

"Of course he is. And he adores me." She sniffed and drew the handkerchief to her nose. "We were supposed to wed before this horrendous war began, but then Samuel thought it best to delay the ceremony until the hostilities were over." Another tear wound its way down her creamy cheek. "And now my parents have dragged me away from everything. From Samuel, from our home, from. . ." She hesitated, looking perplexed. "Well, from simply everything!" She gazed down at her pink petticoat peeking from behind cream-colored skirts fringed in Spanish lace. "Look at me. I'm a mess! I look like a street urchin. Or so Daddy told me this morning."

Eliza didn't know whether to feel sorry for the lady or chastise her for her spoiled attitude. She could find no flaw in the woman's appearance. In fact, she could pass for any Southern lady ready to receive guests for afternoon tea. Still, it had not escaped Eliza's attention that Mr. Scott rarely had a kind word for his daughter. Though Eliza's own father had been stern, he'd never berated her. And never in public. What would it be like to grow up with a father like Magnolia's? And then to be dragged away from her entire world, and worse, the man she loved? The poor girl. "I'm sure your parents are doing what is best for you. No doubt your plantation was ruined as many were by the Northerners."

Magnolia looked down, hesitating. "We could have stayed and recovered our losses. But Daddy was so angry—angrier than I've ever seen him—at the Yankees. He's been that way ever since my brother Allen was killed at Chancellorsville. He said we needed to get as far away from them as we could and start over. But I don't want to start over." She began to whine again, an ear-shattering whine that set Eliza's nerves on edge. She poured the girl a cup of tea, hoping it would keep her mouth—and vocal chords—quiet.

Thanking Eliza, she took it, but her hands shook so violently, tea spilled over the edge. "Don't you have something for my nerves?" Blue eyes that held a deviant twinkle gazed at Eliza. "You *do* look so familiar to me."

Ignoring her, Eliza grabbed the cup to settle it. "This is chamomile tea. I know it's cold, but it will help calm you."

Magnolia bit her lip. "Mercy me, I was hoping for something a bit stronger."

Eliza cocked her head. Shaking hands, nervous twitch at the corner of her mouth, desperation in her striking eyes—Eliza had seen those symptoms before. But never in a lady. Nor one of such high breeding. Eliza wondered if her parents knew. "I have nothing stronger. But never fear, the trembling will subside in a few days."

Magnolia set the tea down, spilling it on the table, then stormed to her feet. "I don't know what you are referring to! Oh why did I ever come to you? You're merely a war nurse."

Yet the girl made no move to leave. Instead, she clasped her hands together and glanced toward the medicines.

Eliza wanted to be angry at her, but she looked so pathetic and sad. "I'm sorry, Magnolia. I wish I could help you." She laid a hand on her arm. "Believe me, your discomfort will pass."

Magnolia huffed, assessing Eliza as if she were a wayward servant. But then something flickered in her eyes before they narrowed into malicious slits. "I *do* remember you now."

Eliza's heart cinched. Turning away, she mopped up the spilled tea. "I fear you are mistaken. We have never met."

"No. You're Seth Randal's daughter. Your aunt and uncle are acquainted with my parents. They run that fancy hotel in Marietta. . . . What was the name? Oh yes, the Randal Inn."

A chill bit Eliza. "I'm sorry, but you have the wrong lady."

"No, I never forget a face. But your name isn't Eliza Crawford. . . ." Magnolia laid a shaky finger on her chin before her eyes lit up with malevolent glee. "Ah yes, Flora. Miss Flora Randal, isn't it? Your father knows my Samuel."

Eliza's blood ran cold. "I know no one by that name." She picked up the teacup and placed it on the tray, fiddling with the spoons so as not to show that her insides had twisted into a hopeless knot. She hadn't heard her given name in a long time. Five years to be exact. Not since she had married Stanton. Not since her father had told her Flora Randal was dead to him.

Suddenly, memories of Magnolia flooded her. Two years before the war, Eliza's aunt and uncle had hosted a party at their hotel for some passing dignitaries. The Scotts had been invited because of their familial relation to the governor of Georgia, who was also in attendance. Though Eliza had not met Magnolia's parents, she and Magnolia had exchanged brief pleasantries. At the time, they had both been girls just coming of age, Magnolia only sixteen and Eliza a year younger. Though Magnolia had changed quite a bit in seven years, Eliza remembered envying her for the way all the men in the hotel had fawned over her. And in the midst of the festivities, she had commented thus to Magnolia. A morbid realization now crawled up Eliza's throat. It was after that playful admission that Magnolia, in what was surely a kind gesture, had introduced Eliza to Stanton, an acquaintance of the family's.

Magnolia gasped and drew a hand to her mouth. "Mercy me! You married Stanton Watts!"

"Shhh." Dashing to the door, Eliza shut it then leaned back against the wood. "Please, Magnolia." Her tone and eyes pleaded with the young woman to keep her secret, but Magnolia only chuckled in return.

"Oh my. The wife of a Yankee general right here in the middle of all these angry Rebels! It is simply too much!"

"That was a long time ago. My husband is dead. I spent the last three years nursing Rebel soldiers on the battlefield." Eliza felt all hope draining from her.

"Never fear. I will keep your little secret, Mrs. *Crawford*." Magnolia adjusted her flowing skirts as a coy smile flitted upon her lips. "If you will do me just one little ole favor."

Eliza narrowed her eyes.

"I believe you *do* have something that would ease my nerves, after all, do you not?"

"You are blackmailing me?"

She pouted. "That's such a nasty word. Let's just say we have an understanding."

Forcing down her anger, Eliza brushed past Magnolia, opened the drawer of the desk, and pulled out a half-empty bottle of rum.

The smile Magnolia offered her could have brightened the darkest cave. Greedily, she snagged the bottle from Eliza's hand like a child after candy.

"That isn't good for you, Magnolia. It will ruin your health and your life."

She pressed the bottle against her chest as if it were the most precious thing in the world. "I don't care. I need it."

Eliza should grab it back from her and shatter it on the deck. She was a nurse, after all. It was her job to look out for the health of others. But what choice did she have? "You know what will happen to me if you tell the others."

A flicker of concern, dare Eliza say, even care, appeared on the girl's face. "I shan't say a word." Hiding the rum in the folds of her skirt, she flung open the door. "As long as you continue to treat my nerves."

"That is the only bottle I have."

"Well, I suppose you'll have to find more, won't you?" She gave Eliza the sweetest smile before sashaying away, flinging the words over her shoulder, "Thank you Mrs. *Crawford*. You've been most helpful."

When the younger woman was gone, Eliza's legs gave out. She leaned on the operating table. Her fate—her very life—was now in the hands of a spoiled, pompous tosspot.

Blake hobbled across the deck of the *New Hope*, drawing in a breath of the briny air. The sun reigned over the seas from its position high in the sky, its bright golden robes fluttering over ship and water. Hammering drew his gaze to a group of sailors working to repair the foremast rigging and the rents in the bulwarks. Yesterday Blake had assisted in plugging up the hole in the hull above the waterline. Thankfully all minor repairs. The frigate's attack could have been so much worse.

Sailors stopped to glance his way, as did Mr. Graves, who puffed on his cigar on the foredeck, along with a group of passengers sitting atop crates, eating their morning biscuits. Whispers sizzled past his ears from behind upraised hands. He knew they spoke about his episode. Shame doused him as he made his way toward the railing. He'd wanted so much to present himself as a strong leader to this group. But he had already failed.

If only the nightmares would stop, maybe the blackouts would as well. He gripped the railing and gazed at the azure sea, sparkling like a bed of dancing diamonds. A hearty breeze spun around him, cooling the sweat on the back of his neck. Every mile south brought them warmer weather and heavier air.

He nodded at Captain Barclay, who stood by the binnacle, and the man returned his greeting. They'd developed a mutual respect for each other these past days. More than once the captain had thanked Blake for his help manning the guns and commanding the crew during the chase. And more than once, Blake had thanked him and his men for not giving away his identity.

Scanning the deck, he found Sarah sitting atop a crate, her skirts spread around her, instructing a group of children at her feet, their sweet laughter a compliment to the creak of the ship and rush of water that had become so familiar to Blake's ears.

Mr. and Mrs. Jenkins, the young farmers, stood behind their daughter, Henrietta, as she listened intently to the story Sarah was telling. The freed slave woman's children stood at a distance, their feet itching to join the other young ones, but Delia's firm hand on each shoulder kept them in place. That and the scowl on Mr. Scott's face as he leaned against the railing beside his wife and daughter. On Miss Magnolia's other side, Dodd attempted to engage her in conversation, but from the young lady's pursed lips and raised nose, Blake doubted the ex-lawman was gaining any ground.

Mr. Lewis, the carpenter, seemed already three sheets to the wind as he clung to the capstan, rolling with each sway of the ship. Parson Bailey strolled around the deck with James, their heads bent in conversation, no doubt regarding some deep theological argument. A call from above shifted Blake's glance to the sailors working the sails. Barefooted, they skittered across the yards as if they preferred balancing on a teetering strip of wood to walking on dry land. The first mate stood on the deck beneath them, shouting up orders. Beside him, Moses, the freed slave, assisted a group of sailors in carrying a barrel of water on deck for the passengers.

They plunked it down beside Hayden, who was polishing the brass fitting atop the foredeck railing. Yesterday Blake had seen him scrub the deck and assist sailors hauling lines. Despite his intrusion on their voyage, the man did not shy from hard work. He'd also proven himself brave and competent during their battle with the Union frigate. In fact, the man had charmed his way so far into everyone's graces that the suspicious circumstances that brought him on board seemed all but forgotten. If he decided to stay on with them in Brazil, Blake could use another strong man to help lead the colony.

Yet still no sign of Mrs. Crawford—Eliza. Her Christian name floated through his mind, longing to appear on his lips, longing for the familiarity it would signify between them. Perhaps all the excitement from yesterday kept her in bed. Or perhaps she was avoiding him. Yes, perhaps he'd been too forward, too open with his thoughts and sentiments. And he'd gone and frightened her away. He couldn't blame her. What would any woman want with a lame man who was obviously going mad?

Speaking of mad, Mr. Graves's dark, piercing eyes assessed Blake from afar. Dressed in his usual black suit, and with his equally black hair, whiskers, and mustache, the man presented a rather somber figure. Spooky was more like it. Yet that impression haled more from his attitude, the way he stood at a distance and stared at people—like he was staring at Blake now—as if he could read his thoughts. A frisson of unease settled in Blake's gut. Mr. Graves smiled, and Blake tore his gaze away. No sense in offering the man any encouragement.

Leaping up the quarterdeck stairs, he made his way to the stern, wincing at the pain radiating through his leg. Which seemed to be getting worse, not better. He guessed that was to be expected with all the heaving and careening and the extra effort it took just to keep upright on the ship. Nevertheless, he would be glad to settle on dry land again.

Leaning over the taffrail, he watched the foamy wake bubble off the stern and dissolve in the deep waters. Just like everything good in his life.

He plucked his brother's belt plate from his pocket and fingered it, shifting it in the sunlight, examining all the facets, the engraving, squinting when it reflected light in his eyes. Which only reminded him of Jeremy's smile, so bright and warm.

Perhaps in a new place, a new country, where no memories of the war or his past existed, Blake would find freedom from his nightmares. In a place where no Yankee roamed, his soul could rest, forget, and find peace.

It was his only hope.

A loud twang crackled over the ship, followed by a snap. Blake spun around. Sailors shouted and rushed across the brig. Rigging parted. The brace on the weather side began to split. One of the yards swung free.

Beneath the urgent shouts of the captain, the first mate joined a group of sailors in the ratlines, scrambling aloft to capture the wayward yard.

Blake started toward them. The ship canted. The yard shifted and struck the first mate.

He fell to the deck with a soul-crunching thud.

On the captain's heels, Blake dashed down to the main deck as men circled the fallen man. But it was the look on Mr. Graves's face that halted Blake in his tracks.

A look of sheer joy.

CHAPTER 11

*S*ink me for a pirate if this voyage ain't under a jinx!" Captain Barclay slammed his fist on his desk, overturning a bottle of ink and sending Eliza's heart into her throat. He righted the bottle before too much of the black liquid spilled on his charts. At least the ones he had left. For in addition to smashing the main compass in the binnacle and stealing the captain's sextant and scales, the thief had also absconded with several of his maps.

Eliza suddenly wished she had not been summoned to the captain's cabin, along with James, to give a report on the first mate's condition. She'd spent enough years enduring her father's temper to last a lifetime. Yet the other men in the room—the colonel, the parson, and two sailors— seemed unaffected by both the captain's outburst and by the furious pace he now took up before the stern windows, growling like a bear.

"Your first mate suffered quite a blow to his head," James stated. "I'm afraid, he's slipped into a coma. There's no telling when he will wake up. Weeks perhaps."

"But he will wake up?" the captain asked, looking concerned.

"I believe so, Captain. In time."

The news did not improve Captain Barclay's mood. He halted, his face hard as quartz. "We are chased and boarded by a Union frigate, my rigging splits and nearly kills my first mate, and"—he tossed the rest of a drink to the back of this throat then slammed the glass down on his desk—"where in Neptune's sea have my instruments and charts gone off to?"

At the man's enraged tone, Eliza took a step back, her ears ringing at the string of curses that followed his statement. The colonel, noting her unease, came to stand by her side.

Always the gentleman. He cleared his throat, drawing the captain's gaze.

"Forgive me, Mrs. Crawford." Captain Barclay said before he poured himself another drink.

"If I may, Cap'n." One of the sailors, the boatswain, whom Eliza believed was named Max, stepped forward. "I might know who took yer instruments."

The deck heaved. Water hissed against the hull. The colonel steadied Eliza with a touch. But the captain only gaped at Max in consternation. "Well, spit it out, man, I haven't all day! Whoever it is, they'll be slurpin' bilgewater by morning!"

"That fine-lookin'"—Max cleared his throat—"the Scotts' daughter, I meant to say." He fidgeted with his hat. "I saw her enter yer cabin yesterday morn."

"And you said nothing!"

The captain's bark sent Max back a step. "How was I to know what the tart was up to?" He shrugged, and his tanned face turned a deep shade of scarlet. "Figured it was none of me business why the lady came to yer cabin alone."

James's eyes widened.

"Oh my." Parson Bailey opened his Bible and began flipping through the pages.

"Oh for the love of. . ." Captain Barclay huffed. "Bring her here immediately. And her parents!"

Within minutes, the Scotts arrived, acting as indignant as if they'd been whisked away from a royal ball.

"What is the meaning of this, Captain?" Mr. Scott grabbed the lapels of his fancy coat.

But the captain's eyes were on Magnolia, who had slipped behind her father's large frame. "I would like a word with your daughter, sir."

"My daughter?" Mr. Scott flinched then turned to find Magnolia cowering beside her mother. With a huff, he dragged her forward. "What could you possibly wish to discuss with her?"

"Miss Scott." Circling the desk, the captain crossed his meaty arms over his chest. Sunlight angled through the window, jouncing over his indigo coat. "Do you have somethin' to say to me?"

Magnolia's eyes widened. Her gaze skittered about the room before landing back on the captain. "I don't believe I do."

"About the cap'n's instruments." Max jerked a thumb toward Captain Barclay. "How ye stole them from his desk."

"An' smashed the compass," the other sailor chimed in.

"Oh dear." Mrs. Scott sank into a chair.

Magnolia's eyes turned to shimmering pools. Her bottom lip quivered, and she stumbled over the deck. Eliza rushed to slip an arm around her back for support.

A real tremble *did* course through the lady, but she jerked from Eliza's embrace and glared at her parents. "I want to go home." Tears trickled down her cheeks. "I didn't mean to hurt anyone. I only wanted the ship to turn around and head back to Charleston!"

Wind pounded against the stern windows.

Mr. Scott gawked in horror at his daughter. "What have you done?"

"There is no place in the kingdom of heaven for thieves and liars," Parson Bailey said, causing Mrs. Scott to whimper.

And red fury to course across Mr. Scott's face. "You stole the captain's instruments?" His voice rose with each word as he glared at his daughter. "What were you thinking?" He grabbed her arm until tears spilled from her cheeks, his jaw tight above quivering jowls. But then his eyes wandered over the group, and composing himself, he faced Captain Barclay. "Do tell me that wasn't the reason we were captured and boarded."

"No, not entirely," the captain said. The ship creaked and groaned as it tumbled over a wave.

Magnolia tripped, never taking her gaze off the deck. "I just wanted to go home," she mumbled. "I just wanted to go home."

"Miss Scott," Captain Barclay said, "you put the entire brig and everyone on board in grave danger." He gripped the edge of his desk behind him and leaned back with a sigh. "Thank God I have a hand compass and an extra sextant. But my charts. What did you do with them?"

"I tossed everything overboard," she said without looking up.

Mrs. Scott's whimpering transformed into wailing, reminding Eliza of a sick cow.

Which seemed somehow fitting, since Mr. Scott, at the moment, resembled a bull penned in a cage. "Of course we will pay for the damages, Captain. Please accept our apology." His tone was one of restrained fury. Then turning, he clutched Magnolia's arm in a pinch and dragged her out the door. "You have embarrassed me to no end, young lady. Incorrigible behavior. Simply incorrigible!" When his wife didn't follow, he shouted over his shoulder. "Come along, Mrs. Scott." As if waking from a stupor, the woman rose, face to the floor, and shuffled out the door.

The parson sped after them, muttering something about repentance and restitution.

Despite Magnolia's actions, Eliza felt sorry for her. She knew what it was like to live with an overbearing parent who insisted on managing every detail of her life. No doubt that was the reason Magnolia had turned to drink. In truth, she and Eliza were not so different after all. Eliza had been no less rebellious against her own father. In fact, she'd been more. She could still picture him standing in his study the day she told him she wanted to marry Stanton.

"You will not marry that man! He is from Pennsylvania of all places. He is not one of us. Besides, it has already been arranged. You are to marry Miles Grisham."

Miles Grisham, the heir to the Grisham railroad fortune. And a mealymouthed weasel of the worst kind. "But, Papa, please. I don't love him."

With a snort, her father strode to the window. Dressed in a fine cutaway coat of gray broadcloth with silver braid trim shimmering in the afternoon sun, he presented such a handsome, commanding figure. "Love only causes pain." He huffed. She knew he was thinking of her mother. Her death when Eliza was only twelve had robbed her father of his youth, his zest for life—his heart.

As if confirming where his thoughts had taken him, he said, "Your mother would approve of Mr. Grisham."

"Mother would want me happy."

He spun around. "And you think I don't? This is for your own good. You'll see."

When Eliza opened her mouth to protest further, he held up a hand. His signal that the discussion had come to an end.

And Eliza's signal to resort to drastic measures—to disobey him and run away with Stanton. Like Magnolia, she had not considered the implications of her actions that day. Now, looking back, she wondered if she'd only married Stanton to get out from under her father's thumb.

The captain's voice jarred her from her thoughts.

"Colonel, I'd like to make you my acting first mate if you'll accept the job."

Colonel Wallace stretched his broad shoulders, which seemed to rise beneath the man's question. "Me? I hardly know what to do."

"The men respect you." The captain sipped his drink then pointed it toward the colonel. "Besides, I've been watching you. You learn fast."

James nodded his approval.

"Very well," the colonel said. "I'll do my best."

Eliza's heart nearly burst with happiness for him. He'd more than proven that he was a leader of men and quite capable of the position.

After the captain dismissed them with a wave of his hand, Max brushed past Eliza, touching her arm as his eyes roved over her, giving her an unpleasant chill—a chill that instantly warmed when the colonel proffered his elbow with a smile. But Eliza begged off with the excuse that she needed to check on her patient. She'd love nothing more than to spend time with the colonel, but it was better this way. Better for them both.

Two uneventful weeks passed. Uneventfully delightful in the sense that they'd not seen another ship, nor had the weather been overly uncomfortable, though it had rained consistently each afternoon. But also uneventful in that most of the passengers had settled into a daily routine and were now complaining of the monotony of company and scenery. And of the food! Porridge and biscuits for breakfast, chicken and biscuits for lunch, and chicken and biscuits for supper. Eliza wouldn't care if she never tasted chicken again. Besides, she couldn't stand the sound of the poor creatures being butchered each morning and evening. Since the Yanks had stolen their rice, cheese, pigs, and most of their produce, the meals had become something to endure rather than enjoy.

Nevertheless, they'd also had a pleasant lapse of medical emergencies. Aside from the first mate, whom Eliza checked daily, there were no other catastrophes except a few rashes and one case of diarrhea. Well, unless running into the colonel every time she turned around was a catastrophe: by the forecastle; on the main deck; by the stern; in the galley, the hold, the sick bay. Wherever she went to try to avoid him, there he was with that hypnotic grin on his face and a request on his lips to join him for a stroll.

What was a lady supposed to do? She could hardly ignore someone on board a tiny brig. And if she dared to admit it, she enjoyed every minute she spent in his company. Minutes in which she'd grown to know and admire him even more.

Sunlight angled across the cabin as Eliza put the final pin in her hair and slipped on her bonnet. Behind her, Sarah's gentle snores filled the tiny space as she swung in her hammock to the movements of the ship. So far along with child, she must be quite uncomfortable and tired. Yet every day she gathered the children together to teach them their lessons. Angeline had already risen and left the cabin sometime in the night, as she often did. Eliza suspected some tragedy ran deep within the poor lady. If only she could get her to talk about it. Perhaps Eliza should pray. Oh fiddle! Of course. Why hadn't she thought of that?

Lifting up a quick prayer for Angeline, she slid a few pins on her hat to keep it in place, took one last glance in the mirror, and turned to leave, looking forward to her daily stroll on the deck. And hoping, against her own good sense, that the colonel would seek her out.

Closing the door as quietly as possible, Eliza made her way down the hall, stopping when a macabre tune floated up from the hold. No, not a tune. A chant of some kind. She'd heard it before in the wee hours of the night. It had slithered down her spine and sent a shiver through her exactly like it was doing now. But who would be uttering such a direful chant?

Shaking it off, she climbed the ladder to the main deck, squinting at the sun, now a hand's breadth above the horizon. Wind tumbled over her, dislodging her hair from its pins and loosening her hat, making her wonder why she bothered to attempt the fashionable coiffeur at all.

Gripping the brim, she proceeded across the deck and spotted Magnolia battling her parasol. Eliza had managed to find another bottle of brandy in the sick bay to lock the woman's tongue, but with the Union frigate absconding with most of their rum, she didn't know how much longer she could appease the girl. Surely Magnolia wasn't cruel enough to ruin Eliza's life when there was no alcohol to be found on board?

A gust of wind tore the parasol from Magnolia's hands, sending it bouncing in the air on its way out to sea. Mable, her slave, dropped the load of books she carried and caught the parasol just in time, handing it to her disgruntled owner, who snagged it from her with a scowl. Moses darted toward them, picking up the books for Mable and handing them to her. Her cheeks reddened like raspberries on chocolate as she nodded her thanks.

Eliza couldn't help but smile at the budding romance. The thought of which drew her gaze to Blake at his usual spot on the quarterdeck. He'd filled the role of first mate as if he'd been born on a ship. How he'd learned all the names and positions of the sails and when they should be raised or lowered, furled or unfurled, she had no idea, but the crew leaped to task whenever he shouted an order. Wind swept over him as he stood conferring with the captain, flapping his white shirt. His dark eyebrows knit together at something the captain was saying, but then he saw her, and his forehead relaxed into soft lines.

Chastising herself for being caught staring at him—yet again— Eliza positioned herself at the starboard railing and gazed out over the blue expanse of sky and sea. She'd never realized how many shades of blue there were: azure, cobalt, indigo, navy, turquoise, cerulean, teal, beryl. And each so beautiful and unique, appearing at the whim of sun, cloud, and wind. As well as the depth of the sea, Captain Barclay had told her.

Closing her eyes, she drew in a breath of briny air tainted with the odor of fish. She fingered the locket hanging around her neck. Thoughts of her mother were interrupted by the clipped gait of the colonel's boots coming her way. Her heart leaped.

"Another fine day, is it not, Mrs. Crawford?"

"It is indeed, Colonel. The ocean grows more magnificent each day."

"I hear it's even more beautiful off the coast of Brazil." The brig flopped over a wave, showering them with salty spray and causing them both to laugh.

Eliza brushed the moisture from her skirts as the colonel's expression sobered. "May I join you, or do you prefer to be alone?" he asked.

If ever there had been a time for her to deny his request, it had been two weeks ago when he'd first asked the same question. But too much time had passed, too many strolls around the deck, too many conversations of happier times in the South before the war, and now Eliza could not imagine denying herself the only thing she looked forward to on the journey. Even though she knew it was unfair to them both. Oh what a weak woman she was! Always led by feelings and not by reason. She should make an excuse that she needed to think, to pray—to do the right thing for once in her life! Instead, she faced him. "I would love the company, but surely you have duties to attend?"

"Ah, you won't get rid of me that easily, Mrs. Crawford. Besides, with a clear sky and a steady wind, there's not much to be done at the moment."

That moment turned into several minutes as the colonel shared with her the reason he started this venture to Brazil. Eliza found herself mesmerized by his words; the inflection of his voice when he spoke; his confident, resonant tone; how the sunlight reflected the ocean's blue in his gray eyes; and the way the wind batted the tips of his coal-colored hair.

"Forgive me, I've gone on and on about my hopes for Brazil," he said.

"There's nothing wrong with wanting a simple life, Colonel. Not after what you've endured. What we've all endured." Eliza sighed and held down her bonnet against a burst of wind. "To work hard, reap the fruit of your labors, raise children, and live in peace. Peace from others lording it over you, peace from oppression and hatred." Yes, Eliza could well understand that. She longed for that kind of life, herself, as well.

"So, you *were* listening to me." He smiled.

"Always, Colonel."

His eyes sparkled pleasure at her response as he leaned on the railing and cocked his head. "Now, what of your dreams, Mrs. Crawford? I would love to hear them."

But she couldn't tell him that her only real dream was to escape the scorn, the hatred toward her in the South. The sun spread sparkling ribbons over waves, and she lowered the brim of her hat against its brightness. "Like you, I simply wish to put my past behind me and start over."

"But you still have family in the States. Why have they not come with you?"

Eliza bit her lip. "We have become estranged, I'm afraid."

"Ah." Understanding flashed across his eyes. "No doubt your father did not wish you to become a war nurse."

Though that was not the reason for the estrangement, it was true enough to allow Eliza to nod in agreement.

The brig rose over a swell, and he touched her elbow to keep her steady. "I'm sure he had your best interests at heart."

She wouldn't tell him that it was her father's own interests, his own reputation, that led his heart. A fact that still weighed heavily on Eliza. Had he ever really loved her? Or was all his meddling, his smothering, his guiding merely a way for him to control her, mold her into the perfect daughter of a prominent solicitor?

Blake hated that he'd somehow caused the sorrow burning in Eliza's golden eyes. Gold like the sun with flecks of silver that sparkled when she laughed. He must bring back her smile. Scanning the deck, he spotted Mr. Dodd pointing to his treasure map and spouting off to a group of passengers. "Well at least you've not got your heart set on a chest of gold like Mr. Dodd."

Clutching the brim of her hat, whereupon ribbons and feathers hopelessly flailed about, she glanced toward the ex-lawman and rewarded Blake with a grin. "Indeed. I am not one for fanciful tales. Can you believe it? Treasure maps and pirates!" She chuckled.

Blake scratched his chin. "And apparently they buried their chest of gold right outside of Rio de Janeiro."

"I hope he didn't pay overmuch for such a forgery." She gave him a sly look. "Though it is rather amusing."

"Then, I take it, you don't believe him?" Blake's attempt at lightness fell flat when, still staring at Dodd, the lady's face tightened. "I find him uncomfortable to be around. But if he does find gold, the better for him. Perhaps then he will keep his eyes off the ladies."

"Yes indeed." The man's obsession with women had not gone unnoticed by Blake. "Let me know if he bothers you, and I will handle it."

She smiled at him shyly and lowered her gaze. Such innocence from a married lady. He enjoyed every moment spent in her company. More than any of the ladies he had courted before the war. When he had thought himself too wounded, too damaged, for any possibility of finding a wife, Eliza Crawford had rekindled hope within him for the first time in years. If only she could overlook his weakness.

Yet the look in her eyes at the moment exuded more respect than pity. And he felt her admiration straight down to his boots. Wind gusted over them. Loose strands of her hair danced over her shoulders in a wildness that was so much like the lady herself. Brave, free, uninhibited. He'd never met anyone like her.

A shout drew his gaze to Miss Magnolia, who was scolding her slave—for some minor infraction, no doubt. After her tirade, she settled onto one of the heavy crates the captain had brought on deck for the passengers. The young lady's gaze drifted above and remained there so long, Blake followed it to find Hayden, stripped to his trousers, his chest gleaming with sweat, working on one of the halyards.

"Odd that she stares at a man she claims to despise," Eliza offered with a chuckle.

Blake cocked a brow at her, noting her eyes were fastened on the man as well. A spike of jealousy caused his annoyance to rise. "Our stowaway is a handsome figure, is he not?"

A coy grin toyed on her lips. "He is no match for you, Colonel." She immediately swept her gaze to sea. "Forgive me. That was far too bold. I fear my thoughts have escaped my mouth again!"

Another endearing quality of hers. "I'm afraid I cannot forgive you, madam." For it meant that, despite his limp, despite his mad episodes, she found him agreeable. And that alone gave him the impetus to ask her to receive his courtship. He wanted to know her better. Wanted to have an understanding between them that excluded all others. She was, after all, only one of four unmarried women aboard, and he saw the way the other men looked at her.

Yet, was it fair of him to pursue her when he had the responsibility of the entire colony on his shoulders? Yes, he'd be busy, especially after arriving at Brazil, but she'd proven herself more than capable of handling any situation. And with her by his side, with her wisdom, skill, bravery, and kind heart, Blake knew he could tackle anything.

After glancing around to ensure they weren't going to be interrupted, he took her hand in his, heart thundering in his chest more than it had on any battlefield. "Mrs. Crawford, I know this is sudden. I know you may think me completely mad, but I would be so honored"—he hesitated, shifting his stance—"you would make me so happy"—he cleared his throat—"if you would allow me to court you."

Instead of the expected smile, the joyful glimmer in her eyes, horror glazed over them then eased onto her face, tightening her features and parting her mouth. Tugging her hand from his, she backed away as if he'd just asked her to climb to the top yard.

CHAPTER 12

$\mathscr{S}$tripped to her petticoats, Eliza ran a damp cloth over her face and arms in an attempt to rid herself of the salty film that seemed permanently glued to her skin. Though she tried, she could not get the colonel's request to court her out of her mind, out of her thoughts. Or out of her heart. Thank God one of the sailors had interrupted them with a complaint of a rash, which was soon followed by a string of infirmities from others that had kept her in the sick bay the rest of the day. Safe from having to answer the question to which her heart screamed, *Yes!* but to which her mind screamed, *No!*

Yet. . .was a courtship possible? Could one tiny mistake several years in the past ruin her chances for happiness? She had thought so. "Oh Lord, I don't know what to do," she said out loud, not really expecting an answer. Not really wanting to know the answer if it meant the colonel was not a part of her future. Which was probably why she wouldn't hear one. She dipped the rag back into the basin of water. The door opened, and she swerved about, covering herself.

"Oh, forgive me, Eliza." Angeline entered the tiny cabin and quickly closed the door. "It's terribly hard to find privacy aboard this ship."

But Eliza had lost all thoughts of modesty when her eyes latched onto the fluffy bundle in Angeline's arms. "Oh my." She stepped toward Angeline and ran her fingers over the black fur. The cat gazed up at her with amber-colored eyes. "Where did you find it?"

Angeline eased into the single chair and set the feline on her lap. "Below in the hold. I went to get some flour for Cook, and I found

116

this wee one pouncing on a rat. A rather large rat, I might add." She chuckled, and Eliza thought how comely she was when she smiled. Which the lady didn't do very often.

"Most women would have swooned at the sight of a rat. You impress me." Eliza knelt to caress the cat, who began purring under so much attention.

"I've been exposed to much worse." Angeline's tone was far too nonchalant for such a statement.

Eliza squeezed her hand. "We've all been exposed to things these past few years that no lady should have to endure." Though Eliza had a feeling Angeline wasn't talking about the war at all. There was something in her demeanor, a sorrow, a worldly knowledge that had stolen the innocence from her eyes. Eyes that now bore shadows beneath them.

"I notice you don't sleep well," Eliza said, bringing the lady's surprised gaze to hers.

"Forgive me for waking you. I try to be quiet."

"I'm a light sleeper." Eliza sat on the trunk beside Angeline. "But that isn't why I mentioned it. Perhaps I can find some medicine to help you rest?"

"Nothing helps. I've been this way since. . .well, since the war."

Eliza nodded her understanding. The dreadful war had changed a lot of people—for the worse. "It must have been horrible to lose your father. Who took care of you?"

"My uncle." The woman seemed to choke on the word. "Then I was on my own."

Eliza wondered what happened but kept silent.

"I did many things I'm not proud of," Angeline added numbly, as if to no one in particular.

"You are not the only one." Eliza sighed.

Angeline's brow wrinkled, and she looked at Eliza, first with curiosity and then with shame. Finally, she gazed down and stroked the cat.

"What will you call her?" Eliza attempted to lighten the mood.

"It's a he, I believe. And he's quite skinny. I fear he hasn't been eating well." The cat leaped from her lap and slinked around the cabin. "I'm going to call him Stowy since he's our stowaway cat."

Eliza chuckled and rose. "Excellent choice. If we keep him in here with us, at least we shan't have to worry about rats crawling on us during our sleep."

Angeline trembled. "At least not the rodent kind."

Her words gave Eliza pause. "Has someone been bothering you?" she asked. "I can have the colonel speak to them." She nearly laughed at her own statement. Did she think the man was her personal bodyguard to share as she desired?

"No. Nothing like that." Angeline's violet eyes swept to the porthole where the setting sun bounced in and out of view. "It's just Mr. Dodd. He keeps staring at me."

"You are a beautiful woman. I fear you'll have to manage the attention. Especially when there are so few single women on this journey."

"Perhaps you are right." She offered Eliza a curt smile then brushed a lock of copper-colored hair from her forehead.

The cat wove around Eliza's feet and then pounced on a shaft of sunlight shifting over the floor.

"Besides"—Eliza turned back to the small mirror, attempting to pin up her unruly locks—"I hear there is a celebration on deck tonight. Apparently some of the passengers and sailors brought along their fiddles and have agreed to play. I insist you join me above. After all we've been through on this voyage, we could use some gaiety."

"Oh, I couldn't possibly." Angeline rubbed her arms as if a chill had come over her.

"Why not?" Eliza gave up on her hair and opened her trunk, seeking her only formal gown, an emerald percale over a bodice of white muslin, trimmed in Chantilly lace. Her fingers touched something hard and cold, and she pulled out the gold pocket watch Stanton had given her. The last thing he had given her. The only thing he'd given her of a personal nature. She flipped it over to see her initials engraved on the back in fine filigree. *FEW.* Flora Eliza Watts. Folding it inside a handkerchief, she placed it back in the trunk and retrieved her gown.

Angeline sat back in her chair with a sigh. "I've never cared for parties or dancing."

"Do say you'll come listen to the music at least. It's better than sitting here alone with a cat."

"Is it?" Stowy leaped at one of the hammock ropes and began gnawing the twines. Angeline smiled. "I'm rather fond of him already."

Yet after much persuasion, Eliza finally convinced her friend to accompany her. Sarah soon returned, begging off from the party with an excuse of exhaustion and promising to watch Stowy while they were above.

So, within an hour and dressed in their finest, Eliza and Angeline emerged onto the deck just in time to see the sun splash ripples of saffron and maroon across the horizon. A jaunty wind held the sails full and stirred the seas into frolicking waves. Everyone was in high spirits as passengers and sailors alike assembled to enjoy the festivities.

Across the deck, the colonel, with one boot propped on the gunwale, was deep in a conversation with James. His gaze traveled her way more than once, and she thought she saw him smile. Which did nothing to becalm the flutter of her heart. She knew she'd have to answer his question sooner or later, but for the life of her, she still had no idea what to say. Perhaps she could avoid him until she did. After all, there were plenty of other men to dance with. Though once the sun had set and the music began, she found her traitorous gaze wandering repeatedly toward him, hoping he would finish his conversation and approach her.

Fiddle, flute, and harmonica joined in a mellifluous melody that swirled like steam into the black bowl circling the ship. Clusters of twinkling stars spanned the inky curtain as if God himself had flung handfuls of diamonds into the sky. The main deck cleared, and couples moved in a country dance. Their efforts to maintain their balance on the shifting wood while performing the steps brought a chuckle to Eliza's lips.

On the quarterdeck, Captain Barclay smoked a pipe and watched the proceedings. Beside him, Parson Bailey prattled on about the evils of dancing. When nobody paid him any mind, he dropped below. The Scotts joined the dancing couples, and Magnolia made her way to stand beside Eliza and Angeline. The smell of alcohol clung to her as tightly as her low-cut bodice.

"Good evening, ladies." She greeted them with a smile. "Seems we are the only single women of any station on board."

Eliza's face grew hot. The audacity of the woman to attempt a friendship with her when she had threatened to destroy her life—continued to threaten her!

Though there was a hearty evening breeze, Magnolia drew out

her fan, waving it flirtatiously over her face. "I find the colonel quite handsome, don't you?"

Eliza ignored the twinge spiraling through her gut.

"However, he *does* have that limp." She sighed. "And then there's James, the doctor or preacher or whatever he is. Oh mercy me, what does it matter? Those devilish bronze eyes could make any woman swoon."

Angeline smiled as her gaze reached across the deck to the good doctor. "I don't believe the doctor is all that he seems to be," she mumbled.

The ship rose, and Eliza clipped her arm through Angeline's. "Indeed, why would you say such a thing?"

"No reason." Her tone carried an intrigue that piqued Eliza's curiosity.

Yet when both ladies glanced at Magnolia, it wasn't the colonel or James her eyes were fixed on, but Hayden Gale, standing beside the aforementioned men, one boot on the bulwarks, one arm on the railing, returning her gaze.

"But you forget our roguish stowaway," Angeline added.

"He's a pig," Magnolia spat.

Eliza restrained a smile. "I believe the pig is heading this way."

Emerging from the crowd like a prince scattering his subjects, Hayden, dressed in a suit of brown broadcloth with silk-lined lapels— no doubt borrowed from one of the colonists—presented quite the dashing gentleman. Especially with his dark hair slicked back and tied in a queue and that devilish grin on his face. To Eliza's surprise, he halted before Magnolia.

"Would you care to dance, Miss Scott?"

Magnolia stared at him as if he'd asked her to walk the plank. "I would not, Mr. Gale." She raised her pert little nose. "Not if you were the last man on board."

Eliza cringed at the girl's rude behavior.

Yet Hayden only grinned as one brow rose over moss-green eyes. "Since it appears no one else will dance with you, it was only charity I had in mind."

"Of all the nerve!" Magnolia blurted. "I have no need to beg for a dance."

"And yet you turn away one freely offered."

"I do not dance with ruffians."

"And I do not dance with swaggering shrews. On board a ship, we can hardly afford to be finicky."

Angeline gasped. Eliza hid a smile.

Magnolia fumed and stomped her foot. "How dare you?" He caught her raised hand—the one aiming for his face—in midair. And after placing a kiss on it, he bowed to them all and left.

"Of all the. . ." Magnolia's chest rose and fell as her gaze followed Hayden across the deck, but thankfully she stewed in silence.

The couples began a quadrille. A sailor sheepishly asked Angeline to dance, his eyes firing with delight when she agreed. Magnolia turned down the next man and the man after that before she huffed away to join her parents.

The ship seemed to sway with the music as water purled against the hull in a soothing accompaniment. Light from lanterns hanging from masts spun dizzying circles over the deck as Eliza strained to see through the miasma of twirling skirts and bobbing crinolettes. Several sailors looked her way, but it was Mr. Graves who finally approached, dressed in his usual black and looking even more sinister in the shadows of night. To make matters worse, Dodd joined him, his eyes aglow with desire. They both asked her to dance at the same time.

To which Mr. Graves frowned and waved the man off. "I was here first."

"First or not," Dodd replied, "it should be the lady's choice."

Eliza closed her eyes and prayed for a solution.

"Mrs. Crawford, I believe you promised me this dance."

That voice—that baritone voice of assurance that caused her stomach to flip and her eyes to open. She placed her hand in his. "Indeed, Colonel. If you will excuse me, gentlemen."

⁓⁂⁓

Blake led Eliza onto the makeshift dance floor, thrilled she had accepted his offer to dance. After her reaction to his question earlier, insecurity had swamped him. Perhaps he had misread her affections for him. Perhaps he had been too bold. Spoken too soon. Perhaps she bore no feelings for him outside of friendship.

"It seems you have saved me once again, Colonel." She smiled, and the lantern light danced in her golden eyes. "First from the hail of Yankee bullets in Charleston, then from the frigate's guns, and now from a fate far worse than both."

Blake chuckled. "It is nothing. I excelled at West Point's training to rescue fair maidens." He hobbled in step, hoping his awkwardness didn't offend her.

She smiled. "Obviously. And a valuable skill it is. Along with commanding troops, organizing expeditions, manning ship's guns, and assuming the role of first mate?" Her approving tone did much to sweep away his insecurities.

"I am at your service." He dipped his head playfully.

She smiled and looked away, her face darkening as if the comment made her sad.

From the moment she'd come on deck, he'd been watching her every move, anxious to end his conversation with James about the price of land in Brazil and the viability of growing corn and cotton, meanwhile hoping she refused any offers to dance. However, when Mr. Graves and Mr. Dodd approached her, Blake excused himself abruptly.

Not that he thought she'd accept their offers, but because both men tended to make the women on board uncomfortable. Mr. Graves because of his unsociable demeanor and the sinister way he stared at everyone from afar and Dodd for his mad gold-hunting dreams and prurient glances toward the ladies.

Placing her gloved hand atop his, he twirled her about the deck. Between the music and laughter and all the spinning and stepping, conversation became impossible. He longed to speak with her in private. He must know her feelings. Though at the moment, Blake was the happiest of all men simply to be near her—to be the one touching her, the one to whom she cast her smiles. They danced a cotillion, a country dance, and then a quadrille. And when the musicians took a break, she stood by his side chatting with the other passengers.

Finally, he could stand it no longer. Begging everyone's pardon, he led her to the larboard railing away from the crowd and fetched her a drink of whiskey-tainted water. Thank goodness, Eliza's smallpox ruse had sent the Union sailors scrambling for the safety of their frigate before they absconded with every ounce of spirits on board, or the *New Hope*'s passengers and crew wouldn't be able to drink the stale water at all. A night breeze wafted over them, cooling the perspiration on Blake's neck, as he strained to see Eliza's features in the shifting lantern light. Why did his chest feel as though an army marched across it?

Eliza scanned the crowd. "Look, Hayden and Angeline are dancing. I'm so glad. I all but dragged her above. I do hope she has a good time." Eliza prattled on as if she were nervous about something. Or worse, as if she were trying to avoid bringing up their earlier conversation.

She cast Blake a sly look. "I'm afraid Hayden received quite a tongue-lashing from Magnolia earlier."

"Yes, I believe the entire ship heard." Blake had actually felt sorry for the man. But he didn't want to talk about Hayden or Angeline or Magnolia. He shifted his stance and gazed over the ebony sea. What was wrong with him? He'd commanded hundreds of men without batting an eye, but he couldn't ask one woman to accept his courtship. Squaring his shoulders, he faced her and opened his mouth to speak when Eliza pointed upward.

A shooting star sped across the black expanse like a fiery rocket, drawing "oohs" and "ahhs" from the crowd. The brig jolted, and Blake took the opportunity to slip his arm around Eliza's waist. To keep her from stumbling, of course. The promise of rain tinged the air, and the musicians packed up their instruments. Some of the passengers and crew went below. Blake's throat went dry. He must ask her before she retired for the evening and it was too late. Before he had to live another moment in this agony. "Eliza." He took her hands in his. "You never answered the question I posed earlier today."

⚜

Eliza drew a nervous breath and glanced across the deck where only a dozen or so people remained. When had the music stopped? When had the couples gone below? She hadn't noticed—she hadn't noticed anything but the man before her.

He caressed her fingers, gently, expectantly. The wind rustled his coal-black hair. Lantern light speckled the stubble on his chin. His eyes found hers. She wished she could see them better in the darkness.

"You have me quite beguiled, Eliza. Tell me you feel something for me."

Eliza squeezed her eyes shut, trying to sort through the jumble in her mind, trying to make the right decision. For once. She had only been married to a Yankee for a year. And she had never been accepted in his circle. Born and raised in Georgia, she was a Southern girl through and through. Did Blake need to know about that one short year? Couldn't she just pretend it never happened? Oh how she longed to erase it from her memory. And her past!

Opening her eyes, she met Blake's gaze, tinged with disappointment, no doubt at her delay in answering him. She hated to see him pained. Longed for joy to fill those wondrous gray eyes. "You know that I do, Blake. How could I not? Any woman would be thrilled to receive your affections."

He blinked as if startled by her declaration. Then a wide grin split his lips, and he lifted her hand for a kiss. "I could never have hoped—" He swallowed. "Then you agree to a formal courtship?"

Against all sense, against everything within her screaming to tell him the truth, Eliza replied, "Yes."

The joy, the hope returned to his eyes. He caressed her jaw with his thumb, gazing at her as if she were a precious jewel. Never had Stanton looked at her that way. Ever. Tremors of heat swept through her, igniting every sense, bringing back to life places in her heart long since dead. His thumb eased to her lips. And finally he moved in for a kiss.

A scream etched across the ship. Eliza jerked to see Magnolia slap a sailor across the cheek. The sharp crack of her hand on his faced shifted all eyes toward the altercation.

Excusing himself, Blake rushed to Magnolia's side, as did several other gentlemen, including Hayden.

Eliza followed. The sailor backed away, rubbing his face. Anger pinched his weatherworn features as he pointed a finger at Magnolia. "She promised me."

"She promised you what?" Captain Barclay stomped into the crowd, scattering it like buzzards on a carcass.

"A kiss," the sailor said.

"I did. . .no such thing." Magnolia wobbled and held her hands out, though the seas were mild.

Hayden clutched the man's arm and jerked him aside. "How dare you assault a lady! He should be locked up below, Captain."

"Wait." Blake stepped forward. "Let's find out what happened first before we go passing sentence."

Magnolia's eyes drifted hazily over the forming crowd.

"She said if I gave her a drink"—the sailor pulled a flask from his pocket and shook it—"she'd give me a kiss. She's been bribin' all the sailors out of their spirits tonight."

"You, sir, are a scamp." Magnolia pointed a finger in his direction, but her hand teetered back and forth. Giggling, she covered up her mouth and started to fall.

Releasing the sailor, Hayden reached out for her, but Eliza got there first. Better to get the lady below to her parents before she made a total fool of herself.

Chuckles filtered through the remaining crowd. Some of the passengers left, shaking their heads.

"Come now, Magnolia." Eliza tugged her arm. "I'll help you below."

"I don't want to go below!" She stomped her foot and swayed in the other direction.

James hooked her arm with his to keep her from falling as he gave Eliza a look of understanding. "But you must, miss. There's a storm on the way." He glanced above as light sprinkles fell.

"Aye, see that she sleeps it off." The captain gave a hearty chuckle then faced the sailor. "Mr. Lenn, don't be makin' bargains for kisses again, or you'll answer to me." The sailor nodded as the captain barged back through the crowd, his pipe smoke filtering behind him.

Eliza and James tugged on Magnolia, but she stood her ground and began singing.

Blake heaved a sigh. "You may have to hoist her over your shoulder, James."

"You will do no such thing. Do you know who I am? I am Magnolia Scott, daughter of Benjamin Scott, owner of the largest plantation in Georgia!" Her eyes slithered over the crowd and landed on Eliza as if she'd just realized she held her arm.

"You." She tugged from her grasp and raised a finger to her lips, smiling. "I know who you are."

Eliza's eyes widened, and she shook her head in warning.

Magnolia's head bobbed atop her neck as if it sat on a spring. "Want to know a secret?" She laughed, first eyeing James beside her and then scanning the few people still on deck.

"No they do not. Now, come along." Eliza grabbed her arm again.

"Mrs. Crawford is not her real name." Magnolia gave a silly smile. "No no no."

Eliza swept her desperate gaze to James. "She's becoming delirious. It may be best to carry her below."

James nodded and bent to gather her up when Magnolia took a step back. "She's Flora Randal Watts"—she hiccuped—"wife of Brigadier General Stanton Watts of the Union army."

CHAPTER 13

*E*liza's blood abandoned her heart. It sped away in a mad dash that left her cold and empty. She couldn't move. Could barely breathe as everyone's eyes snapped in her direction. Some of them registering shock. Others sparking with disdain.

Thunder cracked a fierce whip across the sky, and it began to sprinkle—drops tap, tap, tapping Eliza's doom on the wooden planks of the deck. Three lines as deep as trenches split Blake's forehead. "Is this true?"

Silence tiptoed around the raindrops as everyone held their breath, awaiting her answer. The ship heaved, and Magnolia stumbled. Hayden caught her before she toppled to the deck. She began to sing a ditty as if nothing were amiss and she hadn't just destroyed Eliza's life.

"I wish I was in the land of cotton,
Old times, they are not forgotten. . . ."

Wiping rain from her face, Eliza scanned the eyes locked on her like cannons on an enemy. The seas grew rough. Lantern light shifted over them in bands of silver and black—black like the bands on their arms, honoring lost loved ones. The blame for their deaths now cast at Eliza's feet. Then suddenly rain pounded the deck. It slid down Eliza's cheeks and pooled in her lashes until everything grew blurry. She wished they would all disappear. She wished she could melt into the deck. Anything but answer the question toiling on Blake's face.

Magnolia continued to belt out her tune,

"Look away! Look away! Look away! Dixie Land.
In Dixie Land where I was born,
Early on one frosty morning. . ."

Of all the songs to sing now!

Eliza shifted her gaze to the edge of the crowd, where Angeline gave her a sympathetic look. The only one. She swallowed. Better to get it over with. Better to tell the truth, come what may. Wiping rain from her eyes, Eliza squared her shoulders. "Yes, it is true."

"*Look away! Look away! Look away! Dixie Land,*" Magnolia continued, instantly silenced by Hayden's hand on her mouth.

Gasps sped through the crowd.

"Well, I'll be. . ."

"I don't believe it," one woman exclaimed.

"A bloody Yankee in our midst!"

Max spit a brownish glob onto the deck near her feet.

Eliza lowered her gaze, not wanting to see the fury, the hatred in their eyes. Not wanting to see it in Blake's.

Captain Barclay shoved through the crowd. "You best all get out of the rain. Looks to be a"—he froze when he saw their faces—"wet night." He uttered the last words slowly as his gaze shifted to Eliza.

Mr. Dodd rushed toward her, eyes blazing. Eliza cringed, fearing he intended to push her overboard. Instead, he pointed a finger so close to her face she could smell the chicken stew he'd had for dinner. "Yankee whore. I say we toss her overboard."

"I agree," one of the farmers shouted. "The Yanks murdered my brother, stole our land! She deserves to die."

"I lost everybody and everything in the war!" Max seethed.

Thunder boomed, confirming their assessment as "ayes" fired into the air.

"I don't want no Yankee going to Brazil with us. Dash it! I'm going there to get away from them!"

Swallowing down the hard lump in her throat, Eliza finally dared a glance at Blake. He hadn't moved. He still stared at her. Rain slid down his face and dripped from the tips of his hair onto his coat, melting away all the affection, the adoration of only moments ago. Replaced by a hatred so intense, she could feel it crackle in the air between them.

Magnolia slouched onto a barrel and lifted a hand to her head.

James and Hayden gaped at Eliza with disgust. A tear trickled down Angeline's cheek. Or was it rain? Graves grinned at her from beyond the crowd.

Lightning flashed silver across the sky, distorting the men's faces into demonic masks.

The blacksmith grabbed her arm and began dragging her to the railing. Others mobbed around her, pushing her from behind, nudging and shoving.

"No!" Angeline screamed. With elbows extended, the lady attempted to plow through the crowd, but they pushed her aside with ease.

Eliza's mind spun. Terror seized her breath. She had expected anger, hatred even, but not this. Not being tossed into the sea. She didn't even know how to swim. Not that it would matter in the middle of the ocean. Closing her eyes, she ceased struggling against the meaty grips, ceased listening to the hate-filled curses. Rain lashed across her back as if God Himself were punishing her. Perhaps He was.

"That's quite enough!" Blake's stern voice opened Eliza's eyes. He shoved his way to the front of the mob and spread out his arms as if he could contain their advancing fury. "We aren't murderers."

"No, but she is!" one man yelled as the seething crowd halted. Rain did an angry dance on the deck and over the shoulders and heads of the venom-dripping throng—pelting and striking and spitting. It stung Eliza's bare skin and soaked through her gown. She shivered. But not from the cold.

Captain Barclay took a spot beside Blake. "No one on my ship is tossing anyone overboard!"

Eliza tried to settle her thrashing heart. *What had taken the man so long?*

"Now what's this about you bein' a Yankee, Mrs. Crawford?"

Eliza tugged from the clawlike grips and rubbed her sore arms. Groans of disappointment ricocheted over her as the mob retreated, oscillating with the sway of the ship like a band of cannibalistic warriors dancing before a feast. Hugging herself, she drew a shredded breath. A mask of determination, of duty, had covered Blake's face, hiding all emotion. But she knew he hated her. The loss of his affection extinguished her last spark of hope.

She raised her chin and met the captain's gaze. "I am not Eliza Crawford. My name is Flora Watts."

More curses punctured the air, followed by renewed admonitions to toss her overboard, but all were quickly silenced by a single shout from Blake.

The ship pitched over a wave, and Eliza nearly slipped. Water soaked through her only decent pair of satin slippers. When the mob grew silent, she continued. "However, I am not a Yankee. I was born and raised in Marietta, Georgia. My father is Seth Randal, a prominent lawyer. Our family owns the Randal Inn."

Rain fell in buckets now. Most of the women ducked below. Yet the men remained, surrounding her like a lynch mob, water pouring off their hats in rivulets that pounded the deck like judges' gavels pronouncing her guilt. They waited, stone faced and determined, for her to put the final nail in her own coffin.

So she did.

"But it is true that I married Stanton Watts, Brigadier General Stanton Watts, from Harrisburg, Pennsylvania."

Thunder shook the sky, sending a tremble through the ship.

"See! She's a Yankee lover. A traitor to the Confederate states!"

One man spit on her, followed by another and another. Eliza squeezed her eyes shut. She supposed she deserved it. She had married a Union officer against her father's wishes, against her family's urgings. But Eliza always did what Eliza wanted to do. She always allowed her feelings to guide her—to toss and turn her like the waves were now doing to the ship.

"Where is your Yankee husband now?" one of the farmers demanded.

"He's dead." Eliza shouted over the roar of the rain and wind. "Died four years ago in the Battle of Fredericksburg."

"And she *did* volunteer as a nurse in the war." That was Blake's voice. He was sticking up for her. It brought her gaze to him, but he still refused to look her way.

"Yeah, but for what side?" Dodd shouted.

"For the South, of course." James gave her a nod.

The captain heaved a sigh, drew off his hat, and smacked it on his knee, splattering rainwater.

"I say we lock her up below," Max, the ship's boatswain, growled. "A prisoner of war."

"We are not at war." The hint of kindness in James's tone sent a ribbon of warmth through her—just a tiny ribbon. At least they all didn't hate her.

The rain worsened. More passengers scurried away, shaking their heads and muttering under their breath. Eliza wished they would all leave, for if she had to endure their hateful stares for another moment, her heart would surely crumble in her chest.

Angeline eased beside Eliza and wove her arm through hers. "It doesn't matter who she married. She's a good woman, a healer, and she's as much a Southern lady as I or any of the other ladies on board are."

James's brow rose at the lady's bold declaration. A declaration that seemed to stun the rest of them into silence. The deck teetered. Eliza's legs turned to mush, and she leaned on her friend for support. But it was the care in Angeline's eyes that renewed her strength.

Until Mr. Dodd sauntered to stand before her, his blond hair slicked back, rain dripping off his pointy nose and licking the gold chain hanging from his coat pocket. "We can't just let her go. She's the enemy!"

Angeline's grip on Eliza tightened. "She's no such thing!"

Blake stepped forward. "She will remain free until we reach Rio de Janeiro. Then we will send her back to Charleston with Captain Barclay." He glanced at the captain. "If that's agreeable to you, sir."

Captain Barclay nodded, slapping his hat back atop his head and holding up a hand against Dodd's further protests.

"Then it's settled." Blake gestured for the crowd to disperse. "Now go on, get below out of the rain."

Grunts of disappointment followed the remaining colonists as they slowly obeyed. Hayden helped a swaying Magnolia toward the stairs. Eliza knew she should feel hatred toward the woman, but at the moment she felt nothing at all.

Nothing but agony.

Without a single glance her way, Blake hobbled toward the hatch and dropped out of sight.

Only Angeline remained by Eliza's side.

Lightning flashed. The ship heaved, and the women clung to each other to keep from falling. But Eliza no longer cared. In fact, she wished she would fall over the railing into the churning sea. Tears spilled freely down her cheeks as Angeline swung an arm around her, holding her against the wind and the rain, saying nothing, until finally she led Eliza below.

The next morning, as dawn broke, a flicker of promise, of hope, teased Blake's groggy mind. Memories of dancing with Eliza, of her agreeing to a courtship paraded through his thoughts, scattering joy like confetti. Until reality came crashing down on him, treading those glittering scraps underfoot. She had betrayed him. Used him. Lied to him. Even worse, she had nearly caused him to betray everything and everyone dear to him. Especially his brother. Anger chased his sorrow back into the dark corners where it belonged. Where it would stay. He would not defile the memories of his family by spending a second mourning the loss of Eliza.

He would not.

After climbing out of his hammock and getting dressed, Blake dragged himself onto the main deck. If only to get away from James's constant badgering. Blake would have expected the doctor to share his fury about Eliza's deception, about her relation to a man who had issued orders that murdered so many young Southern men. Especially after the doctor had witnessed the result of those orders firsthand. But perhaps James was more preacher than doctor as he proclaimed, for his forgiveness had come swiftly on the heels of Eliza's confession.

A confession she would not have offered had her ruse not been uncovered by Miss Magnolia.

And Blake would still be pursuing a courtship with a woman who was his enemy.

Fisting his hands, he emerged to a shaft of bright sunlight that was quickly gobbled up by a dark cloud. One sweep of the horizon revealed seas as agitated as his stomach. Foamy sheets of dark water soared then sank as they raced across the wide expanse as if trying to escape some upcoming disaster. Black clouds roiled on the horizon, sparking with lightning, like witches' cauldrons. The ship plunged into a trough, and Blake hung on to the companionway railing.

Only a few passengers braved the weather. Some huddled beside the capstan while sailors hauled lines, scrubbed the deck, and attended their duties. Mr. Graves leaned against the foredeck railing, his black hair blowing behind him, face lifted to the breeze as if he rather enjoyed the menacing weather.

After the deck leveled, Blake started toward the quarterdeck to take his post. That's when he saw her, standing at the larboard bulwarks. Her loose curls tumbled in the wind down to her skirts. Lacy gloves covered her hands as they gripped the railing. Her eyes were closed, and her lips moved as if she prayed.

Prayed indeed. For forgiveness, he hoped.

Or did he? If there was a God, surely He wouldn't grant this traitor absolution so quickly. She must pay for her crimes—for her betrayal to him and to the South.

And for breaking his heart.

She *knew* what the Union had done to him. What he had lost. Yet still she had received his attentions, even encouraged them! What sort of person did that? A heartless, cruel one.

Brigadier General Stanton Watts! Yes, he knew the name. Had heard of his atrocities, his brazen orders that had cost so many lives on both sides. Her association with that madman made her as culpable as he in those acts.

He could never forgive her. Never. She was the enemy, and the sooner they got to Brazil, the sooner he could rid himself of her.

Eliza *felt* Blake behind her. The *thu-ump thu-ump* that marked his hobbled gait scored a groove across her heart. She held her breath. Was he coming to speak to her? Coming to say he'd behaved horribly last night, that he'd thought things over and her past didn't matter? But then the *thu-ump* passed, hastening in both pace and tempo until, out of the corner of her eye, she saw him climb the quarterdeck ladder.

Releasing her breath, she gripped the railing. The seas blurred in her vision. Gray, riotous seas this morning, not the usual smooth turquoise of the Caribbean. Above, clouds swarmed like a flock of predatory birds seeking victims, blocking out the sun that had ascended from its throne only a few hours earlier. After spending a fitful night crying and tossing—if one can toss in a hammock—she'd come above at dawn to pray, to think.

To cry alone.

She knew she took a great risk standing at the railing where some spiteful passenger or sailor could grab her legs and fling her into the sea, but somehow in her dizzying anguish she didn't care. Perhaps she deserved it.

Thoughts of Brazil, of its golden shores, lush jungles, and fertile soil, caused tears to flood her eyes once again. She would never live there, would never be a part of the new world these colonists were building, never have a chance at a new life, a new beginning.

Wiping the moisture from her face, she breathed in the salty air tainted with the sting of rain. No, she would be forced back to a land that writhed beneath the cruel boot of the North, a land where she didn't belong. To either side. Ostracized by her own family as well as her husband's, with no friends, she had nowhere to go. No way to survive.

Angeline slid beside her and placed her hand atop Eliza's, jarring her from her misery. Sarah appeared on her other side. "How are you this morning?" The compassion in Angeline's voice nearly caused a fresh outburst of tears.

"We know you didn't sleep well," Sarah said.

"I'm sorry if I disturbed you." Eliza gazed out at sea. "Be careful ladies, I'm not sure you wish to be seen with me."

"Don't be silly." Sarah gave an unladylike snort. "God has no preference for Rebel or Yankee. He loves everyone equally."

Eliza knew that. She remembered that from her years at church. Yet hearing it now, in a tone that was ripe with sincerity and love, helped settle its truth in her heart.

"Besides." Angeline batted a strand of hair from her eyes. "They had no right to be so cruel to you last night. It matters not that you were once married to a Yankee general. It's not like you were on the battlefield fighting our troops."

"You are both kind," Eliza said. "But I wouldn't want the other passengers to hate you on my account."

"God asks us to befriend the downtrodden, Eliza." Sarah's tone offered room for no other possibility.

Angeline pursed her lips. "I don't give a care what the others think." She grew pensive, almost sad, before she continued, "We all have our secrets, do we not?"

"Indeed." Sarah wove her arm through Eliza's, making her wonder what secrets these two wonderful women could possibly possess that were as bad as Eliza's.

A man cleared his throat behind them, swerving them around to see James. Drawing a deep breath, Eliza braced herself for the doctor's chastisement.

Yet only sympathy gleamed in his eyes.

Wind tossed his sun-glinted hair and rustled the collar of his shirt as he greeted the ladies with a smile that angled the scar alongside his mouth. He faced Eliza. "Mrs. Crawford. . .or Watts, is it?"

"Eliza will do, James."

"Eliza, I want to apologize for the barbaric behavior of the other passengers last night. A ferocious, shocking display."

Not shocking to Eliza. She had become more accustomed to such brutality over the past three years than she cared to admit. Still, she didn't know quite how to react to the man's kindness.

He studied her. "Do I surprise you?"

"It's just that after all you saw on the battlefield, I wouldn't expect. . ."

"Ah, but God commands us to forgive."

Eliza's gaze found Parson Bailey sitting on the foredeck reading his Bible. When he'd come above earlier, he'd cast a loathing glance her way before choosing a spot on the other side of the ship. "It seems Parson Bailey does not share your view."

James chuckled. "The good parson and I do not agree on many things." With that, he tipped his hat and bade them good day. Angeline stared after him as he left. "Such an agreeable man."

"Indeed." Eliza said.

"Blue-coated harpy!" one of the passengers shouted from the starboard railing where a small group had clustered.

"Traitorous fink!" another added.

"Baudy turncoat!"

"Pay them no mind, Eliza." Angeline tugged her around to face the sea. A sea that now heaved and throbbed, flinging foam onto the bulwarks. The ship bolted, and Eliza gripped the railing. Seawater soaked through her gloves. The light of day retreated behind clouds as dark as coal.

"Oh dear." Sarah squeezed Eliza's hand. "I believe a storm is coming."

No sooner had she uttered the words, than the captain's voice bellowed across the ship. "Everyone, below deck, if you please!" Turning, Eliza watched as the captain spoke to Blake, who immediately barked a list of commands: "Hands by the topgallant halyards! Shorten sail! Reef topsails! Set storm mizzen!"

The crew scrambled to do his bidding while passengers hurried below. Looped arm in arm with Sarah and Angeline, Eliza made her way to the hatch, hearing the captain say just before she dropped below, "We are in for a wild ride with this one."

CHAPTER 14

Twenty-four hours later

&liza's fingers burned. Her lungs filled with water. Yet she hung on to the railing of the brig with all her remaining strength. If these were the last minutes of her life, she wouldn't give up. She would fight to the bitter end. Lightning notched the black sky in silver. Thunder bellowed for her to release her grip. *No! I will not!* The brig flopped back and forth like a child's toy in a pond, plunging Eliza into the sea one minute and flinging her into the air the next. She wanted to cry. She wanted to scream. But the wind tore her voice from her mouth. What did it matter? She was about to die. If she didn't fall, her fellow passengers would toss her over anyway. At least that's what they threatened to do when Eliza was below decks with them only moments before. Those threats had forced her above into the belly of the beastly storm.

Maybe she *was* a Jonah after all.

Her fingers slipped. Pain radiated into her palms, her wrists. The brig heaved and canted like a bucking horse.

God, is this how I am to die? Perhaps it was. She'd run from God long enough.

Rain slapped her face, filled her nose. She couldn't breathe. Her fingers slipped again.

A strong hand grabbed her wrist. A face appeared over the railing. "Hang on! I've got you."

He gripped her other hand just as her fingers slid from the railing. The ship teetered, dunking her into the raging sea. Water enveloped her, sloshing and gurgling and pulling her down. But whoever held her did not let go. Then just as quickly as it had tipped to the side, the brig lifted from the water, slinging her upward. The man hauled her on board. They landed like two sacks of sodden rice on the slippery deck, his body atop hers.

It was Blake. He lifted from her, water dripping from his anxious face before the deck lunged again. Grabbing her, he clung to the hatch combing. "Foolish woman!" was all she heard as the bow tilted so far up, she thought the ship would topple over backward.

Once the deck leveled, Blake took her arm, yanked her to her feet, and dragged her to the companionway. "Get below!" Rain streamed down his face. His hair hung in strands of ink.

"I can't go back down there!" she shouted. "They want to toss me overboard."

Grimacing, he untied the rope from around his waist and handed it to her. "Go to your cabin and tie yourself to something."

"But you—"

"Now!" He thrust the rope into her hand and turned to leave.

Clinging to the railing, Eliza made her way below, unsure whether to be happy or sad that she was still among the living.

❦

Grabbing another lifeline, Blake tied himself to the capstan. On the quarterdeck, Captain Barclay gripped the wheel beside the helmsman, their expressions strung tight as they strained to control the ship. Tension constricted the captain's voice and lined his face, causing Blake's terror to rise. If the hardened seaman was so worried, they must be in real danger.

Strands of hair stung Blake's cheek. He jerked them back and dove into the wind, making his way to his post alongside Hayden, where Moses and a group of sailors battled lines attached to yards above. *Foolish, mad woman!* She'd almost gotten herself killed! He hadn't noticed her until a flash of violet skirts tumbling over the deck caught his eye. He'd darted toward her as fast as the heaving ship would allow, but he was too late. She had gone over.

And his heart had gone overboard with her.

He'd thought he'd lost her. And in that brief moment, his life lost all meaning. His anger fled him, and he'd dashed to the railing. When he'd seen her dangling there barely able to breathe, wave after wave slamming her, terror had taken over all reason. And he knew he'd do anything to save her.

But he didn't have time to ponder that now as a wall of water slammed into him, sweeping his feet out from beneath him and sending him careening over the deck. Gripping his rope, he shut his mouth against the torrent and hung on. The waters subsided. He struggled to rise. The captain brayed orders that were quickly stolen by the roar of the storm. Above him, sailors clung to yards and masts that swung back and forth like demonic pendulums. How much more could the brig take before it split in two? Sailors appeared from below, dragging trunks, crates, and barrels to the railing. Blake helped them hoist them over the side, knowing they were losing what was left of their food, their water, their tools, and other necessities for the new world, wondering how they would get by without them.

If they survived the storm.

❧

Eliza didn't like being told what to do. She would have rather stayed above with a lifeline tied around her than be tossed back and forth like a bale of hay in a wagon—a wagon that felt like it was tumbling over a cliff. But after Blake had so graciously offered his own rope, leaving himself in temporary peril, what else could she do? So she tied herself to the table in her cabin and curled into a ball on the deck, praying for God to save them. Now two hours later, the roar of the storm lessened, the crash of waves against the hull subsided, and the thunder retreated.

Either she had died and this was her own personal hell—being on board a ship full of people who hated her—or they had survived and were still afloat.

Untying herself, she crept from the cabin to emerge onto a sodden deck with equally sodden crewmen slouching in various positions of exhaustion—looking much like the remaining sails: drenched, torn, and tattered. Soon passengers popped above. With white faces and open mouths, they gazed around at the bare-masted ship. Though only hours before, some of them had demanded they toss Eliza overboard, now they paid her no mind.

Captain Barclay remained on the quarterdeck. Water dripped from his blue coat, which was angling off one shoulder. His hair, stiff with salt, stuck out in every direction, making him look like a drenched porcupine. A very angry porcupine. He growled orders, sending some men to assess damage and others below to assist with the pumps.

Were they taking on water?

Water dripped from yards and spars, plopping on the waterlogged deck. Electricity crackled in the air as a brisk breeze chilled Eliza. She hugged herself. Angeline and Sarah sped toward her, and together they surveyed the storm retreating on the horizon. Like a monster tucking its tail between its legs, it rumbled away, baring angry teeth of lightning as it went.

Blake, his shirt plastered to his chest, molding every muscle and sinew, gave her a cursory glance before he assisted the sailors in cleaning up the shards of wood and torn lines that littered the deck.

His disregard stung her, destroyed the hope that had sprung when he'd risked himself to save her. But that was the kind of man he was. A noble man who would risk his own life. . .

Even for an enemy.

After all were present and accounted for, the parson, at James's urging, said a prayer of thanks for God's rescue and that no lives had been lost. As all heads bowed, the *drip-drop* of water from the rigging above was the only reminder of the terror they had endured. Eliza said her own prayer of thanks. She didn't know why God had saved her, but she had to admit she was glad to be alive.

The damage report of torn sails, a cracked mast, one split yard, and a hold full of water etched a deeper frown on Captain Barclay's face, but his subsequent decision to set sail for one of the nearby islands seemed to encourage everyone after their near watery grave. There they could restock their food and water supplies and allow the crew a few days to make the necessary repairs.

The next day the *New Hope* hobbled into the bay of an island so lush and beautiful, Eliza wondered if they hadn't found the paradise they were seeking. Emerald water caressed glistening ebony sand that led to a canvas of mossy forest in every possible shade of green. As they drifted closer to shore, the air filled with the melody of a myriad of birds chirping and singing their greeting.

The island of Dominica, the captain had announced, though how he could be sure of their location after the storm, Eliza had no idea. But he had his remaining charts and some instruments and the sky to guide him. Not to mention his vast experience on the sea.

After being confined to the tiny brig for three weeks, everyone declared the sight was more precious than gold. Well, everyone except for Mr. Dodd. And perhaps Mr. Graves, who seemed impervious to joy.

As Eliza made her way through the crowd to the railing for a better look, people scattered as if she had malaria. Spiteful glances and foul words shot her way, but she did her best to ignore them. Swallowing the emotion burning in her throat, she drew a deep breath of air filled with life and tropical flowers, while the captain issued orders for the crew to begin repairs.

"It should take no more than two days," he shouted to the passengers. "Two days to stretch your legs upon the shores and replenish our water supply."

This turned everyone around to face him, including Eliza. Her gaze immediately shifted to Blake standing beside the captain. No longer looking like a drowned rat from the storm or even a military man, he appeared more like a hardened sailor as he stood, boots spread apart, on the swaying deck, black hair in wild disarray, arms crossed over his chest, and necktie flapping in the wind. His eyes grazed over her for a second. A mere second in which she no longer saw hatred. Dare she hope?

"We need everyone's help," the captain continued, "to search for edible fruits, coconuts, and freshwater."

"I know this island well." Parson Bailey's voice rose in excitement. "I was sent here as a missionary several years ago." His beady eyes shifted over the crowd as if seeking approval. "I can find water and food. Just send me ashore with some men and barrels. I know where to look. There's also a settlement across the island. Roseau, I believe. We can buy supplies there."

"We must save our money to purchase land and tools in Brazil," Blake said, his tone begging no argument.

The parson shrugged.

James nodded his agreement. "We'll have to live off what we have left in the hold and whatever we can scavenge from the island for the remainder of the journey."

Mr. Jenkins, one of the farmers, placed an arm around his wife and their young daughter and held them close. "But you tossed over my crate of farming implements."

"And my trunk of pots and pans," a rather robust lady declared.

"And my chest of gowns!" Magnolia sobbed from the edge of the crowd where she stood between her parents. Gazes shot her way, whispers hissing through the air. Ever since she'd made a besotted spectacle of herself, her parents had kept her close.

"What am I to do without them?" she continued to wail.

"Zooks, how will you survive with only *five* gowns?" Hayden chuckled, drawing her viper stare.

"I only have two left, if you must know." She gave him a petulant look.

"You won't have much need for them in Brazil." Angeline wove through the crowd to stand beside Eliza.

Hayden's and James's gazes followed her as did most of the men's, including Mr. Dodd's.

The captain cleared his throat. "My apologies for bein' forced to lighten the load, but it couldn't be helped."

"No apologies necessary, Captain." Blake gave the man an approving nod. "We owe you our lives."

One of the men jerked a thumb at Eliza. "I say we leave the Yankee on the island."

Words of agreement rang from both passengers and crew. All except Angeline, James, and thankfully, Blake.

"Aye," Max, the boatswain, added. "She can catch the next ship back to the States."

"The parson said there's a settlement on the other side of the island," a woman offered.

The blacksmith stepped forward. "We can return her money, and she can purchase passage home."

Their words twisted a cord around Eliza's stomach until she worried the breakfast she'd consumed earlier would reappear.

More agreements zipped through the air. Angeline squeezed Eliza's hand and tried to shout above the clamor, but it was James's voice that stopped them. "We cannot leave a woman alone in the midst of untold dangers."

"It's more than she deserves." Dodd gave her a malignant grin.

Moses, his sister, and her children clung to each other on the other side of the ship, their wide eyes blaring a concern for Eliza that their lips dared not voice.

Her gaze shot to Blake. She wondered if he would say anything. But he simply stood there, eyeing the mob and rubbing his chin. Finally, he spoke. "She stays with us. No matter what she's done, we cannot abandon her to die."

Eliza released a breath.

"Why not?" a sailor spoke up. "We should let God decide, shouldn't we, Parson?"

Parson Bailey gripped his Bible and forced piety onto his face. " 'Vengeance is mine. . .sayeth the Lord.' "

"I say she's bad luck!" one of the farmers shouted. "Ever since she came on board, we been attacked by a frigate, the first mate got injured, and now we been hit by a storm."

Mr. Lewis teetered through the mob, swirling the scent of alcohol in his wake. "Ah, let her stay. She's a good woman. We all need a fresh start." Clipping his thumbs in his suspenders, his kind eyes met hers. She smiled in return, wondering if the drunken carpenter would be the only man to speak up for her.

"Leave her here!" the blacksmith yelled.

"But she's our nurse!" Sarah spoke from the hatchway, where she emerged onto the deck. "We need her." Her eyes locked with Eliza's.

"James can handle things. He's a doctor."

Eliza's harried gaze sped to Blake. As leader of the expedition, wasn't the decision his? Surely, he would demand that she stay and order the mob to silence. Instead, he faced the captain and uttered the words that sealed her fate. "This is your ship and your decision."

Her heart plummeted.

Captain Barclay scratched his salt-encrusted hair. "In truth, I ain't so sure that she didn't bring all this bad luck on us. Besides, her presence here only causes trouble. And I don't need no more trouble, if you know what I mean."

Blake studied the captain, a stunned look on his face as if that was the last thing he expected the man to say. "How can a woman traipse through the jungle alone to Roseau without getting mauled by some animal, attacked by natives, or dying from exposure?"

"I'll send a sailor with her. Max"—Captain Barclay pointed to the boatswain—"you can get Mrs. Crawford to Roseau in a day and get back before we sail, can't you?"

"Aye. Gladly." He grinned as his eyes absorbed her.

"No. You can't do this." Angeline's tone bordered on hysterical.

"I agree." Sarah gazed up at the captain. "It's inhumane."

"I protest too," James added. "Even if she makes it, even if she manages to barter voyage on a ship, she'll still be in danger sailing unescorted."

Blake shook his head and clenched the railing until his knuckles whitened.

"You gave me the decision, Colonel," the captain said, "and this is what I say. For the good of the voyage and all aboard."

Blake's eyes met hers. "Then allow me to escort her."

The captain waved a hand. "I need you here to organize your people to search for food. Max will do."

"But Captain"—Blake's suspicious gaze took in Max—"you might as well sentence her to death."

Captain Barclay's jaw stiffened as he surveyed the mob and then glanced at Eliza. "Very well. Let's put it to a vote then. Those in favor of leaving Mrs. Crawford, or whatever her name is, on Dominica with provisions and money, say, 'Aye.'"

Ayes blared across the ship like trumpets.

CHAPTER 15

$\mathcal{E}$liza dug her toes into the black sand, allowing the grains to cover her feet, enclosing them in a warm cocoon. She wished she could do the same with her entire body—bury herself right there on the beach, hide away from everyone on board the *New Hope*, everyone who hated her. Everyone who would rather see her dead than spend another minute with her.

New Hope, indeed.

New hope for everyone but her.

Gentle waves the color of glistening turquoise stroked the shore as a myriad of brightly plumed birds warbled happy melodies from waving palm and plumeria trees. A balmy breeze soothed her face and frolicked among her curls. All traitors to the angst roiling within her. As soon as Max finished his duties, he would escort her through the jungle to the city of Roseau, where she would supposedly barter passage aboard a merchant ship heading to the United States.

Alone.

Alone, ostracized, forsaken. Once again.

Tugging the chain around her neck, she pulled out the locket her father had given her on her sixteenth birthday and opened it. Her mother's face stared back at her, so graceful, so beautiful. Eliza ran a finger over the lock of hair. "Oh Mama, I miss you so. I need you. If only you hadn't died, maybe Papa would have been more reasonable. Maybe he wouldn't have suffocated me with his rules. You always had a way of soothing his dour moods." Yet the more she stared at the tiny portrait, the more it reflected her own image. Not only did Eliza look like her mother, but she'd been told they were alike in many other ways. No wonder her father sought so desperately to protect her. He couldn't

144

bear to lose her mother all over again. But in the end, Eliza had caused his worst nightmare to come true.

A wayward tear coursed down her cheek, cooled by the wind. She wiped it away. She would not give these people the satisfaction of seeing her sorrow. Her devastation. Not that anyone paid her any mind.

Laughter drew her gaze down shore where several passengers gathered coconuts while the children played tag with the crashing waves. Dark sand—formed by a volcano, one of the sailors had told her—spread a blanket of shimmering onyx across the beach. Dodd sat on a fallen tree, speaking to one of the farmer's wives. Mr. and Mrs. Scott, Magnolia between them, sat beneath the shade of a mango tree while Mable waved a palm frond above their heads. After their sorrowful parting, Angeline had joined a group scouring the jungle for bananas and other fruit. Sarah wasn't feeling well and had stayed on board. And true to his word, Parson Bailey and six sailors had headed off into the jungle, barrels hoisted on their shoulders, in search of freshwater.

Blake, James, Hayden, and some of the other men had grabbed axes and swords and disappeared into the tangle of green looking for wild boar the parson said inhabited the island.

"Blake," she whispered. Despite her aching heart, just saying his name made her smile. He had stood up for her. And James had as well. She was grateful for that, even though now they seemed to have all but forgotten her.

But how could she blame them?

"Oh Lord, I've made a mess of things again." Snapping her locket shut, she let it dangle down the front of her bodice then picked up a shell and tossed it in the water. "I should have asked whether it was Your will that I join this venture. Instead, I just forged ahead, giving no thought to the consequences." As usual.

"Praying, Mrs. Crawford?"

Eliza jumped at the voice and turned to see Moses, Delia, and her two children approaching. The young man—about twenty years of age—towered over his sister by at least a foot, but the woman made up for the discrepancy in the width of her hips. Hips that had born the precious boy and girl now grinning at Eliza as if she were a princess. Joe and Mariah, if she remembered correctly. She looked into Moses' kind eyes. "Yes, it seems the only recourse left to me."

"An' a good recourse it be, missus. God loves t' answer His children's prayers."

"Let's hope so, Moses."

"Hope you don't mind de interruption." Moses tore off his hat. "But Delia an' I want to say good-bye proper an' thank you for your kindness to us on board de ship."

Delia smiled. "You ne'er had a bad word to say 'bout us, missus, an' you heped my Joey when he got sick."

Eliza struggled to rise against her confounded crinolette, but finally stood and shielded her eyes from the sun. "There's been far too much damage, far too much heartache inflicted on your people. It is enough. You are free and should be treated as equals."

"'Fraid dat's gonna take some time to come about, missus." Moses fumbled with his floppy hat.

Eliza sighed. "I fear you are right."

Giggles from the other children drew the longing gazes of both Mariah and Joseph. Moses frowned and released a sigh. "Seems to me, you be getting a taste of how we feel."

Eliza glanced at the people gathering food downshore and then over at the ship where the cadence of hammer and saw filled the air. Mr. Graves, in his usual black attire, stood at the railing. Even from a distance, she could feel his dark gaze boring into her.

Outcast. Ignored. Belittled. Yes, she did have an inkling of how it felt to be a Negro. All except for the shackles, of course. "I'm so sorry," was all she could think to say.

Moses nodded and slapped his hat atop his head. "Godspeed to you, missus."

"We wish you well," Delia added, lowering her gaze.

"And you." Eliza knelt before young Joe. "Now, you take care of your mama, young man, and your sister here."

The little boy smiled.

After they left, Eliza scanned the beach for any sign of Max, but he was nowhere in sight. She glanced at the sun nearing its zenith. Surely he hadn't forgotten her. Not by the way his lecherous grin had raked over her when the captain had assigned him the task of taking her across the island. Despite the heat of the day, Eliza shivered at the memory. Perhaps God was giving her a chance to escape the clutches of the unsavory sailor. Oh fiddle! Why had she not thought of that? She should leave now, head out without him. Surely it would be better to die alone in the jungle than take her chances with a man she hardly knew. Swinging about, she slipped on her shoes, plopped her bonnet atop her head, and gathered her valise.

She cast one last glance at the passengers on the beach, the children playing in the surf. No sign of Blake. She had hoped he would come to say good-bye—that despite the captain's orders, he would insist on taking take her to Roseau himself. But she'd clung to silly dreams her entire life. Perhaps it was time to forsake them and grow up. Turning, she raised her chin and plunged into the web of green.

Blake hacked a trail through the thick greenery, thankful the Yankees hadn't taken his service sword. He and this sword had fought many a battle together, and it had saved his life more than once. He couldn't imagine wrestling against a foe, or these tangled vines, without it.

Ahead of him Hayden trounced through the forest, hefting a machete. The other men had separated in order to cover more space. All except James whose heavy breaths sounded from behind Blake. Entering the jungle from the breezy beach had been akin to flinging oneself into a fiery furnace. The deeper they went, the hotter that furnace became. Moisture dripped from leaves and branches and puddled around shallow, snaking roots. The air, quiet and dank, barely stirred by their passing. Yet the jungle was anything but silent. Life teemed in buzzing and chirping and croaking all around them. It saturated the air with the smell of damp earth and sweet flowers. But Blake didn't care. He was thirsty, hot, and his leg burned. None of which was the reason for his foul mood.

Raising his sword, he sliced through a thick vine, releasing the anger that burned a hole in his heart. Sending a lady alone on a sea voyage. It was unheard of. It was cruel! With no one to stand up for her and protect her, anything could happen. He'd heard how most sailors talked. He knew how lonely they were after months at sea. The presence of a beautiful woman on board could cause them to do things they'd never consider otherwise.

James came alongside him. Stripped to the waist, sweat glistened on his chest and dampened his hair. His gaze scoured the ground, looking for pig droppings. Whatever *they* looked like. Yet, James seemed to know. He'd borrowed a pistol from one of the passengers, ready to shoot a boar as soon as they spotted one. Blake doubted they would. They'd been searching for two hours and had seen nothing but monkeys and parrots and iguanas. In front of them, Hayden halted, drank from a canteen, then passed it their way.

Blake took a swig. "There must be something we can do." He wiped his mouth on his sleeve.

"Eliza?" James dragged a handkerchief across his neck and tipped the canteen to his mouth.

Blake nodded as squawking drew his gaze upward. A green parrot, with a red band around his neck, paced back and forth across a branch as if trying to tell them something.

Taking back the jug from James, Hayden grunted.

"I understand people's anger, I do." Blake planted the tip of his sword in the dirt. "Blast it, I'm angry at her too. My entire family was killed by Yankees. We've all lost someone. But this. It's wrong."

"She'll be all right." Hayden stared at him with eyes the same color as their surroundings, eyes that harbored no sympathy. "She's bad luck. The sooner she's gone the better."

"Bosh! It's murder, pure and simple." Blake ground his teeth together. "We can't know that she will arrive safely in Charleston. What difference does it make if she spends another month with us and then returns safely with Captain Barclay?" By the way Max looked at Eliza, Blake couldn't be sure she'd even arrive in Roseau unscathed. Though the captain had reassured him of such.

"She's not bad to look at, I'll give her that." Hayden corked the canteen and swung it around his shoulder. "But she is a Yankee by marriage, and has no business coming on this journey."

"She shouldn't have deceived us." James gazed up at the parrot that was still squawking above them. "But in truth, her sympathies don't lie with the North."

"Once a Yankee, always a Yankee." Hayden hefted his machete and stomped away.

Blake shook his head. He should let her go. Eliza had brought this on herself. But something inside him refused to loosen the knot she had on his heart. A knot that had formed during moments they had shared these past weeks, the things he'd told her that he'd told no one else, the care he'd seen in her eyes. Was it all a ruse? Had she used him for comfort, for companionship, all the while knowing she was his mortal enemy? Anger simmered in his belly at her deception. Still, Yankee or not, she didn't deserve this.

"All we need do is convince everyone else that her nursing skills are indispensable," James said, mischief twinkling in the corner of his eyes. "If their own safety is at risk, they'll allow her to stay—I guarantee it."

Blake couldn't help but smile at his friend. "But how do we orchestrate a medical emergency? Aside from shooting one of the passengers, that is." He chuckled and shifted his weight off his bad leg. "Not that there aren't a few I wouldn't mind shooting."

"I am in agreement with you there." James snorted. "Whatever we decide, we must hurry before she travels too far away."

Blake grinned at the devious look on the doctor's face. His scheming was unexpected, to be sure. But welcomed with exuberance. "An injury of some sort." Swinging about, he darted back down the path. "Not life-threatening, of course. But one requiring her attention."

"Something quite bloody, which would preclude me from assisting." James hastened behind him.

Blake lifted his sword. A ray of sunlight broke through the canopy and glinted on the metal. "I know just the thing."

CHAPTER 16

*M*isery. A fitting word to describe Eliza's present predicament. Perspiration coated her from head to toe and glued her underthings so tightly to her skin that she doubted she'd ever pry them asunder. Sharp branches clawed at the lace on her sleeves and tore her gown. A monkey had absconded with her hat. Mosquitoes and God-knew-what-other flying pests dove at her from all directions. Twigs and leaves twisted her hair into knots. Her throat gasped for water; her legs ached, and she was lost and alone in the jungle.

And she'd only been walking for a few minutes!

The idea of making it to Roseau on her own, the idea that had fired her determination to cross the tiny island without aid from man nor beast—or even permission from God—crumbled into nonsensical pieces in her mind. What had she been thinking? She hadn't even brought along food or water.

Halting, Eliza drew a handkerchief from her sleeve and dabbed it on her forehead. She gazed up at the greenery crisscrossing the sky where dozens of colorful birds flitted about and laughed at her foolishness. Oh fiddle! Let them laugh. No doubt once the passengers of the *New Hope* discovered she'd ventured out on her own, they'd all be laughing at her.

Holding her valise before her like a shield, she forged ahead. Unable to take her trunk, she'd been forced to select only a few of her things: a clean chemise, petticoats, an extra pair of stockings, one other gown, two books, her journal, and the pocket watch Stanton had given her. The rest she'd given to Sarah and Angeline.

A faint sound met her ears. Not the sound of a bird or insect, but the shout of a human.

"Help! Help!" Muffled but desperate, the voice spun her about.

Nothing but flora met her gaze. Still the sound continued. Wait. She recognized that voice. James. He sounded frantic. And that was enough to send her barreling back the way she had come. As she did, the voice grew louder, more defined, until within minutes, the shore appeared in shifting glimpses through the foliage. She halted and brushed aside a fern for a better view.

Several yards down shore, Hayden and James emerged from the jungle, carrying Blake between them. Blood coated one of his legs. Or at least she thought it was blood. Passengers darted toward the men. Eliza spotted Max among them. If she showed herself, no doubt the beastly sailor would drag her back into the jungle to begin their journey, and her situation would disintegrate even further. Yet. . .

The doctor broke from the crowd and leaned forward on his knees. He shook his head and turned away, clearly unable to bear the sight of so much blood. Several people tried to tug him toward the patient, but he resisted them and backed farther away. If he couldn't treat Blake's wound, Blake may be in danger of bleeding to death or infection.

Alarm charged Eliza's legs into action. Hoisting her skirts with one hand and her valise in the other, she swatted aside the leaves and dashed toward them. The crowd parted, surprise at her presence registering on their faces. But Eliza didn't care. Trying to settle her thumping heart, she searched Blake's prostrate form. The trousers on his left leg were ripped to the knee. A handkerchief, soaked in blood, covered the wound.

"What happened?" She dropped to the sand beside him and gazed at Hayden.

"Apparently, a sword accident." Hayden's tone carried an odd cynicism.

"It's nothing." Blake groaned. "Help me up."

"We will do no such thing," Eliza snapped. Her gaze traveled to the blood dripping on the sand beneath his leg. A shiver coiled around her. She peered beneath the cloth. "I must stop the bleeding. You're going to need stitches."

"Oh my." One woman sounded as though she would faint. Another drew her away from the crowd. Still the men huddled closer, staring at Blake as if he were performing a circus act. James pushed his way past them. Beads of sweat lined his face. His eyes locked on Eliza, avoiding the bloody leg. She knew from the terror flashing within them that he would be of no help.

Drawing a deep breath, Eliza scanned the mob. "Give me your neckerchiefs, ties, anything you have to press on the wound." The men stared at her numbly at first but finally began tossing her sashes, handkerchiefs, and neckties. She pressed them onto Blake's leg. He moaned.

"We need to get him to the ship."

"The doc can take care of him." One man jerked his head toward James.

"I quite agree. Let the doctor perform his duties," Mr. Scott added. "You should be well on your way, Mrs. Crawford."

James's gaze skittered over the crowd, at the sky, the trees, the shore, anywhere but on the blood oozing from Blake's leg. "I fear I cannot, gentlemen." He gripped his belly, dashed for the trees, and emptied the contents of his stomach.

Dodd studied him, his brow wrinkling. "Well, I'll be. I heard you were afraid of blood. I just didn't believe it!" He burst out laughing and slapped his hat on his thigh.

James ran a sleeve over his mouth and faced the crowd. "I told you I'm not a doctor anymore. Mrs. Crawford is all you have."

"If I don't treat him properly, he could die," Eliza said.

The ship's helmsman shoved through the throng, assessed the situation, then gestured toward the small boat. "Aye, we'll allow the lady to tend to him."

⁂

Leg propped on a stool, Blake leaned back in the chair and watched Eliza tend his wound. He was pleased his ploy had gotten her back on the ship, not so pleased at the pain that coursed through his leg. Blast it, he hadn't meant to slice so deep. He'd only meant to nick a bleeder so it would look far worse than it was. After all, he was accustomed to injuries such as this on the battlefield. What was one more if it saved Eliza's life? Still, with the depth of the cut, he'd put himself in danger. Now, being so close to her made him wonder if it was worth it, for her presence only caused him more pain. Not the physical kind, but the kind that came from longing for her so desperately while hating her so intensely.

James stood on the other side of the sick bay, guiding Eliza with words, eyes on anything but the bloody mess.

Tenderly, she removed all the sashes and kerchiefs, now stained beyond use, and stared at the gash Blake had painstakingly made across his skin. The bloody gush had reduced to a dribble. She dabbed it with a clean cloth.

"Ouch."

"Don't be such a baby." She smiled. "I'm sure you've endured far worse than this in battle." She tossed the cloths into a basin and began peering and poking at the wound.

Wincing, but duly chastised, Blake kept his outbursts to himself. Of course he had suffered worse injuries. That was expected in battle. But not expected from one's own hand. Somehow, it made the pain far worse.

Eliza wiped her hands on her apron and addressed James, who had taken to picking at a splinter in the bulkhead. "Stitches and a nettle poultice, Doctor? Is that what you would recommend?"

"Precisely. Though a rinse of spirits would aid greatly as well." He continued plucking the wood while Eliza opened the cupboard and then slammed it with a frown. "I seem to be fresh out of alcohol at the moment."

"Not to worry," James said. "The nettle will do. Well"—he rubbed his hands together—"I can see that I am not needed here. I believe I'll get some fresh air." And before Blake could protest, the doctor fled the room.

Leaving him alone with the traitor.

Eliza's gaze sped over Blake. Long enough for him to see the anguish in her eyes. The light that had sparkled so brilliantly in them the past three weeks had been doused by the hatred and anger from the crew. From him.

"This will only take a minute." She opened the glass case filled with medicines. "I know how difficult it must be for you to be in the same room with me." Her voice carried no bitterness, only despair.

Blake bit back the measure of sympathy that kept trying to rise. He had only done this to save her life, nothing more. Any honorable man would have done the same. Then why couldn't he keep his eyes off her? With her back to him, she drew instruments and vials from the cabinet and arranged them on a tray. Her hair fell in spirals the color of maple syrup, dripping over her tiny waist. Even though it was embedded with twigs, Blake longed to run his fingers through the silky threads. Small tears littered her gown, and an abrasion marred her left arm, reminding him of what he'd heard while the sailors rowed him to the brig. Max accused her of leaving without him, of forging into the jungle alone, to which Eliza had responded that she'd rather be eaten by a panther than travel with him. Even in his pain, Blake had smiled. He swallowed. What was he thinking? He must not allow any sentiments to rise for this woman who had betrayed her countrymen—who had betrayed him.

If his scheme worked and the passengers and captain allowed her to stay, he would tolerate her presence on board, but other than this single necessary moment, he would avoid her at all costs. He had done the honorable thing. Saved her from probable death.

That was where his duty ended.

Swerving around, she knelt before him and placed a tray on the cot. "This will hurt a bit, Colonel. Would you care to bite down on a piece of wood?"

"I'll manage, thank you."

She drew a deep breath and threaded the needle. "How did this happen? Seems an odd thing to occur while looking for pigs."

"Boar." Her scent filled his nose, tantalizing his senses. Blake cleared his throat. "I was hacking through the jungle when my blade slipped."

"Hmm." She slid the needle through his flesh.

It felt like she'd set his skin on fire. Blake closed his eyes, listening to the slap of water on the hull, the hammering and shouts from above, the screech of pelicans. Anything to distract him from the searing pain.

She must have noticed his discomfort, for she uttered a "sorry" that sounded genuine.

Yet the pain was nothing compared to the suffering she had already caused him. "Pains of the flesh I can handle," he muttered.

She met his gaze and swallowed before continuing her work. "I never meant to deceive you."

Blake had never seen such lustrous eyes. "You didn't even tell me your real name. How can that be unintentional?"

She slipped the needle through and tugged on the thread. Her lower lip trembled. "You are right. I should have been truthful." She continued stitching his wound, but Blake could no longer feel the pain for the agony in his heart. He'd hardened himself to it.

"But then you wouldn't have let me join your venture, would you?" she asked.

Lantern light crowned her head and glistened on her moist lips—lips he had almost kissed. He licked his own. "No."

"I had to get away." She clipped the thread and tied it. Then dipping her fingers into a poultice, she spread it over the stitches.

"We all needed to get away." Blake couldn't tear his eyes from the way her delicate fingers caressed his skin. "From Yankees." He sighed. "You betrayed everyone on board." Good, now the anger returned.

She cut a swath of bandage and wrapped it around his leg. "I was born and raised a Southerner just like everyone else on this ship." She looked up at him. Her breath filled the air between them, her eyes just inches from his face.

Blake looked away from the pain he saw in her gaze. He offered a caustic snort. "At least some of your story was true."

"It was all true." Her eyes narrowed. "Everything I told you about my past. I simply changed the names and omitted one year of my life."

"A year in which you betrayed your country."

She jerked the bandage tight. Blake hid the pain from his face. With a huff, she gathered her tray and stood, turning her back to him. "Doesn't my service as a war nurse count for anything?"

"Ah, so you hoped to make restitution."

She spun around, her skirts knocking a tin cup to the deck with a clank. "No, that's not why I served in the war."

"Why didn't you just stay with your husband's family? I hear the Yanks love Southern traitors."

"They tossed me out, if you must know." She stooped to pick up the cup, her skirts billowing around her. "Although I wouldn't have stayed anyway. They hated me for my Southern ties as much as you hate me for my Northern."

Emotion clambered up Blake's throat at the agony in her voice. No. He would not allow any compassion to form for this traitor. His gaze dropped to the locket dangling against her bodice. She'd mentioned strained relations with her family in Georgia. Now he knew why. Still, why had they not taken her in after her husband died? "And your doting father? Was he the one who forced you into nursing? To recover the family name, perhaps?" He hated the sting of sarcasm in his voice.

"My father is Seth Randal III, adviser to Jefferson Davis," she announced, rising to her feet.

Aghast, Blake stared at her. An adviser to the president of the Confederate States. With a traitorous daughter!

"So, surely you see how a Yankee daughter would have ruined his career. He had no choice but to disown me the minute war was declared." She swallowed and looked away. "I had no home to come back to."

Blake tore his gaze from her, clenching his jaw against his rising sympathy, despite his best efforts to push it down.

She set the cup on the table. "I hope someday you'll find it in your heart to forgive me."

Forgive her? Blake fingered the five black bands circling his arm. How could he forgive any Yankee for what they'd done?

His thoughts drifted to Lieutenant Harkins, who had rushed to him from the battle of Antietam—blood splattered across his uniform, eyes wild from the insanities of war—to tell Blake of his brother's death. Wounded, Jeremy had lain on the battlefield after the hostilities had ended while Union soldiers scavenged for valuables among the dead. Rebel doctors also wove among the injured, attending to those who could be saved. But they hadn't made it to Jeremy in time before one particularly vile Union officer ran his injured brother through with his sword.

All for a gold pocket watch the lad refused to give him.

Blake knew that watch. Their father had given it to Jeremy when he enlisted. It had been their grandfather's, who'd fought in the War of 1812, and his father's before him, who'd fought in the Revolutionary War. A good luck piece, since neither had died in battle.

Oh Jeremy, why didn't you just give it to him?

The thud of a boat against the hull jarred Blake from his nightmare. Orders and commotion filtered down from above. Hayden poked his head inside the cabin. "Parson Bailey's gone missing."

Setting his injured leg on the deck, Blake rose, ignored the pain, and headed for the door. "I will never forgive you, Mrs. Crawford. Or any Yankee."

CHAPTER 17

*B*lake stormed out of the sick bay, leaving a trail of loathing in his wake that sent Eliza reeling backward. Fighting back tears, she picked up the basin of bloody rags and placed it on the table. She would prefer to stay below and clean up, away from the scorn and hatred of everyone above, but Hayden's statement that something had happened to Parson Bailey spurred her to wash her hands and follow Blake.

The arc of a golden sun dipped behind palms, flinging glistening jewels over the bay. A breeze cooled the perspiration on Eliza's brow and neck as she emerged from below. Passengers and crew mobbed the deck, encircling something in the center. Hayden and Blake shoved through them, and Eliza followed to find the sailors who had accompanied Parson Bailey in search of water. One of them leaned against the mast, holding a bloody rag to his head. Clutching her skirts, she started toward him, but his eyes, as sharp as black darts, halted her.

"What is she still doing here?" Mr. Scott straightened the jeweled pin on his embroidered waistcoat, his voice incredulous. "The colonel appears well enough to me."

"Aye, I thought she was long gone," a sailor said.

Blake limped to stand beside the captain. "She tended my wound. And now she'll tend Mr. Simmons." He leveled a pointed gaze at the man in question. "Unless he prefers his injury to putrefy and rot his brain."

The sailor's face blanched, and he beckoned Eliza forward with his eyes.

"What happened?" Blake asked.

Captain Barclay scratched his gray beard. "Seems our parson struck Simmons over the head and took off."

157

"Yep, that's what he did," another sailor added. He pointed to the man standing beside him. "George and I was"—he cleared his throat—"well, we was relievin' ourselves when we heard Simmons yell out. When we found him, he was on the ground moaning, and the parson was gone."

Eliza inched toward Mr. Simmons, making no sense of their story. Lifting the bloody cloth, she peered at the swollen knot atop his head. Nothing too serious, though she should clean it and apply a poultice as soon as possible.

"Is that true, Simmons?" the captain asked.

"Aye, Cap'n. I sat down on a tree trunk to rest a spell, and the next thing I know, I'm waking up to these two ugly mugs swirling in me vision." He gestured toward the other sailors with a chuckle. "And the parson is nowheres to be found."

"Perhaps he was taken by natives," Hayden offered.

"But why wouldn't they take all of us? And they didn't take our barrels or weapons. Don't make sense."

"No, it doesn't." Blake shifted his weight. Pain clouded his features, but at least no blood appeared on the bandage around his leg.

James huffed. "And we still have no water."

"We found a creek." The sailor's eyes lit up beneath a brow furrowed with sweat and sand. "We can get water tomorrow."

"Aye." Captain Barclay planted his hands at his waist and squinted at the setting sun. "At first light, we'll search for the parson and gather water." He glanced toward the men still hammering in the yards. "Repairs will be finished tomorrow, and we need to get sailin'. I've wasted enough time as it is. There's cargo in New Orleans waitin' for me to pick it up after I drop your colony off in Brazil."

"We can't just leave the parson here." Angeline spoke from her spot across the deck, drawing curious gazes her way.

"Yes we can, miss." Captain Barclay's tone bore neither rancor nor sympathy. "Especially if he struck my man here."

"We don't know that for sure." Sunlight glinted gold in Dodd's wavy hair—most likely the only gold he'd ever find. "He could have been kidnapped. Why, when I was a sheriff in Richmond, I dealt with many a kidnapping. There was one in par—"

"We didn't hear no struggle or no screamin'." The sailor crossed his beefy arms over his chest.

"An' we saw no one else there," the first sailor said.

"What about *her*?" Graves stroked his black goatee and gestured toward Eliza.

Her breath caught in her throat as all eyes speared her with a scorn so real, she felt its punctures in her chest.

"I need to bandage this man's wound," she squeaked out, frustrated that terror revealed itself in her voice.

Blake stepped forward. "We need her. She's the only person on board who can tend to our sick and injured." He pointed to his wounded leg. "Are you willing to risk your lives for your blasted pride?" Though Eliza knew the only reason he stood up for her was for the benefit of his precious venture, his words warmed her.

"And we'll need her when Sarah's baby arrives," Blake added.

"That's not for another two months," Dodd said. "We'll be in Brazil by then and can find someone there."

"Besides, we have the good doctor." Mr. Scott declared. "He'll get over his fear of blood soon enough."

But James shook his head. "I doubt it. I've been like this for over two years."

"What good is a doctor who's afraid of blood?" one of the soldiers spat with disdain.

"But you can tell one o' us what to do, Doc," one of the farmers added.

The statement fired a plethora of comments into the air like grapeshot, most of which hit their mark in Eliza's heart, and one that sank deep. "Her husband probably killed some of our kin!"

"Aye, she's bad luck to be sure," one sailor shouted. "And now, the parson's gone missing."

"Don't be silly." Angeline moved to stand beside Eliza. "There's no such thing as bad luck."

"But there's such a thing as God's curse, ain't there, Doc?" Max asked. "Aren't you a preacher too?"

James rubbed the back of his neck. "There are curses in the Bible. But not for—"

"There you have it!" Mr. Scott huffed. "The woman is cursed."

"It doesn't matter," Blake shouted. "We would be cursed far worse if we lost her."

Captain Barclay finally raised his hands in a gesture that silenced the mob. "I, for one, have had my fill of bad luck." He faced Blake. "Beggin' your pardon, Colonel, but it's still my decision, and I say the Yankee goes. Max will escort her halfway to Roseau first thing in the morning. She can find her way from there." With eyes like a hawk, he scanned the crowd, daring any to disagree. "I've been at sea long enough to know there *is* such a thing as bad luck. We'll put her ashore, get water, and search for the parson, but we will set sail tomorrow afternoon, and that's my final say on it."

Not wanting anyone to see her fear, Eliza had been successful at keeping her tears at bay, but now, hours later in her cabin, she could not stop them from trickling down her cheeks. Nor could she stop from trembling like a palm frond in the wind. She'd accepted her fate that morning, but to have her hopes revived only to be dashed again had wreaked havoc on her emotions. Darkness slithered outside the porthole of her cabin, teasing her with its temporary reign as every minute ticked by until the sun would rise and she'd be put ashore.

"What shall I do, Stowy?" She kissed the top of the feline's head and snuggled against his furry cheek, but the only answer she received was the contented rumble of a purr.

Unable to eat, she'd refused dinner and instead had paced her cabin, pleading with God for another chance. Sarah had joined her shortly after sunset. But after praying with Eliza and encouraging her to trust her fate to the Almighty, she had retired, complaining of a sore back. Poor food, the constant movement of the ship, and the oppressive heat did little to ease the discomfort of the woman's condition. Yet thankfully, she now swayed calmly in her hammock, sound asleep. In a way, Eliza had much in common with Sarah. They were both alone in the world, and both had huge obstacles to overcome. Yet while Sarah slept peacefully, believing God would take care of her, Eliza's restless soul drove her mad with worry.

The door creaked, and Angeline entered. "I thought you'd be asleep," she whispered after glancing at Sarah.

"I can't." Eliza hugged herself and plopped down in the only chair.

Skirts swished. Angeline sat on the trunk beside her and took her hand.

"It isn't fair." Stowy leaped onto Angeline's lap and curled into a ball. She stroked his fur as if he were her only friend in the world. "Why don't I go with you?" Her voice lifted in excitement. "Two are better than one."

"Don't be absurd. Why should both of us suffer? You haven't done anything wrong."

Nothing but the creak of the ship and Stowy's purrs replied. "You don't know that," Angeline finally whispered.

Eliza squeezed her hand. "Surely nothing that would warrant them hating you as much as they hate me."

"I'm not so sure." Angeline's voice weighed heavy with regret. "I don't even know why they hate you. I mean, you're not really a Yankee."

"They are hurting. They need someone to blame."

Rising, Angeline bundled Stowy in her arms.

"Thank you, Angeline. It's nice to have friends on board." Even if Eliza could count them all on one hand.

Moonlight swayed over Angeline with the rock of the ship. Silver, black, silver, black. Much like the woman's moods. Happy then sad, bold then timid. Eliza could not forget how Angeline had nearly fainted when the frigate captured them. Or, alternatively, how she boldly stood beside Eliza when the passengers threatened to toss her overboard. Eliza longed to know Angeline's story. She longed to help her. But now she'd never have the chance.

"Won't you try to get some sleep?" Angeline asked.

"I don't think I can. You go ahead. I'll just sit here awhile."

Within minutes of undressing and crawling into her hammock— with Stowy curled by her side—Angeline's breathing deepened, leaving Eliza alone again. A loneliness that cloaked her in a familiar, heavy drape. Minutes passed. The muffled sounds of voices echoing through the ship faded one by one until nothing remained but the lap of waves against the hull. Nothing save the frantic thump of her heart and the horrifying visions of her future. She tried to pray, but out of her hopelessness, no words formed. Instead, she crept out of the cabin and made her way above to the starboard railing. Perhaps some fresh air would clear her head and give her a new perspective.

A quarter moon flung silver and blue braids across the choppy bay as a breeze stirred the palms ashore in a gentle swishing cadence. Bowing her head, she clasped her shaky hands and began to pray.

Against the rolling of the ship, Magnolia clung to the ladder and made her way above deck. Her parents snoring away in their stifling cabin afforded her the perfect opportunity to slip from their watchful gazes and steal a few moments alone. She hadn't slept in four nights—not since she'd made a spectacle of herself at the dance and revealed Eliza's secret to all. Slipping her hand into the pocket of her gown, she withdrew a peppermint leaf and plopped it in her mouth. Just in case she came across anyone on deck. She'd tried to control her drinking after that night but found the incident had only increased her need for the vile liquor. Vile, wonderful elixir that took away the pain and made life bearable.

A night breeze, laden with the scent of wild orchids and sweet mangoes, swirled about her, nearly wiping away the stench of the ship and its filthy crew—an odor that seemed permanently lodged in her lungs. She peered into the darkness, seeking Mr. Lewis. The aged carpenter always carried a flask of brandy on him. And Magnolia always managed to talk him out of a sip. Or two. But he was nowhere in sight. Only a few slouching shadows loomed on the fore- and quarterdeck that were most likely watchmen fast asleep.

Another figure stood at the starboard railing, just outside the light from the lantern hanging from the mainmast. Magnolia took a step forward, squinting into the darkness. Mercy, it was Eliza. She was the last person Magnolia wished to see! She imagined the feeling was mutual. No doubt the woman hated her for what she'd done. Turning, Magnolia intended to return to her cabin when an alarming and utterly foreign idea halted her. *Perhaps I should apologize.* That would be the right thing to do, wouldn't it? After all, Magnolia hadn't meant to say anything. In fact, she hardly remembered saying anything at all. But, for goodness' sake, since Eliza was to be cast off on the morrow, an apology was the least Magnolia could offer her for the trouble she'd caused. Bracing herself for the lady's rage, Magnolia crossed the deck and slipped beside her. Eliza's lips moved beneath closed eyes.

Praying? *How quaint.* Yet Magnolia supposed she might be reduced to prayer if she were being stranded on an island in the morning. She leaned toward her, longing to hear how laypeople prayed. All she'd ever heard were the prayers recited in church.

Eliza's eyes shot open. She reeled backward with a start. "Magnolia, you frightened me."

"Forgive me. I didn't mean to."

Eliza's gaze scoured her from head to toe. "Do you need medical attention?"

The true concern in her voice only heightened Magnolia's guilt. "No. I'm quite all right." She sighed and glanced over the inky sea. Inky and dark like her soul.

Eliza's brow knitted. "As you know, I won't be around after tonight, so if you have a question or a complaint I can help you with. . ."

Magnolia swept a shocked gaze her way. "You would help *me*?"

Moonlight trickled over Eliza's smile as she glanced toward the island.

"After what I did?" Magnolia leaned on the railing. Across the bay, dark shadows churned and swayed, making the island look like a breathing, living entity. A monkey howled. Or at least Magnolia thought it was a monkey. She shivered at the thought of being in the jungle alone.

"I came to tell you how sorry I am." Tears burned behind Magnolia's eyes. "I never meant to break my promise. I was. . .well, I was. . ."

Eliza covered Magnolia's hand with hers. "I know." She gave a tiny smile of understanding. "You weren't yourself."

Though Magnolia heard the words, she could not process them. All she could do was stare at the woman whose life she had ruined.

"We all make mistakes, Magnolia. Believe me, I know how it feels to be punished for something you can't take back."

Magnolia swallowed.

Eliza patted her hand then gripped the railing again. "You are forgiven."

A tear slid down Magnolia's cheek. "Just like that. You could die because of me."

"My life is in God's hands, not yours. Here," she said, handing her a handkerchief. "What's done is done."

Magnolia dabbed her face. "But I blackmailed you."

"Alcohol does strange things to people."

Magnolia sniffed, wondering why she smelled smoke all of a sudden.

163

"I suppose you must think me a spoiled tart, a spoiled, besotted tart."

Eliza turned toward her. "No, I don't. I think you are hurting. I think you drink to cover something up. Something deep inside."

Indignation flamed up Magnolia's spine. "Mercy me, of all the nerve! You don't know me." How dare the woman gaze at Magnolia as if she were somehow beneath her? "What could possibly be wrong with my life? Aside from being forced on this despicable journey, that is. I'm wealthy and beautiful and educated. I can play the piano and paint a masterpiece, and I speak French and Italian. Men adore me, vie for my hand in marriage."

Eliza's lips folded, but still the look of pity remained. "I meant no offense."

"I wish you the best, Eliza. Good night." Magnolia spun around. She needed a drink, and she needed one badly.

⚜

Eliza stared after the beauty as she flounced across the deck and disappeared below. What an odd conversation. What an odd woman. One minute apologetic, the next riding her high horse. Yet Eliza found no anger within her toward the woman. Regardless of her list of accomplishments and abilities, Magnolia seemed haunted by something, desperate even, and a bit broken inside. Despite the airs she put on to impress others.

Something Eliza need not worry about. She knew where she stood—with these people, with her family back home. With the entire country, in fact.

The smell of smoke curled her nose. She scanned the ship. A white haze floated over the deck. A shadow shifted to her left. Blake dropped from the quarterdeck and darted to the main hatch where a misty vapor pumped into the air.

"Fire!"

CHAPTER 18

Grabbing the bucket, Blake tossed the seawater on the last dying embers in the hold. The coals sputtered, closing their red, glowing eyes with the final hiss of their demise. The line of exhausted men that extended up the ladder cheered. Faces creased with soot shone with glee in the lantern light as the crowd broke up and headed above.

Hayden slapped Blake on the back. "Good thing you saw the smoke in time." With his dark hair, soot-covered face, and wide eyes, the man looked more like a startled owl at midnight than their tenacious stowaway.

Running a sleeve over his forehead, Blake chuckled at the sight.

Hayden gave him a knowing grin. "You're quite a mess yourself, mate."

Captain Barclay, sweat dripping from his beard, stared at smoking ashes. "Souse me for a gurnet, I can't figure what started the fire. Especially in the hold. My men know better than to leave a lantern lit down here."

"Perhaps a passenger. . ." James spoke from the ladder as he descended to join them.

Moses emerged from the shadows, ashes blotching his meaty arms. "No sir. No passengers down this far. We was all asleep above."

James stared at the smoking remains of what had been a pile of old sailcloth. "Thank God the flames were put out easily."

"Aye," Captain Barclay said. "Or we'd *all* be marooned on this island."

Like Eliza. The smell of smoke and bilge bit Blake's nose as the thought bit his heart.

"This trip be cursed, says I," one of the sailors said, his voice heightened with fear. "We'll be lucky to make it to Brazil alive."

The captain huffed his response and waved toward the man. "Gather some men and get this mess cleaned up and the water pumped out. Then inspect the hold for damage." As the sailor sped off, Captain Barclay faced Blake. "We should question Miss Magnolia. If she's desperate enough to toss my instruments overboard, who's to say she wouldn't start a fire?"

Blake shifted his boots in the sludge and winced at the ache in both legs. Though he'd love to draw suspicion toward the spoon-fed tart and away from Eliza as the source of their bad luck, he could not do so in good conscience. "Don't think it was her. I saw her above with Eliza when the fire started."

"Ah yes, Mrs. Crawford. Lenn!" The captain shouted at the sailor, who poked his head back down the hatchway. "Tell Max to get ashore with Mrs. Crawford straightaway. I want to set sail in a few hours." Then turning, he headed toward the ladder muttering, "Cursed woman."

Blake hung his head. Why had he gone and reminded the captain of Eliza?

An hour later, washed and wearing fresh clothes, Blake stood at the railing watching a boatload of sailors row Eliza ashore. She hadn't pleaded or groveled or begged or cried. She'd merely stared straight ahead. All except one glance. One glance at Blake before she climbed down the rope ladder. It was enough to see the remorse, the anguish, the fear in her eyes. Not hatred. Not anger as he'd expected.

He hadn't meant to eavesdrop that morning. Another restless night had driven him above, seeking solace in the gentle waters of the bay—seeking solace for a mind not only tortured with recurring battles, but swamped with thoughts of Eliza's perilous future. Then she had appeared, as if his dreams had taken form. He watched as she gazed over the sea, wistful and morose, before she clasped her trembling hands together and bowed her head in prayer. He watched her for several minutes from his position in the shadows of the quarterdeck, feeling like a muckraker for intruding on her privacy. He watched her because he could do nothing else. Then when Miss Magnolia had joined her, his curiosity got the better of him. All right. So he *had been* eavesdropping.

But what he'd heard sent his mind reeling. She'd forgiven Magnolia! She'd forgiven the pretentious, spoiled lush without so much as a blink of her eye. The woman who had ruined her life and shoved her into a future riddled with uncertainty and danger. Astounding!

Now as the men rowed Eliza to that treacherous future, she cast one last glance over her shoulder at him. If he were a praying man, he'd petition God for her safety, but he'd given up on prayer long ago. Instead, he ran a hand through his wet hair and cursed.

Blast it! He could not reconcile a lying Yankee with the woman he saw last night. How could he keep his anger toward her blazing when her honor, kindness, and generosity doused the flames at every turn? Sunlight sliced swords of silver across the bay as if angry at Eliza's fate. Steam rose from the jungle, blurring the island. Yet no breeze stirred to offer comfort to those witnessing the lady's judgment. Blake dabbed the sweat from his forehead, resisting the urge to follow her. To escort her to Roseau himself. Forfeit his journey to Brazil. His dreams. But his brother's howl as a Yankee sword plunged into his gut, his family's screams as they burned to death, haunted him with voices that had been silenced far too young, voices demanding justice.

And he couldn't do it.

James appeared beside him, his gaze following Blake's. "You did your best to save her."

"It wasn't good enough."

"God will take care of her. I've been praying, and I sense He's already answered."

Blake snorted and shifted his weight.

"How's your leg?" James asked.

"Healing." Blake stretched it out. Even after standing on it for hours, no blood stained the bandage she'd applied.

"She's a good nurse," James said.

Blake was about to agree when Angeline dashed to his side, her face twisted in fear. "It's Sarah." Her gaze shifted to Eliza nearly on shore then back to Blake.

"What about her?" James stepped forward.

"She's having her baby. And something is terribly wrong,"

James assisted Eliza over the railing. "How is she?"

"In a lot of pain and bleeding heavily. She's asking for you." James took her arm and swept her past the onlooking passengers and crew and down the companionway ladder. A scream that sounded as though Sarah's limbs were being ripped off one by one filtered from below.

"Have you ever delivered a baby, James?"

"No." He stopped at the door to the sick bay, fear skittering across his eyes. "I did most of my doctoring on the battlefield. Regardless, I can't do this. Not with all that blood."

Eliza nodded and grabbed the handle. "Hot water, clean rags. Lots of them, please. Oh, and rum if you can find it."

"Already got them. I'm sorry I can't be of more help." Another ear-piercing howl split the air. Eliza's heart raced. "Not to worry, Doctor, I understand. Besides, I'd rather be here than out in the jungle."

He smiled and opened the door, ushering her inside. Sarah lay on the cot gripping her belly, terror contorting her features. Angeline sat beside her holding her hand. Both ladies' expressions softened when they saw Eliza.

There was so much blood. Eliza withheld the shriek that jumped to her throat as she moved toward Sarah. "So, your little one decided to make an early appearance? Doesn't she know she's not due for another two months?"

She smiled, and Sarah's breathing seemed to steady.

"I need to examine you, all right?"

"I'll be waiting in the hallway." James started to close the door when Magnolia pressed through, her slave, Mable, in tow.

"You shouldn't be here," Eliza snapped, washing her hands in a basin of water.

"I want to help."

"Neither you nor Angeline should be here, being unwed."

"We can hardly stand on propriety at a time like this." Angeline dabbed a rag over Sarah's face.

"Besides," Magnolia leaned in to whisper, "my slave has delivered babies before."

Eliza spun around. "Why didn't you tell anyone?"

"If I had, you wouldn't be here, would you?" Magnolia's cultured brow rose above her knowing smile.

Confusion tumbled through Eliza at the woman's kindness. "Thank you, Magnolia." She faced Mable. "Is this true?"

The girl lowered her gaze. "Yes'm. I's delivered a few babies."

"In that case, I would love your help."

But the examination revealed Eliza's worse fears. Forcing a look of composure, she stood, washed her hands again, and took Mable aside. "Have you delivered a breech baby?"

Every scream, every agonizing wail sent hot needles down Blake's back. He'd never been this close to a birthing, and he never wanted to be this close again. At least not within earshot. It reminded him far too much of the screams of agony on the battlefield. And they said women weren't courageous enough for battle. From the sounds of what Sarah was going through, he'd bet her bravery and endurance would surpass most of the men he'd commanded.

The captain paced before the wheel, hands locked behind his back. Blake knew he was anxious to get under way. So was Blake. Several passengers mulled about the deck in the blaring, afternoon sun. Mr. Graves, cigar in hand, stood at the bow of the ship overlooking the bay as if he were in charge of the entire expedition. The Scotts huddled beneath the shade of an awning erected for their benefit. Mr. Lewis nursed a flask while playing a game of whist with a group of ex-soldiers. Moses and his sister and her children kept to themselves by the capstan. Dodd smiled and tipped his hat at every passing lady. And sailors scattered about, whittling wood or tying ropes as they awaited their captain's orders.

Soon the men emerged from the jungle, kegs of water propped on their shoulders. Blake released a breath. Finally, something to divert his mind from the incessant screams. Within minutes they rowed to the brig, and with the help of the other sailors, they hoisted the kegs aboard. The captain met them. "No sign of Parson Bailey?"

"No Cap'n. We looked everywhere. He didn't leave a mark, footprint, nothin'." The man jerked his head toward another sailor. "You know old hound nose here can track anyone." A torturing wail filtered through the ship. "Is someone dyin'?" the sailor asked.

"No. Just deliverin' a baby." The captain's voice was matter-of-fact, but his mind seemed elsewhere. "I have no choice then. I have a schedule to keep and can't hold it up for one man. We must set sail if I am to make it to New Orleans in time."

The sailor removed his tarred straw hat and wiped the sweat from his brow. "Don't make no sense. The man couldn't just disappear."

Disappear. An idea sprang into Blake's mind like a predator on prey, an idea that chilled him to the bone. Hobbling across the deck, he leaped down the ladder, hoping with everything in him that he was wrong.

"What's got into you, Colonel?" Captain Barclay followed him down the companionway.

He halted at the door to the captain's cabin. "Parson Bailey was the last person to handle the funds for our colony."

Understanding flickered across the old man's eyes. The men barreled into the cabin behind the captain, who darted to his desk. Kneeling, he felt for a latch beneath the bottom drawer. A click echoed through the cabin. Blake's breath caught in this throat. A secret lever swung open. The captain pulled out a tray. Empty.

All their money was gone.

CHAPTER 19

*E*liza cringed as Sarah let out another deafening scream.

"What's happening?" The poor woman panted. A sheen of perspiration covered her face and neck and glued her brown curls to her skin. Fear sparked from her eyes. "Why does it hurt so much?"

"All birthing hurts. Nothing to worry about." Eliza feigned a calm tone and pressed her hands on Sarah's womb, feeling for the position of the child. Still upside down. But the pains were coming closer now, within minutes. Eliza's palms grew damp. Her mind spun in terror. Women often died in childbirth. Especially when the baby was not in the correct position. What was she to do?

Calm. Remain calm. Eliza drew in a deep breath and lifted up a prayer. The same thing she'd done during the war when men's lives were in her hands. But back then, she'd had a bevy of doctors to call to her aid. Here she was alone.

"It be best if she squats," Mable said in a timid voice, her gaze barely meeting Eliza's. "It will hep de baby come out."

"Then let's get her up." Eliza stood and gestured to Magnolia, who'd been pacing the tiny room, and to Angeline beside the bed. "Ladies, the baby is coming. Grab Sarah's arms and assist her to a sitting position."

They complied, though alarm pinched their expressions, an alarm Eliza felt strangling every nerve. Sarah moaned as they maneuvered her. Grabbing a stack of blankets, Eliza laid them on the deck beneath the woman and rubbed her hands together to settle the trembling.

Lifting her face, Sarah wailed for what seemed minutes. The sound of her pain sliced a hole in Eliza's heart as the metallic smell of blood filled her nose.

"Mercy me, is she going to die?" Magnolia whimpered, her lip trembling. "I can't stay here if she's going to die."

Angeline shot her a seething look.

"Then go," Eliza spat. She had no time for weakness. "But no one is going to die."

Sarah's face reddened. Her grunts and groans joined the creaking of the ship.

Mable knelt. "Don't push, ma'am. Try t' not push."

Sarah's eyes flashed. "Are you mad?" she ground out, her face so mottled in agony, Eliza barely recognized her.

The slave girl cowered beneath the woman's chastisement, and Eliza laid a hand on her shoulder for comfort.

Sarah panted. "Forgive me, Mable." Her chest rose and fell. Angeline dabbed the sweat on her forehead. Magnolia's face had gone bone white.

Amazed that, in her pain, Sarah still considered the young slave's feelings, Eliza clasped her sweaty hands. "When you feel like pushing, squeeze my hands instead."

Sarah nodded. Angeline rubbed her back and whispered in her ear. "It will be all right, Sarah. All women go through this. It's perfectly normal."

Eliza didn't have time to wonder where an unmarried woman like Angeline would have witnessed a birthing, for another pain soon hit. Sarah slammed her eyes shut until tears streamed from their corners. She squeezed Eliza's hands. They grew numb with pain. Eliza bit her lip, tasting blood.

Mable held Sarah's skirts out of the way.

The woman howled for what seemed an eternity, not stopping to catch her breath.

Finally one tiny foot appeared.

Then the other.

"Wrap his legs in de blanket," Mable instructed. "Or he'll get too cold before the rest comes out."

Eliza grabbed a clean spread and covered the baby's legs, holding him in her hands. He or she wasn't moving. Neither did any more of the babe appear. Sarah's wail turned savage. All color drained from her face.

No Lord, no. Please don't let them die!

Blake couldn't believe his eyes.

"Gone! What do you mean gone?" James shoved his way through the crowd mobbing the captain's cabin and peered into the tray. He exchanged a harried glance with Blake.

Rising, Captain Barclay slammed the empty tray atop his desk, grabbed a bottle of brandy from his cabinet, and poured himself a glass.

"The good parson stole our money." Blake voiced what his mind refused to accept.

"Parson Bailey?" Dodd exclaimed.

"It makes sense now." The sailor pressed the bandage wrapped around his head. "That's why he hit me."

"Zooks. The parson. Who would've guessed?" Hayden snapped hair from his face.

"This is preposterous!" Mr. Scott stormed forward, his jowls quivering. "I cannot believe it!" His wife seemed ready to faint beside him.

"How will we buy land? Food? Building materials?" One of the farmers, Mr. Jenkins, held his young daughter close.

"That was all I had left in the world," the blacksmith said.

"We trusted you with our money!" one man pointed a finger at Blake.

"You shouldn't have allowed the parson to know where it was!" the baker's wife shouted.

James lifted his hands. "It's not the colonel's fault. Every one of us trusted Parson Bailey."

"I agree." Hayden rubbed the back of his neck and scowled. "What's done is done. The man was a thief. He fooled us all."

"Quite easy for you to say, sir." Mr. Scott fumed. "None of the money was yours. Most of it was ours." He glanced at his wife, whose expression had frozen in shock, then over to Blake. "Isn't that true, Colonel?"

"You were quite generous," Blake mumbled, still too shocked and angry with the parson to deal with Mr. Scott's concerns. Still, since the war had stripped most of the colonists of their wealth, the Scott's contribution, meager as it was, had constituted over half of their combined funds.

"So, we have lost more than anyone else." Mr. Scott all but growled.

Blake wondered what difference it made. "Once you gave me your money, sir, it became part of our colony's combined wealth to be used for land and supplies. Besides, there is naught to do about it now."

Captain Barclay refilled his glass.

Blake wanted to slam his fist on the bulkhead, wanted to grab his pistol and shoot someone. But he'd learned on the battlefield to set an example for his men. And now as he glanced over the passengers, all eyes looking to him for answers, he swallowed his fury and slipped into his role as leader and provider. "Money can be earned again."

"We should go back home." Mr. Graves slithered into the room. "Better to be in a familiar place with nothing than a foreign country destitute."

"Aye, aye," some expressed their agreement.

But Blake didn't want to go home. Going home meant failure, defeat. Going home meant his death. He'd invested all he had in this venture, and he wasn't about to give up now. But these people had also invested their fortunes. They had entrusted him with their money. And he had let them down. Blake had failed at war. He had failed to save his brother. Failed to save his family. Now this. Though Blake's father had always loved him, he'd held both his sons to a high standard. Failure was never an option. Failure was for the mediocre, the riffraff of society. Never for a Wallace.

"Why don't we go lookin' for the parson?" Max tugged on his red neckerchief.

"Where?" the sailor whom the parson had struck asked. "He's probably already at Roseau by now or some other port where he can catch a ship."

Graves stroked his goatee. "Agreed. We'll never see that money again. All the more reason to go back to Charleston."

"We should put it to a vote," the captain said.

Blake squeezed the bridge of his nose. He didn't want a vote. A vote meant the possibility of returning. But the captain was right. After the loss of most of their cargo and now their money, it wasn't Blake's decision to make.

"Very well," he conceded. "Gather all the passengers on deck."

Minutes later, Blake took a spot beside the captain on the quarterdeck and gazed down at the passengers crowding below. Beyond the ship, the island of Dominica waved like a mirage upon the turquoise bay, taunting him with the loss of their money. Somewhere amid its teeming jungles and coal-black shores, Parson Bailey strolled, his pockets heavy with gold. Or perhaps the sailor was right, and the thieving barracuda had already set sail for home.

Per the captain's orders, sailors eased across yards, untying furled canvas in preparation to leave. Others loitered on the deck, casting interested gazes at the proceedings. Blake swallowed. His fate, his very life, lay in the decision of these people he'd handpicked to come on this voyage.

He gestured the crowd to silence then cleared his throat. "I'll not deny that we have suffered many losses. But there is still hope. I've heard the emperor of Brazil is willing to sell land on credit, as well as provide food and supplies to help new colonies until their first harvest."

"I don't want to be beholding to some foreign emperor!" one man shouted.

"What if we can't pay up and he throws us in jail?"

Hayden braced his boots on the rolling deck. "I say we continue. Most of us have nothing to go back to anyway."

"A stowaway doesn't have a say!" Mr. Scott bellowed. Hayden sent the man a scathing glance.

"Say or not, the man is right," James piped in. "We all left because our homeland wasn't our homeland anymore. The Yankees stripped us of everything we loved dear. Why would anyone want to return to that?"

"I lost my wife and only child." Mr. Lewis's hopeless tone stifled Blake's disdain for the drunk carpenter.

Graves sauntered to the front of the crowd, brushing imaginary dust from his black coat. "We should return because it is still a better choice than starving or being eaten by a wild animal in the jungle."

"Oh ye of little faith, Mr. Graves." Blake planted fists at his waist. "You insult the competence of this fine group. I chose each of you for your exceptional skills. Why such dire predictions?"

"Because I am a pragmatist, sir." He gave a slanted smile. "And I know when we are beaten."

Grunts of agreement chipped away at Blake's patience. He wiped the sweat from the back of his neck and squinted at the sun high in the sky.

James leaped onto the quarterdeck ladder, clung to a backstay, and addressed the crowd as a breeze flapped his open shirt. "Our forefathers came to America long ago with much less than we have here. They fought the elements and the natives, and forged a living in an untamed wilderness. Why should we do any less?"

"I quite agree." Dodd clipped his thumbs into his belt. "Besides, there's gold to be found in this new land. I have the maps to prove it." He surveyed the mob, his eyes twinkling. "And I'll cut a share to anyone who helps me find it."

Some of the men's eyes widened.

"I'll drink to that." Mr. Lewis lifted his flask in the air and took a sip.

"Rubbish." Mr. Scott chortled.

"I couldn't agree more," Graves snickered, sounding like the politician he was. "Chasing dreams and fantasies is not for grown men and women. We created successful lives in America once. We can do it again!"

Nods of affirmation bobbed across the deck.

Blake studied the odd man. "Why did you sign on for this voyage if you are so intent on going back?"

"I am a politician, Colonel. I don't vote for risky ventures doomed to fail. And this venture has become far too risky for my tastes."

"Life is full of risk." Hayden crossed his arms over his chest. "Returning home would hold as much a risk as sailing ahead."

James gave him a nod, and Blake followed with an approving glance. "Let's put it to a vote, then," the captain intervened.

"Agreed." Blake drew a deep breath. "All in favor of returning raise your hand and say, 'Aye.'"

"Ayes" echoed across the ship, piercing Blake's heart like musket shot as he counted the hands. Twenty.

"All those against returning, say *nay*."

Nays in equal volume and number filled the air.

Blake scanned the deck. His stomach constricted with the count of each hand. "Twenty." He sighed. "We are equal." Yet there were forty-four colonists in all. Yes, of course. The women below. Since the screams had ceased, he'd all but forgotten them.

"What'll we do now?" one of the farmers asked.

"I vote with the ayes." Magnolia emerged from the companionway, blood on her gown and a grin on her face.

"Hush up, girl!" Her father seethed. "You don't know your own mind. And what in the tarnation is all over your gown? Good heavens,

Mrs. Scott, look at your daughter." Covering her mouth, the lady sped to Magnolia and dragged her below.

"Twenty-one to twenty." Blake felt as if a piece of rope had lodged in his throat. Four additional votes could seal his fate. Eliza would no doubt vote to return, since she was to be sent back anyway. Miss Angeline might as well, considering the bond the two women had formed. That left only Sarah. And her one vote wouldn't be enough.

CHAPTER 20

$\mathcal{N}$othing happened aboard a ship that was not soon privy to all who had ears. Which was why Eliza knew, from the shouts and the tapping of feet above her, that something important was taking place on the main deck. Something that, no doubt, had some bearing on her future. Yet even though Sarah had delivered a healthy baby girl, Eliza hesitated to leave her until mother and child were resting comfortably. Instead, she sent Magnolia to see what was happening and report back immediately. But when the lady did not return, Eliza settled the baby in Sarah's arms, gave Angeline final instructions, and headed above.

Even before she reached the top of the hatch, she deduced the reason for the gathering from the heated discussion. "I vote with the nays," she said, popping onto the main deck. Eyes darted her way, some scanning her with contempt, some blinking at the blood splattered across her apron, others shifting their gazes away as if she were a leper.

Blake grinned. Or at least Eliza thought it was a grin—hoped it was a grin.

"She doesn't get to vote," the baker said. "She's a Yankee."

"Aye, that's right! She shouldn't even be here," one of the ex-soldiers shouted.

Blake's jaw flexed. "She paid the same as the rest of you."

"I simply refuse to accept the vote of a Yankee." Mr. Graves's tone was incredulous. "I doubt any *true* Southerner would."

"This Yankee just saved Sarah's life." Angeline's voice spun Eliza around to see the lady emerging from below. Lifting her chin, she cast a stalwart glance over the passengers. "Saved her life and the life of her baby through a difficult delivery. A healthy baby girl." She smiled at Eliza and squeezed her hand. "So if you won't accept her vote, surely you'll accept mine. I vote we continue to Brazil. And so does Sarah."

Batting hair from her face, Eliza looked up at Blake, wondering what the final count was. Relief reflected in his gray eyes before he looked away. "That makes twenty-three to twenty-one in favor of continuing on to Brazil."

Some shouted in victory. Others moaned. Mr. Graves skulked away.

"Never fear. We will survive," Blake shouted, gripping the quarterdeck railing and halting the retreating mob in their tracks. "We will create a new land, a land where we can keep our freedom, our honor, our integrity, and our Southern ways. A land where no one can tell us how to live."

The confident tone of his voice, the determined assurance lining his features, and the commanding spread of his shoulders all combined to create an aura of ability, of trust, that drew people to follow him. He must have been magnificent on the battlefield. Even now all eyes latched on him and all grumbling ceased.

"Here, here." Dodd thrust his fist into the air, followed by Mr. Jenkins, Mr. Scott, and several other men.

Captain Barclay gave Blake an approving nod before bellowing orders that raised sails, weighed anchor, and set their course. As the crowd dispersed, Blake assumed his duties as first mate with ease. Leaping to the main deck, he brushed past Eliza. Drawing in a deep breath of his masculine scent, she remained in place, stunned. Afraid to move. Afraid that if she did, someone would remember that she wasn't supposed to be on board at all—that she was supposed to be marooned on the island, whose waving palms now taunted her from beyond the starboard quarter.

Shouts echoed across the ship. Sails lowered and flapped in the breeze as men heaved on the capstan to raise the anchor.

James approached, a mischievous twinkle in his eyes. "Good work, Eliza. Shall we check on your patient?" He proffered his elbow with a wink. "Out of sight, out of mind, eh?"

With a grin, Eliza placed her hand on his arm and allowed him to lead her below.

～⚓～

Eliza woke with a start. Darkness saturated the cabin. Grabbing the hammock rope, she pulled herself to sit and listened. Nothing but the creak of the ship and deep breathing of her friends met her ears. But she thought she heard. . .well, it didn't matter. She was no doubt dreaming. Lying down, she closed her eyes and tried to fall back asleep. Much needed sleep ever since Sarah's baby was born. Little Lydia woke up hungry two or three times a night. Yet once Sarah started feeding her, she slipped back asleep in no time. Eliza wished she could do the same. But more often than not, she lay awake for hours pondering her fate.

Wondering if it wouldn't have been better to have remained on Dominica. At least there no one knew who she was. Here, on board the brig, almost everyone hated her. They ignored her, avoided her, and cast disdainful glances her way. To make matters worse, Blake had not said a single word to her in a week, nor even graced her with a glance. His rejection hurt her the most. At least Angeline and Sarah still spoke to her, as did Magnolia, James, and a few of the farmers' wives. She should be thankful for that.

An eerie song filtered through the bulkhead, raising the hairs on Eliza's arms. So she *had* heard something. Sliding from her hammock, she nearly tumbled to the deck. What she wouldn't give to sleep in a bed again. After slipping into a blouse and settling a skirt over her nightdress, she left the cabin and inched up the companionway ladder. Ribbons of light and dark swept over the deck from a lantern hanging at the mainmast. A warm breeze, ripe with brine and a hint of dawn, toyed among the strands of her loose hair.

The chanting stopped. She peered into the darkness but could not find its source. Odd. Probably one of the sailors, embarrassed at seeing her at this hour. Grabbing her skirts, she braced herself on the heaving deck and made her way to the railing. Dawn would break soon, and with each mile they sailed southward, the sun's ascension grew more and more beautiful. She knew because she had often been up at this hour— the perfect time to enjoy fresh air without being assailed by reproachful glances and bitter comments.

Gripping the railing, she drew a deep breath of the sea and prayed for strength to endure another day. Inky water bubbled and churned beneath a sky lit by a thousand twinkling stars, so incredibly beautiful. It was hard to remain morose for long. The warm air suddenly chilled. She glanced behind her. A dark shadow slithered across the deck and disappeared into the shadows. Eliza's skin crawled. "Who's there?"

When no answer came, she faced the sea again and nearly bumped into Mr. Graves. He eyed her with a predatory look that sent her leaping backward. "Mr. Graves, you frightened me."

"Sorry, my dear. Unintended, I'm sure." A burst of wind blew his dark hair behind him. "What are you doing up on deck this time of night?"

"I could ask you the same thing." Eliza gripped the railing and took a step away from the strange man.

"I don't sleep, Mrs. Crawford."

"At all? Or just tonight?"

"Rarely."

"I seem to be having the same trouble lately," she muttered, more to herself than to him.

"I would expect so."

His features were lost to her in the shadows, yet she sensed a hostility—no, something deeper—a malevolence that chilled the air around him.

She rubbed her arms and took another step away, thankful the roar of rushing water drowned out her thumping heart, lest he sense her fear. Leaning one arm on the railing, he turned toward her. The smell of tobacco bit her nose as silence made the passage of time unbearable.

Eliza stepped back yet again. "Why do you tarnish your reputation by speaking to a traitor?"

"When I saw you here alone, I thought you might be in some sort of trouble."

"As you can see, I am quite well." She used a dismissive tone, hoping he'd let her be.

He paused. "There are many people who would not wish that so, Mrs. Crawford."

"Are you one of them, sir?"

He chuckled. The first time she'd ever heard the man chuckle. "For instance"—he waved a hand through the air—"with you standing alone at the railing, anyone could come along and toss you overboard."

Eliza gulped.

"All they need do is grab your feet, and *voila*"—he flicked his wrist and gazed at the churning foam below—"over you go." He sighed. "Who's to stop them?"

"I would." Blake emerged from the darkness like a leviathan from the deep.

Eliza's heart lurched into her throat. Mr. Graves plucked a cigar from his coat pocket. "Never fear, my good colonel. I was merely warning the lady of the possibility, not advocating the action."

Blake crossed his arms over his chest, inflicting Graves with his silent stare.

Finally, the man dipped his head to the two of them. "Well, I suppose. . . Good evening. Or should I say good morning to you both." Then turning, he strode away, whistling a disjointed tune.

Eliza's legs gave out, and she gripped the railing. "Thank you, Blake."

"Colonel." His jaw tightened. Yet he made no move to leave.

"Of course. We are back to formalities."

"Do you blame me?"

Eliza flattened her lips. "Then why not allow Mr. Graves to toss me overboard?"

"Because I am not a murderer, Mrs. Crawford. . .or Watts."

Eliza drew in a ragged breath, trying to settle her nerves. Still he stayed, taunting her with his presence. As agonizing as it was, she wanted him to stay. She wanted to talk to him. Make him see how sorry she was. "Why are you awake so early?"

A hint of gray circled the horizon. "Nightmares. I can't seem to rid myself of them." He approached the railing, sorrow weighing his tone.

Eliza longed to touch him, longed to smooth the lines on his forehead. "Quite normal for men suffering from the war."

He cleared his throat as if embarrassed about his malady. "How is the baby? I have not seen Sarah above deck."

"Lydia. She is small but healthy. The difficult birth taxed them both."

"I doubt either would be alive without you."

Eliza gobbled up the compliment like a starving woman would a scrap of bread. Yet just like a scrap, it did nothing to ease her hunger. "Mable, Magnolia's slave, was a great help."

"Hmm. Regardless of what the crew thinks, they are fortunate to have you on board for the journey."

Another compliment? Dare she hope he was softening toward her? "And you? What do you think, Colonel?"

He faced her. His eyes as hard and unyielding as steel. "I wish I had never met you, Mrs. Crawford. That is what I think."

Blake regretted both his words and his tone the minute they left his lips. Not because he didn't mean them, but because Eliza's sweet face melted into a puddle of despair. Yet it couldn't be helped. When he saw Mr. Graves harassing the lady, as an officer and a gentleman, Blake was obligated to step forth. It was his duty and the only reason he had broken his vow of silence to the lady.

But that was all it was. She was still a liar and a traitor. Two things he could never forget.

Or forgive.

Then why had he stayed?

It was as if some invisible force had kept his feet fastened to the deck, some rebellious need to hear her voice, to look into those golden eyes once more. Eyes that now flooded with pain and turned away. Excusing himself, Blake mounted the steps to the foredeck, seeking solace at the bow where the crash of waves drowned out his conflicting thoughts. In the east, the sun peeked over the horizon, but instead of tossing golden spires across the water, a strange darkness immediately stole the light. A gray mass, thick and black—like storm clouds, yet not storm clouds—appeared in the sky. It settled on the water and began to grow and tumble toward them like a dust storm on an open prairie. Yet this dust storm soon spanned the entire horizon and rose into the sky, shoving back the sun and obscuring all stars in its path. The helmsman eased beside him, his eyes wide.

"What is it?" Blake asked.

"I dunno, Colonel. I ain't seen nothin' like it."

"Wake Captain Barclay."

Within minutes, the captain and most of the crew flooded the deck, along with some passengers who had woken during the commotion. Telescope pressed to his eye, Captain Barclay examined the approaching monster, his body stiffening. He lowered the glass. The lines on his face deepened.

"There's no thunder," he said. "No lightning. No rain. It's not a squall. But what is it?" He tapped the telescope into the palm of his hand then turned and bellowed orders to the crew to lower sail.

James slipped beside them.

More people came above, rubbing their eyes and turning to look at the hungry cloud churning and swirling and moving toward them, eating up the ocean in its path. The air fled Blake's lungs. He glanced over his shoulder to see Eliza, staring at the foggy beast, hugging herself. Angeline stood beside her. Concern for their safety, for *her* safety, bit at his conscience. Before Blake could act, James headed toward them, but Hayden leaped in front of him and beat him to the ladies, leading them beside the quarterdeck.

Then it hit. The gray mass swallowed up the brig without so much as flapping a sail or stirring a lock of hair. No breeze. No wind. No sight. Nothing but gray covered everything: the sea, the sky, and the ship. It was as if a bowl had been dropped on them by the spoiled child of some unearthly giant. Eerie silence reigned. An odd smell, like sulfur, burned Blake's nose. Sailors lit lanterns. Passengers huddled together as voices shot through the fog calling to friends and family.

Blake groped his way toward the main deck, looking for Eliza, but he couldn't see a soul in the thick smoke. Voices sounded hollow as if coming from within a deep well. "Eliza!" His voice bounced across the deck and returned to him, ringing in his ears. Sails flapped above. The sea dashed against the creaking hull, telling him that at least the ship still sailed.

Then the coughing began. At first a few coughs pumped into the fog from all around, then more and more until they coalesced into a crescendo that reminded him of corn popping in a kettle.

"All hands stay where you are. No one move." Captain Barclay's shout muffled through the fog. "Stay calm." Yet his voice was far from calm.

Shadowy figures drifted in the haze. Fearful muttering tickled Blake's ears. What in the blazes was going on? Heart seizing, he found the railing and slid his fingers along the damp wood, thrusting into the smoke toward the spot where he'd last seen Eliza.

Crackling sounded. Light speared the darkness. A single ray at first, striking the deck and scattering the mysterious vapor. Then another shaft and another until the deck, railing, wheel, the masts, the entire brig took form and shape and the mysterious gray shroud disappeared, leaving the ship in full sunlight. Scanning the horizon, Blake squinted at the brightness but found no trace of the gray mass. How could it have dissipated so suddenly? His stomach tightened. The last time they'd been cloaked in fog, the Union frigate had fired on them. This time he wasn't even sure the strange cloud *was* fog. Whatever it was, he shivered at the possibility that it brought an even worse disaster.

He glanced over the brig, making sure no one was hurt. Dodd toppled to the deck. Then two other passengers. Mrs. Scott fainted in her husband's arms. Mr. Jenkins coughed then slouched over the railing. Hayden collapsed beside Eliza.

Captain Barclay opened his mouth to speak, but only garbled words emerged before he fell to the deck with a thud.

CHAPTER 21

Thunder bellowed in the distance. Eliza gazed at the dark, roiling clouds—dark and heavy like her heart. She hugged herself against a sudden chill and forced her attention to the two canvas-bound forms lying lifeless on the plank: Mr. Milner, one of the ship's seamen, and the baker's wife, Mrs. Flanders, with her husband crouching over her body, tears streaming from his eyes.

James opened his Bible and began to read:

"'And as we have borne the image of the earthy, we shall also bear the image of the heavenly. . . . So when this corruptible shall have put on incorruption, and this mortal shall have put on immortality, then shall be brought to pass the saying that is written, Death is swallowed up in victory.'"

The words sounded hollow in Eliza's ears. Hollow like the empty threat of thunder in the distance. After all the catastrophes they'd thus endured, what damage could any storm do to them now? What curse could be worse than the deadly disease that had plagued them ever since the strange, ethereal mist had enveloped the ship? *Was* it a curse? Were there such things? Yet three days later, with over half the passengers and crew sick, and these two precious lives gone, what else could Eliza think?

Worst of all, though Eliza and James had tried every cure and medicine at their disposal, nothing seemed to work. Tears blurred her vision as she glanced over the morbid assembly, faces filled with shock, despair, and, in some, contempt as they met her gaze. Nearly everyone on board had a loved one or friend sick or dying below in the hold. And now, these deaths stole any hope that they'd ever see their loved ones returned to health.

Frantic as any caring doctor could be, James had searched through all his medical books, staying up long into the night until his eyes were red and his face haggard. Now, as he stood reading the scriptures, even his voice bled frustration. Over his shoulder, Mr. Graves leaned casually on the foredeck railing, watching the proceedings with a detachment that sent unease slithering all the way to Eliza's toes.

"O death, where is thy sting? O grave, where is thy victory? The sting of death is sin; and the strength of sin is the law. But thanks be to God, which giveth us the victory through our Lord Jesus Christ."

Eliza shifted her gaze away from Mr. Graves only to land on Blake, beside James, his face a mask of control that defied the outrage in his eyes. He would not look at her. Hadn't looked at her all day.

James closed the Bible, said a quick prayer, and nodded to the sailors standing at the end of the plank. They lifted the wood. The bodies slid over the railing and plunged into the agitated sea with a resounding splash.

Lightning carved a jagged knife across the sky.

The crowd scuffled away, all save Mr. Flanders, who stood at the railing staring at the last remnants of his wife's body before she sank to the bottom of the sea. Eliza longed to comfort him, but the hatred she'd seen earlier in his eyes kept her in place.

Hatred that now spewed toward her from the friends of the dead seaman.

"It's her fault!" one of them shouted. "She's bad luck!"

"Aye, she's the cause of this," another sailor said, darts of malice firing from eyes red with grief.

People turned to stare at her. Thunder rumbled.

James marched forward, Bible pressed to his chest. "Now, gentlemen. No one can cause an illness."

"The devil can!" one of the passengers shouted.

Eliza glanced over the mob, seeking a friendly face—any friendly face. But she found none, save James. Wind blasted over them, whipping her hair onto her cheek. She brushed the strands aside. She was so tired. Tired of being hated. Tired of being threatened. Tired of tending the hopelessly sick. So tired in every way possible. A detached numbness overtook her.

Mr. Graves stared at her from the foredeck, his lips sliding into a grin. Blake, who had been gazing out to sea, finally turned toward the ruckus. A battlefield of emotions stormed across his face. He opened his mouth to say something when James continued, "This woman has been helping your loved ones get better. She's been up for three days straight with no sleep and little food tending their every need."

Lightning cast their faces in a deathly gray. Rain drops splattered on the deck. Women and children darted below. The men lowered their gazes and shuffled off, from the rain or from the doctor's speech, Eliza couldn't be sure. And she didn't care. Wiping water from her face, she smiled at James and headed below deck. His footsteps followed her.

The sour stench of illness nearly sent her back above, but she pressed on, determined to do what she could to ease the suffering. She sat on the stool beside the first hammock and rubbed her aching legs, thankful for the temporary relief. Settling the swinging bed with one hand, she pressed a damp rag over the feverish face that sank deeper among the canvas folds with each passing day. Poor Mrs. Jenkins hadn't woken in two days. Eliza had barely been able to get enough broth down her throat to keep her alive. Her husband looked up from the chair at the end of the hammock, their young daughter, Henrietta, in his lap. His brows teetered in anticipation of good news but quickly sank when Eliza shook her head.

Rising, she moved to the next patient. Raindrops tapped a death march on the deck above. Swaying lanterns cast undulating shadows across the sick—light and dark, light and dark—as if trying to decide which ones would live and which ones would die.

Eliza's gaze met James's across the way. He attempted a smile, but she could see from his face that hope was slipping away, replaced by a brewing frustration and anger. Beside him, Angeline held a cup of water to Hayden's lips. At least he was still conscious and hadn't slipped into delirium as some of the sick had done. Beyond her, Magnolia flitted from patient to patient like a hummingbird, hovering over each one long enough to offer a kind word or a sip of broth. She split her time between those below and her mother in their state cabin above. Still, the sight astounded Eliza. She never would have thought such charity existed in the self-absorbed woman.

The ship dove, and Eliza clung to a mast to keep from falling. Patients' groans and grunts rose to join the creak of wood and pounding of water against the hull. Though the captain lay ailing in his cabin, with the first mate recovered from his injury and Blake's assistance, the ship sped heartily on its way. She only prayed they wouldn't arrive in Brazil a ghost ship, with not a living soul left on board.

Eliza shivered at the thought.

She lifted a mug of broth to a young ex-soldier and, once he'd taken a sip, wiped the dribbles from his chin. He mouthed a "thank you" before closing his eyes once again. In the next hammock, Sarah, with Lydia strapped to her chest, read the Bible to the blacksmith's wife. Though Eliza had told her she should rest and avoid contact with the illness, she insisted on helping, stating that if it was God's will for her to get sick, she'd get sick no matter what.

As Eliza made her way to a table to fetch a fresh rag and some more broth, Moses glanced at her from his spot beside his ailing sister, his eyes filled with anguish. Little Joseph and Mariah, one on each knee, stared at their mother with longing. Eliza looked away before tears spilled down her cheeks. So much agony. So much pain.

A man groaned and held out his hand to her. Stopping, she clasped it and offered him a smile.

"Am I going to die, Mrs. Crawford?"

⚜

Holding a hand to his nose, Blake hobbled down the ladder, deeper and deeper into the bowels of the ship, into the darkness and death that lurked below. With each inch of descent, his heart sank lower in his chest. Lower where no shreds of hope remained. At the bottom, hammocks swayed with the movement of the brig, looking more like a school of ghostly sardines than humans. He scanned the precious passengers who'd volunteered to care for the ill, and his traitorous eyes landed on Eliza—forever drawn to her like a ship to a lighthouse. She leaned over the blacksmith, one arm behind his shoulders, as she pressed a cup to his lips.

Blake inched closer.

"There, there, Mr. Murray. Get some rest now." She smiled and lowered him to the hammock then wiped his mouth.

"But am I going to die?" Terror etched his pale face.

She dabbed the cloth over his forehead and took his hand in hers. "Of course not. You're far too ornery to die." She smiled, and the man's chuckle turned into a cough. But it was the look in her eyes that set Blake aback. Concern and kindness. Not an ounce of resentment or malice for the man who, two weeks ago, had insisted she be fed to the sharks.

In fact, as Blake watched her move to the next patient, it occurred to him that most of the people she tended had demanded that she be left on Dominica to die. Each had said hateful, vile things to her. Yet here she was sacrificing sleep and her own health, wandering among the filth and stench, to bring them a modicum of comfort.

Tearing his gaze from her, he headed for James, the man he'd come down here to see in the first place. Blake had to know if any progress was being made in determining the cause or cure of the illness.

"Cure?" James rubbed the scar on his cheek and blew out a long sigh. "I have no idea." I've studied every book I have, tried every medicine. Nothing." He gestured toward someone over Blake's shoulder and then turned to call Sarah before facing Blake again. "Now as to the cause, I have my suspicions."

Just then Eliza appeared beside them, followed by Sarah and baby Lydia.

Motioning them to follow, James led the group deeper into the shadows, away from patients' ears. Blake ducked beneath a beam and took a spot as far from Eliza as he could.

Rubbing the sweat on his neck, James shifted his stance as if unsure how to proceed. Several seconds passed before he leaned toward the group and raised his brows. "I believe this is a demonic curse."

Mrs. Swanson finally drifted off to sleep. Releasing a sigh, Angeline pressed a hand to the base of her aching back and stretched her shoulders. Even though she was accustomed to hard work and little sleep, caring for the sick and dying was taking its toll on her physically—and emotionally. She hated that there was nothing she could do but offer broth and comforting words. Words that, in truth, brought no comfort at all. They all knew they were dying. She could see the fear, the agony, in their eyes. Some took it well, almost submitting to the angel of death who lurked in the shadows of the hold. Others fought, thrashing in their hammocks and screaming in delirium. It was to those patients

Angeline went. She'd had much experience with angry, maniacal men. She knew how to handle people who were out of their wits.

And besides, she deserved the worst they gave her.

Easing strands of hair from her face, she walked down the narrow path between rows of hammocks, looking for someone else in need and avoiding the one person she could never face, Mr. Dodd. Thank goodness, James didn't seem to recognize her. It had been dark the night she'd met him a year ago, and he was. . .well, he was. . .a very different man back then.

Dodd was another story. As she passed him, one glance told her his fever had increased. Blond hair matted to a forehead and cheeks that were moist and red. Feeling a pinch of guilt, she stopped and slid beside him. What harm could he do to her now? In his delirium, he probably wouldn't recognize his own mother, let alone Angeline.

Pulling a clean cloth from her apron pocket, she wiped his face and eased hair from his brow. Yes, she remembered that pointy chin and crooked nose. Too well, in fact. The sight of it so close brought back memories she'd sooner forget.

Music from a pianoforte drowned out the rush of the sea against the hull. Hammocks disappeared, replaced by tables laden with cards and mugs of ale all surrounded by patrons and doxies instead of those tending the sick. His puckered lips swooped down on hers. Angeline turned her face away as she forced a playful giggle.

"Come on, sweet pea, you shouldn't tease ole Dodd." He pinched her chin and forced her mouth to his. He tasted of sour fish and ale, and she struggled to be free. But he clamped his arms around her waist and shoved her against him. The other men surrounding the table chuckled and whistled their encouragement. Angeline pushed against his chest, but he only laughed and fell into a chair, drawing her onto his lap.

"Ah, ah, ah, miss. You're far too comely a catch to toss back into the pond. Far too comely." He took a long draught of ale and grinned her way, foam lacing his mustache.

"You best be obeying the man, miss," one of his friends said. "He's the law here in town."

Angeline's repulsion turned to terror. "Law." She gulped.

He opened the flap of his coat, and candlelight flashed on a badge.

A sheriff's badge. "So, you see, you're in good hands, miss." He nibbled on her neck.

Angeline allowed him. Allowed him because she could barely breathe.

Mr. Dodd moaned, tearing her from the horrid memories. She dabbed his forehead again. He hadn't recognized her back then. Perhaps he'd been too drunk. Perhaps he hadn't seen the posters. Whatever the reason, she'd earned a reprieve that night.

That long, despicable night.

Now, with her unpainted face and more modest clothing, perhaps she'd earn another reprieve. Especially if he died. Oh sweet saints, shame on her! What a horrible thing to think. Truly she wished that fate on no one.

Dodd groaned again. He drew in a breath, and for a few long seconds, it seemed he stopped breathing. Angeline leaned her ear toward his mouth.

He clutched her wrist. Pain shot into her fingers.

Shrieking, she tried to pry her hand free, but his clamp on it was as strong as it'd been two years ago.

His eyes popped open and snapped toward her. "I know who you are," he hissed. "I know who you are!"

"That's absurd!" Blake huffed and turned to leave.

James grabbed his arm. "Hear me out. We all believe in God, right?"

The ladies nodded. Blake remained silent.

"Then we must also believe in the devil. The good Word says he roams around like a roaring lion, seeking to kill and destroy us."

"Yes, that is true," Eliza said.

Sarah nodded. "I see where you are heading, Doctor."

But Blake did not. "What has this got to do with anything?"

"It has to do with healing these people and stopping this nonsense." James's voice grew determined. "I've never seen anything like that gray mist, have you?" Before Blake could answer, James continued. "There's something evil about this sickness. I can feel it in my spirit."

"All you feel is discouragement like the rest of us." Blake snorted.

"Demonic or not, what can *we* do about it?" Eliza sounded as wilted as a lily in the desert.

"I propose we fast and pray. Gather whoever wishes to join us to fight this evil force."

That was his plan? His great, marvelous plan? Blake couldn't help the chortle of disbelief that tumbled from his lips. "Go ahead and pray. With the captain sick, I have a ship to run." He turned to leave when Angeline screamed, tore her hand from one of the patients, and fled up the ladder.

Blake released a heavy sigh. "Now what?"

CHAPTER 22

*E*xcusing herself from James and Sarah, Eliza hurried after Angeline. She glanced at Mr. Dodd in passing. He appeared to be sound asleep. Even if he wasn't, what could he have done in his condition to upset her to the point of screaming and dashing from the hold?

Eliza found her in their cabin, sitting on the chair, head in her hands, sobbing. Stowy circled her feet and rubbed against her ankles, omitting a pathetic *merow* at being ignored.

At the intrusion, Angeline turned her face away and wiped her tears. "Forgive me, Eliza. I didn't mean to alarm you." Stowy leaped into her lap and plopped down as if he owned it, drawing a tiny smile from Angeline as she stroked his fur.

Sliding onto the trunk, Eliza handed her a handkerchief. "What happened?"

Two shimmering pools of violet swept her way. "It's nothing."

"Did Dodd say something to you?"

Was it Eliza's imagination, or had the sound of his name sent a tremor through the lady? Angeline straightened her shoulders and glanced toward the porthole where gray skies spread a gloomy sheen through the cabin. Minutes passed with only Stowy's purrs and the dash of water against the hull to tantalize their ears. Angeline blew her nose. "I thought I could escape my past. I thought I could start over."

"Of course you can." Eliza squeezed her hand. "We all can. That's what this voyage is about."

"It hasn't turned out that way for you." Sharp eyes assessed Eliza.

"No." Eliza stared at the nicks and scratches marring the wooden floor.

Angeline sighed and eased a copper curl behind her ear. "I fear it

194

won't be a new start for me either."

"I don't see why not." Eliza reached over to pet Stowy. "Unless you married a Yankee general we don't know about."

Angeline gave a sob-laden chuckle. "No." She scratched Stowy beneath the chin, and the cat's purrs rumbled through the cabin. "Far worse, I'm afraid."

Eliza shivered at the look of despair on her friend's face. "I don't see what could be—"

"He knows me." Angeline's lip trembled. She gathered Stowy in her arms and stood. "He remembers me."

"Mr. Dodd?" Rising, Eliza wrapped an arm around her shoulder, pulling her close, desperate to comfort the lady but not knowing how.

But Angeline stiffened and pulled away. She batted tears from her cheeks as if they were rebellious imps.

"It's okay to cry, you know," Eliza said.

"I've cried too many tears already." Angeline sniffed and drew the handkerchief to her nose as she took up a pace, her skirts swishing. Two steps forward. Two steps back. That's all the space the tiny cabin afforded. "And a lot of good my tears have done me." Her breathing steadied, and the next time she looked at Eliza, a shield covered her eyes. But a shield from what?

"So what if Dodd knows you? He can do nothing to you here." Eliza said. "You have friends. You are protected."

"What he knows about me would destroy those friendships."

"Not with me." What could this poor woman have done? "Whatever your past holds, you can start fresh in Brazil. It's a new land with unlimited possibilities."

"You don't understand. Once my secret is known. . ." Angeline set Stowy down and hugged herself. "Let's just say no one will want me around."

Eliza sighed. "I certainly wouldn't wish that pain on anyone."

Stowy leaped into a hammock and reached a paw out to touch Angeline when she passed, but the lady was so deep in thought, she didn't notice. Halting, she raised remorseful eyes to Eliza. "I'm so sorry, Eliza. I'm being insensitive to your predicament."

Eliza shrugged. "What's done is done. Your worst fears are my reality. But I've survived, and you will too." She plucked Stowy from the hammock and nuzzled the feline against her neck. Though she longed to know what horrible thing Angeline had done, it wouldn't be proper to ask. If she wished Eliza to know, she would tell her. "We've all made mistakes, done things we've regretted. People may not forgive us, but God does. He has taken care of me, and He will do the same for you."

Angeline gave a unladylike snort. "I'm afraid there are some things even God does not overlook." She fingered the lace fringing her neckline and gazed out the porthole.

"That's not true. There is nothing He cannot forgive. But He will have to reveal that to you in His time."

"You've been very kind to me, Eliza." Angeline's tone had the tenor of a farewell. Stowy reached for her from Eliza's arms, and she gathered him up and drew him to her chest.

"Seems you've made another friend, as well," Eliza said.

Angeline smiled and kissed Stowy on the head.

"Whatever happens"—Eliza touched her friend's arm—"you will always be welcome wherever I am." Though with no home, no family, and no prospects, she wouldn't tell the lady that might be the poorhouse.

"Thank you, Eliza." Angeline sniffed and waved her away. "Now, you go on. There are people who need you far more than I."

After hugging the lady, Eliza left and headed down the hall. Fear clambered up her throat—fear for Angeline, fear for the sick people below.

Fear for them all.

⚜

Eliza's stomach grumbled. Embarrassed, she pressed a hand over her belly and glanced over the assembled group: the doctor, Sarah with Lydia strapped to her chest, and two other passengers. That was everyone the doctor could find who was willing to fast their evening meal and come together to pray against the evil that had invaded the ship. Eliza had been disappointed not to see Blake. His quick dismissal of the power of prayer broke her heart. She knew the war had wounded his faith. What she hadn't realized was that it had ripped it from his soul.

The small group joined hands when a knock on the storage room preceded Moses who entered, floppy hat in hand. "D'you mind if I pray wid you?"

An uncomfortable silence was the man's only answer. One passenger, a farmer named Gresham, coughed and shifted his stance.

Moses turned to leave when Sarah stretched out her hand. "Of course, Moses. We'd love to have you."

James shifted a pointed gaze over the group. "Yes, we would."

"I ain't praying with no colored." Mr. Gresham's tone hardened, along with his jaw.

Moses froze. James closed his eyes. "God accepts all of His children, Mr. Gresham. If you do not, I suggest you leave."

Eliza raised her brows, pleased with the doctor's strong conviction and a bit embarrassed at her own hesitation. Most people had been raised to believe that Negroes were a lower breed of humanity, less capable, less intelligent. It would take some time for that mind-set to change. Yet she, of all people, should understand what it felt like to be judged for something that had nothing to do with who she really was on the inside.

Scowling, Mr. Gresham stomped out.

"And you, Mr. Bronson?" James asked.

"A prayer's a prayer. I don't suppose it matters who it comes from."

Moses hesitated, but at James's prompting, he finally joined the circle.

"Very well, let's pray, shall we?"

James proceeded to deliver the most eloquent yet powerful prayer Eliza had ever heard. He went on for at least twenty minutes, expounding the mercies and grace of God and praising Him for His goodness and love. He continued by thanking God for His power to answer prayer and His presence among them. Standing beside Eliza, Moses, filled the air with "amens," confirming the word James spoke and bringing a smile to Eliza's lips at the man's faithful exuberance.

Finally, James brought the prayer to a close. "And now, Father, we speak to the evil on board this ship, the evil that has caused so many to fall ill. And we command that evil, that sickness, to depart and never return, in the powerful name of Your Son, Jesus."

"Yes Lord!" Moses shouted, startling Eliza.

"We thank you for hearing our prayer, Father," James concluded. "Let Your will be done."

"Amens" parroted around the group as eyes opened. Eliza and Sarah wiped tears from their cheeks. The men nodded, smiling.

A heaviness seemed to lift. Eliza couldn't explain it, but the room, the air, seemed lighter, the heat less oppressive, the smell less offensive. Even the light from the single lantern seemed to glow brighter.

"God is here among us." James scanned the deckhead.

"I sense Him too, Mister James," Moses said.

Sarah seemed equally delighted, thanking God for making Himself known. Yet aside from the airy feeling, Eliza felt nothing. Oh how she envied their closeness to the Almighty.

Mr. Bronson clapped James on the back. "Never heard such a good prayer."

James smiled. "We know God heard us. Let us pray His answer comes swiftly."

And that it did! The very next day, Eliza noticed slight changes in most of the patients: their fevers were reduced, their breathing was steady, and some of the sick were able to eat. In the corner of the dark hold, the prayer team reassembled to thank God for His healing, lifting words of praise and worship. Overcome with joy, Eliza slipped away to see how the captain fared.

Now as she sat by his side in the big cabin, she noted that he, too, seemed much improved over yesterday. Color had returned to his weathered face, and he slept so peacefully, he hadn't heard her enter.

"Father, You healed everyone on board. Just like we asked." Eliza could hardly believe it. Yes, she believed in God, believed He could do whatever He wished, but she'd also seen so many prayers go unanswered. Her own, as well as a multitude of soldiers' prayers as they lay dying in a hospital.

Taking advantage of a moment alone, Eliza caressed the back of her neck and rubbed her tired eyes. She'd hardly slept in four nights, and her eyelids felt as if cannonballs sat atop them. Every movement renewed aches throughout her body, resurrecting memories of her time nursing the wounded right after a major battle. With the distant sound of cannons and muskets peppering the sky and the stench of blood and gun smoke saturating the air, bodies had poured into the tent hospital like some macabre theater of horrors. So many of them, Eliza had no idea where to start. Screams and moans and pleas for help assailed her from all around. Outstretched bloodied arms reached for her as she hurried past. She couldn't get to them all. She could never get to them all.

Blake halted and gazed at Eliza as she sat on the stool beside the captain's bed. With her head in her hands, rebellious trickles of silken hair dribbled about her face. Was she sleeping? Praying? He took a step toward her. She didn't move. The poor lady was no doubt beyond exhaustion, yet here she was checking on the captain, tending to a man who would have marooned her on an island without so much as a "by-your-leave."

Sunlight angled in from the stern windows, shifting over the captain's desk with each sway of the ship. Thank God they'd had good weather these past days and no ship sightings. Nothing Blake and the first mate couldn't handle alone. And now that they'd passed the fourteenth parallel, Blake had been sent down to inform the captain of their progress.

But he couldn't keep his gaze off Eliza. Sunlight sprinkled her hair with glittering amber and shimmered over the green sash tied about her coral-colored gown. He swallowed. She must be asleep, poor girl. Blake took another step forward, unable to resist staring at her when she was unaware, unguarded. With her face anchored in her hands, her lashes fluttered over her cheeks like dark ribbons on ivory sand.

He knelt beside her, studying her, wondering how such a caring lady could have betrayed her country, her family, her friends. Him. The planks creaked beneath his boot.

Her eyes popped open. "Oh!" She leaped from the stool and threw a hand to her throat, her chest heaving.

"I didn't mean to startle you." Blake stood.

She rubbed eyes that were firing with anger. "You have the audacity to stare at me inches from my face while I am asleep, and you didn't mean to startle me?"

"I was merely curious as to whether you had stopped breathing." He bit down the lie, for he could never reveal the truth. Nor could he reveal his overwhelming urge to take her in his arms and kiss away the pain and stress on her face.

"Sorry to disappoint you, Colonel." Her shoulders lowered, and she widened her eyes as if straining to keep them open. "I must have fallen asleep." She gathered an empty teacup and then leaned over to lay the back of her hand against the captain's cheek. Her locket dangled in the air—back and forth, back and forth—hypnotizing Blake. Or maybe it was her feminine scent.

"His fever has broken," she said.

"I hear everyone is recovering."

"Yes. God chased away the evil on board. It truly is a miracle."

Blake huffed and crossed arms over his chest. "If you say so, Mrs. Craw. . .Watts."

His use of her real name sent a rod through her spine. She raised her chin. "I do say so, Colonel. There is no other explanation." Zeal burned in her golden eyes.

"There is always another explanation," Blake said, regretting his combative tone. Blast it, he hadn't wanted to fight with her. Quite the opposite in fact. These past two weeks, his mind had been at war with both his emotions and his mouth. And though he had commanded a regiment, he seemed incapable of ordering them to task. He ran a hand through his hair and sighed. "You should go. Get some rest."

"Yes, I'm sure you find my presence bothersome." Clutching her skirts, she turned to leave.

Blake blinked at the woman's change in demeanor. Ever since her secret came to light, she'd been remorseful, sad. Now she had turned defiant, angry. For some reason, instead of igniting his anger, it brought a smile to his lips.

"Regardless, I thank you for caring for the sick these past few days. You've sacrificed much for people who wished you ill." He wanted to say something, anything to keep her from leaving.

Halting, she faced him, her eyes searching his. "I'm a nurse. It's what I do." She started to leave again but stopped. Her eyes dipped to his recently injured leg. "However, I owe you a great debt for wounding yourself on my account."

Blake blinked, studying her, his mind spinning. "How did you know?"

"I didn't." One corner of her lips raised in a delightful grin. "But it was quite a noble act."

Blake resisted the smile pushing against his lips. "No matter what you've done, I couldn't allow a woman to be in danger."

"It does seem that God wishes me to remain on your precious voyage." Anger laced her tone.

If her words were true, then Blake owed God a debt, for despite himself, despite his fury, despite his pain, he was glad Eliza was on board. He wanted her to stay on board. And he hated himself for it.

"Perhaps God wishes me to stay on at Brazil? Surely you will need a nurse."

His right leg ached, reminding him of the bullet wound he'd received at the siege of Petersburg. Reminding him that the lady's husband—the man with whom she'd shared a name, a home, a bed—was responsible for many of his soldiers' deaths, his friends' deaths, even his brother's. Guilt tore his recent sentiments for the lady to shreds.

Steeling himself against those luminous gold eyes, he stared at her. "God has no say in that, Mrs. Watts. You will head back to the States as soon as we reach Rio. And that's final."

She spun around and slammed out the door, but not before he saw her eyes moisten. Fisting his hands, Blake hung his head.

CHAPTER 23

$\mathscr{S}$teadying the hammock with one hand, Magnolia wiped a cool cloth over Hayden's head with her other. Hair the color of dark coffee fell away from his moist face, once tanned and healthy, now pale and blotched in red. Most of the other patients had awakened and were recovering from the terrible illness that had plagued half the ship's passengers.

All except Hayden Gale.

Why Magnolia cared, she had no idea. The man was obnoxious beyond all toleration. Obviously of low birth and morals. Uneducated. Uncouth. Mercy me, he was a stowaway! Probably a thief and murderer. Or worse, a ravisher of innocent women. Which she was still certain was the reason for his presence in her cabin when they'd first set out from Charleston. It mattered not that he had a bullet in his side; his kind didn't allow such trivial matters to keep them from their lecherous desires. She dabbed his cheeks as her gaze took in his masculine features. Dark stubble circled his mouth and sped a trail up his jaw where sideburns reached just below his ears. A strong Roman nose, prominent cheeks, and brows and lashes as dark as night completed the noble visage.

"I suppose you *are* handsome in a provincial, boorish sort of way," she breathed out. Actually, now that the man was asleep and not assailing her with his sarcastic quips, he did remind her of someone. A man equally as handsome but with a heart as dark and fiery as Hades itself. She gulped the memory away.

Her association with that man had cost her everything.

The ship canted, and Magnolia clung to the hammock. Cheery voices rose around her from recovering passengers as they ate their noon meal of hardtack soaked in chicken broth. But why not Hayden? Dipping the cloth into a bucket, she wrung it out and pressed it on his chapped lips. Something about the man intrigued her. His mysterious past, his wolfish good looks, or was it the way he looked at her when he thought she took no note?

"Yes, you are quite a fascinating man, Hayden Gale. What brought you to our ship? What secrets do you hold in that handsome head of yours?"

"Wouldn't you like to know?"

Magnolia gasped and snapped her hand back.

One eye open, he peered at her as a grin quirked the edge of his lips.

"How dare you? How long have you been awake?" Magnolia stomped her foot on the moist deck, the hollow thud muffling the impact she intended.

Hayden opened his other eye. "Long enough to know that you find me handsome and fascinating."

"Ohhhhhh!" Magnolia tossed the cloth on his face. He snatched it away, but his grin remained.

She narrowed her eyes. "It isn't polite to listen in on other people's thoughts. And besides, I was just being nice. They say people can hear things even when they are delirious with fever, and since you hadn't woken up like the others, I thought saying something nice—though it carried not a speck of truth—would help you recover quicker. That's all. Oh mercy me, don't look at me like that! I'm telling the truth. You are a true cad, you know." She planted her hands on her hips. "What do you have to say for yourself? Stop smiling at me!"

Hayden instantly forced a frown, though laughter twinkled in his eyes. "How can I get a word in with all your blabbering?"

"Uhhhh!" Magnolia grabbed the rag and dropped it into the bucket. "You are the most infuriating man."

"Yet you are still here."

"Magnolia Scott!" The commanding voice filled the hold, drawing all gazes to Magnolia's father as he stormed down the middle aisle, handkerchief over his nose. "Your mother and I forbade you to tend to the sick in this cesspool." His outraged glance took in the hammocks then the crates and barrels lining the hold. "This is beneath your station. Simply beneath you!"

Magnolia closed her eyes, wishing she could disappear, mortified that her father continued to berate her in front of everyone.

"And look at you! You're a mess. Stains on your dress, hair jumbled like a bird's nest, and what is that?" She could feel his breath on her neck. "Perspiration!" He said the word as if it weren't a natural condition, as if she'd purposely bathed herself in sweat to offend him.

She opened her eyes to see Hayden gazing at her with pity.

She hated pity. Especially from someone like him. "Papa, I like helping the sick. It makes me feel useful."

"Useful, humph." He grabbed her arm. "Come with me. Your mother is feeling better and is asking for you. If you want to feel useful, attend to your own."

Magnolia glanced over the myriad eyes staring at her with sympathy—eyes of the patients, Eliza, Sarah, and the doctor—as her father dragged her like a ragamuffin up the ladder. Would she ever be free of her debt to him?

⚜

Within three days, nearly all the sick on board had fully recovered and everyone was back to their normal routines. Though shipboard life could be incredibly dull, Eliza discovered that after all they'd endured, she quite enjoyed the mundane pace. Now, at the starboard railing, she looked in awe of the most beautiful sky she'd ever seen. A pearly ribbon circumscribed the horizon. On it rested a broad belt of vermilion, interspersed with streaks of gold, followed by a swath of bright cream that extended to a delicate pale blue. Another day had dawned, and Eliza thanked God that the horizon was not only stunning but clear. No storms, no weird mist, and no pursuing ships. At this rate, they should sight the coast of Brazil within a day or two. A warm breeze flowed over her, fluttering her hair and casting a pinkish hue into the air. She glanced up to see red powder dusting the windward side of the sails and rigging.

"African sand, Mrs. Crawford," Captain Barclay said as he joined her. "At least that's what I've heard it called." Sunlight accentuated the lines on his face and sparkled silver in his beard. "Always see it at this latitude sailing windward of the islands."

"What causes it?" Eliza feigned a casual tone, though she was glad the man actually spoke to her.

He shrugged. "Just dust saturatin' the atmosphere. All the way from Africa they say."

"Well, it is very pretty. It's as if God were painting us with vibrant color."

He scratched his whiskers then dropped his gaze to his boots. "I wanted to thank you, Mrs. Crawford, for helpin' the sick on board, and for tendin' to me as well. The doc told me what you did."

"It was my pleasure, Captain."

She had barely finished her sentence when Captain Barclay turned and charged back across the deck. Despite his abrupt departure, Eliza was warmed by his attention. In fact, as she glanced over the ship, several passengers met her gaze with a nod or a smile, not with the loathing glances of before. James stood by the foredeck talking with Angeline and Sarah. The Scotts sat together on chairs beneath a sailcloth while Mable attended to their every need. Mr. Dodd, thumbs stuck in his waistcoat pocket, talked to a group of passengers about his favorite subject—gold. At the far end of the foredeck, Delia and Moses laughed as Delia's children dashed across the deck. The Jenkins's little girl, Henrietta, gazed up at them from the main deck as if she wished to join them. And Mr. Graves stood at the stern smoking a cigar and staring into the frothy water bubbling off the back of the ship.

Even Hayden smiled at Eliza as he made his way to Angeline. Halting before the lady, he said something and proffered his elbow. She hesitated, glanced at James and Sarah as if obtaining their permission, then slipped her arm through his. Both Magnolia's and the doctor's gazes followed them as they took a turn around the deck.

Blake stood at the bow of the ship staring straight ahead as if he could make Brazil rise from the ocean by sheer will. If anyone could move continents purely by resolve, it was him. She'd never met a more bullheaded man. He glanced over his shoulder, and their eyes met, but he quickly turned back around. If only his heart would soften like the others' hearts, perhaps she could convince him to allow her to stay in Brazil.

"Oh Lord, let it be Your will." For she didn't know how she'd survive back home. Yet wasn't it like her to ask God to conform to what she wanted? Or worse, to go ahead and do what she wanted and then ask God to bless it? Oh fiddle. She would try to change. She truly would.

Closing her eyes, she tilted her face to the sun, basking in its warmth. It was far too pleasant a day to think of past mistakes. There had been no ill tidings since the deadly mist, no freak accidents, no inclement weather. Perhaps their luck was about to change. She felt rather than heard someone slip beside her. The spicy scent of cigar smoke swept past her nose, and she tensed, knowing she would find Mr. Graves close by. Sure enough, when she opened her eyes, the politician stood not a foot away. His smile lacked the warmth of most people's. In fact, it chilled her to the bone.

"Good morning, Mr. Graves."

He leaned an elbow on the railing. Pink dusted his black hair, giving it a mahogany sheen. "You astound me, madam."

"How so?"

"You care for people who would just as soon throw you to the sharks as look at you." Yet his tone was not one of astonishment but more of disappointment.

"Regardless of their sentiments or intentions," Eliza said, "it isn't right to allow them to suffer."

He cocked his head and studied her as if she were an anomaly. Yet his frown remained. In fact, his intense perusal forced her gaze back out to sea. Perhaps if she got to know him a bit better, he wouldn't frighten her so.

"Where are you from, Mr. Graves?"

"Northern Maryland." He puffed on his cigar.

"Do you still have family there?"

Wind tore puffs of smoke from his lips before he'd had a chance to exhale. "My mother and father are dead, if that's what you're asking, madam." His tone was one of annoyance. "Murdered in their beds by Yankee soldiers."

Wonderful. Someone else on board who had every reason to hate her. "I'm sorry." The words fell impotent from her lips.

"My father was a senator from Maryland, only recently retired," he continued. "I was to take his place, you see. I'd been trained to do so my entire life."

"You were running for the Senate?"

"Yes." His black eyes brightened for the first time since she'd known him. "And doing quite well, I might add." But then his expression soured, and he peered down his nose at her. "That is until the South ceded from the Union and all my dreams were obliterated."

He stroked his black goatee and stared out to sea. "I was to eventually run for president, you see. It was all planned from my birth. Every moment, every second of my life was spent working toward that single endeavor."

The ship rose on a swell, and Eliza gripped the railing, thinking how strict and disciplined and terribly unhappy his childhood would have been. Even now, a dour cloak seemed to cling to the man.

"Why did you not remain behind, Mr. Graves? Surely you can still run for president."

Eyebrows as thick and dark as night bent together as his chortle filled the air. "A Southerner as president? That will not happen in my lifetime. No, the war changed everything."

"Then perhaps you need a new dream, Mr. Graves."

Taking one last puff on his cigar, he flicked it into the sea. "There is no other dream." The veins in his neck pulsed. "But I do have plans to rectify my reputation." He twisted a gaudy ring on his finger, drawing Eliza's gaze to the tiny golden snakes that formed the band.

Her blood ran cold. Part of her wanted to ask him what plans. Part of her didn't want to know. "I do hope they are good plans, Mr. Graves. For the good of the colony. Perhaps you can run for office once we get established."

"Ah yes, it is all about power, isn't it?"

Eliza flinched at the insinuation. "I beg to differ, sir. It's about service to one's community."

"Bah. That's what they tell you, but it's the power most politicians are after."

"Is that what you are after?"

He shrugged. "Of course. But one can use power for good."

True. But too often those who yearned for power weren't good at heart. Eliza remained silent, wishing the disturbing man would leave.

A few moments of silence passed, ushered by with the rustle of water against the hull.

"I sense in you a rebellion against authority, Mrs. Crawford."

Eliza swallowed. How could he know that? "I have had my problems obeying orders."

His smile was brighter than she'd ever seen it. "Perhaps we are more alike than you think."

Not wanting to consider that option, Eliza asked, "How can one so obsessed with power approve of rebellion?"

"Only by rebellion can you obtain power, no? Look at Lucifer. Once he was merely an archangel. Now, he rules an entire kingdom."

A shiver coiled down her back. "A dark, evil kingdom."

"A kingdom, nonetheless."

CHAPTER 24

$\mathscr{B}$lake woke to the ominous *rat-tat-tat* of drums. War drums. Drums that signaled his troops were on the march. Drums that meant they were about to face the enemy. Scrambling from his hammock, he nearly toppled to the deck in a frenzy to find his sword and pistol. Shadows leaped at him from all around. He batted them away, groping for his weapons. His men needed him. Were they already on the field? How had he overslept? A moan sounded. He swerved. Shapes formed in the darkness. A hammock swung to the rhythm of creaking wood.

"Another nightmare, my friend?" James's groggy voice carved a trail of reason through Blake's delirium. He rubbed his eyes as the bulkhead, the hammocks, the tiny desk and chair took shape and form. Drawing a deep breath, he ran a hand through his sleep-tousled hair.

"Sorry for waking you yet again."

Thump thump thump sounded from above. Voices blared. One glance out the porthole told Blake it was still dark. Something wasn't right. Jumping into his trousers, he hefted suspenders over his shoulders, grabbed his pistol, and flew out the door. Ignoring the pain in his leg, he sprang up the ladder and emerged on deck to a warm breeze and a starlit sky. Instead of harried screams, spirited laughter met his ears as the crew darted back and forth gathering something off the deck. Fish. Blake tried to focus in the dim light of a single lantern. An object flew over the railing. He leaped out of the way. It landed by his feet with a thud. A fish. But no. A bird. No. A fish with wings. Blake closed his eyes. He must still be in his nightmare. Either that or he'd gone completely mad.

"Well, I'll be." The astonishment in James's voice reassured Blake of his sanity. He opened his eyes to see his friend, loose shirt suspended over his chest, sword at the ready, gaping at the odd scene.

"You see them too?" Blake had to be sure.

James slapped him on the back. "God is raining fish, my friend!" Then setting his sword aside, he rushed to join the melee.

Stooping, Blake picked up the wriggling fish by its tail and examined it.

"Flying fish. They're attracted to the lanterns at night," Captain Barclay shouted from the quarterdeck. He rubbed his hands together. "We'll be eatin' well for supper."

Blake laughed and shook his head, depositing the fish into a bucket one of the sailors held out to him.

"Ain't it a miracle, Colonel?" the man said.

"Indeed." Though Blake would hardly label it so. A freak of nature perhaps, but a miracle? Why would God send fish when clearly all the disasters He'd allowed proved He intended them nothing but harm?

After helping the crew gather the suicidal fish, Blake went below and finished dressing then spent the day assisting the captain and his officers with the sailing of the brig. Now, as evening descended, he took a position at the side rail, enjoying the unusually fair weather they'd been having recently. Temperatures ranged in the seventies to eighties from day to night. And with a fair wind and calm sea, Blake hoped their troubles were behind them.

His troubles, however, did not seem to be at an end, for he could not get Eliza out of his mind. It didn't help that she recently came above looking beyond lovely in her cream-colored gown, its skirt split at the front and back to reveal a lavender petticoat beneath. Nor that her complexion glowed fresh and healthy from sea and sun. Neither did it help to hear her sweet voice as she giggled in glee watching the flying fish that were still swimming around the brig. Though they no longer jumped aboard, schools of fifty to one hundred kept pace with the ship on either side of the bow, skipping over surface like swallows looking for flies. Fascinating creatures, to be sure.

"I can hardly believe they are not birds," Eliza said to Angeline and Sarah as others gathered around to watch.

Pushing from the railing, Blake made his way to the other side of the ship as far away from Eliza as possible. The smell of roasting fish sent his empty stomach convulsing, and he had to admit that as interesting as the creatures were, he was rather looking forward to having one for supper. The deck heaved. He staggered and gathered a steady grip on the railing. Salty spray covered his face, leaving a touch of cool refreshment as he gazed at the stunning sunset. Above him, blue sky bled into swirling emerald and maroon at the horizon where the sun spanned its golden wings over a cobalt sea.

"No one can deny the existence of God when looking at such beauty." James joined him.

Blake grew tired of the man's constant talk of God. "And what can one deny when they gaze upon severed limbs and spilt entrails upon the battlefield?" His tone was caustic, and he regretted speaking.

James merely smiled. "One cannot deny that mankind is fallen and in desperate need of salvation."

"Then why didn't God save us? Why didn't He stop the war, all the killing?"

"Because He gave mankind a wonderful yet dangerous gift." James leaned on the railing and gazed at the foam riding high on the hull, his mood somber. "Free will. We are the ones who start wars, not God."

Blake shook his head. "But God could still intervene if He wanted to."

James rubbed the scar on his cheek and shrugged. "Yes, He could. But then we would be nothing but puppets in His hand with no will of our own. No choices to make. Like the North inflicting their will on us, telling us how to live our lives, stripping us of our power, our freedom to decide. Is that the kind of God you want to serve?"

In truth, Blake didn't want to serve any God. Yet James's last description was exactly how Blake had always thought of the Almighty—a strict ruler in the heavens toying with mankind for His own pleasure. It stunned him to consider He might be a more benign sovereign who actually cared enough to give man his freedom. "Still, God could stop us from making bad choices and just allow us to make good ones."

James's lips slanted in skepticism.

Blake sighed. "But that wouldn't be free will either, I suppose."

"I believe it hurts God a great deal to see us suffer from our bad decisions. Which is why He sent His Son to endure all the consequences, the punishment due us for our sinful choices. But love isn't love if it's forced. That's true slavery." James stared out to sea. "Someday He will set all things right. In the meantime, we should try to choose more wisely."

Blake huffed. "I should have brought you along as preacher, not doctor."

"If you are offering me the position, I gladly accept." James held up his hands. "Especially since these are useless for doctoring." He gripped the rail with those hands that were now steady as solid oak. "Thank God, Eliza is still with us."

Blake cringed at the sound of her name. "Don't get used to having her skills. I still intend to send her back."

"And have no nurse or doctor?"

"We have your knowledge. Someone else can follow your instructions until I can find a replacement."

"Not if I can't watch the surgery."

Voices drew Blake around to see the lady in question strolling across the deck with Sarah and Angeline. No longer did people steer clear of her. In fact, several spoke directly to her, including a few of the farmers' wives, and the blacksmith's wife. Even Mrs. Scott acknowledged her in passing.

James arched one eyebrow, his eyes twinkling. "Perhaps we should put her fate to another vote?"

Eliza took a seat on one of the chairs the sailors had brought above for the ladies. She smiled at Angeline perched on one side and Sarah and baby Lydia on the other and then glanced over the happy group, chatting and laughing as children wove to and fro among people, barrels, and chairs strewn across the deck. Platters of fish were passed among the throng, along with bowls of biscuits and dried bananas. For the first time in two weeks, Eliza's heart felt a pinch lighter. Dare she say, even hopeful?

Even the enigmatic Mr. Graves, who normally stood afar watching everyone, joined the festive crowd, smoking his cigar and piling food on his plate. Beside him, the liquor-loving carpenter, Mr. Lewis, consumed his meal with exuberance. His fiddle lay at his feet ready to serenade the passengers and crew after dinner. Moses gathered several plates in hand and returned to the foredeck where his sister and her children ate by themselves. Eliza wondered how long it would be before the group accepted him. Or if they ever would. Yet despite the possibility that nothing might change for him in Brazil, the man always wore a smile and gave glory to God.

Eliza's eye caught Max's, gaping at her from the quarterdeck, a hungry look on his face that she surmised had nothing to do with the food. Shifting her gaze away, she found the baker whose wife had died of the mysterious illness, standing at the starboard railing, staring blankly into the darkening shadows. Eliza longed to comfort him but knew she was the last person he wished to see. Besides, she'd seen James speaking with him earlier, perhaps even praying with him, as she'd noted their heads dipped together.

Lanterns hanging on the main and foremasts cast shifting braids of light over the scene with each movement of the ship. Above them a curtain of clouds hid the usual parade of sparkling stars from view. Speaking of hiding, Blake stood across the deck, as far away from Eliza as he could get without falling overboard, James at his side. After a few moments, the doctor stepped forward and tapped his spoon on a mug, stifling the chatter and drawing all eyes toward him. "Bow for the blessing, if you please."

Mr. Lewis covered his mouthful of food in shame, drawing chuckles from the crowd as all eyes closed. James proceeded to bless the food and thank God for the bounty and the good weather and for God's healing and His careful watch over them.

"Amens" rang across the deck, along with the clank of spoon and fork on tin plates.

"I've never had flying fish before." Angeline nibbled on a piece. "It's quite good."

"I'm sure to love it as long as it isn't chicken." Eliza giggled and sampled a bite, delighting in the subtle nutty flavor as a heavy gust flung strands of hair into her face. Brushing them aside, she wondered where the wind had come from. Only moments before, the air had been so calm. Even the dash of water against the hull seemed to heighten in tone and volume. Yet no one appeared to notice.

"A veritable feast!" Mr. Dodd exclaimed from across the main deck. "And a sign of good fortune to come." He raised his glass.

To which others raised their glasses and shouted in agreement.

Sarah gazed lovingly at Lydia snuggled against her breast.

"She's a good baby." Eliza sipped her water. "She hardly cries at night anymore."

"She's a happy baby." Sarah smiled. "I am thankful she doesn't disturb your sleep too much." She ran a finger over Lydia's plump cheek. "She looks so much like her father."

It was only the second time Sarah had spoken of him. But the sorrow in her voice forbade Eliza to question her further. Instead, she bit into a piece of hard banana. The sweet crunchy flavor burst in her mouth, reminding her of Mrs. Tom's peach pie back home. She wondered if the woman still cooked for her family's hotel in Marietta. And if she still made those delectable pies and cakes Eliza enjoyed so much. The ones Papa and she had shared so often together. The one and only thing they had in common. Memories both sweet and sour flooded her much like the sweet and salty taste filling her mouth. She would never enjoy those pies again. Nor ever see her father.

"Magnolia Scott!" Mr. Scott's bellow brought all eyes to the overbearing plantation owner as he drew his daughter aside with a stiff hand and bent his head toward hers, eyes aflame.

"Poor girl," Sarah said.

"Cruel father," Angeline added with such spite, it jarred Eliza.

"Did you have a difficult father?" Sarah asked her.

"No, my parents were wonderful." She glanced down at the plate in her lap. "My father was. I never knew my mother. She died giving birth to me."

"I'm sorry." The deck canted, and Eliza clutched the edge of her plate to keep it from falling off her lap. Others did not fare so well as clanks and clinks followed by groans bounced over the deck. She glanced up to assess the damage and found Hayden staring at Angeline from his position by the starboard railing. Not just staring, seemingly mesmerized by her. Eliza leaned toward her friend. "I believe you have an admirer."

Angeline followed her gaze to the handsome man, her face pinking. "I hope not. He's agreeable enough, albeit a bit mysterious, but I didn't come on this voyage to find a husband." In defiance of her statement, her eyes searched the ship as if looking for someone. But then her smile instantly snapped into a tight line, and she lowered her chin. Eliza looked up to see Dodd staring at her with neither the same attraction nor the interest of Hayden. But rather a look of puzzlement, coupled with a hint of contempt.

Angeline coughed and drew in a shredded breath.

"Whatever is wrong, Angeline?" Eliza handed her a cup of water. "Here, drink this."

"Nothing. It's nothing." She took a sip, her quivering hand nearly spilling the fluid. She set her plate and cup on the deck and pressed fingers on her forehead. "I'm not feeling well."

"So sudden?" Eliza stared at her quizzically then back at Dodd, whose gaze had not left the lady. Whether he recognized her from somewhere or not, it wasn't polite to stare. Setting down her own plate, Eliza intended to march over there and tell him just that when Angeline stayed her with a touch. More like a tight grip on her arm. Fear blazed in her eyes as she shook her head. "Please don't."

"I don't know why you fear him or what happened between you," Eliza said. "But at the very least, he should be instructed on proper decorum. I can have the colonel speak to him if you'd like."

Angeline swallowed. "No, please. Let it be."

"Very well." Eliza sat back, noting that Dodd had the audacity to continue staring at the lady, though her discomfort was obvious to all. Tearing her gaze from him, Eliza turned to tell Angeline that if she'd only confide in her, maybe Eliza could help, but a large crack, like the snapping of a giant whip, split the sky above. Then without warning, rain gushed on them as if they'd sailed under a faucet. Eliza assisted Sarah and her baby toward the main hatch, where people, hunched over, fled in mass. She only hoped this new storm wasn't a portent of another coming disaster.

CHAPTER 25

$\mathcal{B}$lake darted across the sodden deck to the railing as fast as his wounded leg would allow. Screening his eyes from the sun, he peered into the distant haze, looking for any sign that the "Land ho" he'd just heard from the crosstrees was indeed true. He glanced over his shoulder to see the captain raise a telescope to his eye and peer through it for what seemed an eternity before he shouted, "Land indeed. We have reached Brazil, gentlemen!"

Clapping and cheering ensued as passengers and crew alike sped to the railings vying for a glimpse of their new home. Blake couldn't help but give his own cheer. After the downpour last night, he had his doubts they'd ever find Brazil. And though they still had several miles to traverse to get to Rio, just the sight of land helped ease his spirit that they were going to make it after all.

Eliza threw a hand to her aching head. She'd heard the cries of land an hour ago and should have risen from her bed—hammock—along with Angeline and Sarah, but she hadn't slept a wink last night. Instead, she'd done nothing but wrestle with the itchy canvas and tangle her sheets into a hopeless knot. Tossing that knot aside, she climbed out of her hammock, her bare feet landing on the deck with a thump. Though she had no interest in viewing a land she would never enjoy, perhaps it was better to go above than to lie here and feel her frustration rise along with the heat.

Ah, what she wouldn't give for a proper toilette: a basin of freshwater scented with lavender, a bar of soap, cucumber cream for her dry skin, her favorite heliotrope perfume, powder to scrub her teeth, a proper mirror, and a maid to comb the tangles out of her hair. Ah yes, and a bath! But all she had was a simple comb, a small mirror, and a bowl of stale water that smelled worse than she did. After doing her best to freshen up and pin up her hair, Eliza dressed and rose onto the main deck to the glare of a full sun and fresh morning breeze.

The first thing she saw nearly sent her scrambling back below.

Blake cradled Lydia in his arms. The tiny baby appeared no bigger than a mouse against his rounded biceps and wide chest. Yet the adoring look in his eyes as he glanced down at her, and the awkwardness in his stance, as if the babe were made of porcelain made Eliza weak in the knees. He gently eased Lydia back to her mother, and Eliza turned lest he see her staring at him.

Making her way to the foredeck, she stopped to glimpse Brazil. There it was. Naught but a flea on the ocean's back, yet the passengers pointed and "oohed" and "ahhed" as if it were Shangri-la itself. All but two of them—Angeline, who stood off by herself, and Mr. Graves, who leaned on the capstan looking as morose as if a relative had died. Eliza was just about to join Angeline when she saw James slip beside the girl and offer her a smile.

Good. If anyone could cheer her up, it would be the doctor. Gripping the railing, Eliza allowed the stiff breeze to wash over her, wishing it would wash away her troubles as well. Above, the sun flung glitter over the earth, turning the sea into silvery ribbons and the distant land into shimmering emeralds.

"Beautiful, isn't it?" Blake's voice sent her heart leaping and plunging at the same time.

She drew a deep breath and gave him a sly glance. "Do be careful, Colonel, fraternizing with the enemy will not look good on your record."

A slight grin tugged at his lips. "I fear my record is already tarnished beyond repair."

"I doubt that. I would guess you served with distinction."

"It depends which side you were on." His melancholy tone defied the humor of his words.

A gust of wind brought his scent to her nose. All spice and male. Unable to resist, she drew in a deep breath, trying to implant the memory of it on her senses. "And no, I do not find the land beautiful, since I am forbidden to set foot upon it."

"You have no one to blame but yourself, Mrs. *Watts*." The lines on his forehead deepened.

Tired of his blatant hostility, Eliza faced him, planting a hand at her waist. "Have you come to torture me, Blake, or is there a reason you suffer my presence?"

A shimmer of amusement crossed his gray eyes before he frowned. "I came to tell you that you are not to disembark in Rio de Janeiro. I will lead the colonists ashore to a hotel the emperor has prepared for us where I will sign the appropriate paperwork and inquire about a loan for the land. Then, if all goes well, we will return to the ship, and Barclay will sail us to our new home before you leave for the States."

"And what if it doesn't go well? What if the emperor won't lend you the money for land? Then what?"

"Then we take a vote on whether to stay and work for the money or head home." Blake said. "Either way, you will return to the States. Is that clear?"

The ship slid down the trough of a wave, and Eliza felt her heart sink with it. She knew he hated her. But she had hoped that hatred had softened a bit. "Never fear, I will not tarnish your paradise with one touch of my traitorous toe."

"Good." He clipped out and stiffened his jaw.

Eliza turned her back to him, not wanting him to see the moisture clouding her eyes. A dark blotch appeared in her blurry vision. Blinking, she focused on a strange mass that rose from the land lining the horizon. At first only a dot, it grew larger and larger as it headed their way. Blake saw it too. Lengthening his stance, he gripped the railing and stared at the anomaly. Several of the crew and passengers joined him, some pointing, some questioning, others heading below.

"What is it?" Eliza asked.

Blake didn't answer. Instead, he glanced at the captain and his officers on the quarterdeck, who seemed equally puzzled. Captain Barclay pressed a telescope to his eye. "Birds!" he shouted. "Birds!"

Eliza spun back around to see that the cloud had separated into distinct dots—flying dots. Birds, yes. She could make them out now. They looked like seagulls. Thousands of them. Sailors stared wide-eyed. Some crossed themselves.

"Grab your muskets and pistols!" the captain bellowed.

Muskets and pistols? Eliza wondered what all the fuss was about. They were just birds after all. . .

But then the flock rushed the ship like an army at battle. The beating of their wings thundered overhead. *Thwump thwump thwump.* Alarm rippled through her. Her breath stuck in her throat. Sunlight fled as the birds landed on yards and stays and railings, squawking and cawing as if scolding the ship for daring to come so close to land.

Sailors scrambled down from aloft and darted across the deck in such a frenzy one would think they were being attacked by pirates. Others came above, pistols in hand.

Blake pulled a man aside. "What's going on?"

"Spirits of departed sailors come for revenge." The sailor's wide eyes skittered to and fro.

"Rubbish," Blake snapped, but the man tore from his grasp and jumped down an open hatch.

"They'll sink us, they will," Max yelled, his face redder than usual. "They're jealous of our life and will try to take it from us."

The remaining passengers fled below. Eliza should join them, but her feet appeared to be melded to the deck. Still more birds came. Their squawking grew louder, the flap of their wings more chaotic. Eliza covered her ears against the thunderous sound.

"Fire at will!" Captain Barclay shouted.

A huge bird landed on the railing beside her, spreading its wings and emitting a heinous screech from a triangular beak nearly as large as its body. Shrieking, Eliza jumped back with a start and bumped into Blake.

His arms encircled her. Two birds dove for them. She cringed as Blake pulled her to the deck and hunched his body atop hers.

She didn't have time to consider his protective actions. The air crackled with the *pop pop pop* of musket fire. *Pop pop pop!* Shrieks spiraled across the sky, followed by thuds and splashes as birds fell to deck and water.

Blake's arms tightened around Eliza. The rough stubble on his chin scratched her cheek. His breath filled the space between them. His tight muscles encased her in a protective cocoon, spinning her heart and mind into a jumble of confusion and ecstasy. Despite the fear, despite the birds, she never wanted to leave.

Then he stiffened. He gripped her shoulders and groaned. Eliza turned to peer at him. His eyes were clamped shut, his lips moving. His chest rose and fell like storm swells. He squeezed her arms. "No! No! No! To the ground, men. Drop to the ground!" he shouted, his expression twisting. Sweat broke out on his forehead as he tightened his hold on Eliza.

"It's all right, Blake. You're on a ship. Not in battle."

Yet the incessant cracking of pistols and thump of dead birds defied her statement. One of the feral beasts landed right beside them. A single vacant eye stared up at Eliza.

Releasing her, Blake began to thrash. "Retreat! Retreat!" Eliza threw her arms around him and held on tight. It was the only thing she could think to do. "Shhh, shhh. Wake up, Blake. It's over now. The war is over."

His eyes popped open. Horror sprang from their depths. "They're dead. They are all dead!" He palmed his forehead and growled in agony. Eliza clutched his arms, trying to get him to look at her. But he fell to the deck in a heap.

⁘

Angeline stood at the stern railing. The eye of a full moon stared at her from just above the horizon, watching her, assessing her with a detached curiosity born to those beings that existed beyond the vain, hollow condition of man. Or woman. Satisfying its curiosity, or perhaps just growing bored in the attempt, it continued to rise upon its nightly throne, flinging silvery lace on the ebony sea and over the wake bubbling off the back of the ship.

Wind whipped over the railing, flapping her collar and sending loose strands of hair flailing about her head. She shivered and hugged herself, ignoring the single tear that broke free from her eyes.

Memories she could not escape seeped into her blurred vision. Male faces, young and old, their eyes filled with desire. Drunken laughter, salacious grunts and groans, hands groping, touching places no one should. Pain, shame, waking to the smell of stale alcohol and bad breath.

Wanting to die.

Then do it. End the pain.

The whisper floated on the wind, swirling around her. Wiping her face, she glanced over her shoulder. No one was there. No one save the quartermaster at the wheel, the night watchman on the foredeck, and Mr. Graves shrouded in a cloud of gloom and cigar smoke at the larboard railing. She faced the sea.

She was alone. So alone.

"Oh Papa, why did you have to die? You were all I had in the world." More tears fell, cooled by a wind that pushed them across her cheeks to dampen her hair. "Why did you have to leave me with Uncle John?"

But what good did it do to think of the past? It was over. Finished. She couldn't change it any more than she could change what she had done.

Or what she had become.

The only question that remained was could she live with the shame—with the pain—anymore? A question that had repeatedly driven her from her hammock in the middle of the night. A question that must now be answered once and for all, lest the uncertainty of it slowly eat away at her until there was nothing left of her soul.

It was only a matter of time before Mr. Dodd told someone about her. And the illusion of her virtue would disappear, along with all her newfound friends. Then the looks would begin—the looks of scorn from the women and lust from the men. And the innuendos would start, the winks and suggestive glances, the nighttime visits. And if they ever discovered the rest of her tale, they'd lock her up below. Or cast her from the colony like they'd done to Eliza.

All hope drained from her and washed away with the foamy wake trailing behind the ship.

She'd been a fool to think she could run away from her past. That she could leave it behind in the States. Like a ball and chain fettered to her ankle, she had dragged it on board with her. She would never be free.

Unless. . .

Yes, end it all. It's the only way to find peace.

Glistening onyx waves beckoned her from another world. A watery world where all was tranquil. Where the voices would not taunt her. Where no one would point accusing fingers her way. Where no one would lock her behind bars. Peace. Freedom.

Come. . .come to me and be free!

A cool mist moistened her skin and sent goose bumps skittering up her arms. She balanced herself over the heaving deck and gazed over the sea. Dark clouds had swallowed up the gleam of the moon and the shimmer of waves, making everything dull and lifeless.

Slipping off her shoes, she sat on the railing and eased her legs over the side. Twenty feet below, froth seethed off the back of the ship and disappeared into the dark waters. Just like she would do. She trembled. It was better this way.

Do it!

Her pain would end. No one need know.

"God, forgive me." She drew one last breath and slipped off the bulwark.

CHAPTER 26

A line of defeated troops trudged across Blake's brain. He raised an arm to rub his temples, but his head felt as heavy as a cannon, and he dropped to the bed again, mission thwarted. The creak of wood and gush of water reminded him he was on a ship. The feel of the lumpy cot beneath him told him he must be in the sick bay.

The troops in his head fired another round of humiliation into his memory. Ah yes, he'd had one of his episodes. And once again in front of Eliza and God knew who else. No doubt the entire crew. He moaned, more from shame than pain. Pain he could deal with.

Soft fingers slipped through his. Like threads of silk against burlap, they eased over his rough skin, bringing him more comfort than he cared to admit.

Eliza.

He peeked at her through slits. Waves of maple-colored hair tumbled over her shoulders and down the front of her gown. She squeezed his hand and cradled it between her own; then lifting it to her lips, she placed a gentle kiss on his fingers.

Blake swallowed at her tender display.

Releasing a heavy sigh, she gazed at him, her golden eyes filled with concern, even fear.

Fear. The birds! The shots. Had she been hurt?

He snapped his eyes open. She jerked back, releasing his hand.

"The birds. Are you injured?" he asked.

She shook her head. "They are gone. Those that weren't killed, the sailors chased away." She dropped a rag into a basin. "It's nearly midnight. You slept a long while."

Blake's body relaxed as his gaze took in the room. At least they were alone. No one else was here to witness his weakness. No one but the one person he least wanted to see him in this feeble condition.

"Who else saw?"

"Only one of the sailors." Her voice was tender, reassuring. "He helped bring you below after you blacked out."

Blast it! Renewed pounding assailed his head, and Blake squeezed the bridge of his nose. "What kind of a leader can I be when I swoon like some limp-hearted female?"

She quirked a brow.

"No offense meant, Eliza."

She gave a tiny smile, no doubt at his use of her common name. A slip on his part. "You're suffering from the war," she said. "It will pass in time."

Blake tried to rise but thought better of it when dizziness struck him. "My last battle was over a year ago. Have you seen other soldiers recover?"

"No."

"Then don't shower me with your empty platitudes, Mrs. Watts."

She swallowed and fingered the locket around her neck. Blake felt like a louse. He remembered the tender way she had kissed his hand while she thought he was asleep. The way she'd gazed at him like no woman ever had. The way it sent an unwelcome thrill through him. "You are kind to tend to me."

"You protected me from the birds." She smiled.

"So, we are even."

"That's not why I'm here, and you know it."

He didn't want to think about why she was here, caring for him, loving him with her eyes. "Ah yes, your obligation to tend to the sick and injured."

She rose and picked up the basin of water sitting beside the bed. "Of course. What else?" Her jaw tightened, and she moved to the side table. "You should rest, Colonel. These episodes tax you, I'm sure."

She was going to leave. He couldn't blame her. But despite his anger, he didn't want her to go. Straining against the throb in his head, he sat and swung his legs over the side of the cot. "Regardless, I thank you."

"As you pointed out so succinctly, there is no need." Her tone was curt.

"Yet you care for a man who is determined to send you home." And who had earlier made a point of telling her just that in rather harsh and certain terms.

She swung to face him. Her skirts swished and bumped the examining table. A tiny smile graced those luscious pink lips—the ones he'd almost kissed the night of the dance—but then sorrow drew them down. "I cannot help caring. As you no doubt cannot help sending me home. I only hope we can part as friends and not enemies."

Her statement jarred him. If they were friends, he would not want them to part. Ever. That she still considered him a friend sent a wave of astonishment through him.

She poured water from a pitcher into a cup and handed it to him.

He sipped it. She started to leave. The pain in his head mounted like a rising storm.

"Don't." His voice came out barely a scratch. "Don't leave."

Halting, she spun around, hair dancing around her waist, and stared at him quizzically.

"Why did you marry Stanton Watts?" He could think of nothing else to say, nothing that would keep her here with him.

She blinked and then searched his eyes. "Why do you wish to know?"

Blake sipped his water and set down the cup, forcing anger from his tone. "I want to understand why you became a traitor to your country. How anyone could do such a thing."

"I married him before the war."

"But things were already tense between the North and South. You knew that."

"I did." She lowered her chin and began picking at the wooden operating table. "I don't know why I married him. He was handsome, charming, intelligent. He promised me a lavish life filled with adventure. Vowed to take me traveling with him to exotic lands. But most of all, it was a chance to be free from my father's control." She released a bitter chuckle. "In truth, I ended up in a far worse prison."

"Did you love him?" Blake knew he didn't have a right to ask, but he had to know. He had to know whether the emotion he now saw in her eyes was for the loss of her husband or because she regretted the marriage.

"That's rather bold, Colonel." She tossed her hair over her shoulder as if she could toss aside his question. But then she blew out a sigh. "I don't know. I suppose I thought I loved him in the beginning. But in truth, the news of his death did not overwhelm me with sorrow. I'd only seen him a few times during our year of marriage."

Her words broke through a hard place in Blake's heart. He studied her, the defiant lift of her chin, the way she held herself with confidence, the depth of sorrow and loss in her eyes. And all his anger fled away. Shaking off the ache in his head, he stood with one thought in mind. To take her in his arms.

Halting just inches before her, he brushed a wayward lock of hair from her face then eased a hand down her arm. Warm and soft beneath the cotton sleeve. She looked up, her eyes shifting between his in wonder, in hope. Vulnerability lingered in her gaze. A trust he didn't deserve.

He rubbed his thumb over her cheek. A tiny moan escaped her lips.

"Man overboard! Man overboard!" The frenzied call threaded through the deckhead, snapping Blake's senses alert.

"Man overboard!" The thunder of footsteps rumbled down the hall.

Blake exchanged a look of terror with Eliza before he barreled out the door.

◦⊹◦

Eliza leaped onto the main deck to the sound of the captain ordering sails furled and the sight of sailors rushing in a frenzy across the brig.

"What's happening?" Blake shouted, making a beeline to the captain, who stood on the quarterdeck.

"Woman overboard!" Captain Barclay gestured with his head behind him before he continued bellowing orders, "Hurry it up there, lads. Ease off jib sheet! Helms-a-lee! Bring her about, Mr. Simmons!"

Eliza's heart felt as though it would burst through her chest as shock transformed into panic. She darted to the starboard railing and scanned the sea. Nothing but inky blackness met her gaze.

James popped on deck, his shirt askew, his hair like a porcupine's. He gazed about wildly then took the quarterdeck ladder in a single leap and met Blake above. Eliza followed them to the stern where several sailors stood gaping at the churning sea.

"I heard the splash," one of them said. "She was standin' right here one minute, and the next she was gone." He shook his head and rubbed his whiskered chin.

"Who was it?"

"The pretty lady with the reddish brown hair."

"Angeline?" Panic clamped Eliza's throat, forbidding further words. She gripped the railing and stared at the dark waters. A tremble punched from her heart down her back into her limbs until she could hardly stand. "We have to do something!"

"Can we lower a boat?" Blake stormed toward the captain as he tore off his boots, one by one.

"Not till we tack. Thank God we weren't sailin' fast."

Spinning around, Blake's eyes met hers, and she knew what he intended to do. He started toward the railing when James muttered "I'll get her" as he tore off his shirt. And before anyone could protest, he took a running leap off the stern of the ship, leaving Blake behind.

James had no idea what he was doing. Not until he plunged into the cool water did the realization hit him that he'd actually dived off a perfectly sturdy brig into the vast ocean. When he'd first heard that a woman had fallen overboard, he'd darted above to offer his assistance. But after he'd learned it was Angeline, he didn't remember a thing. He must have taken off his shirt, because now as his head popped above the waves, salty water thrashed his bare chest. He glanced behind him at the *New Hope* beginning its turn into the wind.

"Angeline!" he shouted, scanning the dark sea from his vantage point atop a swell. "Angeline!"

He'd been fascinated with the woman ever since she'd come aboard. There was a sweet yet somber spirit about her that tugged on his heart, and though he'd engaged her in conversation as often as she would allow, she'd been hesitant to share much of her past. He only knew that she'd lost her parents and had lived with an uncle. And that something terrible had happened to her. The last part he surmised. Yet she'd bravely stood up for Eliza more than once, putting herself in danger for her friend. And she'd worked tirelessly to aid the sick stricken with the mysterious illness.

Regardless, she was a human being. And after James's fall from grace, he had vowed to God to save as many as he could from death—both physical and spiritual.

Something caught his eye in the distance, but then the wave passed, and he sank into the trough. He started in that direction, happy his father had taught him to swim in the lakes back in Tennessee. Still nothing had prepared him for such huge waves. What appeared like mere ripples from the deck of the brig now became giant swells rising like monsters from the deep. He hesitated as another wave swept him up toward the starlit sky. Focusing his gaze in the direction where he'd last seen something, he shouted, "Angeline!"

"Help!" A tiny squeak, barely audible, bounced over the sea.

Heart thundering in his chest, James pounded his arms through the water. "Lord, please don't let her die."

As the crest of each wave propelled James toward the sky, Angeline came more clearly into view before she disappeared behind the next ebony wall. James's arms ached. His legs felt like rubber, but still he pressed on. Water filled his mouth with brine. Coughing, he spit it out only to take in more.

Angeline's arms flailed as she bobbed in the churning water. One minute her drenched copper hair popped above the waves, the next she vanished below the surface. James didn't have much time. Groaning, he plowed forward. The water became sand, his limbs weak as noodles.

One more wave. Just one more wave, and he would reach her. Gathering his remaining strength, he ground his teeth together and punched through the sea then slid down the final trough. There she was! Her head sank beneath the water. He gulped in a deep breath and dove. Feet pounding, he swept his arms about in a frantic search. Water that felt as thick as molasses oozed between his fingers.

Lord, help.

His lungs begged for air. He touched something. An arm. He grabbed it and dragged her above. Limp and heavy like a sodden sack of rice, her dead weight nearly forced them both back below.

Treading water with one arm, he held her with the other and leaned his ear to her mouth.

She wasn't breathing.

⚜

Stripped to the waist, Blake clung to the lifeline. His bare feet dragged through the sea while foam licked his legs and spray blinded his eyes.

Above him at the quarterdeck railing, the crew and a few passengers stared across the sea. Their shouts and hysterics had faded to whispered prayers and anxious pauses as all eyes were on James swimming their way, towing Angeline behind him.

Captain Barclay issued orders to the helmsman and topmen to make adjustments that would halt the ship as close to James as possible.

Finally, James's heaving breaths could be heard above the slap of water as he and Angeline slipped down the side of a particularly large wave. Cheered on by those above, Blake reached toward them, bracing his feet against the hull. But the sea shoved them farther away, and they disappeared again behind an obsidian swell. Blake groaned, squinting to see in the dim moonlight. There! They reappeared, this time nearly within reach. James's single arm rose and fell in the water like an anchor. Methodical. Determined. As if moved by a strength not his own. His head dipped beneath the surface. Stretching as far as he could, Blake fisted the water and grabbed the man's arm. He pulled with all his might and finally drew James and Angeline to his side. He handed one of the lines to James, who barely managed to grab hold.

"Get her above. She's not bre–breathing." James clung to the rope, mouth open and breath coming hard.

Blake nodded and removed his own rope, tying it beneath Angeline's arms. "Haul up!" he shouted. Then grabbing the rope with one hand and Angeline with the other, he planted his feet on the hull and inched up as sailors pulled from above. Hayden grabbed the woman from Blake and laid her on the deck.

"Let me see her." Eliza pushed the crowd aside and fell by her friend, leaning her ear toward the lady's mouth.

Blake hoisted himself onto the railing and glanced down to see if James needed help, but the man was right behind him on a second rope. Still breathing hard, he leaped onto the deck and dashed toward Angeline, shoving Hayden aside.

Eliza lifted hollow eyes to his. "She's gone. I'm sorry."

"No!" Dropping to his knees, James placed an arm behind Angeline's neck, and angled her head to the side. Water spilled from her lips. "Blankets! Lots of blankets!"

Sailors sped off, returning in seconds with coverlets and spreads, which James quickly wrapped around her, placing some under her feet to lift them from the deck. Then gently yet firmly, he applied pressure to her abdomen. More water spewed from her mouth.

Everyone stared aghast, including Blake. Only the flap of loose sails echoed through the night, along with James's groans as he attempted to empty the woman's lungs. Eliza sat numbly watching. Tears streamed down her cheeks and dropped into her lap. Finally, when no more water came, James leaned down, placed his lips on Angeline's, and breathed into her mouth.

Blake had never seen such a thing. He raked his wet hair, hoping the doctor knew what he was doing. Yet how had the lady slipped overboard in the first place? She would have to have been sitting on the railing in this mild weather. But why would she do that? He glanced over the horrified faces of the sailors, the captain, Eliza, and Hayden, his gaze finally landing on the lady's shoes sitting neatly on the deck.

Coughing and sputtering drew his gaze back to Angeline. James turned her over, and more water spewed from her mouth onto the deck. She gagged and coughed. Eliza threw her hands to her chest and squealed with glee.

"Sweet, merciful Heaven!" Captain Barclay said with a smile.

Sailors cheered. James leaned back on his legs and breathed out a "Praise God!" Then leaning over, he scooped Angeline into his arms and rose.

Eliza, coming out of her shock, leaped to her feet and followed the doctor below. Blake shared a glance with the captain, who gave him a nod before turning and spitting a trail of orders to get the brig back on course.

❧

Angeline wasn't dead. She knew, because as the doctor carried her to the sick bay, his touch sent warmth tingling over her skin. Certainly one didn't tingle in hell, and certainly not in the pleasurable way she was tingling at the moment. His light hair hung in strands, dripping on his bare shoulders. His breath came heavy. He smelled salty and fresh like the sea. Had he dived in after her?

Kicking the door open, he laid her on the cot then bent to brush saturated strands of hair from her face. Concern sped across his eyes, those bronze-colored eyes that seemed so wise, so full of kindness.

"You're going to be all right now." He attempted a smile, but in that small grin, Angeline found a hope that made her almost believe him. Almost. Unlike Dodd, James didn't seem to recognize her from their brief exchange nearly a year ago. At least that was one thing to be thankful for.

Hayden stormed into the cabin, Eliza on his heels. He moved to the edge of the bed, squeezing James aside, and took Angeline's hand, caressing her fingers. "Angeline. . .Zooks. Thank God James found you." He seemed genuinely distraught.

Angeline tried to respond, but her throat felt like sandpaper.

"All right, gentlemen," Eliza said, her skirts swishing as she moved forward. "I must ask you to leave. I need to get her out of her wet clothes, and she needs to rest."

Hayden stood, but James seemed hesitant to leave. In fact, he continued to stare at her as if he'd almost lost a prized possession. "I'll come back to check on you later."

Angeline stared at him, confused. Why was he acting so oddly? She was anything but prized. Sculpted arms and a firm, molded chest sprinkled with light-colored hair filled her vision. Arms strong enough to swim out to save her and bring her back to the ship. Water dripped from his breeches onto the floor. He shoved back his wet hair, and she had a vision of his lips on hers, his breath inside of her. "You saved me." Her voice sounded like rough rope.

He merely smiled in return.

"Thank you."

Still, he said nothing, but instead followed Hayden out the door. After they left, Eliza took Angeline's hands in hers. "Thank God you are safe."

But Angeline knew God had nothing to do with it. And if He did, her being alive was only further punishment for her crimes.

CHAPTER 27

After the incident with Angeline, Hayden headed up on deck, too frustrated to go back to sleep. Dawn would be upon them in a couple of hours, and he could use the time to think. Think about what he was doing on this crazy, ill-begotten venture with these befuddling passengers. And especially how was he going to find his father once he got to Brazil. A vision of Angeline's lifeless form lying on the deck caused his fists to clench as he made his way to the port railing. Aside from a possible friendship with the colonel—as odd as that would be—his few brief moments with Angeline had been the only thing to stir his interest on this otherwise dismal journey. Well, besides his time with Magnolia. He rather enjoyed teasing the spoiled sprite. But Angeline was different. There was something about her that went far beyond appearance: a meekness he'd rarely seen in other women, a deeply imbedded sorrow he could well understand, and a fiery spirit that enthralled him. Of course there was also the fact that her comely face had stared at him from a WANTED poster in Norfolk, Virginia. Five hundred dollars was a lot of money for the capture and arrest of such a stunning woman. If he hadn't been so anxious to leave town before the constable discovered who he really was, he would have searched for her himself. The lady intrigued him, and he longed to discover her secrets. But a certain someone kept getting in the way.

"James," he spat out the name as he reached the railing, striking the wood with his fists. The righteous doctor had to go and play the hero. But a hero he was not. More like a liar and a hypocrite from what Hayden remembered. Hayden would have happily jumped in after Angeline if he'd been there in time. As it was, he arrived on deck after the good doctor had already disappeared into the sea.

Moonlight spread a silvery sheen over the inky water as the brig plunged through a wave, showering Hayden with spray. It did nothing to cool his humors. Pushing from the railing, he crossed his arms over his chest and snapped hair from his face. Wealthy, learned, privileged men like James thought they had the upper hand in everything. Life, business, women. But Hayden had spent a lifetime proving them wrong, and when it came to Angeline, he wasn't about to forfeit her to the likes of him.

A hiccup tickled his ear, and he turned to see a lady sitting atop a barrel by the foremast. Her shimmering gown clued him to her identity long before he was close enough to see her face. That angelic face of creamy skin, plump lips, pert little nose, and catlike eyes.

She stared blankly out to sea, lost in her thoughts, and Hayden found her nearly tolerable in her silence.

"Miss Magnolia."

She leaped. "You frightened me."

He gave a mock bow. "My apologies."

The smell of alcohol—brandy, if he wasn't mistaken—filtered to his nose and caused his lips to curve.

"What do you want?" She rubbed a hand beneath her nose.

"A sip of whatever you're having."

Eyes as hard as silver met his. "Whatever are you referring to, sir?" Her voice lifted in a sweet Southern drawl.

Hayden chuckled and leaned on the railing beside her. "You can cease the coquettish theatrics, princess. I'm not one of your fawning beaus back home."

She flattened her lips. "That is an understatement, Mr. Gale."

"Call me Hayden." He extended his open palm. "Since we'll be drinking mates now."

"Drinking—ahhhh," she ground out through clenched teeth, then reached within the folds of her skirt and handed him a flask.

He took a sip. The spicy liquor with a hint of orange slid down his throat with ease. Yes, brandy, indeed. "And just where does a lady find alcohol on board a ship?"

"Hard as it may be for you to believe, some people like me and wish to give me gifts."

Hayden snorted. "By that you mean you've been flirting with lonely sailors again."

Her eyes narrowed before she swept her gaze out to sea. "You won't tell my parents?"

"Not as long as you're sharing." He grinned.

"Petulant cur."

Hayden took another drink and handed it back to her. "I've been called worse."

"No doubt."

Sails flapped above as the brig hefted over a wave. Peering into the darkness, Hayden longed to see her expression. "Pray tell, princess, why is such a cultured and lovely lady as yourself drinking spirits on deck in the middle of the night?"

She wiped the lip of the flask with her handkerchief, tipped it to her mouth, and gulped down the pungent liquor like a hardened sailor. Then shoving the hardwood stopper into the spout, she set the flask aside. "After all the commotion caused by that woman, Angeline, I couldn't sleep."

"That woman nearly drowned." Hayden's anger flared.

"I'm not"—she hiccupped—"without sympathy, Mr. Gale." Magnolia pressed fingers to her temple. "But word among the sailors is she jumped."

Jumped? He flinched. "Perhaps she loathes being on this ship even more than you," he said.

"If you are suggesting I throw myself overboard"—poison laced her tone—"prepare to be disappointed."

"Too late."

The brig tilted. She shifted on the barrel, and Hayden reached for her, but she slapped him away. "If you find my company so distasteful, then leave."

"Not until you tell me why you need to saturate your senses with alcohol."

"I don't want to be on thissss horrid, ill-fated ship. I want to go back home where I belong." Though her words slurred, her despondency rang clear, eliciting a speck of sympathy for the lady. But only a speck.

"Hmm." Hayden fingered his chin, studying the way the moonlight sprinkled silver dust over her hair. Lovely. Too bad she was such a priggy shrew. Priggy, yes, but belittled by her father. "And what is waiting for you back home that you cannot live without?"

Wind tore a flaxen curl from her pins. She stuffed it back with a huff. "My fiancé, if you must know. He's a wealthy lawyer from Atlanta, Samuel Wimberly."

"Indeed?"

"Yes *indeed*. Do you doubt me?"

"I only wonder why he isn't here with you, that's all."

"Because he is a very impotent man. He worked side by side with Jefferson Davis through the entire war."

With difficulty, Hayden restrained a chuckle at her slip of tongue. "That still doesn't answer my question."

Magnolia blew out an exasperated huff. "Audacious brute!" She stood, stumbled, batted him way, and staggered to the railing. "You shouldn't even be on this voyage. I don't believe your story, by the way."

Hayden slid beside her, hovering his hand over her back to prevent her from toppling with the next wave. "So you have informed me."

She turned to him, her eyes swirling over his face as if looking for a place to land. "Why didn't you leave us in Dominica, Hayden? Just what do you hope to accompliss in the middle of an uncivilized jingle? I mean, jungle."

He cocked his head, quite enjoying her inebriation and noting the way the moonlight made her skin look like porcelain. "I'm looking for someone."

"In Brazil?" She giggled then hiccuped and covered her mouth.

He wouldn't tell her of course. Wouldn't let anyone know his true purpose. Stepping closer, he leaned toward her. "Perhaps I am looking for you."

She backed away, brow furrowing. "Leave me be. I shouldn't even be talking to you. You are nothing but a—"

"Handsome rogue, if I remember." He grinned.

Was that pink blossoming on her cheeks? "You prove my point, sir." She jutted her chin. "A gentleman would not remind a lady of such a thing."

He eased closer, his gaze unavoidably dropping to her moist lips. "I have never been accused of being a gentleman."

She gave an unladylike snort. "No doubt you have been acoosed of much worse."

He ran a finger down her arm. "Aren't you afraid to be alone with such a scoundrel?" He gave her his most mischievous grin, enjoying the opportunity to put this pompous brat in her place.

Instead of shrinking back from him or dashing away in fear, she studied him with. . .*interest*? Moonlight glossed her eyes in sapphire as her brandy-drenched breath filled the air between them.

She shoved her lips onto his.

Hayden was so shocked, it took him a second to react. Well, less than a second if he was truthful. Reaching his arms around her waist, he pressed her curves against him and caressed her lips with his own. Her passionate moan encouraged him to trail further kisses up her jaw to her earlobe then down her neck. She quivered in his arms. He brought his lips back to hers, hovering, tempting, as their heavy breaths mingled in the air around them. Heat soared through him. Unexpected. Mounting. Fiery. Passion crackled in the air. She swallowed his lips with hers. He tasted brandy on her tongue. She moaned again.

Then stiffened.

Jerking from his embrace, she gaped at him in horror before gathering her skirts and dashing across the deck like a cream puff sliding over a wooden plate.

❦

After one last peek at Angeline sound asleep in sick bay, Eliza eased the door shut and started toward her cabin, deep in thought over the events of the night. Intermittent lanterns created wavering spheres of light on the bulkhead, making the hallway seem even narrower and more compressed than it was. It didn't help, of course, that her crinolette bounced off the sides with each jerk of the ship. She felt like a fat mouse squeezing through a tiny maze, and the sensation did nothing for her already taut nerves. The ship canted to larboard. She braced a hand on the rough wood as thoughts of Angeline filled her mind, resurging the terror of nearly losing her friend, of the horrible death she would have suffered. And most of all, the question of how she could have possibly fallen overboard.

Lost in her musings, Eliza barreled into something solid. Rock solid. And warm.

Leaping back, she turned to run, thoughts of the lecherous Max spinning her mind into a frenzy, when a familiar voice stopped her.

"Forgive me. I didn't mean to startle you."

Blake. She spun around to see his head bent beneath the low deckhead, his body filling the hallway, his presence sucking the air from every corner—from her lungs. The memory of their near kiss in sick bay sent her heart into wild thumping. Or had the affection she'd seen in his eyes been her own wishful thinking?

"If you'll excuse me," she said, trying to control the quiver in her voice, "I was heading to my cabin."

"I came to inquire about Angeline."

"She is sleeping. James is with her."

"James? Is that proper?"

She huffed. "He's a doctor, Colonel. And he insisted."

He grew serious. "What did she tell you about. . .about what happened?"

Lantern light angled over his firm jaw, shadowed by morning stubble. But his eyes remained in darkness.

Eliza stared at the bulkhead, the staggering light, anywhere but at him. "She said she slipped."

"Hmm." He shifted his stance, still not moving to let her pass.

"You don't believe her?"

He scratched his jaw, suddenly bunched in tension. "She would have had to have been sitting on the railing to have accidentally fallen overboard, no?"

Eliza hugged herself and leaned on the bulkhead, giving up hope that he would allow her to pass and not sure she wanted to go anymore. Mainly because his tone no longer harbored hatred, just as it hadn't in those precious moments they'd shared in the sick bay earlier. "Perhaps. I don't know."

"Her shoes were on the deck."

"They were?" Eliza's heart twisted in her chest. "Then that must mean. . .Oh, I cannot consider what that means."

The lantern shifted, and she saw the deep lines on his forehead and the way his eyebrows nearly melted together when he was frustrated. "I'm concerned for her," he said. "If she attempted it once, she may try again."

"I agree. I'll talk with her tomorrow. Perhaps Sarah can help. She has a comforting way about her that makes people want to confide in her."

He seemed pleased with her answer, yet still he did not move. His scent saturated the air around her, shoving aside the stench below deck.

"Did the captain have an explanation for those odd birds?" She regretted bringing up a topic that might cause him stress, but she longed to extend their time together.

"No." His tone indicated neither offense nor burden. "He's never seen anything like it. At least not so many birds at once."

She felt his eyes search her in the darkness. She would give a fortune for a peek into their gray depths, if only to assess what he might be thinking.

"Was there something else, Colonel?"

Something else? Blake stifled a chuckle. Yes, there was something else—he didn't want her to leave. He couldn't get her out of his mind. He thought she was the most astounding, amazing woman he'd ever met. He cleared his throat. "No," he said and turned crossways to allow her to pass when Magnolia's voice stormed down the companionway.

"Stay away from me, you. . .you. . .wanton reprobate!"

Hayden sauntered behind her. "I'm not following you, princess. I'm heading below to get some sleep."

Blake faced the intruders. Magnolia halted when she saw him. Her eyes shifted to Eliza and filled with tears before she tore down the hallway, stumbled, and toppled to the deck, petticoats and lace bobbing in the air. "Now look what you've done," she sobbed.

"Me?" Hayden knelt to assist her, but she swatted him away, instead allowing Eliza to help her to her feet. Then after flinging a spiteful glance his way, Magnolia fell into Eliza's arms and unleashed a torrent of tears. "That man assaulted me. Again." She pointed at Hayden, who huffed in frustration and rolled his eyes as if she'd said he had two heads.

Brushing past the ladies, Blake stepped toward him. "What happened?"

Hayden folded his arms over his chest. "She kissed me."

"I did no such thing!" Magnolia stomped her foot, took the handkerchief Eliza handed her, and drew it to her nose. "I have no need to steal kisses from disgusting men."

"Apparently you do," Hayden quipped.

Blake rubbed his jaw and speared Hayden with a look that had sent lesser men cowering. "This is the second time the lady has accused you of assault, Hayden. I'm starting to wonder if there isn't some merit to her claims."

"Blake, a word, if you please," Eliza said from behind him.

Hayden's eyes narrowed. "I may be many things, but I've never harmed a lady."

The man's honest, indignant tone lent truth to his statement. Besides, why would he do such a thing on a ship where there was no place to run? "Until we sort this out, perhaps I should lock you below," Blake said.

"Yes. Yesss. . .Lock him up! No woman is safe with him raining loose," Magnolia wailed.

"Blake," Eliza called again. Blake clenched his jaw. Couldn't the woman see he was dealing with a potentially volatile man? He faced her. She tipped an invisible glass to her lips and gestured toward Magnolia, who seemed to have fallen asleep on her shoulder.

"Now, let's get you to bed, dear," Eliza said as she led the young lady away.

Blake scratched his head and faced Hayden. "Did you give her the spirits?"

"Quite the contrary," Hayden said. "I found her above like that. We spoke. She kissed me. That's that."

Blake rubbed his temples where a slow, dull ache began. "Do me a favor and just stay away from her." He didn't give Hayden time to answer before he brushed past him with a growl. Two more weeks until they reached Rio. He couldn't wait to get off this mad ship!

CHAPTER 28

"I've brought you some breakfast." Eliza squished through the narrow space between the operating table and bulkhead while trying to balance a tray laden with coffee, some sort of odd-smelling porridge, and a biscuit.

Angeline offered her a languid smile, tossed her legs over the cot, and rubbed her eyes. "Thank you, Eliza. I'm not hungry." Salt-encrusted curls hung limp around her face.

"After your swim in the sea, I should think you would be." Eliza set the tray down, hoping her jovial tone would lighten the lady's mood.

It didn't.

"At least have some coffee. Cook brewed some up just for you." Eliza handed her the cup and slid onto a chair beside her. The chair James had occupied until just an hour ago. The poor man must be exhausted after keeping vigil over Angeline all night.

Though the heat in the sick bay had significantly risen since dawn three hours ago, Angeline warmed her hands on the cup as if it were winter. She took a sip.

"What happened?" Eliza asked. "We were so worried."

Angeline stared at the black coffee in her cup oscillating with the movement of the ship. "I guess I slipped."

Eliza gave a sigh that held more doubt than frustration. Leaning forward, she took one of Angeline's hands in hers. "I wish you'd tell me. Maybe I can help."

Angeline set the cup down. "No one can help."

"Is it Dodd? Is he threatening you? One of the sailors? You must know you are not alone."

Her eyes grew misty, and she squeezed Eliza's hand. "Oh Eliza.

240

You've been so nice to me. Thank you for being my friend."

"I'll always be your friend. No matter what."

"I'm sorry I worried you all so much. And James, risking his life to save me."

"Hayden was about to jump in as well. And Blake. That's three men willing to die for you, Angeline."

"I'm truly humbled by everyone's concern." She released a heavy sigh and picked up the coffee again. "I'm much better now, Eliza." Violet eyes swung to hers, brimming with sincerity. "I truly am."

Eliza had never had so much trouble getting anyone to open up to her before. Oh the stories she would hear in the battlefield hospitals— the secrets soldiers would share with her during the long hours of the night. They'd said she was a good listener. Someone who cared. She'd prided herself on not only being able to tend the wounds on their bodies, but the wounds on their hearts as well.

But Angeline was an iron chest. With a thick iron lock. And there was no key in sight. "I only hope that you will come to me if you need to talk or if you have a problem. Will you promise me that?"

She nodded. "Honestly, I don't know what came over me." She shook her head and swallowed. "I didn't mean to put anyone else at risk."

So, she *had* jumped. The truth bore a hole in Eliza's heart. She brushed hair from Angeline's face. "Nothing can be so bad that you forfeit your life. Whatever it is, you can count on me to always stick by your side."

Angeline gave a halfhearted smile. "Thank you."

"Very well." Eliza rose. "Eat your breakfast, and I'll go fetch some water to rinse that hair of yours." Yet, as Eliza made her way down the hall, she couldn't shake the feeling the poor lady's troubles were only just beginning. And the worst of it was, once they got off in Brazil, Eliza wouldn't be around to help her.

⚜

Twelve days later, Eliza peered into the darkness, trying to make out the features of the continent just a half mile off their starboard side. Nothing but murky shadows met her gaze. Shadows that had snaked around her hammock, strangling her and jarring her awake. In fact, the closer they sailed toward their destination, the more agitated her sleep had become, as if Brazil toyed with her emotions, taunting her with the fact that she'd never set foot on its shores. Or perhaps she was merely depressed because in a few days, everyone she'd grown to know and care for would abandon her for their new home, leaving her all alone once again.

Forsaken. For one mistake.

Myriad stars reflected off a sea as slick as polished onyx, creating a mirror image of sky on water, while a half-moon smiled down on her as if trying to reassure her all would be well. But she knew it was a lie. With most sails furled, the ship barely whisked through the liquid pitch that seemed as thick as the coating around her heart. Eerily peaceful. She guessed it to be around midnight, though she couldn't be sure. The helmsman paid her no mind, and the only night watchman snored from the foredeck.

Not that she minded the company of other passengers. They no longer shunned her or insulted her or even cast disparaging looks her way. In fact, most of them were quite courteous. She supposed it had much to do with her willingness to treat their complaints without hesitation. Everything from the ague, to corns, earaches, sore gums, and diarrhea to heartburn.

"Love does conquer all, Lord." She gazed into the dark void, allowing the night breeze to trickle through her hair, warm and soothing. "And good does conquer evil." For some people anyway. Aside from those few precious moments nearly two weeks ago, Blake had remained at a distance, speaking to her only when forced. She couldn't make heads nor tails of his behavior. Hadn't he almost kissed her in the sick bay? He'd seemed so kind then, so interested in hearing her side of things. Then, as quickly as donning a uniform, he had switched from warm, loving Blake to cold, impervious Colonel Wallace.

Even so, during the past weeks, she'd caught him looking at her more than once from across the deck. Sometimes he gazed at her with such intense admiration it seemed they were the only two people on board. Other times, anger—no, confusion—shadowed his stormy eyes before he looked away.

Frustration soured in her belly. If he wished to hate her, then hate her, but the occasional moments of interest, the glimpses of affection, and the flickers of hope they lit in her heart would be her undoing.

No doubt that was another reason she stood staring into the darkness instead of lying fast asleep in her hammock.

Yet she was the one who had married a Yankee general. Against her father's wishes. Against her entire family's wishes. And if she admitted it, against her own conscience. She hadn't loved Stanton. Not really. She'd been enamored with him. With his position, his power, his commanding presence. The way he made her feel like an adult, not like the child her father always reduced her to. Under her father's roof, she was told what to wear, what to eat, whom to associate with, where to go. But with Stanton, she'd been given the run of her own house. Stanton was her ticket to freedom, her road to living life by her own rules. That was, until the war began and he was called away and she moved into his family's home in Pennsylvania with his parents and siblings. They had never accepted Stanton's marriage to Eliza and made no excuse for their cold behavior. Nor did they hesitate to monitor her every word, correspondence, and movement. As if she were a Southern spy!

The brig rose over a swell, and Eliza braced her slippers on the deck. She'd gotten so used to the rolling of the ship, she hardly had to think about steadying herself anymore. In fact, she'd grown to love the sea for all its wildness and passion and unpredictability. She felt free on these waters—more than she had anywhere else. Her chest grew heavy at the thought of being forced to disembark back in Charleston—back to a land where she didn't belong.

Clutching her locket, she rubbed a thumb over the fine silver. "Why am I so rebellious, God? I'm so sorry. Why don't I ask for Your wisdom before I jump into things? Why don't I listen to Your voice and obey?"

No answer came, save the rush of water against the hull and flap of sail. She breathed in the warm, briny air and then released it in a long sigh. Her rebellion had cost her everything. And now it would cost her the chance at a new life and the love of a man she adored.

Closing her eyes, she gripped the railing. When would she ever learn?

"Well lookee what we gots here." The male voice gave Eliza a start, and she looked up to find Max leaning on the railing beside her, a gleam in his eyes that sent terror slithering up her spine.

"What do you want?" Eliza inched away from him, casting a glance over her shoulder at the helmsman. He was no longer at the wheel.

Max snorted, a maniacal, lethal sort of snort that tightened the noose around her heart. "I'm thinkin' you should be nicer to yer enemies, Mrs. Watts."

"I've been more than polite to you, Max. Now if you please." She clutched her skirts and turned to leave.

He yanked her arm. Pain spiked into her fingers, numbing them beneath his squeeze. "Yankees like you killed me wife and me only son. Took everything from me."

"You're hurting me." She attempted a calm tone. He gripped her harder, drawing her close until his mouth hovered over her ear.

"Yer goin' to pay for what your husband did, Yankee whore. An' when I'm done with you, I'll feed you to the sharks."

A line of bluecoats emerged from the trees like garish devils. Another row appeared behind them. Then another and another as the first line spread out and took their positions, rifles at the ready. At the sight of so many troops, gasps and moans spilled from Blake's men while others merely stared in numb horror. The young private standing next to Blake swallowed hard, his Adam's apple bobbing with each nervous swallow. Henry Swanson had just turned seventeen last week. The camp cook had made him a small cake of cornmeal and molasses, and his company had thrown a celebration, complete with fiddle and harmonica. He was the same age Jeremy would have been. Had he lived. Which made Blake's need to protect Henry all the more desperate. Blake gave the lad a reassuring nod, which had no effect on the terror flashing in the boy's eyes.

The *rat-tat-tat* of drums and the eerie sound of a flute filled the air. Why were battles always accompanied by music? As if a patriotic tune could somehow rebuild the morale of a troop of dejected, defeated boys. Boys who should be back home on their farms helping with chores and courting pretty girls instead of facing an early death.

Grabbing the saddle horn, Blake planted his boot in the stirrup and mounted his thoroughbred. He stroked the horse's sweaty neck. "That a boy, Reliance." The steed pawed the muddy ground. Steam blasted from his nostrils. In over twenty major battles and thrice as many skirmishes, Blake had not once been injured while he rode atop Reliance.

Sensing the upcoming battle, horses pawed the ground and snorted while men muttered prayers. Officers bellowed commands. Cannons fired, shaking the ground. Smoke filled the air. Blake drew his sword, leveled it before him, and gave the order to charge.

If there was a hell, it surfaced on that field near Richmond, Virginia, on that cold October day in 1864. A barrage of smoke and fire and terrifying screams surrounded Blake. He slashed his way through the enemy ranks, dispatching Union soldiers left and right. Cannon fire pounded his ears—sent tremors through his body. Sparks from muskets lit up the smoke-filled air like fireflies at dusk. Blake gasped for a breath. Sweat stung his eyes. He swerved Reliance around to check on his men when fire ignited his leg. Reliance let out a pain-filled screech and started to fall. Blake tried to jump from the tumbling beast, but a Yankee soldier thrust a blade into Blake's side. Gripping the wound, he toppled to the ground. Reliance dropped on top of his leg.

Sounds of battle faded into the distance as his own heartbeat thumped in his chest. *Thump, thuuump thuuuump.* The beat slowed, grew dimmer. He was going to die. He could no longer feel his leg. One glance told him that Reliance was dead. Pressing a hand over the blood oozing from his side, Blake turned his head in search of help. The vacant eyes of Henry Swanson stared back at him, a bullet in his forehead.

"No!" Blake screamed, unable to stop the tears flooding his eyes—unable to stop the vision of his brother, Jeremy, lying in a field like this poor lad, dying all alone.

"No! Jeremy! Jeremy!" Blake leaped from his hammock and landed on the deck on all fours. The brig rocked gently beneath his hands. Sweat dripped onto his fingers. He gasped for a breath. An ache rose in his leg. He rubbed it, struggling to rise. The bullet had struck an artery. If not for Reliance's weight upon it, Blake would have bled out on that field.

"Jeremy?" James's groggy voice sifted through the air.

Blake rose and leaned his hands on his legs, gathering his breath and settling his heart. "Go back to sleep." Rubbing grief from his eyes, he pulled on his trousers, tossed a shirt over his head, and left the cabin before James could say another word. Blake didn't feel like talking. He didn't feel like thinking. All he wanted was some peace. Yet before he even made it above, thoughts of Eliza flooded his mind. After a nightmare like the one he'd just had, he would expect to feel nothing but fury toward her, yet all he found was an affection that, if she returned, promised to soothe away his bad dreams forever.

He'd been avoiding her for just that reason. After the incident with the birds and the tender moments they'd shared in the sick bay, Blake's mind and heart had taken up arms and once again engaged in a fierce battle on the field of confusion. The worst of it was they often switched sides. One minute his mind wanted her to stay, but his heart demanded justice for his family. The next, his heart ached to be with her, but his mind refused entrance to a Yankee. At one point, the fighting became so intense, Blake believed he was going mad. Still, he had no idea what to do. But he did know one thing. Every day he spent on this brig, watching her care for everyone and forgive everyone who'd wanted her dead, both his heart and mind seemed ready to forfeit the battle.

He climbed on deck to a gentle night breeze and the smell of salt and damp wood. Scents he'd grown quite fond of these past months. A muffled squeal brought his gaze toward the foredeck. He peered into the darkness, but nothing seemed out of the ordinary. *Thump. Groan.* Blake limped toward the sound.

A woman's moan made him charge around the capstan. "Who's there?"

A bulky shadow spun around. Lantern light reflected off the blade of a knife. "None of yer business, Colonel." Max spit to the side.

"Blake." The voice emerged as a pleading squeak, barely audible above the rush of the sea, but it grabbed his heart and wouldn't let go.

The brig shifted and moonlight shimmered over maple-colored hair. *Eliza.*

Fury tightened every nerve, every muscle within Blake. "What is the meaning of this?"

"Run along, now, Colonel." Max pointed the knife at Blake. "The Yankee strumpet's gettin' what's comin' to her, that's all."

Blake studied the lecherous fool, weighing his choices. He could reason with the man, threaten to tell the captain, and have him locked below. Or. . .

With lightning speed, he clutched Max's wrist and tightened his grip like a vise. Surprise turned to anger and then fear and finally pain in the sailor's eyes. Blake squeezed harder, feeling the crack of bone.

Max released the knife. It clanked to the deck by Blake's bare feet. Before Max could react, Blake slammed a fist across his jaw then slugged him in the gut. The sailor bent over with a groan. One final pounding of Blake's fists on Max's back sent him toppling to the deck.

Eliza stepped into the light. A cascade of hair tumbled around a pale face and trembling lips. Her gaze took in Max lying on the deck then shifted to Blake as if she didn't believe he was real.

"Are you all right, Eliza? Did he hurt you?" Blake reached for her. She hesitated. Not waiting for her to respond, Blake gathered her in his arms.

⁕

Eliza sat on the cot in the sick bay, already missing the feel of Blake's arms around her. Like steel bands of armor, they did much to assuage her trembling. A trembling that still racked her body.

Sitting on a chair beside her, he handed her a glass of stale water. The mug quivered in her hand, spilling water over the side. He cupped his hands around hers and helped her take a sip. That was when Eliza knew she must be dreaming. The tender way he held her hands, the lines of concern furrowing his brow, the look of adoration in his eyes. Yes, she was surely dreaming. No man who had ignored her for nearly two weeks would be looking at her like that. "Thank you."

Setting down the cup, he eased strands of hair from her face. His eyes widened, and horror claimed his expression. "You're cut."

"I am?" Eliza pressed fingers over her neck. She touched something warm and wet. And painful.

Blake headed for the side table, returning in a moment with a damp cloth.

"Here, let me." He tugged her hand away and dabbed the wound, his warm breath filling the air between them.

"I didn't feel the knife."

"You were in shock."

In truth, she felt like she still was.

She reached up to stop him. "No need to do that."

"Let me care for you. Lord knows you've tended to me enough times." His commanding tone stopped her from further complaints. It had been a long time since someone had cared for her.

After he cleaned and bandaged her wound, he retrieved a blanket from a drawer and flung it over her shoulders. Her breath heightened as memories of the attack assailed her. "Thank God you came when you did."

Blake's jaw knotted. He leaned forward, elbows on his knees, and gave her a look of reprimand. "What were you doing on deck alone at night?"

She lowered her gaze. "I couldn't sleep."

"Couldn't sl—" He stood and took up a pace. "There are still those on board who wish you harm."

Eliza kept silent—both elated and confused at his display of emotion on her behalf. "Why should you care?"

He halted and studied her. "I do not wish you harm, Mrs. Watts."

"Then stop calling me that. It hurts me every time you do."

He huffed. "Would you prefer, Mrs. *Crawford*?"

Ah, there was the bitterness she'd come to expect. Eliza drew a shuddering breath.

He knelt beside her. "Forgive me, Eliza. You're trembling." Thick, rough fingers swallowed her hands. His eyes never left hers, searching, caressing her with his gaze. "You've been so kind to everyone on board, even those who have been cruel to you. Why?"

"God commands us to love our enemies." At least that was one thing in which she'd been obedient. "Besides, I truly do care for them."

"I've never met anyone with such a kind heart."

"Have a care, Colonel." She gave him a coy smile. "You speak blasphemy of a Yankee."

His eyes twinkled in amusement.

An uncontrollable shudder waved through her. No doubt mistaking it for fear, he drew her close, encasing her in the shield of his arms. "You're safe now."

The words dissolved in her heart like honey in tea, erasing all the pain, the rejection of the past months. She began to sob.

Nudging her back, he wiped tears from her cheeks with his thumbs—hard and calloused but they felt so wonderful against her skin. His gray eyes swirled like gentle storm clouds, not churning in their usual tempest. He cupped her face in his hands, his gaze shifting between hers. His chest rose and fell. His masculine scent filled her lungs. He brushed his thumb over her lips and licked his own. Eliza's breath caught in her throat. He was going to kiss her.

CHAPTER 29

$\mathscr{B}$lake's lips met hers.

Eliza's heart sputtered like the flame of a candle, flooding her belly with heat. He caressed her cheeks with his fingers. His lips brushed over hers as if afraid to land.

"Eliza, sweet Eliza."

His mouth melded with hers. He tasted of salt and man. Meaty arms swaddled her with protection and strength.

Eliza submitted, allowing him to kiss her fully, all caution, all sense, tossed overboard. How could she do anything else? She'd never been kissed with such need, such urgency, such tender yearning. Such love. She never wanted this moment to end.

⬥

The kiss was like none Blake had ever experienced. His body reacted. His mind spun with delight. He felt Eliza's hunger, her affection in every touch of her lips across his. Pressing her close, he relished the way her curves molded against him.

But no. He withdrew. Passion glazed her eyes. She moved to kiss him again. Grabbing her arms, he pushed her back.

"Blake." His name emerged breathless on her lips. "If that is the kiss of an enemy, then I fear I am captured."

He chuckled. The woman never ceased to amaze him. Pulling her close, he pressed her head against his shoulder and ran his fingers through her hair. "It is I who am defeated." Something he should have accepted a month ago.

She peered up at him with a trust he did not deserve. "I do not wish to defeat you, not ever."

"Shhh now, get some rest. We'll discuss terms of surrender in the morning."

She released a heavy sigh and snuggled against him. It took every ounce of his remaining strength to resist the soft morsel in his arms, but thankfully, she fell asleep within minutes. Easing her down onto the cot, he covered her with a blanket and slipped from the room before he tarnished her reputation forever.

Four hours later, as dawn broke in an array of glorious color, Blake stood at the bow of the brig, watching a school of dolphins play tag with the *New Hope*. *New Hope*, indeed. For the first time in weeks, he felt new hope springing within him. Not only because they were to arrive in Rio within a few days, but because he'd made up his mind about Mrs. Watts—Eliza.

Shame pinched him. He shouldn't have kissed her without an understanding between them. He shouldn't have kissed her at all! But she had been so sweet, so frightened, so trusting, he'd been unable to resist. He'd gotten caught up in the moment, severing the string between his heart and mind. Sighing, he raked a hand through his hair. Now that he *had* kissed her, what was he to do? Could he truly consider a courtship with a woman whose husband had killed his countrymen?

Moving to the starboard railing, he crossed his arms over his chest and gazed at the Brazilian landscape as the sun lured sand and trees out from hiding. Coconut groves and plantains popped into existence, shading lazy fishing villages—all set against a background of ominous blue mountains.

"Have you ever seen a more beautiful morning?" James appeared beside him, faced the opposite direction, and lifted a hand toward the rising sun. "With water as smooth as glass, the sun rises upon its glorious throne, trailing robes of crimson and gold." He smiled.

"Doctor, preacher, and now poet as well. Is there no end to your talents?" Blake said.

Splashes drew their gazes to dolphins and bonitos playing in the foam coming off the bow.

"Aha, a good sign! Dolphins leading us straight to Rio's harbor." James rubbed the back of his neck. "Though, I must say, if it's already this warm, I fear we are in for a searing afternoon."

"Get used to it, my friend. I hear it's even more scorching on land."

"You'll get no complaints from me. Reminds me of Tennessee summers."

Blake had heard that Brazil mimicked their familiar Southern climate, minus the cold winters, of course. He hoped that would aid the colonists in acclimating to the new land, for they would have problems enough just surviving. But he wouldn't think of that now. For now he would enjoy the panorama of green lowlands passing by the brig as hundreds of small gulls whirled above a forest of palm trees. If all of Brazil was this beautiful and lush, their new home would be a paradise, indeed.

James's yawn reminded Blake of his nightmare. "Sorry to wake you last night. And all the other nights." He gave a sheepish grin.

"Don't trouble yourself over it." James spun around and gripped the railing. The lines at the corners of his eyes grew taut as he gazed at the sea. "It was another dream about your brother? Jeremy, was it?"

Blake nodded. "Killed at Antietam."

"I was at that battle."

Blake snapped his gaze to James as agony weighed down his heart. Surely the doctor wouldn't have crossed paths with Jeremy. And yet hope surged within him, hope for any tiny morsel about his last moments on this earth. "Private Jeremy Wallace of the 7th Georgia Infantry. He died on the battlefield." The brig pitched over a wave, shifting his brother's ever-present belt plate in Blake's pocket. Pulling it out, he ran fingers over the initials, *JSW*, picturing his brother standing in the parlor of their Atlanta home, dressed in his fresh uniform, excitement bursting from his brown eyes. He'd looked far too young to be dressed like a soldier. Far too young to be heading into rising hostilities that would become war. Hadn't it just been a year earlier that he'd roamed the city streets playing pranks on the neighbors and flirting with pretty girls? Blake's mother had cried. His father had embraced the young lad with pride. And Blake had felt sick to his stomach. None of them ever saw him again.

"I'm sorry," James said. "Is that his?"

"All I have left of him." Blake slipped it back into his pocket as shame burned a hole in his heart. How could he have tossed his brother's memory aside so flippantly, defiled it so vehemently, by kissing Eliza? Or had he? Perhaps her brief marriage to Stanton did not make her a traitor at all. Ugh, the confusion was driving him mad! But he did know one thing. He would not kiss her again until he was sure they had a future. Until he was sure a relationship with her would not betray everything he held dear.

"I tended some of the wounded after the battle. Perhaps I came across him." James loosened his necktie, as if the memory of that day stole his breath.

"I doubt it. He was sliced through by a Union officer on the field after the battle was done, or so I was told." Blake clenched his fists until they ached. "For a pocket watch."

James froze. His mouth hung open.

"What is it?" Blake asked.

"Nothing."

"You remember something."

James snapped his gaze toward the mainland as pain tightened the corners of his mouth. His long silence threatened to unravel Blake's carefully wound control.

"It was a horrible battle," the doctor finally said, rubbing his eyes. "We lost thousands that day. I don't remember specific soldiers. Though I do recall that many of our wounded were finished off by Union troops scouring for treasure."

Blake huffed his frustration. "Brutal savages."

"We were no better." James rubbed the scar on his cheek.

Perhaps. Blake drew a deep breath of morning air, hoping to sweep away the foul memories. Slapping his palms on the railing, he lifted his face to the breeze. "Let's talk of brighter things, shall we? Like arriving at our new home soon."

"Hard to believe we are almost there."

"Especially with all the bad fortune that has come our way." Voices brought Blake's gaze to a few passengers emerging from below. On the foredeck, Mr. Graves stared at Brazil, rubbing something between his fingers. When had he come above?

"I'd say." James chuckled. "Chased and boarded by a Union frigate, nearly sunk in that horrendous storm, the strange illness, the rigging splitting and injuring the first mate."

"The fire," Blake added.

"Parson Bailey stealing our money." James shook his head.

"And that baffling bird attack."

James stretched his shoulders and sighed. "It almost seems like someone or something is trying to keep us from our destination."

Blake's gaze unavoidably swept once again to Mr. Graves. "Yet they have not succeeded, have they?"

James cocked a brow, a twinkle in his eye. "We aren't at Rio yet."

Eliza woke to the smell of Blake on her skin and the memory of his lips on hers. She smiled and stretched her hands above her head. What a wonderful, incredible night. Well, all except Max's attack. But even that had brought Blake to her rescue and lowered the shield around his heart. She only hoped it remained lowered and didn't lift again with the rising of the sun. Swinging her legs over the cot, all the sweet sounds she'd grown to love cascaded over her: the thumping of feet above, the creak and groan of the ship, the purl of water against the hull, the shouts of sailors. She listened for one particular voice, the one that sent her heart crashing against her chest. There it was. That commanding, confident shout calling for everyone's attention.

Rising, she examined the scratch on her neck in the mirror and did her best to pin up her hair and smooth the wrinkles from her gown before heading above. From Blake's tone, whatever he wished to tell the passengers sounded important.

Weaving through the mob amassing on deck, Eliza spotted Sarah, Lydia in her arms, standing beside Angeline. Thank goodness Angeline seemed to have recovered from her leap into the sea nearly two weeks ago, though she still refused to discuss the reason she'd wanted to end her life.

Now as she looped her arm through Eliza's, she leaned toward her and whispered, "Where were you last night?"

"I slept in the sick bay." At Sarah's concerned look, Eliza added. "I'll tell you both later."

"Your attention, please." Blake's voice drew all gazes toward him as he stood on the quarterdeck beside the captain. Since she'd seen him last, he'd shaved and donned a proper vest over his shirt, a necktie, and a pair of tall, leather cavalry boots. Eliza thought him the handsomest man in the world.

A breeze tore at her hair, cooling the perspiration forming on her brow, and flapping the sails overhead. The ship rose on a swell, and everyone braced their feet against the canting deck.

"I'd like to take a vote on a rather important question." Blake's tone carried a hint of nervousness. "It concerns Mrs. Crawford." His gaze sought hers and remained there for several seconds as if no one else existed on board the ship. The remembrance of their kiss sent heat flushing through her. She tried to ignore the lingering sensation and focus on the matter at hand, hoping beyond hope that the vote he spoke about had to do with her future on this venture. As if confirming her thoughts, he smiled, and her heart felt as though it were pounding a hole in her chest.

"What about her?" someone yelled, jerking Blake's gaze from her.

He drew a deep breath. "I believe the lady has more than proven how valuable she is to our group. In fact, she has been nothing but kind to all of you, even those who would have abandoned her on Dominica."

Eliza's heart beat even faster.

"Aye, she healed my earache," one man shouted.

"And she delivered my baby," Sarah added.

"And stitched up my cut," a sailor said.

Affirmations of all she'd done flipped into the air like huzzahs after a victory until the captain finally called for silence.

"I realize she married a Yankee officer," Blake continued. "But she is still a true-blooded Southern lady. And let's face it, we have all made mistakes."

Nods of affirmation bobbed through the group.

"Raise your hand if you agree to allow Mrs. Crawford—Eliza—to continue with us."

Eliza couldn't believe her ears. She wanted to rush into Blake's arms and shower him with kisses. Instead, she gripped Angeline's and Sarah's hands and said a silent prayer.

Arms went up all across the deck.

Eliza closed her eyes, afraid to count them, afraid they weren't the majority. Seconds passed like hours. The roar of the sea pounded in her ears. The rumble of sails thrummed on her heart. She squeezed her friends' hands as a trickle of perspiration made its way down her back.

Finally, Blake's voice boomed over the ship. "It's settled then. Eliza stays."

Groans and grunts from those who disagreed buffeted her ears—and her heart—like pistol shots. Yet when she opened her eyes, she found Blake gazing at her once again. The intensity of his look weakened her knees and opened her heart to the possibility that maybe dreams did come true.

Sarah and Angeline squealed in delight and tugged on her arms, dragging her gaze from Blake's. Batting a wayward tear, she hugged them both and allowed herself a moment of bittersweet victory.

Bittersweet because there were still many who wanted nothing to do with her. Mr. Dodd among them, as he snapped his pocket watch shut, gave her a snide look, and strolled away.

Some of the passengers crowded around, offering their congratulations. The Scotts raised their noses and dropped below, while Magnolia gave Eliza a sincere hug. Even Mr. Graves offered his best wishes, though from his tone and demeanor she couldn't be sure that was a good thing. From across the deck, James nodded and smiled. Hayden approached and placed a gentlemanly kiss on her hand and then gave her a mischievous wink that no doubt had charmed a thousand women. A thousand and one from the look on Magnolia's face.

However, a dozen or so people scattered away, scowling at her as if she were the devil himself. How could she settle into a new colony when so many still hated her?

When the crowd dissipated, Moses and Delia, children in tow, approached Eliza, beaming smiles on their faces. "We's so glad you can come wid us."

Mariah, Delia's youngest girl, dashed toward Eliza. Horrified, Delia tried to extricate her daughter from Eliza's skirts, apologizing profusely and cowering as if she expected to be chastised. But Eliza knelt to take Mariah in her arms. "No need to apologize, Delia. I love children." Though Eliza's father would probably die on the spot if he saw her embracing a black child. Surprise dashed across Delia's eyes before she smiled and took young Mariah from Eliza's arms.

The family soon left, and Eliza turned to see Blake standing a short distance away, watching her with interest. "No need to try and impress me further with your extraordinary kindness, Eliza," he said as he approached. "I said you could stay." His grin was sly and charming.

She gazed up at him, her body temperature rising with each step he took toward her. "I don't know how to thank you, Blake. I. . .I. . ."

He placed a finger on her lips. Her pulse raced. "No need," he said, offering her his arm. "It was the right thing to do."

Slipping her hand into the crook of his elbow, Eliza allowed him to lead her to the railing. "And is that the *only* reason you took a vote?" Her tone was teasing. But instead of bolstering her hopes with an amorous response, his silence pounded them into dust. Those stubborn lines on his forehead appeared again. Which meant he was either frustrated or confused.

"About those terms of surrender, Colonel?" She made another attempt to revive the Blake that had made an appearance in sick bay the night before. But he remained hidden beneath a somber exterior.

Leaning one arm on the railing, he faced her. "Eliza, I want to apologize for kissing you. It was wrong of me to take advantage of your frightened condition."

A stone sank in Eliza's stomach. "I wasn't frightened. Well, not then. And you didn't take advantage of me. I wanted to kiss you. I know that is improper of me to say and you must think me far too forward, but it's the truth, nonetheless."

A hint of a smile touched his lips then faded. "Still, I promise you it will not happen again."

"Colonel!" Captain Barclay bellowed from the quarterdeck. "A moment, if you please."

Without another word, Blake excused himself and left. A chill settled on Eliza in his absence. Facing the sea, she pounded her fists on the railing.

What a fool she'd been! Blake didn't love her. The kiss had meant nothing to him. Eliza was no innocent. She understood men. The passion she'd felt in his kiss was just that. Passion. Physical passion in a moment of weakness. If not, he would have made his intentions clear. He would have professed his love to her, asked to court her. Instead, his contrite tone gave her no room for hope. All the blood drained from her heart. Bowing her head, she fought to keep tears from her eyes.

She loved Blake. She loved him so much it hurt. And she knew one thing. It would be impossible to live side by side with him, see him and talk to him every day, perhaps even watch him love another, and know she would never be his.

CHAPTER 30

Anticipation crackled across the ship. It sizzled in every creak and moan of wood, every thunder of sail, every dash of water against the hull. It buzzed in the excited murmurs of the passengers as they stood at the railing in breathless anticipation of their first glimpse of Rio de Janeiro.

Pressed between Sarah and Angeline, Eliza stood among the excited throng, most of whom had been awakened by Captain Barclay's shouts announcing their soon arrival. How the man knew they were so close, Eliza had no idea. The passing vista was much of the same glistening white beaches and luxuriant greenery they'd been seeing for days.

At the bow, Mr. Dodd kept rubbing his hands together and pacing back and forth, shifting his gaze over the mainland. Did he actually believe he would simply set foot on land and forthwith find the illusive pirate treasure? If it even existed. Eliza smiled and glanced at Mrs. Scott, sitting atop a barrel, an expression of abject misery twisting her face as Mable fanned her profusely. Mr. Scott stood by her side, not a speck of enthusiasm peeking from behind his austere expression, while Magnolia leaned against the foremast, looking more bored than usual. That was, until Hayden sauntered by and gave her a roguish grin before tipping his hat at her parents and joining James at the railing. Magnolia's gaze followed him, a pout on her lips and her creamy skin pinking, making Eliza wonder what, if anything, had happened between them.

Moses, Delia, and her children stood on the other side of the ship, but Moses' gaze was on poor Mable, whose arms must surely be aching from so much fanning. The children's gazes, however, were on little Henrietta Jenkins and two other youngsters playing a game of cup and ball on the main deck. A few feet beyond the young ones,

257

Mr. Lewis sat atop the capstan, face down and hunched over, most likely from overindulgence in alcohol last night. The man must have brought along his own stash, since the ship's meager supply was dwindling fast. And at his usual spot at the larboard railing, Mr. Graves stood apart from the others, dressed in black from head to toe, with an equally dark aura hovering around him. Thank goodness Max was nowhere in sight. Locked below, Eliza had heard, by the Captain's orders after Blake told him what the man had done.

Lydia's gurgles brought Eliza's attention back to Sarah, who adjusted the baby's blanket to cover her eyes from the sun. Dabbing the perspiration forming on her neck, Eliza wondered how the child endured a blanket in this heat. Yet she seemed quite content as she smiled at her mother and reached for the shiny cross hanging around her neck. The love sparkling in the child's eyes brought back memories of Eliza's own mother. She felt the loss in the pit of her stomach. How different her life would have been if her mother hadn't died of fever when Eliza was only twelve. Most likely, Eliza never would have married Stanton, nor would she be on this voyage. Nor would she have met Blake. And while his commanding voice continually bounced over the deck, causing her heart to skip a beat with each deep intonation, she almost wished she *had* never met him. She hadn't spoken to him since he'd apologized for their kiss and dashed off to attend his duties yesterday. And she wasn't altogether sure she wished to speak to him. As painful as it was, she knew now what she had to do. There was no other option.

Straightening her shoulders to give an appearance of an inner strength she didn't feel, she stared at the passing web of greenery. Water the color of emeralds caressed golden sands leading to patches of foliage interspersed with tall cliffs and boulders that seemed to grow out of nowhere.

Something moved in the jungle. At first Eliza thought it must be an animal, but then the rustling leaves parted and a person emerged onto the beach. A man dressed in Union blues. His gaze locked on Eliza's. Her blood ran cold. She rubbed her eyes then peered at the spot again. Alarm sped through her. It couldn't be. *Stanton?* It was Stanton! She'd know him anywhere. His thick brown beard. The way he clasped his hands behind his back. The gold winking at her in the sun from his shoulder straps. She closed her eyes again and shook her head, trying to dislodge the vision. Her breath cluttered in her throat, nearly suffocating her. When she opened them again, he was gone.

"Did you see him?" Eliza asked her friends, hearing the quiver in her voice.

"See who?" Following the tip of Eliza's pointed finger, Angeline stared at the passing spot.

"I don't know. I saw someone in the trees. A soldier. A Union soldier." Eliza threw a hand to her throat.

"Impossible." Sarah laid a hand on Eliza's arm. "Oh, my dear. You've gone pale. I'm sure it was an animal of some sort. Do you wish to sit down?"

"No." Eliza tried to settle her heart. "Thank you. I am sure you are right." Her attempted smile felt tight on her lips. She was going mad. There was no other explanation. Stanton was dead. She'd seen his dead body lying in a casket. Of course he wasn't standing on a beach in Brazil. In the agony of her recent decision, her mind must've conjured him up—to torture her for all her bad choices. That was all. *Lord, how many times must I repent? When am I to be free of the guilt?* She lowered her chin and stared into the foam swirling and crashing off the hull.

"There she is!" Captain Barclay shouted. "Sugar Loaf. You can't miss her!"

All eyes shot off the bow where a black mass jutted toward the sky. The excitement rippling through Eliza erased all memory of Stanton. Men returned to their posts, everyone "oohing" and "ahhing" at the gorgeous view. Beyond Sugar Loaf, mountain ranges appeared through the morning mist, their rounded summits covered with verdure and tropical forest, while the faint outline of a much larger range loomed in the distance, rising above a heavy belt of snow-white clouds.

Eliza felt Blake's overpowering presence behind her long before he spoke.

Overpowering, thrilling, and. . .unsettling.

"Sugar Loaf is a huge slab of black granite, ladies," he began. "Towering over us by some thirteen hundred feet. Isn't she magnificent?"

"Indeed, she is." Angeline craned her neck as the monstrosity rose before them. "See how the sunlight washes her in purple."

Shielding her eyes from the reflection, Eliza admired the beauty as Blake swept his hand toward the mountains surrounding the bay.

"The square tower of the Gavia, the crested Corcovado, the pinnacle of Tijuca. All the familiar mountain faces which stand like sentinels looking down upon the loveliest expanse of water in the world. The bay of Rio de Janeiro."

Eliza had never heard such excitement in his voice. "How do you know their names?"

"I've been studying Brazil for months. Ever since I first decided to gather a group of colonists to come here."

Captain Barclay shouted orders to lower sail and set course toward a fort perched on a large rock in front of Sugar Loaf. The Fort of St. Cruz, Blake informed them. Uniformed men scurried from the gate to spread across the front of the large building. One of them raised a speaking cone to his mouth and uttered a string of words in a language unknown to Eliza. Yet Captain Barclay seemed to understand fully as he replied through his own cone.

"What are they saying, Colonel?" Sarah asked.

"I have no idea, though I imagine they are asking who we are and where we are from."

Eliza raised a brow at him. "You mean to say you didn't learn Portuguese as well?"

His grin sent her heart racing again, and she faced forward. Perhaps it was better not to look at the man.

Finally, the signal for them to pass was given, and the *New Hope* skated into the bay. Like jagged teeth, the surrounding coast jutted into the water, forming innumerable smaller lagoons. Charming islets dotted the bay, their borders filled with orange and banana trees, the lush greenery interrupted only by small villas. A sky of the most superb blue spanned overhead while myriad kingfishers dove beneath the water, only to emerge seconds later with fish in their beaks. Catamarans and fishing boats, as well as a few larger ships drifted over the aquamarine water, which was as calm as a lake. Rio de Janeiro itself extended from the bay upward. Several hills sat in its midst, layered in small houses, while in the valleys, countless fine homes, churches, and public buildings sprawled out in all directions. Beyond the city loomed a lofty chain of mountains, their peaks lost in the mist.

Aside from a few gasps and murmurs, most of the passengers stood in stunned awe of the beauty before them. But Eliza felt only sorrow.

Though she should be happy to at least witness such an exotic place, her insides grieved already at the loss. She had made her decision.

Excusing himself, Blake went to assist the crew in lowering sails and anchoring the ship. A small boat soon arrived carrying the port physician, or so the lithe, dark-skinned man claimed to be. After inquiring whether anyone on board was sick and casting a cursory glance over the passengers, he told the captain to wait for the customs house boat and promptly left, dabbing the perspiration on his neck with his handkerchief.

And wait they did. For an hour. The rising heat soon leeched all enthusiasm from the passengers and crew. Some went below. Others sought out shade on the deck, while still others endured the heat at the railing, unable to pull away from the splendid view of the city.

"I cannot believe we are finally here," Angeline said, her tone a mixture of excitement and sorrow. A breeze flirted with her copper curls, and Eliza's heart went out to the lady. She wished she could stay and help her with whatever troubled her, but that was not possible. She would, however, entrust her to Sarah's capable care. And of course Eliza would pray for her daily. For all these people she'd come to love.

Finally, the dockmaster arrived—a short man with a corpulent belly and a wide straw hat. He leaped on board from a small boat rowed out by Negroes, who were stripped to the waist, their ebony skin shimmering in the sun. After inspecting the hold, he, Captain Barclay, the first mate, James, and Blake disappeared into the captain's cabin for what seemed an eternity. An eternity in which the sun became even more oppressive, boiling the pitch out of the deck seams and extracting an equal amount of sweat from each passenger. Eliza went below to gather a few things to go ashore but found her cabin akin to an oven and quickly returned to the breezes above.

Since they were only to stay in Rio a short while before they set sail for their new land, Eliza saw no reason not to join the others ashore. It would give her time to explain her decision to her friends. To Blake. Besides, she longed to set foot on dry land again and to see more of this wondrous city.

Soon the men emerged from the captain's cabin. And after shaking hands, the dockmaster whistled to a group of men waiting at the docks alongside boats, sending them leaping to task and rowing out to retrieve the passengers. Within an hour, Eliza, along with Angeline, Sarah, and several other passengers bumped against the wharf pilings and were assisted onto land by several Negroes, who seemed none too inhibited to stare straight into Eliza's eyes. Other people, some white, some black, and some in all shades in between came to greet them. The men wore white trousers, broadcloth frock coats, and black silk hats, while the women, all with black hair and fine eyes, wore brightly colored skirts and blouses. And all of them strode about barefooted. They chattered in Portuguese and other languages Eliza couldn't place and extended hands to shake in greeting and fingers to stroke the newcomers' arms and clothing.

Unsure of the proper response and uncomfortable with their familiar touches, Eliza thanked them, grabbed her valise, and hobbled down the dock toward dry land, not used to walking on the unshifting surface. She planted her foot on the sandy soil, raised her face to the sun, and drew a deep breath of tropical air. She was in Brazil. The land of new beginnings.

Unfortunately, those new beginnings were not for her.

Hefting a duffel bag over his shoulder, Blake headed down the cobblestone street, wishing more than anything he could spend time with Eliza alone. Was it his imagination, or had she been avoiding him since the vote yesterday morning? Even today she seemed aloof, reserved. He couldn't imagine why. He thought she'd be thrilled to stay with the colonists—with him. Or at the very least, more appreciative. But perhaps he hadn't given her enough time for the good news to settle firmly in her mind. Then with the dock mate's arrival, he'd been too busy with paperwork to seek her out. And now there were far too many citizens and workers crowding the streets and threading through the throng, all gawking at the newcomers.

Negroes and mulattoes—men, women, and children of every shade, from the deepest black to the palest white—carried sugarcane, bananas, oranges, and other fruits and vegetables in huge baskets across their backs, and they thought nothing of bumping into others as they went along.

The smell of fish, sweat, and waste pricked Blake's nose. He coughed, and his legs wobbled. James gripped his arm. "Steady there, mate. After being on the brig for nearly two months, it will take awhile to get our land legs again. I can hardly walk a straight line myself."

Blake thanked him and ran a sleeve over his forehead. "That isn't the only thing that will take some getting used to. This heat is unbearable."

James glanced across the sky, which was devoid of clouds save for a dark patch on the horizon. "It's still early in the afternoon. No doubt it will cool down later."

"It's not so much the heat as the humidity." Blake leaped out of the way of a mule-drawn cart.

"Humidity or not, I'll be glad to sleep in a bed tonight," Hayden said from Blake's other side.

"Let us pray this immigrants' hotel has enough beds for us all." Though Blake would be surprised if that were the case. The lodging was, after all, provided by the Brazilian government at no expense to the colonists until they signed all necessary papers and were deeded their new land.

"I doubt we'll have anything but a straw tick." James chuckled and rubbed his neck.

"Ah, come now." Blake smiled. "The city seems quite civilized to me." At least more civilized than he'd expected. He scanned the narrow street. Houses on either side sported brightly colored stucco and red-tiled roofs. Inhabitants sat on glassless window ledges while others peered around the corners at them. Gardens filled with colorful trellises and gilded, flower-strewn screens surrounded each building.

"See, look." Blake pointed to a line of tramcars clacking over a track. "They even have a tramway."

"But these roads are a disgrace." Hayden squeezed between a passing wagon and the front of a house as thunder rumbled in the distance.

"My biggest concern"—Blake felt his jaw tighten—"is being able to convince the Brazilian immigration authorities to lend us money for land and supplies. At least until we can bring our first crops to market."

"Thank God we still have some farm implements and seed left," James said.

"But not enough," Hayden added. "Do you think they'll be generous? From the notices I read, it seemed they really wanted us here."

"I hope so." Blake ran a hand over his forehead with a sigh. "I've heard nothing but how benevolent the Brazilian government is. Now that we *are* here, let's pray they see us as a worthwhile investment."

James smiled. "Pray?"

"Figure of speech." Blake snorted. "You pray. I'll hope."

"Peixe! Camaroes!" The cries brought Blake's gaze to Chinamen standing beside open carts filled with fresh fish and prawns. Beside them every imaginable fruit bounded from baskets lining thatched stands: bananas, mangoes, watermelons, pineapples, lemons, pears, and pomegranates. The sweet smell permeated the air, and Blake licked his lips. He hadn't had fresh fruit in weeks. Other peddlers, bearing long bamboo poles over their shoulders with huge baskets filled with fruits and vegetables, wove through the mob with an ease that belied the enormous weight they carried. Hawkers conveyed clothing and jewelry in brightly painted trunks strapped to their backs. Naked children by their side, Negresses, wearing turbans, squatted on mats, selling fruit and vegetables. And in the midst of all the chaos, tiny monkeys and parrots of every color and plume squawked and chattered and flitted from stand to stand.

Blake couldn't help but glance repeatedly behind him at the group of women. And in particular, to the luxurious maple-colored head bobbing among the crowd. Surely, with all their petticoats, the heat was getting to them, yet they seemed so enamored with their surroundings, they didn't utter a single complaint. In fact, most of the colonists hobbled along, gazing at everything with wonder, offering no protests about the heat or the long walk, all except the Scotts, who seemed quite miserable, especially once the road began to ascend.

Hayden seemed equally oblivious to the city's charms. In fact, he appeared to be searching for someone—or something—as his gaze stretched down the street.

"I'm surprised you decided to stay with us, Hayden." Blake transferred his duffel bag to his other shoulder.

"I thought I'd investigate what Brazil has to offer. Besides, just like the rest of you, there's nothing for me back home."

The sun disappeared, offering them a reprieve, and Blake looked up to see a mass of dark clouds. Where had they come from? A breeze tore in from the bay, cooling the sweat on his skin.

They turned down Rua de Direita. Fine shade trees lined a broad paved road edged with flagstone shops, restaurants, and stores. Scents of fresh-baked bread, garlic, and oranges swept away the stink of the city. Blake halted and rubbed his sore leg. "This could be any street in America."

"Indeed," James said. "I am quite astonished."

Hayden stretched his neck to see over the crowd. "If you'll excuse me, gentlemen." And without another word, he sped off as if he had a pressing appointment.

"But you won't know where to find us," James called after him.

"I'll find you; don't worry." He shouted over his shoulder before disappearing into the crowd.

As if nature was unhappy with the man's curious departure, thunder cracked the sky and released a violent deluge. One minute, all was dry as a bone. The next, sheets of rain fell on them as if they stood beneath a waterfall. Though some citizens ducked into shops and houses, most of the workers continued onward as if nothing was out of the ordinary.

"Keep going!" Blake shouted to the colonists behind him. "We are almost there!" Yet he could no longer make out their faces through the wall of water. He longed to backtrack and ensure Eliza was well, but he was the only one who knew how to get to the immigrants' hotel. Raising his duffel bag against the rain, Blake plunged forward. Lightning scored the sky. Thunder shook the sodden ground beneath his boots, and within minutes, water flooded the streets and gushed down gullies and alleyways like a raging river. Blake had never seen so much water rise so quickly. It covered his boots and stormed around his ankles, making his feet sink into the mud like anchors. He glanced at James beside him, who, with head down and breath heaving, forged through the torrent as best he could. Then just when Blake thought they might be in danger of being washed away, the rain ceased and the hotel appeared before him.

What he expected was a large shack or a small stucco house at best. What he saw before him was quite the palatial setting. Rain dripped from the eaves of a grand, white, two-story building that would rival any hotel in Charleston. In front, rows of imperial palms lined a walkway that led from the gate to the steps while marble fountains and benches dotted a garden rich with beautiful flowers. Sunlight chased the clouds away, transforming puddles into shimmering pools and sending steam rising on the marble steps. Setting down his duffel, Blake shook the water from his hair and turned to find Eliza.

Clutching Blake's hand, Eliza allowed him to help her up the slick porch stairs. With her legs still wobbling from the sea and the rain making everything slippery, she could imagine tumbling onto the walkway in a heap of stockings and petticoats. His chuckle brought her gaze to his, and she wondered if he was reading her thoughts. Water pooled on his lashes, dripped from the tips of his dark hair, and covered his skin and clothes with a slick sheen that brought a musky smell to her nose. She couldn't help but smile. "You look like a drowned raccoon."

"And you, a beautiful mermaid." He brushed a saturated lock from her cheek. The tender gesture only further befuddled her mind. Oh fiddle, but she would miss him. At the thought, she lowered her gaze.

His finger on her chin brought her eyes back to his. He cocked his head, studying her. "Why the frown? I much prefer your smile."

Laughter emanated from within the hotel as the colonists congregated in the lobby for further instructions. The men who brought up the rear leaped onto the porch, drew off their hats, and slapped them against their legs. After nodding toward her and Blake, they slipped inside.

Eliza swallowed. She might as well get it over with and tell him now. Turning, she gazed over the gardens where sunlight transformed raindrops into diamonds, and then beyond to the odd city with its hilly streets and brightly colored houses. The *drip-drip* of water tapped a nervous cadence on her heart. "I cannot stay, Blake."

His eyebrows collided. "What are you talking about? The vote was in your favor."

"Barely." She bit her lip, still not meeting his gaze. "I came on this voyage to get away from the hatred. At least back home I have a chance to change my name, move somewhere where nobody knows me. Perhaps Kansas."

"They will grow to love you in time. As the rest have." Gray, pleading eyes swung her way.

As you have? She waited for words that never came. "Perhaps." A breeze chilled Eliza's damp gown, and she hugged herself. "Perhaps not." She wouldn't tell him the truth. That it was her love for him that drove her away. Instead, she fought back tears and forced a smile. "Thank you for wanting me to stay. That means more to me than anything."

"Then stay." He grabbed her arms and turned her to face him. "We need you."

But did *he* need her? Want her? She nearly crumpled beneath the pain in his eyes, the desperation—desperation for her as a nurse or for her as a woman? His breath warmed the air between them and filled her with memories of their kiss. She tried to tug from him, but he wouldn't let go. "The doctor can handle things," she said.

"I cannot believe you're giving up so quickly. After all we've been through."

Eliza met his gaze, those stormy eyes filled with angst. "Don't you see it's because of what you've been through, what they've all been through, the pain and loss of the war, that I must leave?" She stared at his necktie and the way the hollow of his throat rose and fell with each breath. "My presence will only be a reminder of your loss."

If only he'd say he forgave her. That he loved her. If only he'd take her in his arms and beg her to stay, she would. For him. Instead, he just stood there, the muscles in his jaw bunching as if engaged in battle. Then releasing her, he took a step back, leaving her cold and shivering.

She faced the yard, which was even blurrier beneath her tears. "After Captain Barclay deposits you on shore near your new home, I intend to sail with him back to America," she finished.

Blake only stared at her in silence. Though she wanted to look at him—to see if there was anything else besides anger in his eyes, she couldn't bring herself to do it. Finally, he spun around, marched into the hotel, and slammed the door behind him.

CHAPTER 31

$\mathcal{B}$lake's newfound joy washed away with the last remnants of rain from the storm. Stubborn, independent woman! After he'd set aside his misgivings about her allegiances, set aside his animosity, his anger. After he'd called for a vote and all but begged her to stay! No doubt she had more Yankee blood in her than she admitted.

The man standing behind a massive mahogany desk stuffed his thumbs into his lapels and shouted over the din in a Southern accent that Blake found comforting. "Ladies and gentlemen! Ladies and gentleman!" Within a few moments, the chattering ceased and all eyes swept his way.

"I am Colonel James Broome, formerly of the 14th Alabama Infantry, and currently manager of this fine establishment. Welcome to Brazil!"

Excitement buzzed through the saturated crowd once again as Blake spotted Eliza slipping through the door to stand in the back. This should be the happiest moment of his life. They had made it to Brazil! Despite all the countless struggles and tragedies, Blake had successfully led these colonists to the promised land. And from the looks of the abundance in town, it was indeed a land flowing with milk and honey.

Then why did his heart feel as though it had been rolled over by a howitzer? Shaking off his grief, he made his way to the front and introduced himself as the expedition leader. Colonel Broome welcomed him adamantly and then began the business of showing the new arrivals to their chambers.

Blake found his room neat and clean, the walls beautifully papered and the ceiling gilded and frescoed. Two iron-framed beds, a washstand,

and a table and chairs—all painted green—bordered the southern wall. After the tight, dirty confines of the brig, Blake felt as though he'd entered a palace. James followed on his heels, throwing his pack onto one of the beds and whistling. "Look at these lavish accommodations. I never would have expected this." The sparkle in his eyes vanished when he looked at Blake's face. "Perchance has the rain soured your mood? We have made it, Blake." He slapped him on the back, the action sending spray over them both.

"Eliza's not staying."

James flinched. "Why not?"

Slipping out of his saturated coat, Blake tossed it on the bed and began unbuttoning his shirt. "Apparently not enough people voted in her favor to suit her."

James walked to the window, his boots squishing over the wooden floor. A breeze ruffled the plain cotton curtains, bringing the scent of flowers and rain-freshened air. "I can't blame her, really. Did you see some of the looks the nays gave her? The Scotts, Mr. Dodd, and those soldiers, Wood and Adams?" He shook his head. "Hard to live so close to people who wish you dead."

Blake tore off his shirt and grabbed a towel from the washstand. "You're supposed to be on my side."

"Which is?" James spun around and struggled to remove his drenched coat.

"For her to stay, of course."

"Stay for you or for her?"

"Why does everything have to be so black-and-white?" Blake sat and tugged off his boots.

"Life is black-and-white. Good and evil. There is no middle ground."

Blake rolled his eyes. Of course there was middle ground—a thousand different shades of gray between black and white. Grays such as killing your fellow American on the battlefield in a nonsensical war, lying to protect a neighbor, stealing to avoid starvation. . .

And courting the enemy that murdered your family.

Standing, he opened his duffel bag and pulled out his best suit. "We need her skills."

James grinned.

Blake shoved his legs into a dry pair of trousers, pulled them to his waist, and sat back on his bed with a sigh.

"It's obvious you adore her." James leaned back on the window ledge. "Yankee husband or not."

Blake stared at his friend but found no mirth, no mockery in his eyes. In fact, he found none within himself. Instead, the words "adore her" settled in a comfortable place in his heart.

"Come now, are you going to deny it?" James arched a brow.

Blake leaned forward on his knees. "Truth is, I can't imagine life without her."

"Then why not ask her to marry you?"

"Marry?" Blake punched to his feet. "Ridiculous notion," he mumbled. Grabbing a shirt, he flung it over his head and fumbled with the buttons—anything to keep his mind off the thought of Eliza as his wife. A thought that was both alarming and thrilling. "Marrying her won't change the way the others feel about her."

"No, but it will change the way *she* feels. The others will come around when she is your wife."

Wife. After the war, Blake had never thought to take a wife. What woman would want a broken shell of a man? Without family, fortune, or name, what did he have to offer a lady?

"If you don't do something soon, it will be too late." James's voice sent turmoil into Blake's already churning gut. "We set sail again tomorrow and will be at our new land by sunset."

Blake tucked in his shirt and reached for his belt.

"Do you love her or not?"

Why didn't the blasted man stop talking? "It's not that simple." Blake eased on his vest and turned to look in the mirror. Yet all he saw staring back at him was a bitter, damaged, used-up ex-colonel whose mind was so tortured from the past, he didn't know what to think anymore.

"It isn't as complicated as you make it, Blake. Come now, you two are made for each other. Anyone can see that." James tugged his wet shirt over his head and tossed it in the corner.

Blake ground his teeth together. But it *was* complicated. More complicated than devising battle plans. More complicated than following orders that sent young boys to their death. More complicated than anything Blake had thus endured.

Even the luxury of a steaming bath had not soothed away the pain in Eliza's heart. Neither had Angeline's noble attempts to cheer her up, nor—once Eliza had told the lady her plans—her vain pleadings for Eliza to remain with the colonists. Not even Stowy balancing on the edge of the porcelain tub and slipping accidentally into the water had lightened Eliza's mood. Though he had looked rather comical with his sopping fur flattened against his lanky body. Why Angeline hadn't left the cat on board the ship, Eliza couldn't guess. Yet when she'd watched the lady gently dry Stowy with a towel and saw the way the cat nuzzled against her and purred, Eliza supposed the two were inseparable.

If only that were true of Eliza and Blake.

Regardless, as Eliza now descended the stairs to the main lobby, she had to admit it felt good to have her skin and hair free of the sticky, salty sheen that had clung to her since she'd boarded the *New Hope*. She wished she could do the same for her gowns, but there'd be no time to wash them here.

The foyer was abuzz with the news that Emperor Dom Pedro intended to visit that afternoon. Several of the colonists sped past Eliza, retreating to their rooms to dress in their finest attire, only to descend within minutes embellished in lace, satin, and beads. Like a flock of colorful parrots, they flitted about the lobby, spilling onto the front porch and stairs, peering down the long drive and chattering excitedly among themselves. As they waited, Eliza gazed at the city from the window, entertaining the idea of perhaps staying in Rio instead of returning to the States, but thoughts of not knowing anyone or the language or culture promptly squashed that plan. Along with the idea of joining another expedition. No doubt another group of colonists would discover her secret just like this one had, and she'd end up in the same position.

Shortly after three o'clock, the royal coach entered the main drive. Everyone clapped in glee as the emperor emerged and ascended the steps. Having never seen a man of such rank before, Eliza stood on tiptoes for a good look at him. Dressed in a plain black suit, with dark hair and a beard streaked with gray, Eliza guessed him to be in his late forties. Stark blue eyes scanned the crowd above a prominent nose. Only a single star on his left breast indicated his royal position. As soon as he entered the building, aides in tow, a shout went up from the crowd. "Viva! Viva! Dom Pedro Segundo!" Hats flew into the air as everyone cheered and celebrated his arrival, offering their thanks to the emperor for taking them in.

Eliza couldn't help but get caught up in the exuberance, if only for a moment. But as soon as she spotted Blake leaning against a doorframe, arms crossed over his chest, staring numbly at the proceedings, Eliza remembered the celebration was not hers.

Blake entered the small room where the leaders of the individual expeditions met briefly with the emperor. Apparently two other groups of colonists were staying at the hotel. One, under the command of an adventurer named Bails, had sailed all the way from Galveston. The other, led by an former naval lieutenant, hailed from Savannah. At the request of one of the emperor's aides, the three men took seats at one end of a long table while the emperor lowered himself into a large ornate chair at the other, two attendants flanking him. An interpreter welcomed them once again. Dom Pedro informed them they could stay in the immigrants' hotel for up to thirty days, during which time food and water would be provided. He also mentioned he would send a band of musicians and a feast to the main gallery that night to help them celebrate their new beginning.

The man's generosity budded hope for Blake's upcoming request, but his mind kept drifting back to what James had said. *Marry her.* At first Blake had thought the idea ludicrous, absurd. Marry a Yankee widow? What would his family think? What would his brother say? What about all the men he'd served beside, those who'd been maimed and disfigured in the war, the men who'd died at the hands of Yankees? Men whose faces still haunted him every night. What would they say?

No. It was ridiculous.

Then why did the idea still float about his thoughts? Prodding him, teasing him—delighting him?

"I am well pleased with the appearance of your people," the emperor's interpreter continued. "My country is here to help you in any way we can."

With that, the leader of Brazil waved them away with a brush of his hand. As the other men exited, Blake approached the emperor with caution, begging a few words of his majesty's time. Twenty minutes later he left the room bearing a much lighter load. True to his word, Dom Pedro, after hearing Blake's sad tale of the loss of their fortune and most of their tools, not only agreed to loan them the money to purchase land, but also to send along donkeys and carts stocked with supplies, as well as a guide to help them acclimate to the Brazilian jungle.

If not for the ache in his heart, Blake would utter a shout of victory—perhaps even thank God for this unexpected blessing. Instead, he wandered onto the porch for some fresh air and found Sarah rocking her baby in a chair. He started to turn, seeking privacy for his thoughts, when her greeting brought him back.

"Exciting day, isn't it, Colonel?" Her knowing eyes assessed him.

He smiled. "Exciting and profitable. I have just procured a loan from the emperor for our land."

"God be praised! That is good news, indeed."

Little Lydia gurgled as if equally pleased.

"Eliza informed me she won't be joining us, after all." Her voice was tinged with sorrow as she gazed at the garden steaming beneath the blazing sun.

"So, I have heard."

"She seems quite distraught."

Blake released a sigh of frustration. The woman would be the death of him yet. "She is welcome to stay if she wishes."

"It must be hard for her to be so hated."

"That, too, is her own doing." Blake cringed at his harsh tone.

Sarah, however, swept eyes as blue and calm as the bay toward him. "Yet you have forgiven her, haven't you, Colonel?"

Blake squirmed and looked away. "For the foolishness of youth in marrying a Yankee? Yes, I suppose."

"It is a good start."

Colorful birds squawked overhead. One landed on the fence post, cocked its head, and stared at them with one curious eye. Blake took a deep breath. There was a smell to the city he couldn't describe. A mixture of sweet, salt, and spice that was rather pleasing. They were indeed in a new land. He faced Sarah, remembering that she had lost her husband in the war. "You had no qualms about befriending Eliza

273

after you discovered her. . .her"—he cleared his throat—"affiliations."

"Of course not. I do not hold my husband's death to her account, or anyone's. That is merely the nature of war. Even if I did, I would forgive her."

"So quickly?" Blake shifted the weight off his sore leg, his ire rising at the woman's ridiculous piety. "And would you forgive the man who pulled the trigger?"

A shadow rolled over her face, and Blake immediately regretted his words.

"My apologies, madam. I'm afraid too much time in the company of soldiers has stolen my manners."

Sincere eyes met his. "Yes, I would forgive him. When God has forgiven me for everything, how can I not forgive others?" Lydia began fussing, and Sarah rose. "Unforgiveness will only make you bitter and sick, Colonel. You came here for freedom, did you not? Then forgive and be free."

⚜

Eliza didn't want to attend the party. Why should she? She wasn't staying in this new land. She had nothing to celebrate. But Angeline and Sarah would not relent with their pleadings, even going so far as to threaten to stay with her in the room and pout all night if she did not attend. Hence, the reason she now descended the stairs between the two aforementioned ladies dressed in her finest, albeit a bit crusty, gown of emerald percale over a bodice of white muslin trimmed in Chantilly lace. Which wasn't nearly as fine as Magnolia's gown of pink silk looped with sprinkles of golden beads. The raving beauty flitted about the guests, flirting with all the young gentlemen from other expeditions as music that sounded very much like a band from back home floated through the room.

Squished between her friends like a petticoat in a clothespress, Eliza followed the crowd into the back gallery, a large magnificent room lit by a hundred candles and overflowing with a profusion of flowers and plants. Along one side of the room stretched a table laden with all sorts of odd-looking food. Chairs and tables framed the rest of the room, surrounding a black-and-white marble floor. Mulattoes and slaves, barefoot and dressed in white trousers and shirts and sporting blue caps, skittered about with drinks on trays. People from the three expeditions filled every crack and crevice, the crescendo of their voices overpowering even the band, which Eliza could now see consisted of three french horns, three drums, a clarinet, and a fife—all played by Negroes.

Eliza hated hotels. She'd practically grown up in a hotel after her mother died, helping her aunt and uncle. In fact, it was at such a gathering at their hotel in Marietta that she'd met Stanton. He was on his way to Atlanta on a military matter and had stopped for the night. She pictured him standing in his brigadier general's uniform with its dark blue tails, its line of gold buttons down the front, and two gleaming shoulder straps. She was only sixteen at the time, and he'd taken her breath away. And even though he'd been speaking to several men who appeared intent on his every word, he'd frozen when she entered the room. In fact, his eyes never left her—though she'd slipped through the crowd, uncomfortable under his scrutiny—until Magnolia had dragged her over for an introduction.

Eliza could remember her feelings even now. Excited, enamored, flattered that a man of his station and reputation would be interested in her.

"I'm starving. Let's see what Brazilian fare is like." Angeline tugged on Eliza's arm, pulling her from the past and dragging her to the oblong table.

"Ladies, I'll join you in a moment," Sarah said, looking very pretty in a red-and-white-striped gown and fringed lacy shawl. "I'm afraid Lydia needs changing again."

A quadrille began, and couples lined the floor as Angeline and Eliza wove through the crowd to examine the feast. Much of the food was familiar: bowls of rice, whole chickens, bananas, guavas, grapes, strawberries, peaches, some sort of cooked pork that omitted a garlicky smell, other indescribable entrees, and coffee and wine aplenty.

"Miss Angeline." Hayden's voice turned them around. In a borrowed suit of black broadcloth—which was a bit short in both sleeve and trouser—clean-shaven with his dark hair tied behind him, he looked nothing like the bleeding stowaway on the deck of the brig two months ago. After giving a gentlemanly bow and proffering his elbow, he raised an eyebrow and asked Angeline to dance. The smile he sent her was dazzling. Angeline shot a questioning look at Eliza, but at Eliza's urging, the two swept onto the dance floor, leaving Eliza to sample the food alone. Or perhaps make her escape back to her room. With just that thought in mind, she turned to see Blake, looking more dashing than ever, making a beeline in her direction.

CHAPTER 32

I hear the *carne seca* is quite good." Blake's presence consumed the space beside her as he pointed to a platter of meat. His eyes, full of sorrow and anger the last time she'd seen him, held a new light. Perhaps he had finally accepted her decision. Still, she had hoped to avoid him tonight, fearing her own heart could not bear the pain. In fact, after his angry exit earlier that day, she wondered why he would speak to her at all.

But none of that seemed to matter now that he stood so close to her—all male and strength. "Carne seca"—she attempted the pronunciation—"what is it?"

"Sun-dried beef."

"And this." He spooned a chunk of what looked like soggy bread from a bowl, placed it on a plate, and handed it to her. "Corn bread soaked in cream and sugar."

"Hmm." Eliza obliged him by taking a bite and was instantly rewarded with a burst of succulent sweetness.

"And this is *biscoito de polvilho*." He pointed toward another dish. "Cakes made from the mandioca root. Very good and nutritious, I'm told."

"And here we have *palmita*." He continued gesturing to different dishes and enlightening her with his knowledge of Brazilian cuisine.

But Eliza wasn't listening anymore. She was so enamored with his lively manner and his presence, she could hardly put two thoughts together. Wearing a single-breasted waistcoat over a white shirt, black trousers, and his usual tall boots, he towered over her by at least a foot. Had he always been this tall? Or perhaps she had shrunk with her recent sorrow. He smelled of soap and shaving balm, and she drew a deep breath of him.

"And this, believe it or not is *tatu*, or armadillos." He chuckled and offered her a smile that reminded her of the days they'd shared before he'd discovered her identity.

She shook her head, trying to dislodge what was surely a fabrication of her desperate heart. "And how do you know all of this?"

"The man who is to be our guide, Thiago Silva Melo"—he gestured to a tall man with a tanned complexion standing by the door—"informed me of each dish when they first set the table." He stared down the line. Plucking a small piece of cake from a platter, he plopped it in his mouth then served her a piece.

Eliza took a bite. Sugar and almonds filled her senses. Their eyes met, his warmly glazed, hers searching for the reason behind his attentions, daring to hope.

"There's a"—he gestured toward her mouth—"a. . ." He brushed her lips with his thumb. "Crumb."

"Oh." Embarrassed, Eliza dabbed a napkin over her mouth still tingling from his touch.

He leaned toward her ear. His breath warmed her neck. "Lucky crumb."

Eliza's heart sped. Her toes tingled. Even as her anger began to simmer. What cruelty was this? Did he wish to torture her into changing her mind about staying? He lengthened his stance. His gray eyes churned like a turbulent sea. He hesitated, opening his lips as if he wished to say something, before flattening them again.

The quadrille ended, and people crowded around them seeking refreshments, but Eliza barely noticed. Blake took her gloved hand in his. "Would you care to dance?"

"No thank you." She didn't want to dance. She wanted to stare into those eyes for as long as she could. She wanted him to keep looking at her as if she were Dodd's lost pirate treasure.

He frowned and glanced across the people lining up for a reel. His fingers loosened on her hand, and for a terrifying moment, she thought he might leave. Her heart braced for the impact. Instead, he tightened his grip. "Perhaps a stroll in the garden?"

Though her insides screamed to run away, to leave, lest her heart suffer a wound beyond repair, she could do nothing but allow him to lead her around the dancers and out the side door. Moonlight dusted the landscape in sparkling silver. Lofty palms swayed above dancing ferns and graceful orchids of every shape and color. Eliza slipped her hand in his elbow as they walked in silence. Lanterns hanging from trees spread snowflake patterns over the grass beneath their feet. Water bubbling from a fountain blended with the fading gaiety coming from the hotel as he led her away from the crowd. She gazed at him, memorizing every detail, every movement, his hobbled gait that was more a march than a casual stroll, the tightness of his jaw, as if he bore all the problems of the entire world, the three lines creasing his forehead, his adorable awkwardness in these social situations. Who would help him when he had one of his episodes? Who would hold him until it had run its course? Who would comfort him?

Sorrow threatened to overwhelm her.

He stopped and faced her, taking both her hands in his. Eliza's pulse raced. He shifted his stance and gazed across the garden.

"Is something wrong?" she asked.

He smiled and released a tiny snort. "I fear I'm not very good at this."

Eliza waited. Her breath retreated back into her lungs.

He kissed her hands then bowed on one knee and gazed up at her. Eliza's heart stopped beating.

"Will you marry me, Eliza?"

Blake braced himself for her rejection. Aghast, she stared at him, her tiny brows bowing together as if he'd asked her to align herself with the devil. Perhaps he had. What was he thinking? He'd done nothing but show her his disdain most of the voyage. And now, without an explanation, he begged for her hand?

Her breath released in short bursts as if she had trouble breathing. Her eyes searched his, confused and conflicted.

"I'm sorry." Blake rose. "Forget I ever—"

Her lips were on his. She flung her arms around his neck, pulling him near. He lost himself in her taste, in her passion, in the beat of her heart against his. He cupped her face and drank her in, desperate for more of her. His mind reeled at the impossibility. His body thrilled at her response. A little too thrilled at the moment. Withdrawing, he nudged her back, but she snuggled close and leaned her head on his shoulder.

"If you're trying to soften me for your rejection," he said, "please don't stop."

She looked up at him. "Rejection? I never kiss a man out of pity, sir." Her voice was teasing, but then she grew sad and took a step back. "Have you forgiven me for marrying Stanton?"

"Yes." Lifting her hand to his lips, he kissed it. "I'm sorry it took me so long to understand, to let go of my bitterness."

She eased her fingers over his jaw. "You suffered so much. I hated it that my marriage caused you more pain." Then a teasing look claimed her face. "Wait. You're only marrying me for my nursing skills, aren't you?"

He gave her a mischievous grin.

She turned her back to him, her skirts bouncing like lilies on a pond. "I won't be married for charity." Her tone was playful.

Blake stepped toward her, longing to bury his face in her hair. Instead, he leaned and whispered in her ear. "It isn't your nursing skills that captivate me." She smelled of gardenias and jasmine. "Eliza, you are the most. . . You are the most. . . Oh blast it all, you enchant me. I can't imagine my life without you." He slipped his arms around her waist and drew her back against him. "It is I who should worry that your yes is but an act of charity."

"Nonsense." She spun around, her golden eyes shimmering with tears. "I love you, Blake. I have loved you from the first moment you took my hand and welcomed me aboard the *New Hope*."

"My heart was lost then as well." He caressed her cheek. He couldn't believe she loved him! "So, you'll marry me?"

"Yes." She embraced him. "Yes. Yes. Yes!"

Gently, he pushed her back and gripped her shoulders. "Some of the colonists may never accept you. Can you handle that?"

"With you by my side, I can handle anything."

Blake wrapped his arms around her. He felt the same way. Nothing would ever come between them again.

ᴄᴇᴙᴆᴐᴗ

Eliza woke to the sound of dozens of birds chirping congratulatory tunes outside her window. Joy! Joy everywhere! In her heart, in her spirit, buzzing over her skin, in the sweet tropical air, in the sounds of life filtering through the halls of the immigrants' hotel. She was engaged to Colonel Blake Wallace! Could it be true? Was it only a dream? Yet when she turned and opened her eyes to see Angeline staring at her, she knew from the twinkle in the woman's eyes, it was no dream.

"Good morning, Mrs. Soon-to-Be Eliza Wallace." She smiled. Stowy leaped on Eliza's cot and performed a balancing act up her side and onto her shoulders before nuzzling his face in Eliza's hair.

"Come here, you little beastie." Eliza grabbed the cat and sat up, placing him in her lap. "I can hardly believe it." She touched her lips where Blake had kissed her over and over again in the garden before escorting her back to the party lest people began to talk. There they had announced the news, much to the delight of many and to the horror of some. But Eliza didn't care what people thought anymore. She didn't care about anything but becoming Blake's wife.

Two hours later, after a light breakfast of mangoes, some sort of bread soaked in milk and cinnamon, and the best coffee she'd ever tasted, Eliza joined the *New Hope* colonists as they made the long trek back to the bay, into boats, and back onto the ship that had been their home for the past two months. Aside from a few compliments over breakfast, Blake had been too busy organizing everyone, checking maps, and signing final papers to speak to her. Still his occasional smiles and knowing glances filled with love were enough to warm her inside as much as the rising heat of the day did to her outside.

Once on board she positioned herself at the railing and gazed at the beautiful city, not sure when she'd be back. With God's help, in a few years their new colony would thrive and they would have no need of constant supplies from the city. Their new colony! Eliza held back a shout for joy as Angeline and Sarah joined her. A colony she would now be a part of creating. A new life in a new world. She glanced over her shoulder at Blake and their new Brazilian guide, both men leaning over a map spread atop the capstan. Her heart leaped. A new life with a man she adored.

"He is quite a catch, Eliza. I'm so happy for you," Angeline said.

"He *is* wonderful, isn't he?" Eliza giggled, surprising herself. Giggling was not something she'd done for quite some time.

"Now we have a wedding to plan, ladies." Sarah laid Lydia over her shoulder and patted the infant's back.

"Yes indeed." Mrs. Scott, Magnolia by her side, approached the group. "I've orchestrated many wedding parties before. Of course they were elaborate affairs, and we have nothing to work with here, but we shall make do. We'll need an archway and lots of flowers and some sweet punch and cakes, and of course some of the ladies can stitch a veil from the lace in our old shawls. Oh it will be such fun!" Eliza wondered at the sudden change in the woman. Hadn't she been one of the more vocal *nays*, alongside her husband? Yet weddings had a way of bringing women together, she supposed.

While the lady continued chattering with the other women, Magnolia gave Eliza a sincere smile. "I wish you every happiness, Eliza."

Other ladies soon joined them, all aflutter about plans for a wedding on the beach, going on and on about what a wonderful way it was to start the colony and how it would bring them all good fortune. They continued to prattle, most completely unaware that the ship had struck sails and headed out of the bay to the open sea. Regardless, Eliza couldn't help but relish in the acceptance of a few ladies who heretofore had done nothing but cast her looks of disdain. Perhaps the rest would accept her in time, after all. Soon a stiff breeze drove the women below, leaving Eliza alone.

"You want to stay near to your beau, I suppose." One elderly lady winked at her before joining the others.

Eliza's glance took in said beau—all six feet of steely muscle—assisting Hayden and a sailor as they heaved a line that led above to the sails. She longed to spend time alone with him, talking about their love and their plans for the future, but she knew that despite the first mate's return, the captain had come to depend on Blake. Instead, she would gladly settle for a lifetime with him.

With a huge smile on her face, she turned to gaze out over the azure sea, bubbling in frothy waves as if it held the same excitement she felt within. The wind tore her hair from its pins once again, but she was thankful for its cooling caress after the oppressive heat of land. She wondered if their new home would be as hot as Rio. No matter. She would grow accustomed to it.

Several minutes passed while she gazed at the lush greenery passing by the ship. She felt, rather than heard, Mr. Graves slip beside her. With him came an outward chill, a shrinking in her soul. She couldn't quite explain it. He stared at the passing shore, the lines on his face drawn and unyielding.

"Good day, Mr. Graves." Eliza forced down her unease.

He nodded but said nothing.

"You do not seem as overjoyed as the rest of the colonists at our arrival in Brazil," she said.

"Quite perceptive, madam." He gripped the railing, still gazing at the land passing by them in an artistic blend of greens, browns, and gold.

"I don't understand, sir. Why did you join the colony if you did not wish to come here?"

Breaking his trance, he turned to face her, leaning his elbow on the railing. "Forgive me, Mrs. Crawford." He smiled. "I meant only to say that now that we *are* here, I am unsure whether the colony will be a success."

"Where is your faith, sir? We will succeed because we must succeed." She would not allow this sullen man to spoil her newfound joy.

"Faith?" He gave a repugnant snort. "Faith in what? Faith in people? Faith in *God*" The Almighty's name spewed from his lips. "No. I have faith in something else."

Anger tightened her jaw. "And what is that, Mr. Graves? Yourself?"

"No madam." He faced the land again, and a smile coiled his lips. "In power. And the pursuit of that power."

"As you have told me." She followed his gaze to the shore, her emotions running the gambit from fear to anger to sorrow for the man.

"There is something here in Brazil I had not anticipated." The snake ring on his finger winked at her in the sunlight.

From the intense longing in his eyes, Eliza sensed his anticipation wasn't sparked by the same thing that had delighted her—the land's lush beauty.

"Can't you feel it?" He gestured toward the land. "An energy, a preeminent, living force that supersedes our limited understanding."

She glanced at the man curiously before he went on.

"I had thought to have my revenge, but I see now that if I had, I would have missed out."

Now, she knew he'd gone mad. Eliza's breath caught in her throat. The man's words had spilled numbly, almost unbidden from his twisted mind. "Revenge, sir? On us?" She remembered that the South's seceding from the Union had ruined his political aspirations.

He flinched and fingered his black goatee. "What does it matter now?"

She thought of all the disasters that had befallen them on their journey. Could Mr. Graves have been responsible somehow? "What are you saying, sir? That you are the cause of our troubles?"

"Me?" An incredulous brow rose above dark eyes burning with victorious glee. "How could *I* have caused those things? I'm simply a man."

Indeed. She eyed him. "Why are you telling me this?"

"Because out of all the simpletons on board, I thought you might understand. You have a rare sense about you, Eliza. You are familiar with rebellion. And you've seen something, haven't you?" He leaned toward her. "I thought perhaps to find a kindred spirit."

Familiar with rebellion? Yet it was his last words that caused the vision of Stanton standing on the beach to reappear in her mind. But that had just been a figment of her troubled imagination, hadn't it? "Mr. Graves, if your intent is to ruin our colony, then, sir, I am most definitely not a kindred spirit."

"Ah." He glanced over his shoulder at Blake. "Your recent engagement has no doubt settled your alliances."

"My alliances have always been with the colony. Where are yours, Mr. Graves?"

"Where they should be, madam. Where they should be." He gave her a malignant smile, tipped his hat, and strolled away.

And the feeling of uneasiness left with him. Eliza drew a deep breath. She would have to inform Blake of her odd conversation with Graves. If he was responsible for any of the disasters that had plagued their journey and if he had any nefarious plans for the future of the colony, Blake should know so he could stop him.

She glanced behind her, noting that she was finally alone. Now was the perfect time to do what she'd set her mind to do. Slipping her hand into the pocket of her gown, she pulled out the watch Stanton had given her. The initials *FEW* sparkled in the sunlight in beautiful scripted letters. Though the watch appeared a bit masculine for a lady, it was the only thing Stanton had ever given her that had a personal touch. He hadn't even picked out the wedding ring he'd placed on her finger, but rather it was an heirloom that had been passed down through his family. One she'd been forced to return after Stanton's death. Why she'd kept the watch, she didn't know. Perhaps, deep in her heart, she mourned the loss of her first love, or what she had thought was love. Perhaps it gave her comfort that Stanton might have truly loved her after all. She sighed and flipped it over, allowing the chain to dangle over the churning waters. She'd retrieved it from her luggage for one purpose. To toss it into the sea. For she wanted no reminders of her past when she married Blake.

James slid beside her and gripped the railing. Hair the color of wheat tossed behind him as his bronze eyes found hers. "Congratulations, Eliza."

"Thank you, James. I am very happy." Perhaps she should tell the doctor what Mr. Graves had said. But no. It was too happy a day to ruin anyone's mood. Even hers. She would put all thoughts of the odd man out of her mind for now.

"God's plans always work out for the best." He slapped the moist railing and lifted his chin to the sun.

"I see that now." She paused and flattened her lips. "It's amazing to see God turn my blunder into a blessing."

"I'm sure most of us have secrets we'd prefer to keep hidden." The way he said the words and the glimmer of shame in his eyes made Eliza wonder just what nefarious secrets an honorable man like the doctor could possibly have.

"I have no excuse for what I did save my stupidity and rebellion." Eliza gazed at the Brazilian coast speeding by in a kaleidoscope of vibrant greens and creamy beaches. "I always jump into things without thinking, without consulting God. Even if I do consult Him, I still do as I please."

"A common human frailty. Submission is no easy feat for any of us." He snapped hair from his face. "But I've discovered it is well worth it, for God always knows what's best for us." He chuckled. "How arrogant we are to assume we know better than our Creator. His ways are perfect while ours are so flawed."

"I'm starting to see that. I could have saved myself much pain if I'd only obeyed."

The air suddenly stiffened as if an invisible wall rose between them. When Eliza looked at James, she found him staring at the pocket watch in her hand.

"You've gone pale, James. What is it?" She laid a hand on his arm.

"Where did you get that watch?" His voice sounded hollow.

Eliza held it up. "From my husband. It was the last thing he gave me."

James's breath gusted from his chest as his dazed look never left the watch. "Your husband? What was his rank again?"

"Brigadier general."

"Do you know if he fought at Antietam?"

She stared at him, her mind spinning with his questions. "I believe so, yes. He was killed only a few months later."

"And when did he give you the watch?"

"You're scaring me. What is this about?"

"Answer the question, please." She'd never seen him so serious.

"I received it in the mail a week before we received news of his death."

"May I?" He held out his palm, and she slid it onto his hand. "These initials. They are yours?"

"Yes. Flora Eliza Watts."

A cloud covered the sun. James lowered his head.

"What is it, James?"

He fisted the watch until his knuckles turned white. "I met your husband on the battlefield."

"You did? Pray tell, where?"

"Antietam."

James finally faced her, and what she saw in his eyes sent the blood retreating from her heart. She swallowed the burst of angst threatening to destroy her joy.

"After the battle, we suffered major losses. Over ten thousand wounded—so many we couldn't count. I went out on the field to assess the injured before we transported them back to the hospital. Body parts and organs were strewn over the field. But it's the screaming I'll never forget."

Eliza's eyes misted at his pain, even as she feared what he would say next.

"Union soldiers canvassed the dead, stripping them of their effects." Nausea bubbled in her stomach.

"I approached a young boy no more than seventeen. He had a leg wound. Not fatal from the looks of it. A Yankee soldier, a brigadier general, appeared out of nowhere. I noticed him because it was rare to see a man of his rank combing the field after a battle. He never glanced my way but instead knelt by the lad and yanked on a chain around the boy's neck. At the end of it hung a pocket watch."

Eliza felt the blood drain from her face. "You think he was my Stanton?"

"Let me finish." The lines on the doctor's face dipped in sorrow. "The boy gripped the Yankee officer's arm and shook his head, pleading with him not to take it. Instead, the man pulled out his sword and thrust it in the boy's heart then yanked the watch from his neck. Afterward, he stared at his new trinket for a minute, smiled, and stuffed it in his pocket."

Eliza's legs turned to mush, and she grabbed the railing. James took her elbow to steady her. "How can you be sure it was Stanton?" she asked.

"This is the watch he took." James opened his palm. "I'm sure of it. I'd recognize this silver etching anywhere. Besides, I saw the initials. See how big the letters are and the way they glitter in the sun? It was a bright afternoon that day."

A sour, putrid taste filled her mouth. Eliza knew Stanton had been cruel, she just didn't know how much of a monster he truly was. She pressed a hand to her belly, forcing her breakfast to remain. "So, he didn't have it engraved just for me. He murdered a boy for it and was pleased when the initials matched mine." And all this time, she'd been carrying it around, admiring it, dreaming that Stanton had harbored a modicum of love for her.

"But that's not the worst of it."

The doctor's tone sent Eliza's heart into her throat.

"The watch was an heirloom passed down through the military men in the boy's family as a good luck charm."

"How do you know this?"

"Because that boy was Jeremy Wallace, Blake's little brother."

CHAPTER 33

As the *New Hope* drifted to a halt and the anchor was cast, Blake sought out Eliza through the crowd amassing on deck. He'd been so busy with his duties, he hadn't been able to speak to her all day. During the one break he'd had, she had gone below, no doubt to rest in her cabin. Now, spotting her at the railing, he shoved through the mob, pleased to hear the exclamations of excitement at the sight of their new home. It was beautiful indeed.

But even more beautiful was the sight of Eliza, her hair springing from her pins in the breeze and tumbling down her back over her small waist. He slid beside her and covered her hand with his.

"It's exquisite, Blake." Her eyes remained locked on the coast, just twenty yards from the brig. Water the color of aquamarine spread fans of ivory filigree on golden beaches that stretched for miles in either direction. A lush tropical jungle in every shade of green fringed the beach and grew taller as it receded on hills that ended in distant mountains capped with creamy clouds. To their left, a wide river reached emerald fingers laced in foam toward the sea.

Blake swallowed. "It is, isn't it? I can't believe we are finally here." He drew her hand to his lips for a kiss then ran a finger over her cheek.

Still Eliza would not look his way.

Captain Barclay spit a string of orders to the crew to lower boats, open hatches, and prepare the blocks and tackles to hoist the cargo above deck. Passengers scrambled to get out of the way and go below for their things.

Still Eliza did not move.

"Are you all right?" Blake finally asked. He felt a quiver run through her, and he settled his arm over her shoulder drawing her near.

"Something has frightened you."

"Me?" She looked up at him then, her eyes red and puffy. "Frightened of a new adventure?" Her laugh faltered on her lips.

Taking her shoulders, Blake turned her to face him. "You've been crying. Did someone hurt you? Say something to you?"

She lowered her chin. "No. Nothing like that."

"Then what?"

She brought her gaze back to his, her eyes flitting across his face, as if too frightened to land. Pain or perhaps sorrow weighed heavy on her features. Then she smiled, and her body seemed to relax. "I suppose I'm far too excited about our new life, that's all. So much has happened."

"You aren't having second thoughts about us, are you?"

She caressed his jaw. "Never"

He drew her close and kissed her forehead, his fears abandoning him. Together, they faced the shore. "James has agreed to wed us on that very beach tomorrow."

"He has?" She flinched as if this news surprised her, but then uttered a sigh that seemed to relieve her of some burden. "I can hardly believe it, Blake. I'm so happy. I pray nothing will ever separate us." A shadow rolled across her face as she gazed up at him. "Tell me nothing will ever separate us."

Confused, Blake brushed a lock of hair from her forehead. "What could ever do that?"

A breeze blew in from the shore, ripe with the sweet smell of life, tropical flowers, and hope. Blake smiled and stared into the jungle that would soon become their new home. Something shifted in the greenery. A shadow sped through the trees then disappeared. "What was that?"

"What?" Eliza followed his gaze.

"I thought I saw someone in the trees. . .a shadow." Blake rubbed his eyes, but when he looked again, nothing but oversized vines and palm fronds met his gaze.

Eliza stared at the spot for a moment, seemingly deep in thought, but then she gave him a placating smile. "You are no doubt tired. As we all are." She leaned her head on his shoulder. "Besides, this place is far too beautiful to harbor anything dangerous."

Eliza couldn't tell him. She simply couldn't. She knew Blake too well. It had taken him weeks, months, to forgive her for marrying a Yankee. He would never forgive her when he discovered that Yankee had murdered his brother. And for a pocket watch, no less.

Eliza clutched her skirts and stepped from the wobbling boat onto the shore. Sand squished beneath her shoes as waves caressed her stockinged legs. Holding her valise in one hand and her skirts in the other, she waded the short distance to the beach where passengers who had already arrived waited. Turning, she shielded her eyes from the sun and watched as Blake helped sailors hoist supplies from the hold using a series of pulleys strung over the yards.

Bare-chested, his back—now bronze from the sun—glistened in the bright light. Beside him, Moses, also bare-backed, and Hayden lowered smaller crates and barrels into the waiting boats. No, she couldn't tell him. She wouldn't. What good would it do? The past was the past. She couldn't change it. Nor could she change what Stanton had done.

She glanced over the other colonists. Angeline, Stowy in her arms, assisted Sarah and Lydia into the shade of a banana tree. Magnolia, along with her parents, perched on a crate beneath a palm, the ever-present Mable fanning them all as best she could. Mr. Dodd's excited gaze shifted from his map to the jungle then back to his map again. Children played tag with the incoming waves, while most of the men assisted in offloading crates and barrels from the incoming boats. Even Mr. Lewis, in his normal sponged condition, hefted a large sack onto his shoulder and hauled it ashore in an effort to help. Graves, however, stood off to the side smoking one of his cigars and staring at the jungle with a most peculiar look on his face. She'd meant to tell Blake about her conversation with the strange man, but the revelation about the pocket watch had pushed all other thoughts from her mind.

Slipping off her wet shoes, Eliza wandered down the beach, watching as her stockinged toes sank into the sand, wishing she could bury her past just as easily. *Why, Lord? Why do you place this truth on me now? When I've finally found happiness? Oh what am I to do?*

"You have to tell him." Though Eliza had not spoken her prayer out loud, the answering voice was as audible as if God were standing right beside her. Heart seizing, she turned to see James looking at her like a schoolmaster with a pupil. Oh how she hated that look! She'd seen it enough on her father's face to last a lifetime.

"What good would it do?" She swung about and continued walking.

He slid beside her. "It may do no good at all, but that doesn't matter. It's the right thing to do."

"He will hate me."

"Possibly."

Eliza kicked a wave, sending foam into the air. "I could not bear it. Not again."

James halted her with a touch, stuffed his hands into his pockets, and stared at her with that look again.

Shielding her eyes from the sun, she forced pleading into her tone as she met his gaze. "You won't tell him, will you?"

"Not my place."

"And you'll still marry us?"

He nodded. "But you must do one thing for me in return."

Eliza's breath huddled in her throat.

"Pray," James said. "Ask God what you should do, and then do it. If you do that, I'll never say another word about it. I promise."

Sounded simple enough. God wanted her to be happy, didn't He? God was a God of mercy. Surely He wouldn't punish her for something Stanton had done.

She barely had time to nod her agreement when Angeline, Sarah, Magnolia, and several other ladies descended on her with excited voices and giddy smiles, all agog with plans for her wedding.

As the ladies drew her away, Eliza cast one last glance over her shoulder at James, who gave her a nod. The praying she could do. The obeying she'd never been very good at.

⚜

"You did good work today, Moses." Blake laid the final hewn log on the pile and turned to see the black man's features in the darkness.

"Yessir. Thank you." Moses wiped a cloth over his brow and stopped to catch his breath.

Blake did the same. They had worked side by side all day. First on the brig, hoisting goods into boats and then on land, chopping wood for fires. And Blake had learned one thing about the large Negro. Well, maybe two. He was a hard worker. He didn't complain. And he was kind. Three then. Yet there was one thing that had troubled Blake all day, ever since Moses had taken off his shirt.

"Moses, the stripes on your back. Where did you get them?" The words had barely left Blake's mouth before he silently chastised himself for his boldness.

But Moses seemed unaffected. "I don't mind, sir." The large man stretched his back. "Dem stripes are the compliment of my former master. Dat man loved his whip." He chuckled.

Blake found nothing amusing about it. "You're such a hard worker. I can't imagine anyone ever being displeased with you."

"He was displeased with everything, sir. Didn't matter so much what any of us slaves did."

"How did you get free from him?"

"We didn't. After de war, he threatened to shoot any of us who tried to run away." He kicked the sand, the first indication of any anger within him. "He shot my wife. My wife in God's eyes, since they wouldn't let us get married proper."

Shock sped through Blake along with a sinking feeling that twisted his gut into a knot.

Moses lowered his gaze. "Shot 'er right in de back."

"I'm sorry." Blake knew the words were meaningless, but he didn't have any others to offer.

"I ran away after dat." Moses lifted his gaze to the dark sky strewn with clusters of stars. "My wife be in glory now. An' I forgive him." He shrugged as if he were forgiving a slap on the face or the theft of a small object, not the stripes marring his back and the death of his wife.

Confusion ripped Blake's reason to threads. "How can you do that? Forgive so easily?"

"Not up to me, sir. I ain't de judge. That be God's place. Besides, He's forgiven us more than we deserve."

Blake wanted to ask him what kind of judge allowed such injustice, but Captain Barclay marched toward him and slapped him on the back. "Excellent work today, Colonel!"

"Thank you, Captain." Blake turned back to see Moses' dark figure fading into the shadows.

"Are you sure you ain't interested in becomin' my first mate?" the captain continued. "You not only learned to handle a ship in two months better'n any seaman I seen, but you've organized this disorderly group into a civilized camp in a single afternoon. I could use a man like you."

Blake glanced down the beach. Flickering light from two massive fires spread a glowing sphere over the sand and pushed back the encroaching shadows of the night. Around them colonists sat on logs and trunks, chattering excitedly about the days ahead. A massive tent for the ladies stood stark against the dark forest. The men would sleep on the sand. He'd already assigned three shifts of two watchmen to stand guard throughout the night.

"I appreciate the offer, Captain, but I believe I owe it to myself and these people to give this colony my best shot."

"Well, if anyone can do it, you can."

Hayden, cup in hand, slogged in the sand toward them, followed by James. "Captain, when do you set sail?" James asked.

Captain Barclay scratched his beard. "Was goin' to leave tomorrow, but I believe I'll stay for the weddin' and festivities and leave the day after. My men could use a good party."

At the mention of the wedding, Blake realized he hadn't seen where had Eliza gone off to. He had left her after dinner over an hour ago. Now she was nowhere in sight.

James slapped a bug on his arm. "We will miss you, Captain. It's been a pleasure sailing with you and your crew."

"Agreed," Hayden added with a quick nod. "Thank you for taking me on board."

"You are a good worker, Hayden. We were glad to have you." Captain Barclay gazed at the *New Hope*, nothing but a dark silhouette against a smoky horizon, and chuckled. "Though 'twas quite a voyage, I'd say. Ne'er had so much bad luck on one trip before."

"But God saw us through," James added with a smile.

Hayden grunted and sipped his drink.

"Indeed," Captain Barclay said.

"What are our plans, Blake?" Hayden asked. "After the wedding, of course." He winked.

Other than the wedding night? Blake couldn't help but smile—and warm at the thought—but he quickly rubbed his mouth before the others noticed. "The emperor said the donkeys and wagons should be here in five or six days. We wait for them to show up and—"

A loud screech blared from the jungle, sounding half human, half beast. The hair on Blake's arms stood at attention as all eyes shot toward the sound. The colonists grew silent. Blake peered into the dark maze so full of life that it undulated and billowed as if it were alive. "I was told there were no longer any natives here, but I thought I saw something earlier. A person."

"Probably a trick o' the sun is all." Captain Barclay spat to the side. "An' that there was probably just a monkey. For such tiny creatures, they sure make quite a clatter."

Blake loosened his tie. That didn't sound like any monkey he'd ever heard. But then again, he hadn't heard that many monkeys in his lifetime. "After the donkeys arrive," he continued, "we pack up and hack our way inland. The emperor told me there is some prime farming land just a mile or two upriver."

James rubbed his hands together. "I can't wait to get started."

Hayden glanced toward the colonists around the fire, his eyes alighting on Angeline—or was it Magnolia?—Blake wasn't sure.

"It will be hard on the ladies," Hayden said. "Going through the jungle."

James followed his gaze and frowned. "They survived a precarious sea journey. They will survive this."

"What of the lady who tossed herself into the sea?" Captain Barclay asked.

"She seems quite recovered," James said, his eyes, too, on Angeline.

Hayden tossed the rest of his drink into the sand.

"Her mood does seem much improved," Blake offered even as the lady's laughter echoed over the sand. "Speaking of moods, mine would be much improved if I could find my fiancée. She seems to have disappeared yet again."

Hayden cocked a brow. "You've got quite a handful in her."

Smiling, Blake started down the beach, turning to face the men as he walked backward. "I commanded a regiment of over a thousand men, how hard can it be to handle one small woman?"

⸎

Eliza knelt in the sand and stared across the dark sea. A half-moon rose on the horizon, frosting the tips of ebony swells. The crash of waves joined the buzz and chirp of a myriad night creatures singing in the forest behind her as the smell of salt and smoke and moist earth filled her nose. She breathed it in like an elixir. This beautiful place was her new home, would be her new home, and she would be Blake's wife tomorrow.

If everything worked out as she hoped. As she dreamed.

She fingered the locket around her neck. "Oh Mother. I wish you could meet him." A shooting star caught her eye, drawing it to the thousands—no, millions—of stars flickering against the dark sky. "Lord, You said all things work together for good." At least she thought she remembered a verse like that. When was the last time she'd even read her Bible? Sarah had been so faithful to read hers every day, even offering to read passages out loud to Eliza, but Eliza had never had time.

"I'm sorry I haven't spoken to You very much, Father. You know I believe in You and I love You. There's just been so much going on. Please forgive me." She bit her lip, waiting for a burst of thunder or maybe lightning to strike, but instead a light breeze whisked over her as if God, Himself, were caressing her face. She smiled, emboldened to continue. "I love Blake. He's everything I've ever wanted in a man. Strong, protective, smart, kind, honorable, and good. And he loves me—can you believe it?" She chuckled. "Me?" Poking a finger into the sand, she began sliding it through the warm grains. "But there's this thing, this unimaginably horrible thing that Stanton did. Well, You know." Even now she felt the weight of the pocket watch in her skirt. She had wanted to toss it into the sea. Should have tossed it. But something held her back. It wasn't hers to throw away. In truth, it didn't belong to her at all.

It belonged to Blake.

A tiny crab skittered up to her leg, stopped, and then dashed away. She glanced down the shore where lights from the two fires flickered in the distance. "I don't know what to do. What good would it do to tell him?"

A tear spilled down her cheek, instantly cooled by the breeze. "I can't lose him. Please." She swallowed the burning in her throat. "But what is Your will? What would You have me do?"

There, she had asked. Now she would wait a few minutes, give God a chance to answer, and if she heard nothing, she'd do what she felt was right. Which was not telling Blake.

A wavelet crashed ashore, spreading a circle of bubbling foam over the sand. Palm fronds stirred by the wind sounded like gentle rain. It was so peaceful here. Yet out of that peacefulness came a voice.

You must tell him, child.

A voice that did not come from within or without. Neither was it a shout or a whisper. But Eliza had heard it, nonetheless. And her heart sank into the sand beneath her.

"Father? Was that You?"

You must tell him.

Tears poured down her cheeks. She dropped her head into her hands. "I can't."

Trust Me. . .for once.

Eliza sat up and looked around. No one was there. Nothing but the crabs and the surf. Yet *"for once"* kept ringing in her ears. No one would know that but God. No one would know that she'd been disobedient her entire life. Gone her own way. Done whatever she wanted. And she'd gotten herself into mess after mess.

If you love Me, you will obey Me.

"I do love You, Father. You've always been there for me, no matter the mess I've made of things. You've always helped me, forgiven me."

Then stop fighting Me.

Eliza wiped the moisture from her face. Who could fight God? Yet, as she thought over her life, she had indeed fought Him. Just as she'd fought her own father. And anyone else who tried to control her, smother her. She'd always thought that if she obeyed God, she'd be restricted, imprisoned, unhappy with choices that were not her own, when in reality, the choices she'd made had stolen away her freedoms even more. Stuffed her in a cage from which there was no escape.

In fact, God had neither smothered her nor reprimanded her. He was the perfect Father, the perfect gentleman. Almost too perfect, for He had allowed her too long a leash. Her rebellion had caused so much pain, not only for herself, but for her father, her aunt and uncle, even Stanton. And now Blake.

"I've been such a fool!" The tears came again, this time sliding down her cheeks in abandon. "I'm so sorry. If I'd only listened to You."

I love you, precious daughter.

Eliza closed her eyes, sensing the caress of God on her face in the gentle breeze. "I love You, too, Father."

Moments later the crunch of sand sounded, breaking Eliza from her trance. Batting tears from her face, she stood and turned to see the shadow of a man coming her way.

"What on earth are you doing out here by yourself, Eliza? It isn't safe." Blake's voice reached her ears. Before she could protest, he took her in his arms, surrounding her with his strength, breaking her resolve to do the right thing.

She pushed away from him. "I must tell you something, Blake."

CHAPTER 34

Air seized in Eliza's throat. She drew a shaky breath. "I must tell you now, Blake, or I never will," she rasped out.

He kissed her forehead. "Whatever it is, it doesn't matter. This time tomorrow we will be wed." The desire dripping from his sultry voice was nearly her undoing. As were his lips touching hers.

Pushing against his chest, she backed away. "Hear me out, please."

He must have sensed her dismay, for he took her hand in his. "What is it, Eliza?"

Waves stroked the shore in a soothing pulse that defied the one thundering within her. She searched for his eyes in the darkness, glad when she couldn't find them. At least she wouldn't see the pain, the anger that would burn within them when she told him the truth.

A wavelet tickled her foot, and he led her aside. "If someone has upset you, tell me, and I'll speak to—"

"It's about my husband."

He caressed her fingers. "Whatever it is, I don't care. I'll be your husband tomorrow." He leaned down to kiss her, but she laid a finger on his lips.

"You're scaring me now," he said. "What is it?"

"Something I learned only yesterday. But something you must know." Her heart pounded so forcefully against her ribs, she worried it would break through. Reaching into her pocket, she felt the watch and slowly pulled it out. Then turning toward the moonlight, she held it out to him.

He stared at it but made no move to touch it. The buzz of the teeming jungle, the crash of waves, and the distant crackle of fire and chatter of the colonists all combined to scrape against Eliza's nerves.

Furrows appeared on Blake's brow, slight at first, then deepening with each passing second. Seconds that ticked out Eliza's last moments with him in an agonizing slowness. Finally, he reached for it, held it to the light, flipped it over. And gasped.

His chest rose and fell like a sail snapping in the wind. He stumbled.

Eliza gripped his hand to steady him. His eyes met hers. Or at least she felt them meet hers—dark, gaping holes staring at her in shock, in confusion so thick she could feel it thicken the air between them.

"Where did you get this?"

She'd found it. She'd bought it. She'd stolen it. A dozen lies forced their way onto her tongue, vying for preeminence. "Stanton."

He released her hand. It fell to her side, empty and cold. "Your husband gave this to you?" His voice rose, etched in pain.

Eliza nodded, fighting back tears.

"This is my family's." He pointed to the engraving. "These letters stand for Frederick Evan Wallace, my great-grandfather." He closed a fist over the watch and glanced at the dark sea, where waves churned and frothed as if heightened by his anger. "The last person to have this was my brother, Jeremy."

"I know."

He snapped his gaze to her. His silence stole the remainder of her hope. She knew James had told him what he'd seen that day in Antietam. She knew Blake was putting the pieces together—laying the bricks one atop the other to form an impenetrable wall between them. "Your husband murdered my brother."

The words hung in the air like a massive judge's gavel ready to pound Eliza into the sand.

"I didn't know, Blake. I didn't know any of this until James saw the watch yesterday. It was a gift from Stanton. I thought he'd had my initials engraved on it. Flora Eliza Watts. I'm so sorry, Blake. I'm so very sorry."

He pulled away from her as if she had a disease. "Your husband killed Jeremy," he repeated numbly. Then, enclosing the watch in his fist, he thrust it in the air, chain spinning about his arm. "For this watch!" he shouted.

Tears coursed down her cheeks. She hugged herself as Blake's breath came out heavy and hard. A breeze flapped the collar of his shirt and the ends of his necktie but did nothing to cool the anger steaming off him. His face grew dark, indistinguishable with the night.

"I'm so sorry, Blake, I didn't know." She laid a tentative hand on his arm.

He shrugged her off and backed away.

"Blake?"

"I never want to see you again." His voice was hard as steel and cold as the chill darting down Eliza's back. Then turning, he stormed back to camp.

Eliza crumbled to the sand in a puddle of agony. Minutes later, or maybe it was hours, Angeline and Sarah surrounded her with loving arms and useless words of comfort before leading her back to the tent, where they tucked her into bed. But her mind and heart refused her sleep. Instead, she watched tree branches cast eerie shadows on the canvas roof, like giant claws reaching for her, trying to pull her into the abyss of despair. Was Blake asleep, or was he as upset as she was? Oh what did it matter? He never wanted to see her again. She would leave with Captain Barclay as soon as he readied the ship to set sail. There was no other choice. Tears slid onto her pillow. Angeline murmured a name in her sleep, and Eliza reached out and grabbed her hand, hoping to comfort her in the midst of her dream. She would miss her terribly. And Sarah. And even Magnolia. And all the friends she'd made among these people.

"Lord, why?" she whispered. "Why, when I obeyed You? When I did what You asked?" Wind flapped the tent, sweeping beneath the canvas and wafting over her.

I love you, precious one.

Despite her agony, despite her pain, Eliza found her anger dissipating. God was with her, and He loved her. In fact, she spent the remainder of the night talking with Him. About her life, her father, Stanton, her bad choices, and her good ones. She prayed for each of her new friends: for Angeline to find peace, for Sarah to find love again, for Magnolia to. . .well, just for Magnolia. For James to find healing from the internal wounds he seemed to carry around, for Hayden's agitated spirit to settle, for Dodd to find a treasure far better than gold, for Mr. Lewis's bitterness and drinking to ease, for Mr. Graves to let go of his quest for revenge and power, and for all the rest to find what they were looking for in this new land.

And finally for Blake. For him to forgive all those who had hurt him in the war, for his nightmares and episodes to stop, and for him to find a woman to love him.

The last prayer was the hardest of all, but once Eliza had uttered the words, she realized what true love was. It was selfless and pure and sought only the best for the object of its devotion.

By the time the first rays of the sun set the tent aglow in pinks and saffron, Eliza felt at peace for the first time in her life. She had done the right thing. Against her own wishes, she had told the truth. She had done the hard thing. She had obeyed God. And though the outcome was worse than she could have imagined, the guilt, the burden of fighting her Creator, of trying to run her life on her own terms, was gone, lifted from her shoulders in the same way the pulley had lifted the cargo from the hold. She had spent the night with God and found Him to be a loving, caring, wise, compassionate Father. Never again would she forge out on her own. Never again would she decide her own fate. Why would anyone do such a thing when there was a God who created them, who knew the past, present, and future? And who always knew the right choice to make, the right path to choose.

Noises from camp drew Blake's gaze to James sitting by the fire, stirring the red coals to life. Men stood and stretched while a few ladies emerged from the tent. Rising to sit from the place in the sand where he'd dropped from exhaustion, Blake rubbed his eyes. The arc of the sun peered over the horizon, the train of its royal robes fluttering over sea and sky in an array of vermilion, gold, and coral. Such beauty should have been prohibited on a day like today. It should be dark and gloomy and stormy, not bright and cheery. Picking up a shell, Blake tossed it into the sea, feeling as empty and devastated as he always had after fighting a major battle. Only this battle had been on the inside, not on the outside. Somehow, it seemed much harder.

People pointed and glanced his way, leaning their heads in gossipy prattle. No doubt word had spread throughout camp of what had happened. He wanted neither their pity nor their advice. Advice he was sure to receive now as James headed toward him bearing a steaming mug.

Leaping to his feet, Blake dusted sand from his trousers and met him halfway—passed him, actually—holding up a hand against the outstretched mug.

"Coffee. You look like you need it."

"Not if there's a price." Blake huffed, continuing onward.

"It's free." James kept pace beside him.

"I don't want to hear it."

"What?"

"Your opinion."

"Good, 'cause I wasn't going to give it."

Ignoring the stares shot his way, Blake wove through the camp, kicking sand as he went, and retrieved the machete from its spot wedged in a tree stump.

"If you intend to hack Eliza to pieces, I'm afraid I *do* have an opinion on that." James gave a wry smile.

"Don't give me any ideas." Blake spun about and marched toward the jungle.

Still James followed. "Telling you the truth was hard for her to do."

Blake spun around. "You knew, didn't you? You knew that soldier was her husband."

Planting his fists at his waist, James glanced downshore. "Not until I saw the watch."

Blake grunted and started on his way again.

"Unforgiveness will destroy you, Blake."

Ignoring him, Blake plunged into the tangled web and began hacking his way through the vines and branches, releasing his fury on the plants. Yet after several minutes, rather than appease his anger, every strike seemed to add fuel to the flames. One glance over his shoulder told him James had not followed him. Good. He faced forward and slashed left and right, back and forth, focusing on the vision in his mind. The one that had been there all night. The one he couldn't shake—Eliza's husband plunging his blade into Jeremy's chest. And her, the adoring wife, sitting at home waiting for him to return. Blake raised the machete. *Slash!* Receiving his family's watch as a love gift from Stanton. Sure, she hadn't known what he'd done, wouldn't have approved, but how could she have married such a monster? *Hack!*

In a frenzied rush, he slashed his way forward. Sweat streamed down his face, dripping off his chin. The smell of musk and earth and life battled against the sense of death invading his soul. Stopping, he wiped his sleeve over his forehead and gazed at the canopy forming an impenetrable roof over the jungle. Birds flitted from branch to branch. The sounds of the ocean faded behind him, replaced by the buzz of insects and warble of parrots.

And a still, small voice. . .

Sarah forgave.

Blake spun around. No one was there. Shaking his head, he forged ahead. *Slash! Hack! Whack!*

Moses forgave.

Halting, Blake scanned the jungle. He must be having another episode. Or worse, he was going mad. Yes, Moses had forgiven the man who had beaten him, killed his wife. And Sarah had forgiven those who had killed her husband. They were better people than Blake. Stronger, with good hearts.

Whack! His fury exploded on an innocent vine. Fury that fueled him. Fury that had kept him going during the war, after the war. And after he'd found his entire family dead.

Slash! Hack! Branches and vines flew in every direction. His chest heaved. His shirt clung to his skin. Thirst clawed at his throat. But he didn't care. He would beat down this jungle until the pain subsided. Until the grief left him. Even if he had to beat a trail to the other side of Brazil.

Stopping, he yanked the black bands from his arm and stuffed them in his pocket then tore off his moist shirt and continued. A spiky vine caught his skin and ripped through flesh. Blood trickled onto his belly.

Sarah and Moses have peace.

Yes, they did. They were happy, not tormented like Blake. He pictured Sarah's kind face and Moses' wide, blinding smile.

Something moved to Blake's left. A dark flicker. A shadow. Blake hacked in that direction. A breeze cooled his sweaty skin. The sound of a crackling fire filled the air. Coming from nowhere yet everywhere. Chilled air twisted around him. Shivering, Blake halted and squeezed the bridge of his nose. He was definitely going mad. The crackling turned into groans, low and guttural.

Ignoring them, Blake raised his machete and continued. How

could he marry a woman whose husband had so brutally murdered his brother? He would be defiling Jeremy's memory—his entire family's memory. They would never forgive him.

He would never forgive himself.

Hack! Thwack! Blake halted to catch his breath. A shadow drifted among the greenery ahead of him. It moved slowly, methodically, the gray mist coalescing into a single shape, solidifying, until the leaves parted and out stepped. . .

Jeremy.

His brother, in his Rebel uniform with gray kepi atop his head, stared at Blake, a blank look on his face. Blake closed his eyes, his heart racing. The episodes had never produced anything so real before. Yet when he peered at the sight again, Jeremy remained.

Blake stumbled forward, reaching out. "Jeremy." But the boy turned and ran into—no through—the tangled shrubbery, stirring not a leaf. A shiver bolted across Blake's shoulders. His hands began to tingle. Raising his machete, he darted after his brother, slashing away the branches as he went.

He burst into a clearing. Jeremy lay on the ground. Blood bubbled from a wound on his chest and trickled to the dirt at his side. His vacant eyes stared into nothing.

"No!" Blake headed for him, his mind spinning at the impossibility. But then Jeremy faded into black smoke and disappeared. The crackling began again, and Blake fell to his knees. "No!"

He choked on his own breath. His leg burned.

"God help me!" he shouted.

I am here, son.

Jumping to his feet, Blake swept his blade across the clearing. The crackling ceased. Sunlight broke through the canopy in shafts of glittering light.

"God?" Blake breathed out the question.

The shafts danced and twirled, growing larger and wider until they spilled over him with warmth, chasing away his chill and forcing the shadows back into the jungle. "You're real?"

Yet what other explanation was there for the intense sensation that now poured down on him? Blake's mind twisted. If there was a God and He was here. . . He raised the machete. "Why did you allow my family to be killed? My brother?"

James's words returned to fill his mind: *"God gave mankind a wonderful yet dangerous gift—free will."*

"But You could have stopped it. All of it." Blake fell to his knees again and hung his head. "But then we would all be puppets without free choice." He tried to recall James's words. "And love given without choice is nothing but empty servitude." Finally, Blake understood why God allowed man to have a will of his own. He lifted his gaze to the canopy. Dozens of tiny white butterflies danced in the light.

A sensation struck him, a flash, a flicker, a vision, and suddenly he knew that Jeremy and his parents were happy and well. He couldn't say how he knew, but he knew—could sense them smiling down on him. Along with God. A sense of belonging, of family, filled his chest till he thought he would burst. There was life after this world, and God would set things straight in the end.

"I'm so sorry I doubted You. I'm so sorry I blamed You." Leaning forward, Blake touched the spot where Jeremy's blood had spilled. But there was nothing there.

His thoughts sped to Eliza.

Sarah had told him unforgiveness would make Blake bitter and sick. That it was a prison. Blake bowed his head, trying to force the picture of Jeremy's bloodied and bruised body from his mind. Yes, he could forgive Eliza. She'd been young and impetuous when she'd married Stanton. How could Blake blame her for the actions of her husband? Still. Would Blake's family forgive him for marrying her? Reaching into his pocket, he pulled out the five bands and gazed up at the rays of sun piercing the canopy. Somehow, he knew they would. Knew they no longer cared about such things. He laid the bands on the spot where Jeremy's body had lain, an offering of his sincerity. "I forgive her, Lord."

Then forgive him as well.

Stanton? Blake swallowed as he realized the man was probably in a very bad place right now. A place Blake wouldn't wish on anybody. Yet anger still burned in Blake's gut. He felt no forgiveness in his heart toward the horrid man, but he could say the words. He could do that one thing. Take that small step. "I forgive him, Lord." Nothing changed after his declaration, yet he'd obeyed. "I suppose I have some work to do on that one." He shrugged as Eliza's beautiful face filled his thoughts.

Eliza!

Blast it, she might already be sailing away with Captain Barclay.

Rising, Blake shouted his thanks to God, grabbed his machete, and raced into the jungle.

CHAPTER 35

*E*liza stood on the beach, arm in arm with Angeline and Sarah. Their support and love had sustained her through many a dark moment on board the ship. And now it sustained her in her darkest moment as she waited to leave Brazil—forever. Above them, the merciless sun hurled fiery blades on sand and sea. Perspiration beaded her neck and brow. But she didn't care. These were her last moments with her friends. Her last moments as part of the colony.

Lydia cooed, and Sarah spread a lacy shawl over the baby's head, rocking her back and forth. Eliza ran a finger over the child's soft cheek, wondering if she'd ever have a baby of her own. Most likely not. Who would marry a traitor?

Shouts drew their gazes to Captain Barclay storming across the deck of the *New Hope*, issuing orders that sent some of his crew skittering up shrouds and others dropping below. Upon discovering there would be no wedding, he'd decided to leave forthwith. Thankfully, he'd allowed Eliza to remain ashore to say her good-byes while he prepared the ship. Yet now as Eliza and her friends watched in silence, those preparations seemed to be coming to an end. Soon he would signal the final boat to bring her on board.

Stowy circled Eliza's feet and rubbed the fringe of her gown as if saying good-bye. Bending over, Angeline bundled the cat in her arms and stroked his fur. From several yards down the beach, where the colonists loitered about camp, wind brought the scent of cooking fish to Eliza's nose. Her stomach grumbled, but she had no appetite. She'd already said good-bye to most of them. Several had expressed their sorrow at the way things had turned out, which gave Eliza a measure of comfort.

However, aside from Angeline and Sarah, James seemed the most distraught. Even now he paced through the camp, glancing occasionally at the jungle as if he expected some miracle to occur and Blake to appear. Over her shoulder, Eliza studied the thick greenery where she'd been told the colonel had disappeared earlier that morning, but there was no sign of him. She hoped—no prayed—he was all right. She would have loved to have had one more chance to apologize, one more chance to gaze into those stormy, gray eyes. But perhaps God was sparing her that pain.

"The captain's signaling the boat." Sarah's voice was solemn, bringing Eliza's gaze to the sailor waiting by the small craft down shore. He gestured for her to come.

Straightening her shoulders, she drew a breath for strength and fought back the burning in her eyes. "I pray you both find the happiness you seek in this grand new world," she addressed her friends, forcing a smile.

Angeline sniffed and raised a hand to her mouth. "It will seem so empty without you."

Eliza squeezed her arm, but no words of comfort formed on her lips. She'd already said them all.

The trio began walking down the beach. Eliza's feet felt like anvils, her heart like a stone. A tear broke free and slid down her cheek. They halted before the boat, and the sailor held out a hand to assist her on board where her valise awaited her.

"I will pray for you every day, Eliza," Sarah said, shifting teary eyes her way.

"And I shall pray for you both as well." Eliza drew her friends into an embrace.

"Finally!" James's voice thundered across the beach. Swiping tears away, Eliza looked up to see Blake hobbling out from the jungle. He scanned the beach, his eyes latching on hers. Raising a hand to ward off James's approach, he started toward her. Stripped to the waist, the muscles in his chest and belly surged and rippled with each step. Sweat glistened on his skin. His dark hair, normally combed, was now ruffled by the wind. Like a cannon to its target, he sped her way. Eliza's heart lurched into her throat. Did he intend to push her into the sea?

"Oh my," Angeline said.

Sarah tugged on the lady's arm. "Come, Angeline, it appears the colonel has something to say to Eliza."

Eliza cast a pleading look at her friends. She opened her mouth to ask them to stay, but a mere squeak emerged from her lips. Sarah offered her a comforting smile and a wink before dragging Angeline and Stowy away.

Blake halted before her. He smelled of sweat and forest musk, and she was afraid to look into his eyes. Afraid of what she'd see. Instead, she stared at his bare chest, raw muscle flexing from exertion.

"Eliza," he breathed. Placing a finger beneath her chin, he raised her gaze to his. Remorse and affection burned in his eyes. Her legs wobbled. He took her hand and led her down the beach, away from prying eyes and ears.

"I've been a complete fool." He halted and stared at their locked hands.

She opened her mouth to speak, but he placed a finger over it and smiled. "Let me finish." He dropped to one knee—his bad leg—and grimaced. "I love you, Eliza. It was wrong of me to hold you responsible for Stanton's actions."

The words trickled over her mind like water over a rock. Cooling, soothing, yet not remaining. Not making sense. It must be a dream. But then that dream spoke again.

"I'm sorry for the way I behaved. I love you, Eliza. I don't deserve your forgiveness, but please say you'll forgive me, and that you'll still marry me."

His voice, the sincere urgency in his eyes, sparked her heart to life like a match to kindling. If this *was* only a dream, Eliza must give it a happy ending. She knelt in front of him and took his hand and placed it over her heart. "Yes. Now and forever, I am yours."

He smiled and gathered her in his arms. And together they laughed and cried and kissed, oblivious to all around them. Until clapping and cheering sounded from down shore.

Eliza's face warmed. "Does this mean I'm staying?" She gestured to the sailor waiting by the boat, a confused expression on his face.

Blake waved him off before facing her again and helping her to her feet. "By my side forever." He picked her up and swung her around and around, their laughter mingling in the air above them.

Within minutes, the sailor rowed back to the *New Hope* where the boat was hoisted on board, and Captain Barclay waved his farewell to all of them. Soon, with all canvas spread to the wind, the brig drifted away.

Three hours later, Blake, bathed and in his best suit, stood beside Eliza beneath a bamboo arbor festooned with passionflowers and seashells. James, open Bible in hand, stood before them. The sound of waves kissing the shore and an orchestra of birds provided the music.

"Charity suffereth long, and is kind; Charity envieth not; Charity vaunteth not itself. . ." James read from the Bible, but all Blake could think of was how glad he was that the beautiful lady beside him would soon become his wife. "Charity. . .beareth all things, believeth all things, hopeth all things, endureth all things. Charity never faileth." Closing the Holy Book, James looked up. "You may face your bride."

Finally. Blake turned and took Eliza's trembling hands in his. Dressed in a creamy silk gown she'd borrowed from Magnolia, she glistened like an angel dropped from heaven. The locket she cherished so much hung about her neck. Sunlight glimmered in the maple ringlets dangling about her shoulders. A violet and pink orchid adorned her hair. She smelled of gardenias and sweet fruit, and Blake licked his lips in anticipation. Not just of their night together. But of their life together. Of making her his.

James opened the Book of Common Prayer. "Repeat after me. Do you, Blake Wallace take Eliza Watts to be thy wedded wife. . . ?" As James continued, Blake focused on each precious word, eager to promise her anything. Finally, the man concluded.

"I do," Blake said emphatically, smiling at Eliza and silently thanking God for revealing Himself to Blake, for forgiving him and helping him to forgive others, and for this amazing woman before him.

Eliza repeated her part, barely audible over the crash of waves, her tone timid and quavering. Nervous? The dauntless Eliza Watts? Blake couldn't help but smile.

". . .till death do us part, according to God's holy ordinance." She finished and gazed up at him, her eyes glossy with happiness.

Blake slid the green band one of the ladies had woven from vines onto her finger. He would buy her a better ring in Rio when he had the chance. And the money.

Yet she glanced down with such pride in her face it may as well have been covered with diamonds.

"I now pronounce you man and wife. You may kiss your bride."

But Blake didn't need an invitation. He swooped Eliza into his arms and pressed his lips against hers.

Cheers and laughter filled the air around them, along with the sound of a fiddle and a harmonica. Eliza pulled away from him, seemingly embarrassed, yet the promise in her eyes spoke of the night to come.

Sunlight brushed Eliza's eyelids like the gentle caress of a wave. Back and forth, warm and inviting, luring her from her sleep. The crash of the sea, the warble of birds, the chatter of people, and deep male breathing swirled in an eclectic symphony over her ears.

Male breathing?

Eliza moved her fingers. Warm, firm—and hairy—flesh met her touch! Flesh that rose and fell like a bellows. Memories flooded her sleepy mind. Wonderful, glorious memories! Rising on her elbow, she propped her head in her hand and stared at the man beside her, still not believing what her eyes beheld.

Blake. Her husband.

Thank You, Father. Thank You. You have blessed me far beyond anything I could have hoped for. And deserved. Wind tore at their tiny shelter of bamboo and palm fronds—a wedding gift from the men to give them privacy. The leaves fluttered, allowing the morning sun to dapple patches of gold over Blake's body.

A magnificent body that reminded her of the night they'd spent in each other's arms. A night that far surpassed her wildest dreams—far surpassed any moment she'd spent with Stanton. She ran her fingers over Blake's bare chest. He moved. Groaned. Opened one eye. And smiled.

He drew her near. "Is that my wife I see?" His voice was groggy with sleep.

"Pray tell, sir, who else would be in your bed?"

He grew serious. "Only you, forever." He kissed her forehead and brushed his hand down her back. "Hmm. Methinks the lady forgot her clothing this morning."

His touch gliding down her bare skin sent a shiver to her belly. "Does it offend you?" She gave him a coy smile. "If so, I can be dressed within a minute."

"Don't you dare." He gently flipped her onto her back and planted his arms around her, pinning her in. "We still haven't finished discussing your terms of surrender."

Five days later, after the donkeys and wagons had arrived, the colonists stood before the jungle, all packed and ready to go. Excitement and uneasiness crackled in the air as everyone waited for Blake's command to forge ahead. And if he admitted it, Blake's own nerves were tight as a drum. He felt as though he were leading troops into battle, not farmers into the forest. Yet just like a battle, the outcome was unknown. They were entering a new land, creating a new world of their own, trekking into a jungle few had even seen. Who knew what struggles, what trials, what triumphs, and pleasures awaited them?

Thiago, their guide—a man Blake found to be both intelligent and kind—stood to Blake's left while Eliza stood on his right. Her sweet scent was driving him mad, but there was nothing to be done about it now. She slid her hand in his and gave him such a look of approval, of love, he had to whisper another thanks to God for allowing this precious woman to be his wife.

In front of them, Hayden, James, and several men held machetes, ready to hack a path through the jungle. Angeline, carrying a cat of all things, and Sarah with Lydia strapped to her chest, joined them, while Magnolia and her parents stood off to the side, looking none too pleased at having to enter the steaming knot of greenery. Nor had they, along with a few other colonists, been pleased to discover the wagons were not meant to carry them, but to haul what remained of their supplies.

Blake glanced across the crowd. Renewed zeal flickered in Mr. Dodd's eyes, causing Blake to chuckle. He truly hoped the man found his blasted gold. Even Mr. Graves seemed unusually excited as he gazed at the jungle like a scientist studying a specimen. Mr. Lewis folded his hands over his corpulent belly as if he hadn't a care in the world, while Moses, Delia, and her children brought up the rear.

Blake faced the jungle again. Waves thundered behind him. Birds and insects chirped and buzzed before him, luring him onward.

Something moved among the leaves. A shadow.

Blake's vision of Jeremy rose stark in his mind. It had seemed so real.

"Are you ready, Blake?" James glanced over his shoulder.

But Blake was still looking at the forest. A chill traversed his back.

"What is it?" Eliza stared at him quizzically.

"We should go before it gets too hot," Hayden urged.

"I thought I saw something in the jungle," Blake said.

"What?" Angeline followed his gaze.

"I don't know. A darkness. A shadow. It's probably nothing." Blake shook his head, feeling silly. Yet the sense of foreboding remained.

James cocked one brow. "Never fear, God is with us, my friend."

Blake nodded and slapped him on the back before facing the colonists. "Move out!" he shouted. Then hefting a sack onto his shoulder, he squeezed Eliza's hand and led her and the band of colonists into the thicket.

James was right. Whatever was in this jungle, they would not face it alone. They had God on their side.

AUTHOR'S HISTORICAL NOTE

Disillusioned by the loss and devastation of war and persecuted under the vengeful thumb of the North, nearly three million Southerners migrated from the former Confederate States in the years following the Civil War. Many of them remained in the United States, moving out west or to larger cities of the North. A great majority traveled to Canada and Mexico. Exactly how many immigrated to Brazil is unknown due to poor record keeping at the time. Southerners were not even required to have passports. They simply boarded ships and sailed away!

Despite much opposition from newspapers, politicians, and even some war heroes, thousands of Southerners risked the long, dangerous voyage to Brazil for the benefit of maintaining their way of life in peace. Conservative estimates derived from newspapers, available numbers, and descendants tell us that perhaps close to twenty thousand Southerners came to Brazil to resettle after the war. It is believed that today more than a hundred thousand of their descendants still inhabit the fair country. But why Brazil? Brazil offered a similar climate to that found in the Southern states, had plenty of land good for growing sugarcane and cotton, had cheap labor, and boasted religious and political tolerance. Also, though the importation of slaves had been outlawed in 1850, slavery within the country was still allowed.

The following letter from Frank Shippey, one of the early Confederados (as they soon came to be called) conveys the sentiment of the day:

> Since the surrender of our armies, I have roamed in exile over the fairest portions of the globe. But it has been reserved for me to find in Brazil that peace which we all, from sad experience, know so well to appreciate. Here, the war-worn soldier, the bereaved parent, the oppressed patriot, the homeless and despoiled, can find a refuge from the trials which beset them and a home not haunted by eternal remembrance of harrowing scenes of sorrow and death.

MaryLu Tyndall, a Christy Award finalist and bestselling author of the Legacy of the King's Pirates series is known for her adventurous historical romances filled with deep spiritual themes. She holds a degree in math and worked as a software engineer for fifteen years before testing the waters as a writer. MaryLu currently writes full-time and makes her home on the California coast with her husband, six kids, and four cats. Her passion is to write page-turning, romantic adventures that not only entertain but open people's eyes to their God-given potential. MaryLu is a member of American Christian Fiction Writers and Romance Writers of America.